D1525509

STARSHIP FOR RENT

STARSHIP FOR RENT
BOOK 1

M.R. FORBES

CHAPTER 1

Hospitals always smelled the same. The scent should have made me gag, but the odor crept up on me slowly. A harsh lavender trying to mask a whole building full of sickness, pain, and loss. Bleaches and sanitizers failed to hide lingering despair, and I guess an occasional bout of joy, which was the last thing I wanted to think about right now, and the last thing I was capable of feeling.

All I noticed at first was how badly I trembled. My teeth chattered uncontrollably despite the heated air blasting from overhead vents. The thin gown draped over me provided no warmth, coverage, or comfort. They had taken my jacket, my jeans, and my Vans. Bandages had replaced them, wrapped tight around my forehead, arms, and knees where the glass had penetrated my clothes and cut me, still burning hot under strips of gauze and surgical tape. Good news, the ER Doc who'd looked me over had said. No broken bones. No internal bleeding or damage. I had made it through relatively unscathed.

A miracle.

No amount of shock could erase what I had seen. What I refused to face but couldn't escape. Mom and Dad were dead. Extinguished in a blaze of shattering glass and shrieking metal. Stolen by Death's cruel hand; the asshole was never satisfied. How many times had I played games with similar plots? Seen NPC families ripped apart by violence meant to inspire the protagonist into making an epic journey.

It was too bad life didn't come with a reset button. It was too bad I couldn't just start a new game and play for a different outcome.

Of course, that didn't stop my brain from trying. As the accident replayed over and over in my head, I analyzed every millisecond, picking out every detail and processing how things had gone so horribly wrong. The most frustrating part was that I didn't need a replay. I understood exactly how I had caused the accident. Dad's distraction in questioning me placed the responsibility squarely on my shoulders. Asking about my day instead of watching the lights and traffic closely enough to have seen the SUV coming. His worry about my lack of outside interests rather than outside hazards had caused their deaths. Simple, mundane stuff leading to catastrophic results.

I both loved and hated him for it.

I loved them both.

And they were gone.

The thought sent me into a fresh round of tears. Burying my face in my thin pillow, I no longer noticed the smell, the burning of my lacerations, or the soreness of my muscles.

I don't know how long I laid there in my bed bawling my eyes out. Ten minutes? More? Time had become immaterial to me. *Everything* but my loss and grief was immaterial.

A stout nurse with curly red hair stood at the edge of my bed as I finally lifted my head, the round of agony subsiding. I could see the compassion in her eyes, and feel it in her presence as she grabbed the thin paper blanket bunched at my waist and tugged it up to my chest before tucking it gently around me.

"I'm so sorry, Noah," she said in a nasally voice, tears coming to her eyes. Since they had brought me to St. Luke's, the same place Mom and Dad worked, she probably knew at least one of them. "My name's Judy," she continued, refocusing on taking care of me. "We need to get you warm again. Your body is still in shock."

Shock seemed almost like a reprieve, the only thing keeping me from all-out despair.

"Can I get you anything? Some water? Maybe a snack or something warm to drink?"

My throat closed at the thought of eating. I shook my head and turned away, gazing toward the window. Raindrops slid in crooked paths down the dark pane of glass. The weather had turned dismal, reflecting my state of mind.

"Okay. I have a few other patients I need to check on, but I'll come back when I'm done. If you need anything in the meantime, just buzz."

I nodded without looking at her. She had started for the door when a rational thought finally made it to the forefront of my mind. "What's going to happen to me?"

"What do you mean, dear?" She asked, pausing at the foot of the bed.

"I won't be eighteen until April." As an only child, without my parents, and not yet considered an adult, my prospects seemed bleak.

She made a face. "You don't have any other family here?"

"No."

"I'm sure someone's already working on it. They'll send someone to talk to you when you're feeling better. Just to try to rest. No one's going to throw you out on the streets to live on your own, and you have enough to deal with right now without worrying about what comes next."

I nodded again. She lingered until she was sure I didn't have any more questions before leaving the room.

My eyes remained fixed on the window, watching the rain rolling down the glass and doing everything I could to focus on the present instead of the past. Or even the future. Easier said than done. My brain still wanted to replay those few seconds when my parents died, the guilt stabbing into me again and again like a knife.

I once again buried my face against the pillow, struggling not to cry anymore. People would understand why I kept breaking down, but it made me look and feel pathetic. Weak. I didn't have that luxury anymore. Maybe I should have been easier on myself. More forgiving. But the longer I sat there and stared at the rain, the angrier with myself I became. The only way I would get through this was with the strength I needed to find somewhere within myself even though all I wanted to do was pull the covers over my head and hide from the reality of my loss.

Twenty minutes passed before the latch on my hospital room's door clacked as somebody pushed the door open. Expecting my attending physician or maybe Judy again, I drew a steadying breath.

A policeman in full uniform entered the room.

Seeing him cemented all my agony at the rock bottom of my gut. I choked back the newest threat of sorrow and refused to get upset again. It was a promise I knew I couldn't keep, but it helped in the short term.

"Hello," he said, stopping beside my bed and removing his cap, tucking it under his left elbow. The name under the badge fastened to the leather case hanging open over his belt identified him as Officer Duncan. "How are you feeling?"

"How do you think I feel?" I snapped. Chilled and

hollow and lost rolled together, hidden in my angry response. "What do you want?"

His neutral expression collapsed. "I know it's tough. I can only imagine how difficult this is for you." He sighed, glancing down to gather his practiced speech. "I'm very sorry for your loss, Noah."

Hearing a total stranger say my name almost broke me. He shouldn't know it. Shouldn't be involved. This was too personal for pleasantries and procedure.

"I hate to bring this up now," he continued. "But I need to ask you a few questions about the accident."

I froze in place, staring at him for who knew how long. I don't think I even remembered to breathe. "What do you want to know?" I barely pushed out.

"Normally, we wouldn't need to do this," he continued. "I don't know if you're aware, but the man who hit you fled the scene."

"He did what?" I snarled, giving him what I knew had to be a scorching look. The raw emotion in my voice made it seem like I was mad at him. "He killed my parents!" Wrong. Lie. I killed my parents. He was only Death's instrument.

"He left the scene before we arrived. A bystander said they saw him heading south but lost track of him when you reacted to the tragedy. I really hate to be here like this, but I need to know if you saw the man driving the SUV. If you did, I need your statement while it's still fresh in your mind."

"If it helps you find him, I'm glad to help."

"Thank you," Officer Duncan said, putting his hand on the back of the seat beside my bed. "May I?" I nodded, and he sat, retrieving a pen and notepad from his shirt pocket. "Did you get a look at him?"

"Sort of," I replied, my mind reverting back to the moment for the hundredth time. At least on this occasion, I could do something useful with the data. "I didn't get a good look at him when he ran the light. I only saw the SUV half a second before it hit us. But I saw him after he got out of the truck. Well, part of him. He had his arm over his face, doing his best not to look at us. I thought it was because he was ashamed, but now…maybe he didn't want to be identified. Do you know who he is?"

"No. The truck was unregistered. It may have been stolen. We're still looking into it. What can you tell me about what you saw?"

"He was young, or at least had a lot of brown hair with no grey or white in it. He had a square jaw, clean shaven. Caucasian."

"Did you notice any identifying marks on his hands or arms? Tattoos or scars?"

In my mind, I watched him climb out of the car, arm in front of his face as he wandered away from the scene instead of toward the wreck he had created. "No. Nothing." I paused. "He was a little overweight, or maybe he had a lot of muscle. I couldn't tell, but he was definitely a lot more filled out than me, although that isn't hard to do."

"What was he wearing?" Duncan asked.

"A suit. Dark. With a red tie. He could have been an Uber Black driver."

Duncan finished writing. "Is it okay if I have an artist come up and take the description, too?"

"I'll do whatever you need to help you find him."

"Great. We might not be able to get Lindsey out here until morning."

"I'm not going anywhere," I replied. "Even though my injuries are all superficial, I don't have anywhere *to* go."

"You don't have any next of kin nearby?"

"No," I answered, the same way I had Judy. A little calmer now, I offered Duncan more of an explanation. "My Dad was an only child. His father died when he was a kid.

His mother just last year. Cancer. My Mom's parents both live in Osaka. So does my Aunt Noriko. I might have some extended family in Germany. I don't really know."

"But no one else in the States?"

I shook my head.

"Okay." Duncan scribbled on a new page in his notepad before looking at me again. "You're how old now?"

"Seventeen. I'll be eighteen in April. It's only six months away, and I imagine my parents had life insurance. I can take care of myself."

"I'm not Child Protective Services, so I can't speak to that with certainty, but in my experience the courts are pretty unbending on cases like this. The rules are the rules, and exceptions for one mean exceptions for many, and then the rules don't mean anything anymore."

I swallowed hard, fighting back tears. "You sound just like my Dad. Everything by the book."

Duncan looked back at me, sadness in his eyes. He must have read the panic tightening my face because he put his free hand gently on my shoulder. The compassionate act almost broke me again. "Don't worry. The system's designed to assist families in difficult situations like this and make sure everyone lands in the most beneficial circumstances."

My throat constricted more. I didn't need reassurances or platitudes. Those belonged to someone else's nightmare instead of my new, devastating reality. And the "system" sucked. I had read enough online horror stories to know it failed way more people than it helped.

I needed to talk to my parents. Have Mom stroke my hair and tell me we would figure things out together, one step at a time. Hear Dad promise nothing would really change. We would endure. Except I was the only one left. And endurance meant shouldering the full burden by myself.

Duncan waited for a response I couldn't force. When the silence stretched too long, he slid a business card from his breast pocket and set it on the table beside my bed. "Call me if you need anything or have more questions. I'll be back in the morning with Lindsey. And take care of yourself, son. There are always people willing to help if you let them, including me."

"Thank you," I replied meekly.

He waited another handful of seconds for me to say something more. When I didn't, he slipped the pad and pen back in his pocket and got up. "I'll see you in the morning then," he said before turning and slipping out the door. I listened until his heavy footfalls faded and the door finally eased closed behind him.

Glancing out the window again, I decided I couldn't stay in bed another minute. I shoved the blanket away and dropped my feet to the cold tiled floor. Shivering, I stood and went to the window, my muscles already sore enough I shuffled along like an old man. Rain continued streaking the pane, denying me a clear glimpse of the city beyond. The melancholy weather perfectly matched my mood. I laid my forehead against the cool glass as reality threatened to suffocate me.

I'd sworn I wouldn't cry again. I knew it was a lie then. I proved it now.

I'm not sure how long I stood there struggling to breathe between guttural sobs. Somewhere in the deluge, I became vaguely aware of a repetitive buzzing against the room's side table. The notification tone echoed from my phone, forgotten since the accident. Wiping my face with my gown, I crossed back to the bed. As much as I wanted to forget the world, the world hadn't forgotten me.

There were two missed calls and a handful of texts waiting when I unlocked the device. All from Tyler Kent. We had four classes together, but our friendship to this point had remained mostly confined to school and group projects, and online, where we were both members of Stinking Badgers, our eSports team.

We shared a lot of interests, yet remained just shy of being truly close friends. Probably because of me. If I would let anybody past my normally stoic defensive perimeter, it was Tyler. But right then my walls felt dangerously fragile. I had to gather my fortitude not to shatter when I responded.

I opened Tyler's texts instead of listening to any voice-mails, reading the last one first:

> I saw what happened. I know ur not ok.
> Nobody would be after that Im so sry
> Noah. If u need anything Ill be there.

My entire body shivered as I read the message. Tyler had been at the scene during the accident? The odds weren't that far-fetched, we lived within a half mile of one another, but still…for some stupid reason, I felt embarrassed that he had seen the family car get creamed.

Had seen my parents die.

My fingers quivered as I typed an honest response. I had never been so real or so raw with anyone but my parents. But Duncan was right, there were people willing to help. I hoped Tyler would be one of them.

> Not ok doesn't begin to cover it. I can't process that they're gone. I wasn't even hurt. Just some glass cuts. It doesn't feel real.

He answered back less than a minute later.

> Are u at St Lukes

> Yes.

Im on my way

The reply stunned me. Sure, Tyler was nice to everyone. But driving halfway across town late on a school night exceeded simple kindness for someone whose house I'd never even been to. I could refuse his offer just as easily over text. But having even one person nearby suddenly sounded a lot better than full isolation. I needed that lifeline more desperately than expected.

You don't have to do that.

ik c u soon

Out of habit, I exited the messaging app and started browsing social media posts. I didn't get very far before realizing that someone had already linked a police bulletin about the accident with the rumor that my parents and I had been involved. Someone else had commented that they'd heard my parents were dead. Despite my experience online, the speed at which the news traveled still took me by surprise. Seeing further comments from classmates who barely knew me was more than I could take. My finger poised over the power button, prepared to shut it all out again. Then Tyler's contact image popped onto the screen. An incoming call instead of another text. I took a moment to gather myself before tapping to accept, taking a deep breath to steady my voice.

"Hello?"

"Hey, Noah. I hope it's cool I called instead of sending another text. I'm pulling into the lot right now. Are you in the waiting room, or—"

"No. I have a private room. I…" I froze, struggling with the decision of how far to trust Tyler. "I'm so damn alone."

"I hear you. Look, I know we've never been besties

outside of school or beyond the Badgers, but none of that matters right now. I'm here for you, man."

I could have cried again. Instead, I laughed softly. His smooth tone flowed like milk chocolate, rich and soothing. The absurd imagery made me chuckle despite the circumstances.

"Yeah, I appreciate that more than you know. You really didn't have to come all this way though."

"Uh-huh," he replied. "I'm already here. I might as well come up." He killed the engine, his door creaking open a second later. "I'll be right there."

The call ended before I could argue further that we weren't truly friends and that he didn't owe me anything. He had inserted himself into my tragedy because he cared. However the connection manifested hardly mattered. I couldn't deny the comfort of simply knowing someone gave a damn.

Whatever happened next, at least I wouldn't have to endure it alone.

CHAPTER 2

Judy's distinctive voice preceded her into my room as she opened the door, a swole teenager trailing right behind her. His brown hair stood up in messy spikes while a hoodie hung over down to black cargos and unlaced high-top skater shoes. "Noah, you have a visitor."

Tyler Kent shifted the cardboard drink carrier into the hand bracing a grease-stained paper bag and offered me a sympathetic grin. "Hey, Noah-san. I come bearing gifts."

I couldn't stop myself from smiling, despite the pervasive tightness in my chest. "Tyler. I...I don't know what to say."

Judy slipped back out the door as Tyler approached my bedside. He extended the food my way. "You don't need to say anything. You're always talking about Miyaki's in team chat. I figured if anything might help ease some of the gut-ache, it would be greasy rice balls and sugary soda."

I took the warm bag and slid out the fragrant white cartons stacked inside. The smell was almost enough to kick-start my appetite. Almost.

"I'm not really that hungry," I said, shifting the cartons to my table. "But I definitely appreciate the sentiment."

"No problem," Tyler replied, placing the drink carrier beside the boxes. "I figured the odds you would eat something were forty-sixty. But hey, you'll get hungry sometime tonight and this has gotta beat hospital grub, right?" He dropped onto the barebones recliner at my bedside. "I would have picked you up something from the gift shop, but I didn't think a teddy bear or flowers and balloons would make you feel any better." His levity faded into a serious and sad grimaced. "We both know nothing will be alright for you for a while. And it'll never be like it was before."

I stared at him in surprise. "Did you come here to cheer me up, or rub it in?" I asked, too weary to put much energy into the question.

"I came here to tell you that I know what you're going through," he replied. "You know I transferred here from Pennsylvania, but you don't know why." When I didn't say anything, he continued. "I had a younger brother. James. But he liked to be called Jumbo. Don't ask me why. He was just a fun-loving little man. Always had a smile on his face. Always joking around with everyone. Mom swore he would grow up to be a comedian. But he never had the chance."

Tyler had never mentioned anything about a younger brother before. "What happened?"

"He was eight years old. Mom stopped at a grocery store to pick up a couple of things. He stayed in the car to play Candy Crush. Couple of guys in the parking lot got into an argument. Next thing you know, they're shooting at one another." He paused, tears rolling. "He got caught in the crossfire. Made it to the hospital, lived another twelve hours before he couldn't do it anymore."

I stared at him, eyes moist again. "Damn, Tyler. I'm sorry."

He wiped his eyes with a sleeve. "Yeah. I'm not here

looking for your pity. Just like I know you don't want mine. I'm just saying I have a small idea of what you're going through. We've got a lot more in common than our love for *League of Legends*."

"Yeah," I agreed. "I guess we do. There is one major difference though."

"What's that?"

"I know your parents are divorced, but you still have your mom, and you can call your dad. They're still there for you whenever you need them. They're still a support system for you, financially if nothing else. Plus, you aren't looking forward to a conversation with Child Protective Services about where you're going to live for the next six months." I paused, shaking my head. "This is all so messed up."

He put his hand on my shoulder, giving me a comforting squeeze. "I hear you, man. Damn, I hadn't even thought about that. Are you sure you can't just stay at home on your own? I'm sure your folks had money saved and life insurance. Maybe—"

"No. I already talked to a cop about it. He said the laws are the laws, so no chance. I expect someone from CPS to show up any second now."

"The cops came to talk to you already? It's only been a few hours. That's kind of cold, don't you think?"

"Nah. Officer Duncan was kind enough. He told me the guy who hit us took off on foot. He asked me for a description."

"Are you serious? The guy murdered your parents and ran away?"

I trembled at Tyler's choice of words. "It was an accident, not murder."

"How do you know? If the guy was high or drunk or running from someone or something like a robbery, that's vehicular homicide. Why else would he run away?"

I shrugged. I couldn't argue his point. Consequently, I also found it more difficult to continue blaming myself. Maybe I had distracted Dad, but the guy in the Escalade shouldn't have blown the light. It hit me now that he didn't even slow down. At the very least, he should have hit the brakes before the impact. "Yeah, you're probably right. I hadn't thought of it like that."

"You haven't had much time to think about anything. I bet you've been reliving the accident in your head over and over again, right?"

"How'd you know?"

"I didn't see Jumbo die, but I still conjured up the scene in my brain and replayed it a thousand times, trying to logic some way that I could have been there to stop it. It's a normal response."

"Nothing feels normal right now. How am I still in one piece, barely injured, and they're both gone?"

"I wish I had answers for you," Tyler replied. "But I guarantee your folks would have gladly traded their lives for you to come out of that accident unharmed if they'd had the choice."

"Yeah," I agreed. "I know that's true." I leaned back in the bed, finally starting to calm down a little. Again, I knew it wouldn't last, but I didn't want to lose the moment. I even gathered enough of an appetite to reach for the bag from Miyaki's.

"There you go," Tyler said. "Your parents would want you to survive. To live. To go on."

"Don't even think about warbling Celine Dione at me," I said, opening the chopstick package and pulling them apart. I flipped the lid of the first box, my stomach growling at the sight of the rice balls. On one hand, my hunger seemed like a betrayal to my folks. On the other, Tyler was right. Mom and Dad wouldn't want me to fall apart without them.

I devoured the rice balls in no time before taking a long pull on the cola to wash them down. Tyler and I got to talking about simpler things. Fortnite and Liz Dern's legs. Judy checked on us a couple of times. The first time, her expression softened when she saw me confiding in Tyler. I kept waiting for someone from CPS, but it was getting late enough that I guessed they were planning to drop by in the morning.

"You know," Tyler said as his soda cup gurgled empty. He mashed it flat before stuffing the crushed container in the bag with my second container of rice balls. "I've been thinking."

"The look on your face suggests you've been doing more than thinking," I said. "I would suggest plotting as a more appropriate word."

"An hour hanging out with me, and you can already read my mind," he replied. "Pretty impressive."

"Do I even want to ask?"

"What do you think about a quick field trip? Help you take your mind off things for a few hours?"

"I think you're crazy," I replied. "I can't go anywhere. I don't want to go anywhere. My parents were killed six hours ago. I can barely keep my mind off that, and I definitely can't wrap my mind around how much bureaucracy I'll need to cut through in the next forty-eight hours. I'm the only one who can make arrangements for them, handle insurance, and all that crap."

Tyler waved off my concerns. "Are you kidding? I know we're more like gamer friends and study mates than actual friend friends, but from what you've told me about your folks, I can't believe they wouldn't have made arrangements if anything happened to them before your adulthood was official. Your dad was in administration, right? A paper pusher."

"I don't appreciate you calling him that," I growled.

"Sorry. I didn't mean it in a negative way. Point being, they wouldn't leave their son to have to handle all that red tape. I guarantee it. Someone other than you can figure all that out. And my idea speaks directly to your second point. Or maybe it was your first point. You can barely get your mind off the accident. I get it. I really do. It's the reason I'm here. I'm suggesting a short break, away from the heaviness of your life. Eight hours. If today taught you anything, it should be that life is precious and short, so live it while you can."

"And what about you?" I asked, putting my excuses on him. "No one expects me to be at school in the morning. And I have no parents waiting up for me to come home. But you do."

"I already told my mother I probably wouldn't be back tonight. She knows I can take care of myself, and she's cool with it."

"You don't have a very good mother, do you?"

I said it without thinking, and flinched, waiting for him to yell at me. He laughed instead. "She's…it was never the same after Jumbo died. It was like she didn't want kids anymore once he was gone. She cares, but in a different way. She's not bad. Just hurt deep to her core."

"I'm sorry. I shouldn't have said that."

"Look man, I know you're raw. I won't use anything you say against you."

"I appreciate that."

"Back to the question at hand. Do you want to break out of here, or do you want to sit there in that dress with your ass hanging out, drowning in your misery?"

I still should have refused on principle. Sneaking out of the hospital hours after losing my last anchors to reality was ludicrous. Except the thought of waiting around for Child Protective Services to swoop in and scoop me up didn't offer much of an incentive to stay. A temporary distraction sounded way better, however reckless indulging the whim might be.

"Like what?" I asked. "It's almost ten o'clock on a Wednesday night. What's even open now besides Wal-Mart and truck stops?"

Tyler smiled, sensing that he was breaking through. Like a shark smelling blood, he went in for the kill. "I've got the perfect spot to lift your spirits. You ever hear of VR Awesome?"

I nodded, the simple mention of the place lifting my spirits. "Hell yeah, I've heard of VR Awesome. I've read every online article about it that I could find. I've seen the TikToks taken inside the one in California. It looks amazing."

"It looks awesome," he corrected with a beaming grin. "And it's open until two in the morning for adult play. I can get us to Des Moines in an hour and a half. That leaves us two hours to enjoy all the wonders the place has to offer, and we'll still be back here before your CPS agent even wakes up. And, if you do need to handle all the legal stuff yourself, you'll still be back to do that."

I nearly jumped at the chance to say yes before reality settled back in. "It sounds fun," I said, losing my excitement. "There's only one problem. The same problem I'm already having. Adult play means twenty-one and over, and neither one of us is twenty-one."

"Oh, ye of little faith! It just so happens that another member of the Stinking Badgers works the late shift there. All we have to do is get in touch with her. I'm sure she'll let us in."

"You mean All-red?" I asked, using her gamer handle.

"Yup."

"I didn't know she lived in Des Moines."

"That's because you don't stick around for the small talk after practice."

"She told me she's our age. How can she work the late shift at VR Awesome?"

Tyler really started cracking up now. "She tells everyone that. Her real name is Alyssa Danson. She's a twenty-one-year-old college dropout. Lives in Des Moines with a roommate and a cat."

"How do you know all that?" I asked, bewildered by his info dump.

His laughter faded, his face reddening. "I may have cyber-stalked her a little."

"How do you stalk someone a little? Don't tell me you doxxed her."

"I won't tell you that," he answered, falling silent.

"That's not cool," I said, the buzz totally killed.

"No," he admitted. "I felt guilty after I did it. That's why I never said anything to anyone."

"You should tell her you did it."

"I agree. And I will. As soon as we get there. It's an apology that should be made in person, I think."

"Did you see what she looks like?" I asked. "So you'll know her when you see her?"

"I found her alternate X account. Her avatar's cuter, in my opinion. She's old." He laughed again, the wild energy creeping back into the room. "Does that mean we're doing this?"

I opened my mouth to say yes, but something else came out.

CHAPTER 3

"I don't know," I waffled, affirmation failing to reach my lips.

As appealing as ditching the hospital and taking off to play the most advanced virtual reality video games in the world sounded, this field trip couldn't erase my problems indefinitely. It couldn't erase my pain either. Only dull it for a while. And regardless of whether my parents had a lawyer to handle things or not, I still had to figure out where I was going to live or if I could be emancipated or whatever other legal nonsense loomed on the horizon.

Was it so terrible that I couldn't force myself to care about those obligations the same way I cared about disappearing into an adventure? I should stay put, be the mature one working out essential logistics. That was the responsible thing, after all. The adult thing. This morning, I still had six more months before anyone expected me to be fully an adult. Surely, I could be a kid for eight more hours. It was so damn tempting. Yet…

"Come on, where's your sense of adventure?" Tyler asked. "I promise, no one will know you stepped outside, much less suspect a covert rescue mission to Des Moines."

"Right now this hospital room represents the eye of the ongoing storm surrounding me. Out there..." I jabbed my finger toward the dismal night. "...waits a metric ton of crap I'm nowhere near ready to process. Besides, nurses are big on checking on patients every couple of hours. What's gonna happen when they find me gone?"

Tyler dismissed my rebuttal with an impatient huff. "I already talked to Judy. Since you're just here waiting for CPS to come scoop you up in the morning, she put a *Do Not Disturb* note on your medical record for tonight. His expression softened marginally. "Look, I get this is crappy timing, and you gotta handle fallout nobody our age should ever have to face. But staying trapped in this soul-sucking box all night while everything outside gets decided for you makes it infinitely crappier. Am I wrong or am I right?"

As bad as taking off might appear, it did beat sticking my head in the sand for a few more hours of denial. I couldn't avoid this forever no matter how fiercely that yearning rooted itself in my psyche. Wasn't it better to grab fleeting snatches of pseudo-independence while the choice remained mine? Before some clipboard-toting crusader redefined my entire existence.

"I see it on your face," Tyler said, getting excited again. "You know I'm right. We're doing this, yeah?"

"Yeah," I finally agreed with a grin.

"Cool. Then we're golden!" Tyler reached for my hand, hauling me off the bed in a single breathless motion. He practically dragged me toward the exterior wall before I wrested my fingers free.

"What gives?" I stumbled sideways, catching myself with a hand against the wall. "I may not have any broken bones or stitches, but I think you just opened up some of my cuts." I could feel their unwelcome sting under the bandages.

He paused. "Right. Sorry. I got a little over-excited. Nice

butt though." He laughed as I grabbed at the back of my gown, jerking the gaping opening back together. "Wait here. You can't jailbreak mooning everybody." He grabbed the door latch and vanished from my room like a tornado swept back up into the sky.

An overwhelming loneliness slammed into me the moment the door latched closed. My brain immediately tried returning me to the accident. Hoping there was one last rice ball from Miyaki's I could shove in my face as a distraction, I scrambled for the second box still sitting on my bedside table. The minute I picked it up, the empty weight reminded me that Tyler had finished them off.

Disheartened, I moved to the window, looking out and down at the front of the hospital six floors below. The sight of an incoming ambulance sent a wave of panic through me. What was I going to do in the morning when they came for me and I lost all control of my future?

I retreated to the bed where I sat down and started to hyperventilate. Enough of that crap. Grabbing up my empty soda cup, I sucked on the straw, pulling up the last bit of almost melted ice as I forced myself to focus on the taste of it instead of my anxiety.

It saved me for the few minutes that passed before Tyler returned. The door swung open, clothes flying at me before he came into view. I caught the sweatshirt, but fumbled the sweatpants.

"These aren't mine," I said, bending down to pick them up off the floor as Tyler entered.

"Nope. They're mine. They'll be big on you, but we can stop at Wal-Mart on the way to Des Moines. I do have your boxers and Vans though. I had to sneak them out of the nurse's station. That was fun." He held up the sneakers. He had stuffed my underwear into one of them, socks in the other. "Get dressed so we can get out of here." He put the sneakers on the bed beside me.

"Do you mind turning around?" I asked.

He laughed as he spun away from me. "You're such an uptight geek, Noah-san."

"So are you. You're just better at pretending you aren't."

"Unlike you, I'm not a virgin."

"Uh-huh." I untied the gown at the back of my neck and tossed it on the bed.

"Seriously, I'm not."

"Only virgins feel the need to try to convince their friends they aren't virgins," I shot back, pulling on my boxers and putting on the sweats. Of course, they were too big, but at least they had a string so I could cinch them tight on my waist. The sweatshirt was big too, and smelled. "What are these, your gym clothes?"

"Yeah. I washed them a couple of weeks ago."

"Maybe I'm better off with my ass hanging out."

"Are you under wraps yet?"

"Just about. Do we have an exit strategy?" I asked as he turned around, chuckling at how his clothes fit me. I scowled back at him. I couldn't help that I was thin as a rail. I ate more than my parents had always thought I had places to put all of it. I just never seemed to gain any mass; I just kept growing vertically.

"Who needs a strategy? Haven't you ever seen a prison break film? We slip out like ninjas and disappear. Poof!"

I rolled my eyes. "Sure, great idea."

Tyler's scheming confidence shattered, his baffled expression less than encouraging. "Okay, admittedly I'm still refining details. What do you suggest, whiz kid?"

"Seriously? This was your idea."

"You're our Stinking tactician, remember?" He countered. "You always have a plan."

I sighed, but my disappointment at the beginning of this escapade paled in comparison to what awaited me if I canceled the shenanigans. Besides, I couldn't stop my brain from working on the problem, and any thoughts that weren't of my parents or the crash were welcome right now.

"First, we need to get past the nurses' station. Then we have to get to a stairwell. Once we reach the ground floor, we can slip out a side exit."

"But why use the stairwell when the elevators go right to the parking garage."

"They also have cameras. We don't want to be discovered, at least until it's too late for them to stop us."

"Good point. That's why you're the plan man."

"Divide and conquer," I said. "Go out past the station, pretend you're hitting up a vending machine or something. Text me when the coast is clear to the stairs. Meet me there."

"Damn, this is like Ghost Recon in real life. Okay, I'm on it."

He went out the door again, and I picked up my phone, going to the door to wait for his text. The focus was enough to keep my mind off the trauma, and when Tyler's message popped up on my screen, announcing it was go time, I hurried out the door, fast-walking past the momentarily deserted nurse's station, turning the corner just before I spotted Judy and another nurse pop into view at the end of the hall. Running to the sign for the stairs, I ducked inside, met by a grinning Tyler.

"Nice work. Let's get out of here."

We hurried down the steps, two or three at a time. No one stopped us. No blaring alarms. No phalanx of orderlies. Not one authority demanding our peaceful surrender across a bullhorn. Every hacked-together thriller and suspense-laced video game I'd seen left those cliches burned permanently into my brain, we made it to the parking garage without incident.

The relative serenity of our escape felt ironically disappointing.

Tyler pointed me toward his ride, a fifteen-year-old KIA that was too beat up for anyone to even want to steal. "Are you sure we can make it to Des Moines in that thing?" I asked, needing to wait for him to push the passenger door open from the inside.

"I could quote Star Wars, but I'm not gonna," he replied. "Get in."

I froze in place, anxiety mainlining into me at the moment of truth. Staring at the torn pleather of the front seat, visions of Mom in that position, her body broken, her bloody head lolled to the side, nearly derailed my sanity. Nauseous and dizzy, I turned away from the car. "I can't do this," I said, afraid I was going to puke. Breathing deeply, I bent over and braced my hands on my knees.

"There's only one way past it," Tyler said. "And that's straight through the fear, full speed ahead."

He was right. I didn't plan to spend the rest of my life riding a bus. I took one more deep breath and turned back toward the car, practically throwing myself into the front seat."Hell yeah, Noah-san!" Tyler shouted as I pulled the door closed and buckled my seat belt. He fumbled to connect an aging iPhone to the sedan's stereo. "I've got the perfect song, too."

He finished establishing the Bluetooth connection, quickly browsing Spotify and hitting play. Starting the engine and throwing the car into reverse, the unfamiliar tune immediately brought a smile to my face. The beat was lively, and while they were singing about drinking, the part about getting knocked down but always getting back up really resonated with me.

"This song is crazy," I said while Tyler guided us to the exit, moving to the automated payment lane to avoid the attendant in the other.

"An oldie but a goodie," Tyler remarked. He finished paying and we headed for the exit.

I let exhaled tension ease tight shoulders, consciously trying to relax my sore, exhausted muscles as my queasiness evaporated into thin air. "It feels strangely normal to be moving again instead of treading water back there. Honestly, I can't believe we made it without security tackling us at the door."

Tyler's face scrunched thoughtfully. "For real, I expected way more fireworks. Figured we would have to hack some keycards or fake a toxin leak or maybe rappel from the third-story ledge on tied together bed sheets.." He leaned across the narrow gap to nudge me playfully. "But you seemed to know where Big Brother might be napping. I bet that divide and conquer trick works killer for taking out zombies or creepers too, huh?"

I huffed a weary laugh. "I wish real leveling went that smoothly. Especially lately. I was two seconds from bailing back there. Your advice was exactly what I needed. So, thanks for that."

"Hey, don't sweat it! I promise you won't regret this."

The weight of my pain lifted off my shoulders, hopefully for at least the next few hours. I grinned back. "I'm sure I won't."

CHAPTER 4

The glowing sign for VR Awesome! stood out like a beacon of hope against the gloom of the rainy Des Moines skyline. Even after midnight on a weeknight, the parking lot remained half full, a testament to the futuristic fun that awaited gamers inside. My foot tapped anxiously against the floorboard as Tyler wheeled his rust bucket Kia into an open space near the back corner of the lot. I knew better than to question whether showing up unannounced in the middle of Alyssa's shift was truly smart.

For once, spur-of-the-moment poor judgment felt totally warranted despite what awaited me come morning. Tyler killed the sputtering engine while I gawked silently through smudged glass at the square building that looked as if it had possibly once been a Bed Bath and Beyond. Giant waterproof-framed posters plastered on exterior walls depicted intense virtual battles between humanoid mechs, sword-wielding elves, and laser-toting space marines. Any one of those immersive game worlds offered guaranteed respite from the desolation I wanted so much to escape.

I made myself focus on electric anticipation rather than

my tragic memories while Tyler punched buttons on his iPhone.

"You owe me for this," he grumbled in my general direction as he put the finishing touches on the missive he hoped would convince our Stinking Badger teammate to let us inside.

"This was your idea," I reminded him.

"Confessing my crimes was your idea," he countered. "And you owe me for following your lead on this one."

"I am the tactician, remember? We didn't come all of this way to be left out in the cold."

He sighed as he hit the send button, foot tapping the floor at a thousand RPMs while we awaited her reply.

You're outside?

Yeah. I told u I want to apologize.

This had better be good. Meet me around back.

Tyler glanced at me. I shrugged. "At least she's still talking to you."

"How do I know some Zangief muscle-head won't be back there instead of her, waiting to pile-drive me into a dumpster?"

"If that's the case, you'll probably be getting what you deserve."

"Maybe, but what I won't be getting is us into VR Awesome."

"Only one way to find out," I said, needing three shoves to get the passenger door open.

"Be careful," Tyler complained. "It's liable to fall off."

Rolling my eyes, I exited the car, hoping for the best when I gently pressed the door closed and it held. Avoiding puddles, I hurried as fast as my sore muscles allowed to catch up to Tyler. Together, we crossed the parking lot, navigating along the side of the building to the rear. Since the place had once been a retail store, there was a red fire door at the back corner next to a pair of delivery bays.

So far, neither Alyssa nor Zangief were out there.

"Option C," Tyler said. "She leaves us standing out here in the cold for the next two hours, satisfied to have taught me a lesson for being a privacy-intruding asshole."

"Playing against her, I never got the impression she was dishonest. Unlike you. If she said she'll meet us, I think she'll meet us."

"Let's hope you're right. And I'm not dishonest. I just stretch the truth a bit too far sometimes."

"Sometimes?"

We were almost to the red fire door when it swung outward, spilling yellow light across the cracked pavement. The woman standing in the doorway didn't match any of the mental images I had built of Alyssa after hearing Tyler's modified version of her general appearance. This woman's brown hair—in her picture she was a redhead—was cut to the ears, not flowing down her back in long curls. The pair of oversized gold-framed glasses sitting on her unexpectedly sharp blade of a nose magnified brown eyes that were supposed to be green. Her thin lips weren't kissably lush. And where were her curves? Her tan VR Awesome sweatshirt hung over her skinny jeans like an oversized gunny sack, showing no figure at all. Either she'd used fake images on her alt-adult accounts too, or the woman eyeing us with open skepticism wasn't Alyssa.. The only thing that was the same was her pale skin.

"Alyssa?" Tyler regarded her with a furtive look. Clearly, he was trying to resolve the discrepancies between this woman and the voluptuous redhead pictured online.

"You must be T-Bone," she said. Her eyes stayed locked on him like a velociraptor hunting prey. "Start explaining.

Now." Her tone was more angry librarian than enraged barbarian.

Tyler reddened with embarrassment. "I… I wouldn't really call it stalking. More like, I don't know…basic curiosity? Just some typical online stuff trying to figure out more about someone I kinda like."

"Someone you like?" she scoffed, incredulity deepening the harsh lines of her scowl. "You don't know anything about me."

"That's not true. We've been gaming together for the last two years."

"You know my online persona. One of them, anyway. A social construct designed to maintain my personal privacy while still participating in something I enjoy. You don't like Alyssa, the twenty-one-year-old college dropout who works at a VR arcade. You like Alyssa, the seventeen year-old hottie who likes to dress as her favorite anime character while she kicks your ass at, well, everything."

"That's kind of the point," Tyler shot back. "I was trying to find out who you are. The real you. Social construct or not, the mind behind that Alyssa is still yours, and I was and remained intrigued by it."

Tyler's Ryu smashed Alyssa's Zangief anger with a solid shoryuken. Her mouth opened, but no words came out. Showing no mercy, Tyler kept talking.

"You're right. I got wrapped up in my interest in a teammate. Started digging without considering boundaries or privacy. It was thoughtless and immature and I apologize wholeheartedly. Please understand I meant no harm."

I glanced at Tyler, surprised by both the formality and sincerity of his apology. It wasn't what I expected from the brash guy I had just spent the last two hours in the car with. But it *was* like the guy who had inserted himself into my tragedy with kind words and a big heart, and brought me on this crazy adventure.

Alyssa appraised him skeptically another moment without speaking. I tensed, uncertain if she would read Tyler the same way I had, mentally preparing myself for a long, painful car ride back to the hospital.

"Okay then." Alyssa's frosty veneer thawed marginally as she thrust a finger at him. "But let's get a few things straight. One, I'm still mad at you."

"Understood," Tyler replied.

"Two, whatever romantic notions of us you had when you started prying into my personal life, you can forget it."

"I kind of tabled that concept after I found out you were twenty-one, not seventeen. But now that we're meeting in real life, maybe we can find common ground as friends?"

"Three, I don't want to be your friend. And I can't let you into the shop. I know you came a long way, but that's not my problem. As far as I'm concerned, you're T-Bone, I'm All-red, and that's the beginning and end of our interactions with one another. Goodbye, T-Bone."

She turned to go back inside, stopping when her eyes lit on me for the first time. Not that I minded. I was glad to have avoided her attention while she took care of business with Tyler. But now, her eyes meeting mine before quickly giving me the once-over, her stiff expression vanished, a hand going to her mouth. "Are you okay?" she asked. "What happened? You look like you were in some kind of accident."

Her unexpected concern caught me off guard. I touched self-conscious fingertips to the gauze wrapped like a headband around my forehead and then down over the bruise on my cheek. Swelling emotion constricted the explanation in my throat.

"This is Noah. Katzuo," Tyler intervened gently as my tears again threatened to fall. "He was in an accident this afternoon. A bad one." I regained some of my composure as he summarized events in the same calm, sympathetic tone that had eased my anxiety hours earlier in my hospital room.

Alyssa's perplexed expression had shifted to empathetic sorrow by the time he finished. "I am so very sorry, Noah. I can't imagine anything worse happening to someone." Without hesitation she left the red door hanging open and came to me, enfolding me in a consoling hug that lasted several seconds. I stiffened instinctively before relaxing into her unexpectedly genuine hug. When she released me, her eyes glistened with tears. "I hate to meet you like this, Katzuo. Noah, I mean. Of course I'll help any way I can. But shouldn't you be at home with your family instead of here?"

"It's...complicated," I said. "The only place open this late was either here or Wal-Mart. And given the...situation, I didn't think wasting time shopping for socks was going to make me feel better. My descent into a waking nightmare can resume tomorrow. Tonight, I just wanted to pretend everything's normal. Maybe even better than normal."

"I guess that's understandable." Sympathy further softened Alyssa's sharp features. "Everything will seem less awful in time, I'm sure, and it's not for me to judge how you process your grief. For now though, let's get you inside before you run out of playtime."

Maneuvering through the maintenance area in the back, Alyssa left us there while she went up front to get us a pair of open-play bracelets. I didn't ask her any questions about how she'd acquired them when she returned, and from her expression when she handed them over, I was pretty sure she wouldn't have answered anyway.

Guiding us to the double doors leading out onto the game room floor, she paused ahead of them, turning to me with a huge grin on her face. "Are you ready for awesome, Noah?"

"I could use a little awesome right now," I replied.

"Then follow me." She pushed the doors open ahead of us, and we stepped out into Wonderland.

VR Awesome felt bigger than any Bed Bath and Beyond I had ever been in. It was probably because all of the non load-bearing supports had been removed and the ceiling tiles ripped out. They had been replaced by hundreds of multi-colored LEDs that flashed and shifted in accordance with the changing game environments. Those environments were clearly separated by glass partitions and wide aisles, which themselves were split in half by classic arcade games. I spotted *Pac-man, Galaga,* and *Dig Dug* right off the bat.

I gawked like the starry-eyed tourist I was while Alyssa led us down one of the aisles. I had seen all of this in TikTok walkthroughs and Youtube videos, but being here in person was a totally different story.

On my left, a dozen encapsulated pods occupied the floor, wires rising from their backs to the ceiling where they vanished, likely to a massive server farm somewhere in the back. A sign at the entrance advertised the game as *Mech Jockey,* and huge screens both inside and out of the game's footprint displayed the gameplay. Two teams of six mechs each crossed a desolate cityscape, hunting one another. It looked cool, and I wanted to play, but I already had my mind set on a specific game. I figuratively had both my fingers and toes crossed, hoping this VR Awesome location carried it and that it wasn't out of order or booked for a private party.

To my right, a dozen patrons occupied all the available omni-directional treadmills. Each person had a helmet visor over their head, the faceplate opaque to prevent the outside environment from bleeding in. Wires snaked out from the glove each player wore, connected to different parts of their dominant arm which allowed them to manipulate the virtual world. Each treadmill also had a rack on either side, carrying different props that went along with the gameplay. In this case, a machete, a short rope, and a shotgun among other plastic stand-ins.

"*Jungle Invasion*," Tyler said, pointing to one of the gamers and his screen. Dark aliens rushed him, pouring through the thick jungle vegetation like molasses. The player struggled to hold them back, picking them off one after another without slowing them down. When he finally decided to retreat it was too late. The aliens caught up to him, the screen turning red as he expended his last available life force. "I want to play that one."

"Bug hunts aren't really my thing," I replied. "Too much shooting, not enough thinking."

"I don't know," Alyssa said. "If he had tried thinking more and shooting less, it might not be game over for him." She pointed to the player as he removed his helmet and slinked away from his treadmill in defeat.

"Maybe. I don't want to start with that one though." I craned my neck, trying to see further down the row of games. "I really want to try—"

And then I saw it. Gleaming like Excalibur, it was the crown jewel anchoring this virtual paradise.

Star Squadron.

CHAPTER 5

"*Star Squadron*!" I shouted, earning sideways glances from a few of the other gamers. I didn't care, hurrying toward the entrance to the futuristic space dogfighting simulator. Tyler and Alyssa rushed after me as I entered the staging area, my eyes immediately drawn to the monitors displaying the current match.

Two teams of five starfighters bearing red and green color outlines wove through a debris field that looked like the remnants of a large space battle. Blue and orange bolts of energy lanced between the ships as they tried blowing one another into expanding clouds of shrapnel. Even with all the chaos, I could tell the players knew what they were doing by how they utilized pockets of debris for cover and how they compensated for their quarry's evasive maneuvers.

"This looks amazing," I said to no one in particular. This was the real deal. I couldn't wait to play the game. A tall, skinny attendant in a faux flight suit emerged from a storage area to greet us. "Are you here to enlist in the squadron?" he asked. Despite the late hour, he looked almost as excited to be there as I was.

"Totally," I replied.

"Yeah, man," Tyler agreed.

He suddenly squinted at us in silence, dread trying to blot out my *Star Squadron* sun as his mouth opened in what I knew was going to be a stone cold question about our ages.

"Hey, Mark," Alyssa said, coming up behind us and forestalling the guy's inquiry.

"What's up, Ally?" he replied.

"This is Noah and Tyler; they're friends of mine."

"Friends?" he asked, confused by their apparent age difference.

"They're older than they look," she confirmed for us. "And they're here on my dime." She also confirmed she had paid for our bracelets, rather than using an employee benefit. I hoped she at least gotten a discount. "I'm going to jump on this one with them."

"You know Shandra doesn't like it when we steal free plays."

"Shandra went home an hour ago."

Mark's eyes brightened. "She did?"

Alyssa nodded.

Mark grinned. "In that case, let's get you dudes suited up and on the roster for the next dogfight!"

"Alright!" I agreed, scrubbing my palms together. My grin felt like it stretched a mile wide.

He pulled out a plastic pistol that doubled as an RF scanner and ran it over our bracelets before leading us toward racks lined with flight suits.

"Looks like Red needs three more players, and Green only one," Mark said.

Alyssa immediately reached for the green flight suit.

"Traitor," Tyler said.

"I'm not going to miss a chance to shoot you down while the wounds are still fresh," she replied.

"Good job, Tee," I said, knowing All-red would be a major problem out on the field. She and Lebowski were our strongest all-around players.

"Bad planning on my part," Tyler agreed. "I never saw myself in this situation."

We each picked a red flight suit from the rack. They were all the same size, and mine ended up stretched in the vertical and loose across the chest. Tyler's fit pretty well, while Alyssa's was baggy everywhere. I didn't say it out loud, but she looked like a turtle in the green suit.

A blaring of trumpets drew my attention to one of the screens. The current match had just ended, with Green triumphant. Two of their fighters remained, and they did barrel rolls as the players climbed out of their pods and headed for the racks, chatting excitedly. Only a few started removing their flight suits, meaning most of the same players would participate in the next match. That didn't bode well for my chances. They were all so good.

And they all knew Alyssa, greeting her as they gathered in the prep area. The immediate acceptance when she introduced us held my general social anxiety to a minimum. Besides, what was this compared to what I had already been through today? I forced my mind away from that avenue of thought. I had come to escape it for a few hours, not fall apart in front of a crowd.

"Looks like we're one short," a heavier college kid who had introduced himself as Jedi said. "You playing, Mark?"

"I guess I'll have to," he replied.

"Like that's such a hardship," another player joked.

"Am I too late for the next game?"

All our heads swiveled toward the latecomer. Around the same age as the others, he was in good shape, with a kind face framed by a mop of dark hair.

"No, you're just in time," Mark said, barely managing to

veil his disappointment as he reached for his scanner, running it across the new guy's bracelet.

"I'm Hondo," he said, eyes sweeping across the rest of us. He caught my gaze, holding it for a couple of seconds before pointing to the flight suits. "Looks like Red is short one, right?"

"That's right," Alyssa agreed.

Hondo made a face, turning to Mark. "Sorry. I guess I stole your thunder."

"It's no problem," Mark replied. "I'll have other chances."

We grabbed helmets from a separate rack, and split into two teams. I joined the rest of the Red squad pilots waiting on the marked side of the staging area.

"New meat better not drag us down," grumbled the oldest and least friendly of the group, call-sign Psych0K1l-l3r. He was the only one in the ten-person scrum older than twenty-five. "What do you guys think of a little added incentive? Twenty bucks says I smoke more Greens than any of you. And survive to the end of the match."

"In your dreams, old-timer," laughed one of the others, who had identified himself as ShottaLotta. "But feel free to toss your money this way when you crash and burn."

"I'm in," Hondo added, grinning.

"Sorry, I can't afford the gas to get home if I lose," Tyler said, bowing out. "And my man Katzuo here is broke."

"What kind of gamer tag is Katzuo?" Jedi asked.

"Katze is German for cat," I replied. "My father is…was German." I paused, fighting to keep myself composed. "Katsuo is a type of sushi, skipjack tuna. My mother was Japanese. It's a play on that."

"So, Catfish?" Jedi said.

"No, Katzuo," I corrected. "If I wanted to be Catfish, I would have chosen Catfish. Or probably Catfish920 or something lame like that." I turned to Tyler. "And I'm not broke."

"How much do you have in your wallet?" he asked.

I reached to my back pocket, only then realizing I had skipped out of the hospital without it. "Okay, I'm broke," I admitted while the others chuckled.

"First time?" Hondo asked.

"Yeah. You?"

"I've flown these things before."

There was something about the way he said it that gave me pause. The slight upturn of his lip? A twinkle in his eye? Either way, I was still trying to come up with something more to say when a buzzer sounded and the others started for their pods.

"Good luck," Hondo said with a friendly pat on my back before heading for his pod.

"This is way better than hanging out alone in a dreary hospital room, isn't it?" Tyler asked. He appeared beside me, face split by a beaming grin.

"Definitely," I replied. "Thank you for rescuing me."

"I thought this didn't qualify as a rescue mission."

"I changed my mind. It totally is."

He laughed, splitting away from me as we reached the last two open pods. I was a little bummed I didn't get Red-5. Of course, Psych0K1ll3r had. I hated him already.

Climbing into the pod, I settled into the padded seat, positioned behind a short steering column with a joystick, a throttle, and a pair of foot pedals. About the size of a small go-kart, the entire pod rested on a set of robotic arms that could raise and lower the platform from each corner. It allowed for up to twenty degrees of pitch and yaw to mimic the sensation of flight.

From what I had read online, the seats also contained a number of haptic sensors to give the player a nice jolt whenever they took a hit. I'd also read that the first version of the system had channeled all the visuals through the visor of the flight helmet. Equipped with the second generation pods, I was delighted when the faux cockpit closed around me and an organic 4k light-emitting diode, or OLED, instantly placed my pod in a star field my brain fell for in point-two seconds.

I was doubly delighted when a hologram joined the display, for the moment only showing the VR Awesome logo. Further examination of the controls revealed a button on the right marked HELP. I assumed it would alert Mark if the player needed anything and probably open the pod, quickly returning the person to reality in case he or she suffered from claustrophobia or airsickness once things really started rocking and rolling.

Not me, of course. All tragedy, sadness, and trauma aside, I really believed I had found myself right where I was supposed to be at this very moment.

Thanks to Tyler.

A soft tone sounded through speakers embedded in the back of the headrest. "Attention. Briefing will commence in thirty seconds," a woman said in a commanding voice.

A second tone sounded about thirty seconds later. The display on the monitor turned to a hangar bay, the outer doors sealed ahead of me and the rest of Red Team deployed as generic pilots in generic star fighters on either side. In the air, just below my eye level, a hologram of a woman wearing a crisp Space Force uniform appeared between me and the surround.. "I'm Commander Abigail Cage," she said. "Welcome to *Star Squadron*."

I nearly cried out in excitement, my heart pounding so hard it felt like it would burst out of my chest. I'd already had the same sensation today on the total opposite end of the spectrum. Swapping pain for pleasure, I could sense myself grinning like an idiot as Commander Cage continued. "If this is your first mission, raise your right hand so I can go over the basics with you. If you're a veteran, tap the thumb trigger on your stick to skip to the next section and standby."

I raised my right hand. Cameras hidden somewhere in the pod caught the motion.

"So, you want to become a *Star Squadron* ace," Cage said. My disbelief ended right there. As far as I was concerned, I was in a starfighter, in space, and Commander Cage was a real person talking to me from the CIC of the starship to which we were assigned. "You should know, it's a dangerous path you've chosen. A path that's claimed the lives of hundreds of aspiring pilots before you. Are you sure you want to continue?"

"Hell, yeah," I said with absolute conviction. There was only one thing I wanted more right now, and I had to force it back out of my thoughts so I could enjoy the moment.

Commander Cage smiled. "Good. The first thing you need to do is enter your callsign and a passcode. You'll only have to do this once to have all of your career information saved to central intelligence and available whenever you are part of *Star Squadron*, become a *Mech Jockey,* or participate in *Jungle Invasion*, among other challenges."

The projection added a floating keyboard, which amazed me by accurately capturing my airborne keypresses. I entered Katzuo and my usual password, eager to get to the next screen.

"Welcome to *Star Squadron*, Katzuo," Commander Cage said. "Next, you'll select your starfighter. All ships have the same basic capabilities, but as you gain experience you'll be able to upgrade to less common skins, and other improvements like better inertial dampeners that will soften the blow from hits. Bundles of credits and unique starfighter non-fungible tokens, or NFTs, are also available for purchase to enhance your gameplay experience."

A carousel of starship skins appeared on the monitor. I

used my hand to air-swipe left until they'd gone full circle. All the usuals were there. X-wing, Y-wing, Viper, Gunstar, Kilrathi Gothri, Warp Fighter, and one I think was from Buck Rogers whose name I didn't know. Among others. The X-wing tempted me, but I decided it was too mainstream and went with the Gunstar instead.

"Excellent choice," Cage said. I was certain every choice was an excellent one. "If you need to go over the control layout, raise your right hand. Otherwise, tap the thumb trigger on your stick to skip to the next section and standby."

I was sure I didn't need additional instruction, so I tapped the trigger and rested back in the seat as Commander Cage vanished. Still inside the hangar, I noticed the cockpit's interior had changed to match the skin I'd selected. Looking around, I saw that the other Red Team fighters had changed as well. Two X-wings and a Y-wing, not much of a surprise there. I was sure Tyler had chosen the Y, trying to be different without breaking pop culture. The last ship caused me to do a double take before leaving me staring.

Larger than the other ships, it appeared to be a robot head, with a corrugated metal grin, a set of spotlights for eyes, and four pairs of rotating turrets. One was mounted on each cheek and behind each armored ear. I definitely hadn't seen it in the standard selection, so I assumed it was one of the unique NFTs. It reminded me of the TARDIS in the way its ridiculousness emitted an aura of comfortable cool.

I was still staring when Commander Cage's voice startled me from my daze. "Attention *Star Squadron*! We've just jumped into the Aurea System. It's a trap! You must overcome the enemy starfighters or the fleet will surely be destroyed. I'm activating your comms now. Prepare to launch."

The dialog bordered on cringeworthy, but the end result was all that mattered. A click in my ears signaled the connection to the rest of Red Team. Before anyone could speak, emergency klaxons blared in my ears. Warning lights flashed at the front of the hangar. The lights on either side of the outer bay doors turned green, and once they opened, I punched the throttle. The pod tilted back and the harness around me tightened to simulate the G-force as my virtual starfighter launched into virtual space.

All of my external cares were temporarily forgotten.

CHAPTER 6

Two massive dreadnoughts exchanged broadsides with a planet-sized battle station, their flashes of energy weapons and missile trails crisscrossing the blackness filling the surround in front of me. Both the battle station and the hulking capital ships spewed out fighter squadrons in a heroic last stand for superiority.

Allyssa immediately broke off, joining the greens in their attack against the battle station. Psych0K1ll3r's voice broke over the comms. "Reds break and attack those greens with everything you have!" Neither side interfered with us as we selected targets and dove onto attack vectors in defense of the battle station..

I nudged the stick gently to starboard, sending my fighter banking away from the others. A glance at the hologram showed it had switched to a three-dimensional display of the battlefield, with both teams' starfighters outlined in their respective colors, along with the NPC warships that surrounded us. Two Greens shot right at us, attempting a pincer maneuver, while the remaining trio split wide to circle behind our squadron.

The lead Greens opened fire, green lasers bracketing me.

I twisted the ship through jinking turns and flew straight into a heavy beam from one of the dreadnoughts, barely avoiding the embarrassment of getting knocked out in the first ten seconds of our entrance into the fight. I turned hard left, trying to get out of the line of fire, and the two Greens gave chase. I wondered if Alyssa was in one of them, hoping to score two quick kills against her Stinking Badgers teammates for Tyler's invasion of her privacy. Considering her compassionate response to my reason for even being here, I doubted she would be so cold, at least toward me.

"You can't shake 'em, Cat," Hondo warned as green lasers flashed all around me, using up most of my nine lives in a hurry. "Lead them back this way."

I risked a quick glance rearward and spotted both Greens still glued to my tail. The better pilot hung further back while his wingmate made constant targeting runs, hoping to catch me off-guard. A floating hull segment spinning languidly ahead, offered a perfect point to change course. I rolled over and pulled my nose hard up, using the debris for a slingshot turn back toward my own support ships.

Sure enough, the overeager bogey kept coming through the turn, unable to adjust before the robot head swept in for the kill. "Your cash is so mine!" Psych0K1ll3r cried, denying the robot head ship first blood as his X-wing cut in front of Hondo, his missile vaporizing the enemy fighter on my tail.

I had initially thought Psych0K1ll3r had to be flying the robot head, but now I knew better. The head had to be Hondo. The other players didn't look like they could afford a ride so unique.

As for Psych0K1ll3r, he was just an asshole vulture.

My marginal gratitude lasted only seconds before another Green pilot cut in to take the place of the destroyed green fighter. I didn't know why they had chosen to gang up on me. Maybe it was as simple as my Gunstar selection.

Had picking something not from Star Wars made me more of a target? If so, then why weren't they going right for the robot head?

It was a rhetorical question. If Hondo had invested the cash for a unique skin, he had no doubt played the game a lot more often than anyone else here tonight. That didn't guarantee he was better than the rest of us, but what he lacked in skill he could probably make up for with dollar bills. Better to take out the obvious newbie first and then deal with the vet. The Stinking Badgers had employed that strategy plenty of times before.

Every trick I knew failed, shaking my determined foe. He matched me move for move, firing only occasional shots to remind me of his presence without overtaxing his weapons. I couldn't sustain breakneck aggression forever, but no amount of juking won me escape. Exasperation turned to alarm the longer we continued our deadly dance.

"Tag 'em and bag 'em!" Psych0K1ll3r crowed across the channel. "That's two for me. One more and I'll go home forty bucks richer."

"Red Three," Hondo said. "Swing around that dreadnought and pull a hard upward vector. Cat, break right, dip low, and go under. We'll swat that pesky fly off your tail."

That he had noticed my predicament impressed me. And his calm confidence nearly had me affirming command without hesitation. I knew it was a team game, but at the same time, I hadn't come here to be rescued. Once in a night was enough.

"Negative, Red Five," I replied. "I've got this one."

"Are you sure?" Hondo asked.

My brain said no. My mouth said, "Yeah. I'm sure."

I juked a few more times, watching how the Green pilot hung behind me, seemingly always one step ahead. Time had already proven I couldn't lose them this way, which in turn dialed my acceptable risk up to eleven.

I dropped all evasion and whipped the ship into a punishingly tight loop, briefly thankful for the limitations of the pod's delivery. Timing would be everything for this gamble to pay off. I turned until I sighted the trailing fighter and kept rotating back onto my original heading. Caught completely flat-footed, the Green pilot overshot wildly. I rolled out, squarely on his six. Squeezing hard on the trigger, I sent a hail of laser bolts into his tail, shattering his engines and sending the ship pinwheeling as it vanished in a fireball.

"Got him!" I cheered, adrenaline and excitement nearly overwhelming me. The desperate move shouldn't have worked against the obviously experienced player, but fortune had favored the bold. Surely that earned me some...

"Watch it, Cat!" Tyler shouted an instant before my ship shuddered under multiple impacts. Alarms blared damage warnings while I yanked the stick and aimed for empty space. "You're attracting the wrong kind of attention."

Annoyance replaced smugness at the cheap shot after winning my one-on-one. Things had suddenly gotten personal. I craned right and then left, seeking the offending ships, wanting names and payback. "Why the hell is everybody picking on me? Tyler's a newbie, too."

Tyler's laughter echoed over the comms. "They don't know who's who, man. They probably think you're me. I figured Ally would have her squad gunning my way. That's why I picked an X-wing."

"I thought you were in a Y," I replied.

"Nope. Fooled you, too."

"Katzuo, focus," Hondo said. "You can do this."

I couldn't guess the reason for his calming support, but I appreciated it, especially as green laser streaks blew by my port side, narrowly missing me. I followed the path back to a modified X-wing. Its black and green overlay definitely wasn't standard, nor was the row of skull decals proclaiming the pilot's aerial victories. Someone else in the fight had put down cash for some upgrades.

"That's Jedi showing off again," Psych0K1ll3r informed me as the modified X-wing banked tightly to reacquire weapons lock. From the looks of the grid, the vulture had no intention of helping me deal with any of my attackers.

Fine with me. I didn't want help before, and I definitely didn't want it now, especially from Jedi.

I punched the throttle, racing across the black toward the middle of a gnarly exchange of battery fire from a pair of opposing warships. Jedi trailed a few thousand meters behind, the other members of Green left too far behind to remain relevant to me. The modified X-wing's thrusters flared from blue to white, the trails extending as his electric boost kicked in, accelerating the ship's ion drive. He closed up behind me in a hurry. Everyone else faded as we rock-eted toward destiny, diving into the middle of the furious crossfire.

Larger, thicker bolts surrounded me as I juked and jinked. Eyes in constant motion, I checked the holographic grid and then glanced over my shoulder, searching for cover from the intense fire of the warship batteries. I barely made it through a few exchanges, escaping to cover behind a chunk of wreckage that went up in a cloud of debris just as I swung past it. Jedi clung tight to me, unleashing barrages I could tell were intended to funnel me toward the point of his real attack. The arrogant bastard had the better ship as if that alone guaranteed success. Too bad for him I remained unintimidated by bullies, especially those depending on such predictable maneuvers.

Jedi's trap sprang as expected, his nearly-algorithmic tactics telegraphing his intent. I had no doubt he expected me to panic without thinking and turn sloppy. My complete focus was on navigating the crossfire while I obliged him and centered us in his kill box. However, I wasn't offering myself up for the kill. I frantically jinked and rolled before nosing hard up. Jedi tried predicting my arc, but he didn't predict me throwing the Gunstar into a tight backflip at the top of my arc. He couldn't replicate it, leaving him squarely in my crosshairs halfway through his own turn.

"Surprise, idiot!" I snapped, mashing the thumb trigger. My Lasers hammered Jedi's cockpit, tearing through and killing his avatar before he had a chance to react. Still moving backward, I kept the dead hulk in the crosshairs until the lasers punctured armor and initiated a sympathetic chain reaction that turned his pretty starfighter into a short-lived blossom of flame.

"You're dogfighting in space, padawan," I cried out to nobody. "Class dismissed."

"Nice shooting, Cat," Psych0K1ll3r admitted begrudgingly. "Didn't know you had the furballs." He cracked himself up. "I guess I don't get the moolah this round."

I checked the grid. While I had been dogfighting Jedi, Hondo had finished off the final Green fighter. I winced when I saw Tyler had been knocked out of the fight, the only one of our team to have their ticket punched.

The simulation ended, the battlefield turning back into a star field. A holographic gold medal appeared on my dashboard, naming me the MVP of the fight.

"Are you kidding?" Psych0K1ll3r said over the comms. "I had two kills, too."

"Jealous?" I asked.

"Nah. Enjoy your fifteen minutes, pussycat," he laughed.

I thought the pod would open on its own, so I waited as the star field repeated and the seconds ticked past. At thirty, I decided something had gone wrong with the mechanism. Still calm, I reached for the HELP button, but before I could tap it, the screen suddenly changed.

"Searching for real adventure? " a voice asked that

reminded me of every action movie trailer I'd ever seen. "Looking for an escape?" The robot head starship shot forward, pausing front and center on the screen. A huge FOR RENT sign slammed down over it. "You've found it! The only question is, are you ready for the ride of your life? Don't miss this once in a lifetime opportunity."

The screen remained static for a few seconds before the robot head blasted away and the star field returned to normal. The pod finally opened while I stared at the screen in confused silence.

I had no idea what I had just seen.

I only knew that I needed to find Hondo.

CHAPTER 7

I scrambled out of the pod, wild eyes quickly scanning the group of players near the staging area. None of them had changed out of their flight suits, including Alyssa and Tyler, who I imagined were waiting to see if I wanted to go another round.

"Hondo!" I called out, searching the small crowd gathered between the pods and the equipment racks. Most of them turned to look my way, but the one person I wanted to talk to wasn't among them.

"Hey, Kitty-Cat, what's up?" Psych0K1ll3r asked. "That was some incredible flying out there." He had relaxed considerably now that the match was over. Apparently, asshole vulture was just his game face.

Even so, I barely registered the compliment, still scanning faces. "Thanks. Have you seen Hondo? The guy in the robot head ship?"

He shook his head with a baffled expression before looking over the gathered players himself. "No. That's strange. We all exited our pods at the same time, except for you."

"Yeah, my pod didn't open right away," I said, leaving it

at that for the moment. Finding Hondo was more important right now.

Where could he have gone so fast? Even with the delay, it hadn't taken me more than a minute to exit my simulator. How could he have made it out of the staging area that fast?

"Hey, Katzuo," a voice that didn't belong to Hondo said. Jedi approached me with a devilish grin, as if he planned to compliment me now for beating him and then jump me once I went outside.

"Jedi, have you seen Hondo?" I asked.

The question took him off-guard. "Who?"

"The guy with the curly black hair," I said. "Showed up late."

"Oh man, that guy had a crazy skin on his ship," Shotta-Lotta said, turning away from his chat with Alyssa. "A freaking giant robot head. LOL." He actually said 'el-oh-el,' which under any other circumstances would have drawn a weird look from me. Right now, I was too focused on the advertisement at the end of my game to care.

It was like Hondo had vanished into thin air.

"Whoa, someone's in a hurry," Tyler quipped, catching up to me. "Where's the fire, Cat? You already toasted one Jedi."

"You, Catman, that was a decent move you pulled on me," Jedi retorted. "I haven't seen anyone take advantage of the physics engine like that, especially their first time."

"Is that a backhanded way of suggesting he got lucky?" Alyssa asked, coming to my defense.

"If the sneaker fits," he replied.

"Someone sounds like a sore loser," Tyler added.

"No, it's not like that. I just think beginner's luck is real, and you had it on your side today."

"You have so many tells in your attack pattern. If we

were playing poker I'd not only beat you, I'd know what cards you were holding," I blurted without thinking.

His eyes narrowed. "What? You little mother—"

"Cool it," Mark said, stepping between us. "It may be adult swim, but we're still a family establishment. If you can't handle being beaten, you shouldn't play."

"Yeah, Jedi," Psych0K1ll3r agreed. "It's not like you've never lost before. Nobody wins every time."

"If he saw patterns in your flying, you should try buddying up instead of getting angry," Tyler said. "You might learn something new and maybe get better."

Jedi stood down with a nod. "Yeah, you're right. Sorry, Cat. I'm still a little hyped after that chase. It was a fun duel." He grinned sheepishly. "Until the end, anyway."

"No worries, Jedi. We're good," I said, not really interested in his argument or his apology. "Did any of you see a weird commercial after the match ended?" I asked, scanning each face, one after another.

Tyler and Alyssa exchanged confused looks. "No advertisements popped up on our end," she said. "The system reset to the home screen like normal."

"I didn't see anything," Psych0K1ll3r and ShottaLotta agreed.

"Me, neither," Jedi said.

"That's so strange." I ran anxious fingers through my already disheveled hair. "It was right there on my monitor. Like someone hijacked the feed to show me that robot ship and post a 'for rent' notice on it."

"He's renting out his NFT?" Alyssa asked.

"How would he get a commercial into the game?" Mark asked, obviously baffled.

"I know this is going to sound crazy," I said. "But it seemed more to me like the advertisement was for a real starship, not the skin he used in the match."

The comment drew laughter all around. I was surprised Jedi didn't just say 'LOL' again.

"What makes you think it was for a real ship?" Alyssa asked.

"I don't know. It just looked so real."

"That's the whole idea of VR, dude," Jedi said, still chuckling.

"You can laugh all you want. Maybe I'm crazy. Maybe it's just the end result of a day that's both the worst of my life and one of the best, as strange as that sounds to even say. Maybe I'm just going completely insane because of what I'm going through. Who knows? All I know is that it sparked something in me, and I need to find Hondo and ask him what it was all about."

"Calm down and think, Noah," Alyssa said. "Did the advertisement include any contact details? A phone number? Email address? Website? Anything?"

I mentally replayed the brief video, paying closer attention to specifics instead of letting my imagination run wild. "No, no info," I admitted reluctantly after a moment. "It didn't even list a price."

"Come on, man," Tyler said. "Who knows why, but it has to be Hondo just messing with you."

"Why would he do that? He seemed like a pretty nice guy during the match."

Alyssa smiled kindly. "I'm sure he didn't mean any harm."

I sighed, coming back down from my irrational heights. "Yeah, you're absolutely right. I'm being ridiculous. Everything else today finally caught up and knocked me for a loop, no pun intended. Just let the crazy be crazy for a few minutes. I'll be okay."

"That's the spirit," PsychoK1ll3r said.

"Regardless of the reasons for the commercial, I'm worried about how he was able to insert a video into the end of the runtime," Mark said. "The thought that some random customer can just hack our systems isn't very comforting."

"You should bring that up to Shandra," Alyssa said.

"I'll leave a note for her tonight. All we need is for our systems to be attacked and user data to end up compromised. I love this job. I don't want us to be shut down."

"Do you think we should close early?" Alyssa asked. "Just in case?"

"Wait, what?" I said. "I only had a chance to play one game."

"If Hondo, whoever he is, was able to stick a video into the end of the game, he's probably a skilled enough hacker to have broken into whatever he wanted to crack," Tyler said. "Shutting down now won't help anything. It'll just add more headaches."

Mark and Alyssa looked at one another, silently negotiating the outcome.

"Please," I said, eager to give another title a shot. Maybe *Jungle Invasion*.

"T-Bone's right," Alyssa said. "If there's any damage, it's already done. Hopefully, Hondo was just having a little fun at Noah's expense. Let Shandra deal with it tomorrow."

Mark nodded. "Yeah, okay. We'll keep this between us for now."

"Thank you!" I shouted in relief, practically coming to tears and leaving no question about the fragility of my current emotional state.

"We've still got a solid hour left on the play clocks if you want to jump into another round. I'm itching for payback against little Miss All-red over here."

Alyssa shrugged nonchalantly. "Promises, promises. But we all know I can run circles around you any day of the week." Her playful retort raised welcoming smiles. Lingering emotional turmoil wouldn't stand a chance against friendly competition. Maybe that had been Hondo's goal in showing me that advertisement. To pull me fully into the moment.

I let the last ragged edges of Hondo's puzzling disappearance go, turning bright eyes Tyler's way. "I hope you've got a few more lives left. Because you're going to need them!"

"Rematch then?" Jedi asked. "Maybe you can brief me on my tells ahead of time, so I can smoke you in this round."

"I don't know," I replied. "I think it might be better to pause my *Star Squadron* career while I'm ahead. At least for tonight. I really want to try the other games, too."

Jedi shrugged. "All right. I haven't played the others as much as this one, but I'm happy to hunt you down wherever you go."

"Dude, let it go for tonight," ShottaLotta said. "I'm sure Noah will be back, assuming Hondo doesn't hack everything and get the place sued and shuttered."

"You'll definitely have another chance," I said. "We made it out this far once, I'm sure we can do it again, right Tyler?"

Tyler grinned and nodded. "Yeah, man. That sounds great."

"If you're coming back, I might have to find another job," Alyssa teased.

"What's your number?" Jedi asked. "I'll send you a text so we can stay in touch."

The request surprised me. "You can all add me to your contacts if you want," I said, giving them my cell number. My phone immediately buzzed in my pocket. Once. Twice. Three times in rapid succession. Finally, a fourth. "I'm on social media, too," I added, digging my phone out to check the messages. "Katzuo, of course."

I looked at the screen. The senders were all listed by

their phone numbers, but I checked the messages to see who was who. Alyssa, Cody (Jedi), and Phil (Psychok1ll3r) had all reached out. The sense of camaraderie nearly overwhelmed me, threatening to break me down again. In the time when I needed real, physical friends the most, there they were. I needed to believe that somehow my parents had something to do with that.

The moment hit me so hard, I almost didn't notice the last message in the group of incoming texts.

See you at Jefferson Farm.

CHAPTER 8

My eyes remained glued to my phone screen, pulse elevating as I read and reread Hondo's text.

See you at Jefferson Farm.

I had barely begun considering the implications of the message when Alyssa's gentle hand on my shoulder drew my attention.

"Noah, are you okay?" she asked. "I know you've been through a lot today. We're here for you if you want to talk."

Five sets of eyes broadcast the same supportive message from where the group had paused preparing for a rematch. I blinked hard, temporarily overwhelmed by their collective kindness. Most of them didn't even know exactly what Alyssa was referring to. I'd only mentioned being in an accident earlier to explain away the bandages and bruises. I hadn't told anyone else my full tale of loss.

"I know." I swallowed the emotional lump in my throat and passed Alyssa my phone. "And I appreciate everyone rallying around a total stranger. I think Hondo sent me a text."

"You gave him your number?" Tyler asked.

"No," I replied, a chill running down my spine. "That's the weird part."

"This whole thing is *the weird part*," he countered. The others murmured in affirmation.

Alyssa studied the brief message, her forehead wrinkling. "Jefferson Farm? I can't say it's familiar." Alyssa handed the device off to Mark with a questioning glance. "Any idea what's out there?"

"Not a clue." After giving the message a quick scan, he passed the phone along to Tyler. "It's some old homestead surrounded by cornfields would be my guess. Shotta, you ever heard of it?"

"No. Jedi?"

"It sounds familiar," he replied. "Maybe they do hayrides and pumpkin picking? It's possible I went there once as a kid. My parents took me to a bunch of farms."

"This is Iowa," PsychoK1ll3r agreed. "I don't know Jefferson Farm, but I can rattle off a dozen others."

"Well, Google makes it look legit," Tyler said. He angled the screen my way, highlighting a web page featuring an antique tractor and weathered barn. "Says they host fall festivals and allow visitors to wander the property."

"Ha!" Jedi exclaimed. "See? I was right."

"Is everything a competition to you?" Tyler asked.

"I'm just saying."

"Why would Hondo send you there?" Alyssa wondered aloud.

I reclaimed the phone, feeling irrationally defensive. "I wish I knew. That's why I need to check it out."

"I wouldn't do that if I were you," Jedi scoffed. "I'll bet cash money he's some creeper who lures people to dark places to murder them."

"For real?" Tyler fired back. "Project much?"

"I've read about this kind of thing!" Jedi doubled down.

"Don't be a chump. You go out there, you're signing your own death certificate."

I waved off his obvious exaggeration. "I'm not afraid. And I'm definitely going, so you can give up the criminal profiling."

"Your funeral, man," Jedi persisted, folding his arms over his chest. "Just don't come back as a haunt and say I didn't warn you."

"Noah, we don't know anything about this Hondo guy," Tyler added. "Except that he hacked into the VR Awesome servers and also somehow got his hands on your cell number."

"Maybe he bumped you while you were waiting for the game to start," PsychoK1ll3r suggested.

"Bumped me?"

"It's the pickpocketing technique they use in the movies. The thief bumps into the mark and uses the distraction to lift his or her wallet, or phone in this case."

"And how did he unlock it to see my number?" I asked. "I have Face ID on."

PsychoK1ll3r made a face, stymied by the response.

"The point is, you can't trust this," Jedi said. "At all. I don't know you that well, but you picked out the tells in my flying inside of a minute and blasted me to space dust, so you must be somewhat intelligent. You have to be able to reason that pursuing this is a bad idea. Serial killer or not, if you go to the farm, you're only going to find trouble."

"I agree," Shotta said. "Let it rest, Katzuo."

I looked at each of them, genuinely appreciative of their sincere concern for my well-being. Part of me knew they were right; I should just drop the whole thing. But the other part of me—the part that hurt so bad that if I paid it any mind, the only thing I felt was numb misery—wanted to see how deep the rabbit hole went. No, it *needed* to see how deep the rabbit hole went.

"You guys don't understand," I said, shaking my head. "I can't let it go. I have to check it out. The only other option is…" I trailed off, not wanting to go there.

"It's nearly one in the morning," Alyssa said gently, draping her arm over my shoulders. It was no easy task since I was nearly a full head taller than her. "Maybe sleep on it and see if he messages you again tomorrow?" Her question came out more as a plea.

I set my jaw obstinately. "I don't have time. It's now or never." I looked at Tyler. "Are you doing this with me, or what?"

"Yeah, if you go, I gotta go; I'm driving," Tyler replied, stepping up beside me wearing his already trademark devil-may-care grin. "I've got your back if things get sketchy."

"Then I should come too," Alyssa decided after a thoughtful beat. "Three makes less enticing bait for serial killers." She tried amplifying weak humor with an unconvincing smile. "Mark, is it okay if I bail an hour early?"

"I'm not your boss," he replied.

"No, but you can cover for me."

He hesitated before nodding. "Fine. But you owe me one."

"Deal."

"Anyone else want to tag along?" Tyler asked.

No one else came forward. They had enjoyed our match, but their sense of adventure appeared to be limited to what could be achieved in pixels.

Jedi eyed us as if we had lost our collective minds. "I warned you. Remember that when you wake up chained inside a pit wearing a face mask made of human skin."

"Noted," I said, refusing further engagement with his morbid scenario. "Well, anyway, it was great meeting you all. Assuming we aren't chopped into little pieces by morning, T-Bone and I will be back for another round sooner or later."

"Looking forward to it, Katzuo," Jedi said. "In all seriousness, be safe out there."

"Thanks," I replied. "We will."

We said goodbye to Mark, ShottaLotta and PsychoK1ll3r before heading for the parking lot, exiting through the front this time.

"I can't believe I'm doing this," Alyssa said as we stepped outside.

"I can't believe you're doing this, either," Tyler said. "I thought you hated my guts."

"I sort of do, but I feel this strange big sister instinct to keep an eye on Noah. Especially since he doesn't have anyone else to watch over him."

"Please don't remind me of that right now," I said, choking back the pursuant emotions.

"Sorry," she replied.

"Well, in that case, do you have a car?" Tyler said. "I mean, we can take my ride, but I have to offer another sacrifice to the Kia gods for every mile she makes it without falling apart."

"Sorry, Tee," she answered. "I took an Uber here."

"That might not be a bad idea," he offered.

"Yeah, good luck getting a driver to take us out to a creepy farm in the middle of the night," she countered.

"You don't know it's creepy."

"I have an idea," I said. "Let's take your car, Tyler."

They both laughed. "Your wish is my command," he joked, waving me toward the back of the lot.

"I owe you one, Tee," I said.

"You owe me at least two. But what are favors among friends?" We exchanged a knowing glance. Not gamer friends or lab buddies. Real friends. He grabbed me by the back of the neck and gave me an easy jostle.

"Aww, you two are so adorable," Alyssa teased, killing the moment.

I hurried to the car at a fast walk, prompting Tyler and Alyssa to do the same. There was no way for me to know for certain why Hondo had summoned me to Jefferson Farm, but by the time we reached the Kia, I had convinced myself that something inexplicable and amazing awaited us there.

We just had to be willing to claim it.

CHAPTER 9

Leaning against the door, I had the Kia's rear bench seat all to myself on our return trip through Des Moines. I watched the city quickly thin into suburbs and then scattered rural acreages before the outlying homes faded into dark countryside. Tyler had started off following Maps, but Alyssa wound up scrolling through satellite views and going audible with turn-by-turn when the algorithm lost the way. I tuned out their aimless chatter about favorite foods and game tropes, my thoughts lingering instead on Hondo's vexing disappearance and subsequent message.

Would he be at the farm when we arrived? Or had his cryptic text intended for us to head out in the morning for a more proper meet? Would he pop out of the corn like Pennywise the clown, knife in hand, ready to skin us alive like Jedi had claimed, or did he have some completely innocent reason for the subterfuge?

Unnervingly, the former felt much more logical than the latter. If Hondo meant no harm, why hadn't he stuck around after the match and spoken to me in person? Why make it into a mysterious game with such dark overtones?

If it was a game, how poorly was I playing it right now? Maybe noting specifics on the robot head advertisement could have provided clues about his identity or intent. Even now, I could only recall the post-credit scene in generic terms. I had been too pumped after winning *Star Squadron* to pay such close attention.

And what the heck were we even doing out here right now? It wasn't only my death and dismemberment at stake. I glanced at the backs of Tee and Ally's heads, second thoughts gnawing at me. Still, my attention returning to the passing countryside, I couldn't bring myself to ask Tyler to turn around. Not when we'd already come this far.

"Stay with us, Noah." Alyssa's gentle prompt nudged me back from gloomy abstraction. "We were just talking about what your parents might think if they knew you rode off into the night with an older woman."

I scoffed mildly. "I think they would have major issues with my life choices right about now." I once again tamped down jagged emotions that the simple reminder brought back to the surface of my thoughts. I turned my tired eyes back to the black fields sliding past the window. Lingering fog diffused occasional electrical poles along the roadside as we barreled past empty pastures. It hurt to talk about my folks in any respect, but maybe counterintuitively, it also helped me work through my grief.

"My folks grounded me for a month when I went to an illegal street race back in sophomore year of High School," Alyssa shared, evidently trying to commiserate. "I lost phone privileges and had to do all the household chores for a month."

"Street racing?" Tyler replied. "You don't seem like the type to enjoy that sort of thing."

"Reminder," Alyssa retorted. "You don't know me." She released her attitude with a shrug. "But yeah, it was stupid.

I just wanted to fit in with the cool people for once. Typical teenage angst, I guess. Instead, the cops showed up and rounded up the newbies who didn't know when it was time to make ourselves scarce."

"You went to prison?" I asked.

"No. They brought us to the local precinct and called our parents. I think I would've been happier to spend the night in the hoosegow."

"Who uses that word?" Tyler laughed.

"What word? *Hoosegow*? It's a great word."

Our chatter devolved into a debate regarding what punishments might fit my crimes. In the end, we determined a final verdict was impossible to reach, but only because I hadn't finished committing my offenses yet. Regardless, the turn in conversation from food and gaming had sucked me in, so much so that I flinched when Tyler shut off the engine. He left the headlights on, the beams dimming when the engine turned over a couple more times before finally sputtering and dying.

"We're heeeeerrre," Tyler announced in a creepy voice, the limited light allowing us to see only a little way out into the open pastures surrounding us. We could make out the entirety of a rambling two-story farmhouse and a detached garage only because they were painted white. A leaning barn and various other outbuildings were nothing more than colorless silhouettes.

"Are you sure this is Jefferson Farm?" I asked.

"You didn't see the sign back at the main road?"

"I guess not. I was neck deep in social therapy."

"This is the place, man," he assured me, finally killing the headlights and leaving us in pitch black. He turned on his phone's flashlight and looked at me over his shoulder. "Maybe no one's home."

"Maybe we *should* come back in the morning," Alyssa suggested.

"Let me see if Hondo sent me anything else. Maybe he saw us coming up the road." I checked my phone. No new alerts waited. "Nope. We're on our own."

"I should've listened to Jedi."

"What happened to taking care of your new kid brother?" Tyler asked.

"We all should have listened to Jedi," she corrected.

"It's not that creepy," Tyler scoffed. "Come on, let's take a look around."

"How? I can't see much of anything out there."

He responded by shining his phone's flashlight out through the window, the action absurd enough to draw my laughter. "That's the spirit, compadre," he said, shoving open his door and hopping from the driver's seat with his customary bravado.

Alyssa slipped out the passenger side wearing a dubious expression. "At least no cleaver-wielding madman or drooling hellhounds have jumped us," she said, closing the door.

"Yet," Tyler replied, sticking the phone under his chin to shine the light up at his face. "Mwahahahahaha!"

"If there is a serial killer out here, do you really want to advertise yourself like that?" I asked.

He lowered the phone, still grinning. "Maybe we should look around for a starship made in the shape of a robot head, ya think?"

"Or a robot head that was converted into a starship," Alyssa suggested.

"Are you two mocking me?" I asked.

"A little," Ally admitted. "It helps with the nerves."

I trailed the pair toward the garage. Once we got close, we could see that the paint on it and the house was starting to peel away. Ty stopped to shine his phone light through the garage window. "No starship in here," he said, looking back at me. "No car, either. It's empty."

We headed up a cracked cement walkway to the front porch, our footsteps sounding abnormally loud given the noticeable absence of the wildlife noises one might expect on rural acreage. I followed Ty up the steps, hoping the porch light was motion activated, letting us know that the place was actually lived in. Naturally, the porch light didn't illuminate. Neither did any lights inside the house.

"Well, go ahead. Knock," I suggested, once we stood at the front door.

"What if this is all a joke, and some pissed off farmer opens the door with a loaded shotgun?" Tyler replied. "Haven't you heard those news stories about the crazies who shoot first and ask questions later?"

"And you thought Jedi's imagination cup had runneth over," I said. "That's not going to happen."

"Yeah, right."

"Look, shotgun or not, if anyone was home, they would have caught our headlights from half a mile out," Alyssa said. "If they're gonna come out shooting, we're dead meat, right where we stand. Knock and get it over with."

"Go for it, Tee," I agreed.

"I don't know," he said, shining his flashlight through the plate glass window beside the door. "From the looks of it, the place has been cleaned out."

"As in, there's nobody alive inside?" I asked.

"Sure seems that way. Or if they are, they Kondo'ed the hell out of the place."

"I don't get it," Alyssa whispered. "Does Hondo live here? Work here? Or maybe this belongs to the guy who custom-painted his starship?" She eyed me in amusement.

"I never said Hondo had an actual ship," I argued.

"You sort of did," Tyler countered. "Starship for rent, remember? The adventure of a lifetime." He breathed in deeply, and before Alyssa or I could slap a hand over his mouth, he released a deep-throated bellow. "Heeeellll-looooooo! Anybody home? Olly-olly-oxen free!"

Alyssa gave out a whimper, and we all froze as Tyler's voice echoed in the darkness, fading away without eliciting a response. "And you gave me crap about hoosegow?" she said.

A brittle sigh escaped my nerve-clenched throat. "This was stupid. I'm sorry. I shouldn't have dragged you both out here. We should probably get going before—"

Suddenly, a trio of floodlights flashed on—one by the barn, another at the closest corner of the cornfield in front of the house, and the third one at the far side of the house—surrounding us in brilliant white light. I staggered toward Tyler, blinded by the sudden illumination. Alyssa yelped and grabbed my arm, gripping fiercely enough to open the cut beneath one of my bandages. I reached over and loosened her fingers, but left my hand there, holding hers to my arm.Tyler stepped bravely in front of us as if preparing to ward off demons with his phone's flashlight as they rushed from the cornstalks brandishing fiery scythes.

No demons appeared. And yet nobody relaxed.

"What the hell?" Tyler said.

I waited for an encounter that seemed a foregone conclusion now that the farm was lit up like a prison exercise yard. As my eyes adjusted to the bright light, I could see a narrow but obvious path worn through the cornstalks. Small, battery-powered LEDs rested on either side of the dirt aisle, waiting for motion to activate them.

"He wants us to follow that path," I said, pointing to the evidence.

"Isn't that how Jedi suggested this would go?" Tyler asked.

"A little too closely," Alyssa agreed. "Let's get out of here." She tugged me down the steps, but I stopped there,

Ty right behind us. Ally pulled on me but she was too small and light to detach my feet from the ground.

My curiosity kept me from heeding Jedi's potential warning. How could something so obviously orchestrated, not to mention incredibly visible, be a forerunner to a grisly demise among the ears of corn? "Let's go check it out," I countered.

Alyssa and I both looked to Tyler for the tiebreaker. "Do you really have to ask?" he wondered out loud, flashing his already familiar mischievous grin. He pointed toward the dirt path. "Tally ho."

The first line of LEDs activated as we neared, kicking off a domino effect that continued onward as we pushed deeper into the corn.

"I wonder if this will turn into a maze," I said, excitement building as we followed the trail.

"With Hondo playing the minotaur," Alyssa said.

"Or Jack Nicholson from *The Shining*," Tyler added.

"To be honest, I'd rather die out here tonight than go home without answers," I decided.

"That makes one of us," Alyssa replied.

We froze and looked back when all three spotlights went out behind us. It left us with only the motion-activated LEDs on the ground that lit up when we got within ten feet of them. Then they shut off when we moved ten feet beyond them, leaving us feeling alone and adrift in the sea of stalks.

"I hate everything about this," Alyssa said, eyeing our predicament with saucer eyes.

"We'll be fine," Tyler said, though his tone didn't convince me. Not that I needed convincing. I had committed fully to the adventure by now. Fear of the dark was nothing compared to what I had already experienced today. Even fear of dying took a back seat. I forged ahead, leaving Tee and Ally to follow.

The path through the corn turned left, then right, and left again. It wasn't really a maze, but it wasn't a straight line, either. As we wandered, I amused myself by thinking about how much all the battery-powered LED lights on the ground must have cost. I grinned, picturing Hondo taking delivery of a thousand AAA batteries from a dusty Amazon truck, the gears of his nefarious plot spinning in his mind as he unpacked and laid them all out. I imagined him waiting at the end of the maze, a huge carving knife in one hand, a taser in the other, and maybe a prepared firepit in a crop circle behind him. Meanwhile, I could still feel the tension emitting like solar flares from Alyssa and Tyler.

We reached the fourth turn. Then the fifth. By turn seven we'd plunged beyond any sense of direction, with no comprehension of where we were within the cornfield. We negotiated turn eight and then nine, still without a clue about the point to all this.

I pushed forward, ignoring the misgivings of my less than steely-eyed companions. Well past the point of no return, it wasn't until the tenth and final change in direction when destiny at last revealed itself at the end of the path.

WTF?

We stopped in our tracks. Wide-eyed, Tyler let loose a low whistle. Alyssa's hand dropped from my arm and she let out a shocked squeak. As for me, I stared without comment, a smile lingering at the corners of my mouth. Inside me, emotions played like a symphony as I tried to make sense of what I was seeing.

A sign had been set out ten feet ahead of us. Red and blue carnival bulbs framed a neatly stenciled proclamation:

Starship Rides - $20.

A dozen feet behind it waited a simple wood and canvas structure. Like the sign, red and blue lights surrounded what was no more than an open-sided lean to, making it clear no one waited inside.

There was no sign of a starship, though the clearing in the midst of the corn seemed plenty large enough to fit the robot head.

There was no sign of Hondo, either.

"Okay, you got us." Tyler shouted, likely assuming Hondo and a film crew waited just out of sight, hidden in the corn. "Come on out and take a bow so we can all have a good laugh before heading out. And make sure to send us the link to the TikTok vid so we can relive the moment again and again."

No one emerged from the surrounding stalks. We remained fixed in place, sharing sidelong glances of confusion, amusement, and remorse. I'd lost out on my last hour of play at VR Awesome to be here. Tyler had put fifty extra miles on his beater, not to mention the gas he'd wasted. And Alyssa had skipped work early and stayed up late.

All for nothing.

"I guess he did mean for us to come in the morning," I said after a pregnant silence.

Alyssa and Tyler both looked at me before bursting out in laughter. Infectious, I started cracking up too.

"At least there's no serial killer out here," Alyssa said. "Maybe if you come back in the morning, there will be an actual starship waiting."

"I can't come back," I replied, the thought deflating me in an instant. "I have too much to deal with to sneak back out again. This was my only shot."

"I'm so sorry, Noah," Alyssa said. "I forgot about that. At least we know where this place is. You can come back once things have settled down. Maybe Hondo will still be here."

"I doubt it," I said, hanging my head. I'd convinced myself that this could be something magical. Instead, it was a total bust.

"You'd better step back," someone said, walking soundlessly up behind us. Startled, we reacted as a single unit, whirling around to face…

"Hondo! What the hell!" I cried, a huge grin splitting my face as my emotions did another one-eighty.

"Hondo's my callsign," he answered. "My name is Benjamin Murdock. You can call me Ben. I thought you came for the adventure of a lifetime."

"I did," I said, nodding like a bobblehead. "I totally did."

"Geez, man," Tyler said. "You scared the crap out of us. What's with all the creepy corn and sneaking around?"

"You aren't going to murder us, are you?" Alyssa asked.

"Murder?" He laughed. "No. I hope you aren't disappointed. Creepy corn and sneaking around? You can't exactly leave a starship sitting out where anyone can find it. The next thing you know, men in black SUVs are showing up looking for you, the Space Force is taking potshots at you, and you can't get from here to the other side of the galaxy without jumping through a thousand celestial hoops. It's just work, work, work, all the time."

Hondo… Or rather, Ben's mention of men in black SUVs froze me in place, a chill spreading across my entire body.

"Noah, are you okay?" He asked before making a face. "Oh, damn. I'm so stupid sometimes. Bad choice of words. I'm so sorry about your parents."

"It…it wasn't the government, was it?" I asked, fighting to recover my composure.

"Not that I know of," Ben replied. "But I don't know everything."

"How did you know about his parents?" Alyssa asked.

"How did you know his name?" Tyler added. "He never gave it to you back at VR Awesome."

"Reasonable questions, with reasonable answers. And I'll get to that soon enough. But first, you really should step this way." He motioned us toward him, and we joined him at the end of the path where it merged with the clearing. As we did, a slight breeze hit me in the back of the neck, ruffling my hair. "Now, turn around."

We did, and what we saw took our collective breaths away.

CHAPTER 10

"How the hell did you do that?"

Those were the first words out of Tyler's mouth as we stared at the robot head starship that had appeared beside the ticket booth as if from thin air.

It looked just like Ben's starfighter skin from *Star Squadron*, except it was significantly larger. At least eighty feet tall, it spiked high into the darkened sky, its corrugated metal grin more sinister in person than in pixels. The gun turrets were there too, huge and menacing, while the unlit spotlights jutted well out, promising a sun-like brilliance when activated.

The surface of the ship itself seemed to be composed from scrap metal, some new, some rusted, most of it drab metal, the remainder in various colors. I spotted a couple of riveted panels that still had bits of text along the edges. I recognized one as Maersk, the shipping company.

There was no way this thing was real.

"That's some David Copperfield level magic," Alyssa agreed, apparently unfazed by the starship itself. "Considering the darkness and the uniformity of our surroundings,

I bet you hid it from this vantage point pretty easily with mirrors."

Ben's grin hadn't faded at all when I glanced back at him, wondering how he would take the comment.

"No mirrors," he replied. "No tricks. At least, not in a traditional sense."

"Is that thing really a starship?" I asked. I had already suspended so much disbelief to keep myself sane today, it was an easy leap to believe it could be, despite all other signs pointing to a scam, a fraud, or a joke.

"It doesn't look like much, I agree," Ben said. "But she's got it where it counts."

Tyler's head whipped around. "Are you quoting Star Wars?"

"I'm not an alien, if that's what you're asking. In fact, I was you four years ago."

"What do you mean?" I asked.

"I'll explain everything once we go inside. First, you need tickets." He pointed to the booth, where a man and woman had appeared. While the starship's appearance may have been magical, it occurred to me that they might have been hiding beneath the counter the entire time. They were both just over five feet tall and rail-thin, with short brown hair, small noses, and soft faces.

"Tickets?" I said. "I don't have any money."

Ben made a face. "How did you pay at VR Awesome without any money?"

"I snuck him and Tyler in," Alyssa said. "They weren't supposed to be there. But you already know that, don't you?"

"What makes you say that?"

"You knew Noah's name," Tyler said. "And what happened to him today."

"Well, you caught me," Ben said. "Badabing badaboom."

"Bada-what?" Tyler asked.

"Sorry. My friend Keep says that a lot. Sometimes it gets in my head and I start saying it too."

"I'm so lost right now," I said, turning to Tyler. "I need to borrow another twenty. You know I'm good for it."

"I know, man," Tyler said, pulling his wallet from his pants pocket and opening it to show he had no cash, "but I'm dry, too…" He looked at Ben. "…unless you take Visa."

"Sorry, it's cash only."

We both looked at Alyssa, who was laughing. "You claim to have a starship for rent, but you don't take credit?"

"It's the processing fees," Ben said. "Our margins are razor thin as it is."

"Are you for real?" Tyler asked. "There's no way you can operate a starship for sixty dollars."

"Let's say I pony up," Alyssa added. "What does this ride entail? Because right now, I'm betting you have a mobile VR setup, not unlike VR Awesome. You already proved you can get into our systems. You probably downloaded the source code."

"I didn't download the source code from your servers," Ben replied, still showing no signs of insult from our accusations. "And it's not virtual reality. Head Case is a real, functioning starship. What your money buys is a ride up to orbit for some sightseeing of Earth from space, followed by an FTL transit to Mars, maybe a stop at Venus if we have time, and then back home. It takes about an hour, total."

"Did you say FTL?" I asked. Excitement at hearing the letters left me tied in knots that I didn't have the down payment. "What kind of system do you use?"

"Standard FTL is based on Alcubierre," Ben answered, which by itself nearly made my head explode. "The original equations had some incorrect assumptions, but they've been corrected and of course, the whole kit has been upgraded over time. It's pretty ho-hum these days."

"For you, maybe," I replied. "What about energy requirements?"

"Meg and Leo will be happy to share more details during the ride," Ben said, pointing to the pair in the ticket booth.

"Ally, please?" I begged, looking at her.

"I've only got fifteen dollars," she replied, holding up a ten and some singles.

I turned to Ben. "Maybe we can wash dishes or something after the ride," I suggested.

"I really hate to be the voice of reason," Tyler said. "Because it's totally unlike me. But why should we believe this ugly-mug giant robot head is anything more than a scrap metal and cardboard construct?"

"If we don't leave Earth, I'll give you your money back," Ben answered.

"But we don't have any money!" I cried, just about ready to fall apart again. At least, until I noticed how amused and at ease Ben seemed by this entire encounter.

"Ben!" I turned my head back toward the starship. A blonde-haired guy in a tight black tee and jeans that showed off his buff physique had opened a door in the center of the ship's grin, making it look as if it had gotten one of its teeth knocked out. The guy spread his hands in question. "Are we taking off or what? Satellite flyover is in less than five minutes."

"What?" Ben pushed back his sleeve to check a regular wristwatch. "We should have at least twelve more minutes."

"You forgot about that new satellite Starlink launched a couple weeks ago."

"They said that was for internet access."

"Yeah. Uh-huh. And you believed that? Its signature is oozing surveillance."

"Okay, I'll wrap this up." He looked at us again as the other guy vanished back into the ship.

"Who was that?" Alyssa asked. "He's gorgeous."

Ben rolled his eyes. "So I've heard. Matt's my business partner. We're co-owners of Head Case."

"Head Case is the ship?" Tyler said, grinning.

"Yes."

"Cool name."

"Thank you." He shrugged. " We like it. Anyway, it seems we have to get moving before our little secret is discovered. Since you don't have any money, I guess this is goodbye."

"Wait!" I said, grabbing Ben by the shoulder. He looked at me, then at my hand, and everything in me down to the last atom told me I should let go immediately. "Sorry," I said, pulling my hand away.

It was then that I noticed a blue squirrel had appeared on Ben's opposite shoulder, glaring at me with huge, contemptuous eyes. It buzzed like an angry swarm of hornets, its fur shivering with the effort.

"Awww," Alyssa purred behind me. "What is that little critter? It's so cute."

The blue squirrel's head swiveled toward Alyssa. His buzzing sounded like he didn't appreciate being called cute.

"Does it understand English?" Tyler asked.

"He does," Ben confirmed. "His name is Shaq. He's a Jagger. Sorry about his attitude. He doesn't like it when people touch me." The creature buzzed more softly in Ben's ear and nuzzled his cheek. "At least she didn't call you a blue squirrel," he answered the creature.

"And you understand him?" Tyler questioned.

"Or course. He's not a pet. He's an ILF."

"An elf?" I asked.

"ILF," Ben repeated. "Intelligent Life Form."

"Oh, like Alf," Tyler said.

"He was an Alien Life Form," Ben said.

"Yeah, I know. Same thing, right?"

"Alf was a puppet. And Shaq's only an alien on Earth."

"Where did you get him?" Alyssa questioned, shoving an elbow into Tyler's ribs to get him off the subject.

"I didn't *get* him," Ben stressed. "I befriended him."

"In a galaxy far, far, away?" Tyler asked.

"Actually, yeah."

"So why aren't we going there instead of Mars? I'd love to see some other ALFs."

"ILFs," I corrected.

"To-ma-to, to-mah-to."

"I think a round trip from Earth to Mars for twenty bucks from each of you is a pretty fair deal," Ben said.

"Except we don't have sixty bucks and you don't take credit," I reminded him.

"Which I can't," he reminded us. "See you around."

He shifted to head for his ship. I jumped into his path. "Wait, please. You know what happened. My heart already broke once today. You showed me that advertisement at the end of the game. There had to be a reason for that. Maybe you know how much I love space stuff. Maybe you got my Google search history so you know how much research I've done. What you offered me is a dream come true. What you offered me…I dragged my friends out here in the middle of the night because it was too good not to look into. Too good to be true, but it is true. I wasn't sure before, but unless you crossbred a squirrel and a tarsier monkey and dyed its hair blue, that's a real alien, and that…" I pointed to Head Case. "…is a real starship."

"See," Tyler said. "Alien."

"Please, Ben. I'll do anything. Work the galley. Swab the

poop deck. Whatever you want." I fell to my knees, clasping my palms together and looking imploringly up at him. It was admittedly a pathetic display, but I'd never wanted anything more.

Well, there was one thing I wanted more, but that was impossible. Unlike this.

"I know you want this, but have some pride," Tyler said in response to my groveling.

Alyssa surprised me, joining me on the muddy ground, getting her knees wet and dirty to beg beside me. "Please, Ben. Noah's a nice guy. He's really hurting right now. I don't think anyone would enjoy or appreciate this more."

Ben gazed at us without speaking, his eyes shifting expectantly to Tyler.

"Are you going to make me beg?" Ty asked.

Ben shrugged.

"Come on, T-Bone," I said.

"Fine," he said at last, dropping to his knees on my other side. "But only because I didn't want to risk the last few miles on the Kia for nothing. Just please don't ask me to swab the poop deck. I don't know what that is, but I have coprophobia."

"What's coprophobia?" Ben asked.

"I'll tell you once we're on board."

Ben nodded. "All right. Get up. You're making me feel guilty. Follow me." He stepped around us as we returned to our feet, leading us to the ticket counter. "Meg, Leo, this is Noah, Tyler, and Alyssa."

"How do you…" Alyssa trailed off before she finished asking how he knew her name.

"Pleased to meet you," Leo said with a smile.

"I'm more pleased than he is," Meg said.

Seeing them up close, it was obvious they were siblings, maybe even twins.

"You are not," Leo countered.

"Sure am."

"We've got three minutes to bounce out of here," Ben said. "Can we stow the bickering until we're airborne?"

"Sorry, Captain," Leo said. They both reached under the counter. Leo produced two robot head shaped badges, Meg one.

"These are both tickets and comm badges," Ben said. "Just like Star Trek, tap it and say the name of the person you want to talk to, and it'll ping them."

"Which one of you is Katzuo?" Leo asked, looking at the back of one badge.

"That's me," I replied, barely able to contain my excitement. I burst once he handed me the badge. "This is so amazing already. I can't believe any of this is real." I froze as Leo handed Tyler his badge.

"Noah, what's wrong?" Alyssa asked, noticing my sudden distress.

"What if this isn't real?" I asked. "What if this is a dream? Or what if I died in the accident, not my parents, and this is purgatory or something? Or what if I suffered a traumatic brain injury and I'm in a coma right now?"I suddenly couldn't breathe, panicked by the idea that things were even worse than they seemed.

Ben moved in front of me, gently gripping my shoulders. "Noah, look at me," he said in a kind but commanding tone. I did as he asked, staring into his eyes. "I know it looks crazy. I know it sounds insane. I know it seems impossible. But this is all very real."

I stared into those eyes, and saw only kindness and sincerity. I couldn't find any reason not to believe those eyes.

"But…why me?" I asked.

Ben smiled. "Because I need a pilot for this mission. Let's go."

CHAPTER 11

"What do you mean, you need a pilot for this mission?" I asked as Ben led us to the ramp that descended from Head Case's grin.

"I think that one's pretty self-explanatory," he replied.

"No. I mean. Well, a minute ago you weren't even going to let us on board because we don't have any cash."

"Oh, that? I had no intention of leaving without you."

"Hold up," Tyler said, pausing at the bottom of the ramp. "What?"

"There's a satellite that's going to pass over this area in less than two minutes," Ben said. "If we're still here when it does, it won't be very long before Space-X knows about it. I don't know exactly how they'll react, but I don't think they'll just chalk it up to crazy Iowa farmers building weird scarecrows. We need to get moving."

"You made me drop to my knees and beg," Tyler said. "I'm not going anywhere until you tell me why you made us do that if you planned to let us on board anyway."

"It was a test," Ben answered. "You passed. Come on."

"What kind of test?"

While Tyler stalled us, Leo and Meg ran past us and up

the ramp with the rental sign held between them, the carnival lights draped over Leo's shoulder. They vanished into the ship and then ran back out without the props.

"I inserted the advertisement for Noah," Ben explained. "I thought you would probably show because you drove him to VR Awesome, which you decided to do on the way to the hospital after we inserted those ads and vids into your TikTok feed."

"I wasn't scrolling and driving," Tyler said defensively before the full scope of Ben's words sank in. "You manipulated me?"

"Isn't that what social media is for?" Ben answered. "To be honest, I didn't expect Ally to tag along." He glanced at her. "No offense. I'm pleased you're here."

"You are?" Alyssa replied.

"But this is a special rental arrangement, provided under special circumstances. So we don't bring just anyone along for the ride. Noah, I tested not only your desire, but also your fortitude. You didn't give up, and that's an important attribute in your circumstances. And as for you two…" He turned to Tyler and Ally. "…I wanted to see how well you supported your friend. And like I said, you passed. So, can we go?"

Ben started up the ramp. Tyler followed without further cajoling.

"I still don't get it," I said, right behind Ty. "Special circumstances? You mean what happened to my parents?"

"Yes." Ben threw me a look over his shoulder.

"People die every day."

"They do. And people are instantly orphaned more often than you would think. But Levi picked you, and she's rarely wrong."

"Picked me for what?" I asked. "And who's Levi?"

"She's our onboard computer, and she picked you to

pilot this mission," he answered, remaining patient with my obtrusiveness.

We reached the missing tooth, passing over the threshold and into what appeared to be a hangar bay. A single small ship, which was as sleek as an Indy race car, sat on the right.

On its knees in the back of the bay, a full-sized war mech loomed over us. With its fists planted on the deck, its stylized faceplate glared angrily at us over Ben's shoulder.

"Whoa," Tyler said in response to it.

"Do we get to drive that thing too?" I asked.

"The Hunter?" Ben replied. "No. Sorry. Normally, I'd start with a tour of Head Case, but we need to launch ASAP. This way."

"I'm starting to think this might be real," Alyssa said, tapping the Hunter's thumb as we passed it by on our way to the metal stairway leading up the right side of the bay to a balcony. Another identical set of stairs led up the bay's left side.

"Yeah," Tyler agreed. "It's so real, it's unreal."

Before we even reached the balcony, our proximity seemed enough to open an elevator door in the rear bulkhead, and Ben hurriedly ushered us into the small cab. The interior of it resembled something out of a Victorian-style bed and breakfast, with ornate wood paneling and thick red carpets.

"This is seriously retro-chic," Alyssa commented as Ben pressed a button on the control panel and the doors closed.

A strange sensation hit me when the elevator climbed, turning my stomach queasy and raising goosebumps on my arms. Ben looked my way, and I thought he might ask me if I was okay, but he remained quiet. The cab doors opened again within a few seconds, dropping us off in an ordinary-looking corridor. As Ben led us forward toward a pair of sliding doors, I noticed how the interior metal of the robot head's hull appeared to be scored and scratched in a manner that left me thinking the marks were intentional. But why?

I didn't have time to ask Ben. The doors opened ahead of him, and we followed him through at a fast walk, stepping onto what was obviously the flight deck.

It was both similar to and completely different from any starship bridge or flight deck I had ever seen on TV. For one thing, the back half had been arranged as though it were a movie theater. In fact, I was pretty sure the three rows of reclining pleather seats with drink holders and swiveling food trays had been picked up at a random theater's bankruptcy proceedings. Just ahead of them, positioned low enough it wouldn't obstruct the view from these seats, a single larger seat rested on an elevated dais. A trio of touchscreens on articulating arms surrounded it. Ahead of that, two additional seats were split in the middle by a center console.

"Those look familiar," Tyler whispered beside me, motioning to the pilot seats.

More than familiar. They were identical to the controls of the VR Awesome *Star Squadron* pods.

The blonde-haired guy, Matt, occupied the pilot station on the left. He'd watched our entrance from over his shoulder, his attention now solely moving to Ben. "It's about time. We have less than a minute."

"Is all our gear on board?" Ben asked, stepping up onto the dais and taking that seat.

"The twins just finished loading the booth," Matt said. "The reactor's online. And our guests..." He waved toward us. "...are onboard. Hey, I'm Matt." He jerked his chin up in greeting.

"Hey, man, I'm Tyler. This is Noah, and Alyssa."

"Hi," Alyssa said, her cheeks darkening, unable to conceal her instant crush on the strapping Ken.

"Noah, why don't you take the co-pilot seat?" Ben suggested. "You two, pick a lounger."

"You want me to co-pilot?" I asked, voice quivering with excitement.

"That's why you're here. You've already proved your mettle back at the arcade."

"Are we expecting a dogfight?"

"Hey, you never know. Head Case has guns for a reason."

"They're not just props to make the ship look cooler?"

Ben winked, using his hands to shoo me toward the co-pilot seat.

"Good to meet you, Noah," Matt said, stretching his hand across the center console the moment my butt touched the seat's padding.

"What do I do?" I asked, shaking his hand.

"Right now, nothing. I'll get us into orbit, and then you'll take over once you get used to everything."

"Sounds good to me. I can't believe this is really happening."

"I remember the first time I said that. You haven't seen anything yet. Here we go."

Even though the flight deck had a huge ear-to-ear window across its face, a screen rose out of the floor in front of me, extending out and overhead on both sides and enveloping me in the same VR view as in the cockpit in the *Star Squadron* pod. Only instead of looking out at space or the interior of a hangar, my view appeared to be from the midpoint of Head Case's full height, looking out and down over the cornfield in every direction.

"Eat it, Jedi," I muttered. His serial killer fear-mongering had cost him participation in this adventure.

"Reactor's online," Matt said. "All systems are nominal."

"Take her up, Matt."

"Aye aye, Captain," Matt acknowledged, glancing over at me. "You're gonna love this."

"I already do," I replied, even though we had yet to leave the ground.

"Punch it," Ben said.

Matt pushed his throttle forward with one hand, his other on the control stick. Head Case shuddered slightly as the force of the thrusters pushed the ship off the ground more quickly than any rocket I had ever seen.

I felt the G-force, but the pressure was nowhere near as strong as it should have been. It was more like feeling the weight of a bowling ball in my lap than being glued to the seat while we climbed vertically up through the patchy fog into a clear night dimly lit by a new moon. The thrust vector changed, tilting the flight deck back and blasting us toward space at a forty-five-degree angle.

A wave of guilt rolled through me in response to my outright enjoyment of the first few seconds of the ride. My parents had been dead less than twelve hours, and here I was smiling and enjoying myself. It felt wrong. Like I should be back at the hospital, mourning and in physical and emotional agony.

Watching the sky darken, I looked to the bottom of the screen to see Earth growing smaller under my feet. It gave me enough of a rush to let go of my self-stigmatization. My folks would never have wanted me to pass up an opportunity like this, no matter the situation. They would want me to live my life to the fullest and enjoy what I was being offered.

And that's exactly what I did.

CHAPTER 12

Head Case continued climbing smoothly, pushing up through Earth's atmosphere in no time flat. I watched in awe as the curve of the planet became visible, mimicking so many images I had looked at online.

"This is unbelievable," Alyssa said behind me.

"It's awesome," Tyler agreed. "But why aren't we weightless by now?"

"Artificial gravity," Matt answered. "And I'm sure you noticed the effects of the inertial dampening."

"The ride up did seem hella smooth. More like gliding along freshly paved asphalt than pushing up through the atmosphere."

"Bingo!" Ben said. "Matt, let's cut thrust and orbit for a few minutes so our guests can get a better look at Earth."

"Aye aye, Captain," Matt replied, his tone hardly formal. Ben had said they were co-owners, so it made sense if they both functioned at one time or another as captains. "Noah, you can access the flight control settings by raising your left hand just above eye level. If you go into the settings at the bottom of the menu, you can turn off the

surround view so you can look out through the front transparency. The view's definitely better live."

I did as he suggested, activating a holographic series of
settings and menus while he gracefully piloted Head Case
into a stable orbit.

"What's this one marked PEW PEW?" I asked.

"Exactly what it looks like," Matt replied. "That's to
enter the settings for the guns, including the Fire Control
System. We won't need that one on this flight."

"But you've needed it before?"

"It's a big galaxy out there. You don't need to worry
about that while we're inside the Solar System."

"What do I have to do to see more of the universe?" I
asked impetuously. "How do I become a permanent
member of the crew?"

"Whoa there, cowboy," Ben said. "Let's not get ahead of
ourselves. This is, or will be, a rental agreement. Two hours,
tops, and then back to Jackson's Farm you go. Keep in
mind, you didn't even pay for this ride."

"But you already know I have nothing to go back to," I
argued. "My parents are dead. I don't have any other
family, not that I've met more than a few times. And I'll be
eighteen in six months. An adult. That has to count for
something."

"Even if there were no other problems, I'm not hiring
right now."

I tensed up, unexpectedly and immediately desperate to
stay out in space forever. To see planets inhabited by blue
squirrels and encounter why Head Case needed so many
guns to defend itself. "Maybe you can connect me with a
captain and ship that is hiring?"

Ben's smile remained fixed as he shook his head.
"You've got moxie, kid. I'll give you that. But this is a one-
time, up and back deal." He sighed, digging a hand
through his curly hair. "It's my fault. I forgot about the new

satellite and didn't plan my intro timing well, so we didn't get to go over the agreement before we launched. It's all spelled out pretty clearly."

"It's okay," I said, disheartened by his veto but still too elated by my current situation to be too deflated. "I understand. You aren't going to wipe my memory of this when it's over, are you?"

"What would be the point of taking a trip you'll never remember?"

I dropped the subject, instead locating the control to retract the co-pilot seat's surround. I gasped in breathtaking awe as the screen shifted out of my view, and I sat there, staring directly at the planet we had just launched from. The panoramic view through Head Case's flight deck transparency left me momentarily speechless.

"How does it feel to be an astronaut, my friend?"

Ben's voice at my shoulder tore my attention away from the spectacle outside. His ever-present grin conveyed sincere delight at my awe.

"This is...I don't have words. Unreal seems inadequate." I gestured helplessly. "It's everything I've dreamed of and more. I don't know why you, or Levi, picked me for this, but thank you so much for the opportunity to be here. To see this. In some ways, you may have saved my life today."

Ben nodded, appreciative of my gratitude. "Don't thank me yet. We've still got plenty to see and do out here. But I'm happy you're enjoying it." He craned his neck over his shoulder to look at Tyler and Ally. "What about you two?"

"I'm just glad I didn't send them home after they drove all the way from Cedar Rapids just to play *Star Squadron*," Alyssa said.

"I'm not mad that you manipulated me anymore," Tyler added. "In fact, I'm glad you did. Just wait until I post this video to Youtube."

"Yeah, about that..." Ben said. I'd noticed Tyler had his

phone out, and had apparently recorded the entire liftoff. Considering what Ben had put us through just to find him and his ship, it surprised me that he hadn't confiscated our phones up front. "Everything will be wiped before you disembark.".

"What?" Tyler complained. "Come on, man."

"Didn't I mention how much of a secret this is? It's in the rental agreement. I just haven't had time to have you sign it yet."

"What if I refuse to sign it?"

"If you don't sign, you can't stay on the ship, which could be a big problem for you at this point."

"You'd airlock me?" Tyler questioned, his voice raising an octave.

"Technically, you'd be airlocking you by choosing not to sign. I'm not a bad guy at all. But I'm not lying when I say I've done worse."

Tyler's face blanched. Even I got goosebumps from Ben's last statement.

He didn't seem bothered by what he had said or our reaction. He returned to forward. "Matt, why don't you let Noah take her for a spin?"

"Uh, are you sure I'm ready?" I asked.

"You flew aces in *Star Squadron*. It's pretty much the same deal, only with more accurate feedback."

"You just need to recover your surround first," Matt said. "You know where it is in the menu."

I nodded, and with shaking hands managed to find it.

"Passing controls to the co-pilot station," Matt said, looking over at me, sharing Ben's grin. "You're up, Noah."

I wrapped relevant hands around the stick and throttle.

"Relax, you'll do fine," Matt encouraged, noticing my white-knuckled grip.

I wished I shared his confidence. Virtual simulations hadn't prepared me for the very real ship responding to my tentative movements. She seemed eager, willing to leap or spin at the barest nudge. What was I so afraid of, anyway? This wasn't the interstate, where a wrong move could…I trailed off, unable to finish the thought. This was outer space, emphasis on *space*. There probably wasn't anything I could do out here that would get us killed.

Matt talked me through the basics while Ben looked on approvingly. Within a few minutes I executed practice maneuvers with growing confidence.

"He's a natural," Matt judged soon after.

"Born to it," Ben agreed.

"Nice job, Katzuo," Tyler cheered from the back.

"I think we're ready to head for Mars," Ben said. "Matt, I assume the coordinates are reset after our last trip?"

"Aye, Captain."

"How many people have you ferried out to Mars?" I asked.

"We've been doing this for a couple of years now. That's why we reconfigured the flight deck and added the loungers."

"And somehow you've managed to keep it a secret," Alyssa said.

Ben shrugged. "It's actually not that hard once you have all the components in place. Since the passengers step off Head Case without any evidence beyond their memories."

"And there's an NDA in the rental agreement, right?" I assumed.

"Exactly," he laughed. "Who would believe them anyway?"

"But twenty dollars isn't making you a profit," Tyler said.

"Not in a financial sense, no," Ben agreed. "But it makes the passengers feel more like they have some skin in the game."

"So why do it?" I asked. "If you aren't making any money, I mean?"

"Besides seeing the looks on people's faces when we give them a tour of outer space?" He paused. "I can't think of another reason, actually. Matt?"

"Some things are more rewarding than money," he added. "We don't take just anyone. A friend of ours wrote an algorithm that aggregates different data points from thousands of sources, cross-references them with other variables, and spits out a list of potential customers. The only thing they all have in common is that they're either terminally ill or have suffered a recent tragedy."

"Wow," Alyssa said. "You're doing all of this as charity?"

"If I didn't co-own Head Case, I would probably be on that list," Ben said. "It's my way of giving back."

"That's incredible."

"It's really nothing. It seems amazing to people here, but where Head Case comes from, it's all just part of normal life."

"How come no one else from that part of the galaxy has come to Earth then?" I asked. "If they have the ships to do it."

"It's pretty far away. And Head Case is a little more special than that."

"He means *he's* a little more special than that," Matt corrected.

"How—"

"We can talk about that later," Ben interrupted. "Matt will walk you through activating the hyperdrive."

"You just said one of my favorite words," I gushed.

"Matt?" he joked.

"Hyperdrive," I replied. "It still blows my mind that it's real."

"Mine, too," Tyler agreed.

"Since the coordinates are already set," Matt said, "we just need to pass them to the Primary Control System for processing, which I'm doing right now." He air-tapped a couple of times. A red diode activated on my control surface, next to a closed toggle switch above the throttle. "When that light turns green, we're ready to go. Open the guard, flip the toggle, and off we go. Easy-peasy."

"And I get to flip the switch?" I asked.

He shrugged. "I can do it if you'd rather not."

"No, no, no. I've got it." I grinned, my eyes split between the view outside and the red diode. "How long does it take?"

"A couple of minutes. We don't want to crash into anything at 10 c."

"Did you just say ten c?" Tyler cried. "As in, ten times the speed of light?"

"We could go faster, but Mars is pretty close."

Tyler cracked up. "You could get to the Proxima system in less than half an hour! Why don't we go there?"

"Most people don't know the Milky Way outside of the planets around the Sun," Ben said. "So we stick to what's familiar."

"I'm guessing most of your passengers aren't like us. Noah and I at least are total sci-fi nerds. Noah most of all."

"I like sci-fi," Alyssa added.

Ben's grin proved he thought the whole thing amusing. "Let's just get to Mars first, take a few minutes to sign the agreement, and then we can discuss changes to the itinerary, okay?"

"Deal," I said, still eying the diode. "So Mars will take what, like thirty seconds?"

"Give or take," Matt agreed. "Almost—" His voice was drowned out by a shrill beep from the console between us. A projection like the one in my *Star Squadron* pod appeared in front of my surround, creating a grid of space around Head Case.

A red shape had just entered that grid, closing on us at lightning speed.

"What the...?" Matt's eyes suddenly widened. "Brace for impact!"

CHAPTER 13

My knuckles blanched bone-white against the controls. I'm sure my face paled as well. My muscles seized so fiercely that my whole body vibrated. I stopped breathing, staring at the red icon hurtling toward us.

"Evasive action!" Ben barked. "Shields up!"

Matt scrambled to comply while throwing Head Case into a wild corkscrew. My heart pounded, trying to beat its way out of my chest. Eyes locked unblinking on the grid, the g-forces of the evasive maneuver overcame the dampeners, leaving me plastered sideways to my seat. It was all for nothing. The projectile reached the center of the grid, blending with the circle that represented Head Case.

The hit rattled the entire ship, sending it whirling out of control while sparks rained down from overhead conduits, followed by intense smoke filling the flight deck. I could hardly believe we had survived the strike. Suddenly more sick to my stomach than excited, I looked over to Matt to find he had barely reacted to the chaos and commotion. His attention remained focused on his flying, as if being smacked with a missile was another day at the office for him.

Maybe it was.

He expertly regained control of the flailing starship, keeping us headed away from Earth.

"Meg, damage report!" Ben said, presumably over the ship's comms since she wasn't on the flight deck.

"The shields absorbed some of the hit, but we lost thruster three and the hyperdrive is offline."

"You've got to be kidding," Ben answered, suggesting the loss of the hyperdrive was simply bad luck.

"I wish I were."

I was about to say something along the lines of, *at least we're alive, and we're safe now.* when I noticed a second, larger icon enter the grid, along with two more of the smaller projectiles fired from it. Apparently, whoever was chasing us hadn't expected us to survive the first blow.

They were still after us.

Matt kept Head Case moving in a random pattern, pushing the thrust to max and juking and jiving to ruin our attacker's aim. With one of the thrusters down, the bogey easily matched our maneuvers, continuing to close the distance between us at an alarming rate.

The two missiles closed even faster.

"Noah, take the stick," Matt said. "I'm on the guns."

He switched control to me before I could argue, leaving me to continue his maneuvers as his surround changed, offering a rear view and a reticle. I could feel the ear turrets swiveling to face rearward, a smooth vibration followed by a pulsing shudder as they opened fire. Matt hit one of the missiles within a few seconds.

The other snuck past the defensive barrage. I yanked the stick hard right, twisting it at the same time while reducing thrust. Head Case jerked and shifted, almost avoiding the missile.

Almost.

The ship shook again, the second hit more glancing

than the first, leaving the shields still fully powered and ready to avoid the next attack. Kinetic force spun us off-course, but years of playing similar games allowed my muscle memory to work out the physics, bringing us back in line. Not as fast as Matt had done it, but not bad for my first time.

Not that it mattered. The bogey remained on our six, still gaining. It was obvious to me we couldn't outrun it. I'm sure Ben and Matt knew that, too.

I threw us into another spiraling evasive, the unchecked inertia dragging at my body as I pushed the ship beyond its dampening ability. I groaned, simultaneously thrilled and terrified, alive with adrenaline.

"Levi, any luck identifying that bastard?" Matt demanded through gritted teeth.

"Negative," Levi reported. Her smooth, almost-human vocals conveyed the same tension I felt. "The craft doesn't match anything in our data store."

"Of course not!" Matt snarled, our tail taking evasive action as the ear cannons continued spewing fury. "Come on! Sit still, you son of a bitch."

The target on the grid suddenly flashed yellow, possibly an indicator that the guns had finally hit their mark. It tried to escape the barrage, but like my bout with Jedi, Matt had figured out the craft's pattern, taking advantage of it until it changed. A trio of projectiles escaped the attack, launching toward us from the bogey.

"Noah!" Matt shouted as if there was anything more I could do. I was flying with every ounce of energy I had left, but it was almost all gone. It had been a long day, emotionally and physically draining.

And this was the poisoned cherry on top.

Matt hit one of the missiles with the guns. I managed to avoid the next one, giving Matt the opportunity to swing the guns around and hit it as it streaked past us. It detonated right in front of us, the debris momentarily lighting up the bow shields like the Fourth of July.

With two projectiles down, I couldn't avoid the third one.

Alarms blared an instant before the deck bucked wildly, yanking me hard against my restraints. Behind me, pained cries hinted that Tyler and Alyssa hadn't fared any better.

"Aft shields are at thirty percent," Meg reported. "We can't take much more of this."

"Whatever this bastard's flying, he's got shields to match," Matt grunted. "The guns should've at least taken a bite out of him by now." He risked a glance back at Ben. "We need to get out of here."

I let my gaze follow Matt's, glancing at Ben just long enough to see the hesitancy in his tight expression. It was obvious that whatever escape option Matt had suggested, it wasn't one Ben wanted to take.

I didn't have time to wait for him to make a decision. I threw Head Case into a sharp dive, initiating an extended burn on a new vector away from the pursuing UFO. I tasted blood as I gritted my teeth, vaguely realizing I must've bitten my tongue during the last bone-shaking hit.

Three more missiles streaked toward us. I briefly glanced at Matt, his expression hardened with furious intensity as he blasted away at the missiles, picking off two while I managed to evade the last one.

"Noah," Ben said, his voice strangely calm. "I need you to keep us straight and level."

"What?" Not sure I'd heard him correctly, I wanted to look his way, but I didn't dare tear my eyes from the surround. I still didn't know that much about Head Case's capabilities, but we had already taken a spanking, and I was terrified by the idea of giving the bogey a clean shot to take us out.

"Straight and level," he repeated as if in a zen trance.

"You'll see a dark line appear ahead of us. It'll get wider pretty fast. You need to fly us down it."

They were the strangest instructions anyone had ever given me. This time, I couldn't avoid looking back at Ben to confirm them. I thought I had seen everything when Head Case appeared from out of nowhere in the cornfield.

Apparently, I hadn't seen anything yet.

Ben stood in front of his station, hands raised as if he was about to catch a basketball. That was weird enough, given the circumstances.

Even weirder, he was *glowing*.

"What the hell?" I cried, my psyche finally stretched to the breaking point.

"Straight and level," Ben said a third time, despite three more missiles coming our way, threatening my ability to follow his simple instructions.

"Do what he said, Noah. Otherwise, we're dead."

I looked at Matt, his expression as hard as his words had been. He turned from me and again opened fire on the approaching missiles.

When nothing made sense anymore, it was better not to question. I looked back at the surround, adjusting our flight pattern to stay straight and level.

The line appeared in space ahead of us. At first, I thought maybe some of the pixels on the surround had died, because it seemed like the darkness wasn't part of the universe. But as the odd black line widened, I got the distinct impression that while I was correct and the dark wasn't part of the universe, I was wrong about its nature.

Somehow, some way, Ben was literally ripping a hole in reality, and he wanted me to fly right into it.

I wasn't sure I would get the chance. Matt had only managed to take out one of the three missiles coming at us. I wanted more than anything to juke or change course, to take evasive action and save us from the remaining projectiles. I didn't think it was crazy that no part of me desired to see what existed outside of spacetime. Then again, it had to be better than ceasing to exist at all.

Countering every instinct I possessed, I kept my hand steady on the stick, rapidly approaching the tear and hoping we made it before the projectiles slammed into our already damaged stern. Matt finally hit another one with the guns, leaving only one bearing down on us.

"When we go into the rift, you're going to feel an immense sadness like you've never known before," Ben said behind me, loudly enough it was clear he was addressing both me and my friends. "It will only last a few seconds, but it'll feel longer. Strengthen your resolve, and remember who you are."

The entire statement left me chilled. The last sentence, vague and enigmatic, froze me completely.

I wanted to go home.

The rift, as Ben had called it, loomed in front of us, close enough now that, in its absolute black nothingness, it was all I could see, both in the surround and through the forward viewport. The missile on the grid had made it inside the cannons' firing arc, meaning another hit was inevitable.

Or was it?

I forced my eyes to remain open as we shot into the rift, the blackness swallowing us up.

CHAPTER 14

As the eerie darkness fell over the flight deck, absorbing the overhead lights, even Ben's glow seemed to be fading. The sadness he'd warned me about hit me like a bull at Pamplona. The air left my lungs, and from one instant to the next, I went from hyped-up anxiety coursing through me to a near-suicidal fugue.

I stared into the black, my chest clenched in pain as my thoughts turned to my parents. What was I doing out here? How could I let them down like this? Why had I distracted my dad when I did? Why hadn't I done more to save them after the crash? The questions assailed me like cerebral missiles, battering my already weary psyche, threatening to steal my soul.

A real or imagined spectral hand—I couldn't tell which—reached out for me from the black void. Either way, it terrified the rational side of me and beckoned to the irrational. It was both damnation and salvation, and I wanted it so bad that I physically reached out for it, hoping to grab the offered lifeline, though I realized life might not be the true outcome.

Ben had warned us to strengthen our resolve and

remember who we are. Those words saved me. Remembering them, I pulled my hand back just as the apparition reached for it, lightly making contact and sending a chill through every nerve in my body and stretching deep within my spirit.

I forced myself to think about happier times. Playing chess with Mom. Playing catch with Dad. Going fishing, to ballgames, to the park. Practicing karate. Gaming with the Stinking Badgers. The memories didn't lift me all the way back up, but they gave me enough buoyancy to tread water.

Ben had also said it would feel like a long time, even though only seconds passed. He was right about that. The journey through the rift felt endless, the darkness all-encompassing. Finally, a light appeared at the end of the tunnel. Or rather, a second hole in spacetime. A way out of this infernal nothingness. We approached it so slowly that it was as if we were slogging through molasses. I wasn't sure I could come up with enough positive vibes to maintain my sanity for the remainder of the crossing. Even Ben's light had faded to a dim glow that barely reached me in the co-pilot's seat.

And then, like a window opening on a spring day, we were through the rift, and the immediate lightening of my emotional load left me practically giddy. Once we were through the entire way and the stars splayed out ahead of us, I remembered the enemy missile that had been right on our tail. Had it followed us into the rift?

I looked for it on the grid. Nothing was there. By the skin of our teeth, we had made it through the rift unscathed.

Well, most of us.

"Help!" Alyssa's panicked screech pierced my celebratory relief. "Something's wrong with Ben!"

"What?" Matt exchanged an anxious look with me

before we both abandoned our stations and stumbled back to where Ben was slumped in his command chair, his body wracked with convulsions. I went down to my knees on one side of him, Matt on the other. Whimpering softly, Shaq was already nuzzling his chin. Suddenly, Ben gave out a sucking gasp and went limp, his lax form showing no signs of life beyond faint respiration. Confused, both Matt and I cast questioning looks at Alyssa, her wide eyes staring past me, seemingly locked onto something beyond normal perception.

"What happened?" Matt demanded.

"I don't know!" She cried, blinking and then looking directly at Matt. "He was glowing. You all saw it" Her eyes swept over my eyes and then Tee's. "But as we went through…w-whatever that was, the glow started to fade, and he was struggling. I could see it in his posture and expression. The growing exhaustion. The glow stopped just as we cleared the rift. Then he collapsed and went into convulsions."

Matt gently shook his friend. "Ben, can you hear me? Ben!" he shouted.

He didn't respond.

"W-what the hell is going on here?" Tyler stammered with rage. "Who was chasing us? Why were they trying to kill us? Why was Ben glowing? And how did he punch a hole through the freaking universe?"

"Relax," Matt snapped, trying to focus on Ben as he checked his pulse.

"Relax?" Tyler cried. "We didn't sign up for this. Technically, we didn't sign up for anything. We never signed the agreement. I'm going to sue your ass. Both your asses. I'll take everything you have for this. You could have gotten us killed."

"Tee, this isn't the time to panic," Alyssa snapped. "Ben's in trouble here!"

"I'm not panicking. I'm angry. These sons of bitches brought us out here without full disclosure. If I had known the freaking Evil Empire was hunting them, I would have taken a hard pass on renting this rust bucket!"

Shaq lifted his head, glaring at Tyler with bared teeth. The lethal look of them was enough to immediately shut Ty up. He pressed back against his lounger, his shoulders tense as boards, the fingers of both his hands clenched in the overstuffed arms.

"We need to get Ben to sickbay," Matt said, ignoring Tyler and looking at me. "The good news is this isn't the first time this has happened. But it's been a while, and he's never gone into convulsions before."

"Not the first time he's glowed?" Tyler asked. "Or not the first time he's keeled over?"

"Can you please shut up?" Matt growled at him. "You aren't helping."

Tyler's mouth closed tight, his face red, his expression clearly one of frenzied terror. I didn't really blame him. This whole episode had been scary as hell. The only excuse I had for not losing it was that I had already drained my emotional pool. Still, Ally and Matt were right. Panicking wouldn't accomplish anything but create a state of chaos, and it wouldn't help Ben any.

Glancing at Ally, she seemed none the worse for wear. She was obviously as fearful as Ty, but unlike T-Bone, she also had it completely under control. So did I.

"What can I do?" I asked Matt.

"I need you to take command of the ship," he replied. "Stay on the stick, make sure we don't fly toward the center of a star and be ready in case that other ship shows up again. It shouldn't be able to transit through spacetime like we can, but it shouldn't have been in Earth's orbit either, so I don't know what to expect from it."

"Who was it?" I asked.

"I don't know," Matt replied, shaking his head. "Maybe Ben does. We'll find out later. For now, just take the stick and keep us out of trouble."

"I'll do my best," I said, returning to my seat.

I grabbed the controls with renewed focus, definitely intent on not flying Head Case into the center of a star and also resolved to remain ready should the UFO that attacked us make another appearance. I couldn't understand how two ships could break reality and come out in the same place, but I figured Matt knew better than me what could happen. I only had sci-fi movies and novels to go off. He had real-life experience.

A glance over my shoulder a few seconds later revealed Matt carrying Ben over one shoulder, Shaq on his opposite shoulder as he rushed off the flight deck, leaving me alone with Ally and Tyler.

"Well, that was fun." Tyler's thick sarcasm only served as fuel to my fire.

"What is your problem?" I ground out, head whipping back around to glare at him.

"Are you serious? We just got into a real dogfight with a real enemy starship. And news flash, it kicked our ass. We almost died, Noah."

"But we didn't," I countered. "Ben put himself on the line to save our lives. He's in sickbay and all you can do is bitch and moan instead of showing an ounce of gratitude and concern."

"Ben put us in this position in the first place. He's responsible. I'm sorry he's hurt, but it's his own damn fault."

"He didn't know we would be attacked. He thought Head Case was the only ship that could reach Earth."

"And obviously, unless the ship came from Earth, he was wrong."

"Can we stop arguing?" Alyssa interjected. "It's not

going to help or change anything. This is where we are now. Get a grip on it, Tyler."

"This is where we are because of Ben," Tyler repeated, refusing to back down. "We deserve an apology and some answers."

"Maybe so," I agreed. "But I think it can wait until, I don't know, the person who can give us those answers is conscious again? That might be a good start."

"Of course you're backing him instead of me," Tyler whined. "He came to Des Moines for you. He let you pilot the ship. He stuck us in the nosebleeds while he gave you the VIP treatment."

"So that's what this is about? Jealousy? Did your parents both die in a car crash today, asshole?" I had reached the end of my rope, and the last outburst left me raw. Tears sprang free as easily as my anger, and I turned away from him, doing my best to focus on the surround, to keep from falling apart, and in that, stay out of trouble.

"What?"

I ignored Tyler's indignant tone of voice, figuring Ally was still oozing disapproval at him. "You *are* being an asshole," she said. "For a while, I thought your creepy online stalker persona wasn't the real you. Now, I'm beginning to think I was right about you in the first place." I heard her get up and glanced at her as she came forward and threw herself into the pilot's seat beside me.

I didn't say anything. Neither did she, choosing instead to look over Matt's controls as a tense silence overcame the flight deck, all three of us spent in different ways.

A few ticks later, Tyler shoved his head between our two stations, turning to me and then to Ally. "You're both right," he calmly admitted. "I'm sorry. I got totally freaked out by this whole thing. We almost died. Can either of you deny that?"

"But we didn't die. That's the whole point," I reiterated.

"Thanks to you, Matt, and Ben," he answered, "while I did nothing to help. That's what this is about. Feeling helpless. Useless. Out of the game. I don't like it."

"You aren't the only one on the bench," Alyssa reminded him.

"Yeah, but..." he trailed off with a long frustrated release of breath.

"If you were going to say, yeah but you're a girl, I might have to punch you."

"It wouldn't hurt," Tyler said with a smile.

"You wanna bet?" Alyssa laughed. Her slightly nasal chortle broke the tension and restored sanity. All three of us cracked up.

"I have to admit," Tyler said. "Even though it was terrifying and we almost died, there's a part of me that kind of enjoyed it."

"Me, too," Alyssa added. "It's like *Star Squadron* came to life."

"I'd rather see that movie though than live it," I said.

"Truth," Tyler agreed.

"Right now, the sensors are clear and there doesn't appear to be any major celestial bodies nearby," I said, looking from the grid to the surround. "So hopefully once Matt comes back, he can give us his side of the story, and later we can get more from Ben."

"Yeah, I guess that's our only move right now," Tyler agreed.

"So, what do you think of Ben?" Alyssa asked.

"Gandalf," I replied.

"What?" Tyler snapped. "No way he's Gandalf."

"Why not? He was glowing. He's clearly a wizard. And he gives sick and traumatized people joy rides in his starship, which means he's altruistic. A good guy. And he just saved us from a Balrog."

"That's a stretch," Alyssa commented.

"He's too young," Tyler countered. "He can't be more than twenty-five. He's more like...I don't know. Newt Scamander?"

"No way."

"He has a blue squirrel for a pet."

"Companion," Alyssa corrected.

"Same diff. The analogy fits."

"Tell Shaq that and see how he reacts."

"Fine, companion. It still works."

"Young Gandalf then," I said.

"Gandalf was never young. He came to Middle-Earth in that form."

"That doesn't mean Ben can't be an analog of a young Gandalf."

"Of course it means that."

"No, it doesn't."

"Sorry, man. It does. Sad for you, really."

"Ally, what do you think?" I asked.

"I think—"

"She doesn't get a vote," Tyler interrupted.

"Why not?" She and I both asked in unison.

"Because she's a girl," he answered. "Duh."

Alyssa feigned socking him while we laughed again. We quieted when the door to the flight deck slid open. Tyler extracted himself from between the stations, turning to see who was there.

"Uh, that's weird," he said.

"What is?" I asked.

"Nobody came in."

"What do you mean? I heard the doors."

"So did I, but there's no one there."

"Glitch maybe," Alyssa suggested.

Tyler shrugged and turned back around, one hand on the back of each pilot station seat. "Where do you think we are?"

"Space," I answered.

"You're very funny," Tyler answered dryly. "I imagine a rift in spacetime can get us anywhere in the universe. So where do you think we are? Not Mars or Venus, that's for sure."

"Another good question for Ben," I said. "We can ask him once we—"

Alyssa let out an ear-curdling scream.

Tyler jumped back.

And I froze in shocked horror as a giant spider lowered itself from the overhead just outside the open door, hanging from a disgustingly thick strand of webbing.

Its menacing eyes stared directly at us.

CHAPTER 15

"Hellossss," the spider clacked, its mouthparts shifting and vibrating to produce the English-sounding word.

We stared at the creature in silent shock. Tyler recovered first. "Uh. Hi. You…uh…aren't going to eat us, are you?"

The spider made a sound that had to be laughter. "Nossss. Not hungryssss."

"You're a friend of Ben's, I take it," I said.

"Yesss."

"See," Tyler said. "Newt Scamander. I was right."

"Are you a spider? Or?"

"Xixitl," it answered. "ILFsss."

"Gotcha," I replied, my initial surprise and fear fading. Positive I couldn't take another attempt on my life, jump scare, or anything else that elicited a strong emotion, I slumped back in my seat, returning some of my attention to the surround. We remained free and clear of external contacts of any kind.

"What's your name?" Alyssa asked, her voice meek while she struggled to overcome an obvious bout of arachnophobia.

"Ixysss," the spider replied.

"I'm Alyssa. That's Noah, and Tyler."

"Nice to meets yousss."

"Are you male or female?" Tyler asked. "Or both? Or none?"

"Femalesss. Lays eggsss."

"Is there a male Xixitl on this ship we should know about? So he doesn't scare the hell out of us, too?"

Ixy laughed again. "Nosss. Xixitl stays on Xixitl planetsss."

"So what are you doing out here?" Tyler asked.

"Was slavesss. Ben freesss. Likes shipsss."

"See," I said, turning to Tyler and using the same tone he had just used to prove his point. "Ben's a good guy."

"Yesss," Ixy agreed.

"Well, maybe he's just a little reckless then," Tyler argued.

"Ixy, do you know what happened to Ben?" I asked.

"Not yetsss. Matts says, keeps eyes on yousss. Keeps out of troublesss." She lowered herself from the overhead the rest of the way to the deck, standing up on her four hind legs between the pilot station and the forward transparency. Her body was easily six feet long, but with her legs extended, she probably doubled that. Seeing her more clearly, I could tell she had some minor differences to Earthbound spiders, mostly in the thickness of her limbs and the shape of her head. "Enjoying the ridesss?"

"Not really," Tyler said.

"Someone was chasing us," I said. "And firing missiles at us."

"Torpedoes," Tyler said.

"What?" I looked back at him again. "They were missiles."

"They're torpedoes. Like Star Trek. Besides, we're in space. That makes them torpedoes."

"How do you come to that conclusion?"

"Because space uses nautical nomenclature. Navies, frigates, battleships, etcetera. Torpedoes. I didn't think this was up for debate."

"It's absolutely up for debate," I replied. "Torpedoes are slow. Those missiles were fast and highly maneuverable."

"And torpedoes are fired in water," Alyssa added. "Missiles in air."

"Space is a vacuum," Tyler interjected.

"Starships fly," I countered. "Fly, as in like air. Air equals missiles. I can draw you a diagram, if you want."

"Starships float," Tyler said.

"On what?"

"Nothing."

"You can't float on nothing. But you can fly through nothing. We just did. We also flew through the air on the way out of the atmosphere. We didn't float through it."

"Well, I'm calling them torpedoes."

I shrugged. "If you want to be wrong, you can be wrong."

Ixy clattered the entire time, cracking up at our stupid argument. But I needed the stupid argument for my sanity.

"What do you think?" I asked her.

"Missilesss."

"Whatever," Tyler said.

"The ship was damaged. I don't know how badly."

"Not too badsss. Megs and Leos will fixssss."

"You've done this sort of thing before, I take it."

"Yesss. Not in a whilesss."

"Do you know who attacked us? Or why?"

"No ideassss."

"We'll have to wait on Ben for that," Alyssa said. "I suppose there's nothing for us to do right now but wait."

"I hope we don't have to wait too long," Tyler said. "Mom knows I might not come home tonight, but if I'm not back in the morning, she'll worry."

"I don't want to miss my shift at the arcade," Alyssa said. "I still have rent to pay."

I opened my mouth, ready to explain why I needed to get back home. To meet with Child Protective Services? To plan my parent's funeral or talk to lawyers? To help the police sketch artist make a composite of the man who killed my folks?

None of it sounded very appealing. "I'm sure we'll get a timeline soon," I added instead.

I heard the doors slide open again and looked over my shoulder as Matt stepped onto the flight deck. He didn't look overly concerned, which I took as a good sign.

"How's Ben?" I asked when he reached us.

"I think he'll be okay," he replied. "Pretty sure anyway."

The lack of definitive positivity wasn't the prognosis I expected. "What's wrong with him?"

"It's complicated, and better if you hear about it directly from his mouth. I see you've met Ixy."

"She scared the crap out of us," Tyler said.

"Yeah, she likes to sneak up on people. I'd say she's harmless, but that wouldn't be true. But she's an intelligent life form. She doesn't randomly grab people with her pedipalps and rip their heads off."

"Good to know."

Ixy laughed.

"I don't know how long Ben will be down. I'm sure that's not what you want to hear, but considering the alternative was being blown to bits, I hope you're okay with the delay." He pointedly looked at Tyler when he said it.

"Yeah, man. I'm good now," Tyler replied. "Sorry I came on a little too strong before. No hard feelings?"

"Believe me, I understand. We're good."

"Cool."

"In any case, since I'm the acting captain right now, I figured I would pick up where Ben should have started. I'll give you a quick tour, and then we can go over the rental agreement."

"You still want us to sign something?" Alyssa asked. "Doesn't that seem superfluous at this point?"

"Probably. And there's no way any of it will hold up in an Earth-based court since we technically don't exist, but should you ever find yourself in the Manticore Spiral, you could sue our pants off without it."

"The Manticore Spiral," I said. "That's where you're from?"

"We're from Earth, originally. The Spiral is where we live now. It's a galaxy a few billion light years away."

"Did you say billion?" Tyler asked. "With a *B*?"

Matt nodded.

"And when you said you could reach Earth because Ben is special, you meant his ability to open rifts in spacetime."

"Exactamundo."

"Are you sure Ben's the only one who can do that?"

"I used to be," Matt admitted. "We never would have brought you on board if we thought there was any risk. Especially this kind of risk. I don't know who attacked us. I don't know where they came from. I doubt Ben does either. This is a bad situation for all of us."

"We just want to help in any way we can," I answered. A moment of silence passed while Matt and I both waited for Tyler to counter the statement. Thankfully, he remained silent.

"You already helped," Matt answered. "I'm sure you have lives on Earth you want to get back to. Once Ben wakes up, he'll be able to reverse the transit and get you home in no time."

"I don't really have anything to go back to," I said. "If there's any chance I can stay on board—"

"I get it, Noah," Matt said. "My mom skipped town when I was young, and my dad never gave much of a damn about me. So I've been there, to some extent. But it's just not possible right now."

I nodded. The answer didn't upset me. He'd given me the bottom line I expected. "Just let me know if you guys change your minds. I won't bring it up again."

"Come on, I'll show you around."

"What about monitoring our flight path? Or watching for enemy ships?"

"Levi, set AP protocol one," Matt said.

"AP protocol one engaged," the computer replied through hidden speakers.

"AP?" Tyler asked. "Is that autopilot?"

"Yep. I wouldn't trust it in a scrape, but it's enough to keep us adrift without worry. If anything shows up on sensors, Levi will let us know in time to deal with it."

I wanted to ask him if he meant like she did before the first missile hit us, but it felt too obnoxious. Maybe the busyness of Earth had made detecting the incoming projectile more difficult. That wouldn't be the case out here. There was nothing for thousands of miles around.

"Did you say adrift? Similar to a sailing ship on the ocean?" Tyler asked.

"Yeah, why?"

He looked over at me with his normal mischievous expression. "Just wondering."

I rolled my eyes as I got to my feet, the excitement of seeing the rest of Head Case helping me overcome my lingering apprehension. "I'm ready to see the rest of this ship if you're ready to show us."

CHAPTER 16

"We'll start from the top down," Matt announced as we departed the flight deck. "Head Case isn't a big ship, so it won't take long. When we reach the lounge, I'll fetch the paperwork and we can make everything official."

"Sounds like a plan," I replied, doing my best to ignore Ixy scurrying across the deck behind us. The clattering of her many legs served as a constant reminder that I had what amounted to a giant spider hugging my six. Spiders didn't normally creep me out like they apparently did Alyssa, but then, Earth spiders didn't weigh hundreds of pounds. "I'm especially interested in seeing the hyperdrive."

Matt glanced back at me, wrinkling his face. "We'll have to check on that. Meg and Leo are working on repairs. That area might be off limits right now."

I didn't let the minor disappointment temper the rest of my improving mood. "It's not the end of the world if I don't see it."

We boarded the elevator, which was already on our deck. Matt hit the button to send us up to Deck Seven. We arrived quickly, the doors opening out beneath the dome of the ship's skull. Being what I imagined was the smallest deck on the ship, Seven didn't have any bulkheads beyond the superstructure, leaving the outer plating bare across almost the entire area. As before, there were score marks in the metal, creating an interesting pattern along the overhead. Noticing how the lines passed from one bolted-on plate to another without interruption left me certain that either one of the crew members was in the midst of creating an artistic masterpiece, or the marks served a purpose I couldn't yet fathom.

"I probably don't need to say it, but Deck Seven is where the Primary Control System is stored," Matt explained. "Levi, say hello to our guests."

"Hello, Katzuo, T-bone, and All-red," the AI replied.

Matt smirked at her reply while glancing at Alyssa. "All-red? That's an interesting username."

"If you'd seen her alternate X account, you'd understand," Tyler replied before she could answer.

It was just as well. She seemed shocked by Matt's direct address, and she stumbled to find even simple words while her face made good on her callsign. "Oh. Uh… yeah." She paused to glare at Tyler with dagger eyes. "My online personas are always redheads. So, All-red."

"Why not Ginger?" Matt followed up.

I imagined that during the course of normal conversation with anyone who wasn't Matt, such a question would have elicited a scathing reply. In his case, she just blushed harder. "Too common," she replied simply. "Depending on the generation of the online creeper, you're either from Gilligan's Island, Dr. Who, or somehow related to Ed Sheeran."

Matt laughed. "Point made. I should have thought of that."

He said something else to her afterward, but I had stopped paying attention as my eyes settled on the PCS unit. A square black box as tall and wide as me, it had a number of thick cables spewing out from the base and vanishing into the deck and overhead, the appearance similar to what an octopus might look like in Minecraft. I almost laughed out loud picturing it with large eyes painted on the sides, and maybe wearing a top hat. A few flashing LEDs proved it was constantly crunching data at a rate I could barely imagine. "How many FLOPS does it do?" I asked.

"Huh?" Matt replied.

"FLOPS," I repeated. "Floating Point Operations. How many does it do?"

"He's asking what Levi's processing speed is," Tyler translated from my geek-speak.

"Oh." Matt shrugged. "I have no idea. I can tell you this is an upgraded unit from the original. Levi, what's your processing speed?"

"Fifty-one point four exaFLOPS," she replied.

My jaw went slack. "Are you serious? That's fifty times faster than the fastest supercomputer on Earth. And you're tiny."

"Thank you. I've been trying to lose weight."

Tyler laughed. "I always wanted to hang on a starship with a snarky AI."

"I'm not snarky. My prior iteration weighed nearly two hundred kilograms more than this form, at twenty percent of the processing speed. It also had a very limited voice module. Would you like to hear me sing?"

"Maybe later," Tyler answered.

"I think you're amazing, Levi," I said.

"Thank you, Noah."

"Levi's different subprocesses handle everything onboard, from the lighting to the targeting systems for the guns, to the hyperspace field compression calculations," Matt said. "We wouldn't be able to get along without her."

"And I wouldn't exist without you," Levi answered. "I believe that makes us even."

"It does," Matt agreed. "Come on, I'll show you Deck Six." He turned for the elevator.

"Before we go," I said, freezing him in his tracks. "What's the deal with the lines on the interior of the hull?"

He turned his head my way, looking at me like I had asked him to solve the Riemann hypothesis. "That...uh... well..." He shook his head. "I'll have to punt that question over to Ben. He can answer it a lot better than me. Sorry."

"No problem. I'll ask Ben later."

Matt continued walking, but I sensed a shift in his demeanor like he had hoped I wouldn't notice the lines. *As if.*

"See you later, Levi," I said, following Matt back toward the elevator, where Ixy had remained during the quick stop.

"You don't have to say goodbye, man," Tyler said. "She's the ship's brain. She's on every deck."

"Talk to you soon, Levi," I added, just to needle him for the comment.

We piled back into the elevator, which barely had to move to get us to Six. Again, we exited onto the deck while Ixy remained behind. I imagined she had no need for the tour. So why had she tagged along?

The question was forgotten as the centerpiece of the deck caught my attention. "What is that?" I asked, rushing ahead of Tyler and Alyssa to feast my eyes on a metal cylinder positioned just below the PCS on the deck above. Looking through the tinted window, I stared at a blue-hued orb of pure energy hanging free in the center of the container.

"That's Head Case's power source," Matt replied. "A fusion reaction creates a miniature star within a magnetic containment field. Those two dark boxes on either side of the cylinder stabilize everything using the energy provided from the star. David built it."

"Who's David?" I asked.

"Ben's brother-in-law. He's a smart guy."

I looked from the mini-star to the two black boxes. They had been shoehorned into an available space between two other machines flanking the open floor plan. One I guessed was life support since it appeared to sit between a pair of ventilation pipes. The other three were harder to discern.

"Deck Six is home to all of our critical systems. Power, gravity, life support. And the main engines." He pointed behind me, so I whirled around, excited to see a pair of thick columns wrapped by wires, pipes, and tubes. Chunky terminals on the outer sides each sported a screen displaying flowing lines of numbers that only David would probably understand. The two columns deployed their pipes and wiring aft, where some vanished through the rear bulkhead and others disappeared into the deck. "The thrusters are fully external," Matt explained. "The two mains are mounted outside and down at the inward curve of the skull. There are also two smaller thrusters at the base of the skull behind the hangar that help achieve tighter vectoring arcs."

"Fully external?" Tyler said. "How do you fix them when they break?"

"Fortunately, they don't break very often. If one does, someone needs to do an EVA to do the repair."

"You mean someone has to go outside and do a real spacewalk?"

"With space suits and everything," Matt confirmed.

"I totally want to do that."

"We lost one of the thrusters in the attack, so I might be able to arrange it."

"Really? Don't tease me."

"Consider it a token of good will for your inconvenience."

"Noah, do you want in on this?" Tyler asked.

"Definitely," I answered.

"Ally?"

"I'm game." Her face suddenly pinched up. "I guess."

Matt laughed. "I'll see what I can do. We just need—"

"—to wait for Ben," I finished for him. "Got it."

"I thought you were co-owners?" Tyler asked. "Why does he need to approve everything?"

"We are, but while he's on board he's in charge. That's what we agreed to back when we bought Head Case. I'm usually in charge of ground ops."

"Ben said you're from Earth, right?"

"Yeah. Modesto, California."

"So how did you end up buying a starship?"

"A real starship," I added, the distinction important in my mind.

"That's a really long story," Matt answered. "Maybe we'll get into the details later. The point is, Ben and I are on the same page when it comes to chain-of-command. Seeing that he's also my best friend, I'd never renege on that deal. Anyway, now that you've seen Six, let's keep going."

We trailed him back to the elevator. He directed the cab to Deck Five, but when the doors opened, Ixy pushed me gently aside so she could exit.

"Excusssssse meeessss," she said, exiting the elevator. I would have followed her out if Matt hadn't grabbed my arm.

"We're not disembarking here," he said.

"But you didn't show us the deck."

"Five doesn't contain anything you need to see," Matt replied. "Ixy's web is in the front, along with a bunch of sand. I think Meg and Leo are working in the rear of the deck. We just stopped here so Ixy could get off."

"Oh. Okay." Of course, I was disappointed not to see everything, but the PCS and the copy of Doc Ock's Fusion Reactor had already set my world on fire.

"Why is there sand on a starship?" Alyssa asked. "Do you have a beach in there, too?"

Matt forced a chuckle. "It belonged to a prior owner. It's a hassle to get it all out, and we don't need the space, so we just left it there."

"Uh-huh," she answered suspiciously. "What did the prior owner use it for?"

"I honestly don't know."

"I see."

"What, you don't believe him?" Tyler asked.

"I want to," she answered, turning back to Matt. "But I feel like there's a lot you aren't telling us."

"You aren't wrong," Matt answered. "But I'm not under any obligation to tell you everything, and you have no right to expect it. You're visitors here. Guests. We want you to have a great experience, but that doesn't include prying into every facet of our operation and history."

"Ouch. Burn," Tyler teased, putting up his hands in mock defense when Alyssa turned her daggers his way. "I was just joking with you."

"Sorry, Matt," she said, returning her attention to her crush. "You're right. I shouldn't have pushed. I apologize."

He waved off the concession. "Don't worry about it. I think that encounter with the other starship left us all a little on edge."

"You can say that again."

We reached Deck Four. We'd already seen the flight deck, but Matt brought us to the other side of the elevator to show us more of Head Case's guts in the form of cables, pipes, wires, and large boxes that carried out various subtasks like waste filtration and assembly. After his response to Alyssa over the sand, I decided not to ask him about anything he mentioned. If he didn't tell us up front, I figured either it wasn't important, or he didn't want us to know.

We headed for Deck Three. Riding the elevator down, I noticed a strange tingling sensation like an electromagnetic charge that rippled through my entire body, leaving my arm hairs standing on end by the time the cab doors slid open. "Did you feel that?" I asked.

"Feel what?" Tyler replied.

"It was kind of like sticking my finger in a low-powered wall outlet," I replied.

"I didn't feel anything," Alyssa added.

"Matt?" I asked.

"Maybe you accumulated some static electricity from the carpeting."

"It went through my entire body," I answered. "And I didn't touch anything to cause a discharge."

He responded with a shrug. "We'll come back to Three to go over the contract. I'm just showing you the level so you don't worry about me skipping another deck." He tapped the elevator controls, closing the cab doors again. Directing it to Deck Two, we descended once more. Thankfully, the shocking sensation didn't recur.

I had a sense that something was wrong the moment the elevator slowed to a stop, though I couldn't quite put my finger on it. A glance at Matt suggested he had picked up on something, too. He tapped on the control panel as the cab doors slid open.

"What's on this deck?" Alyssa asked, glancing over at Matt while heading for the exit.

Except the deck wasn't there. Instead, what appeared to be a twenty-foot drop between the cab and the deck below.

"Ally!" I cried, as she went to step out. Suddenly realizing her dilemma, she lost her balance, windmilling her arms to regain it. I lunged for her, my arm snaking around her waist. I threw my weight backward, pulling her with me, away from the edge. Matt caught us both before we could fall.

"What the hell?" Allyssa cried. All four of us looked out through the open doors, the passageway in front of us looming larger than life in comparison to our heights.

"Is it just me, or did we shrink?" Tyler asked.

CHAPTER 17

I stared wide-eyed at the impossibly huge corridor leading away from the elevator doors, my thoughts racing nearly as fast as when we plunged into the spacetime rift.

"What the hell happened?" Tyler demanded.

"I don't know." Matt's stunned expression morphed quickly into confused concern. He tapped his comm badge. "Meg? Leo? Something's up with the elevator."

"Matt?" Meg replied. "What do you mean? You sound funny."

"We're on Deck Two, but we're still half-sized."

"Uh, that's not good."

"Yeah, no kidding."

"Standby, I'll check the system."

Matt glanced over at us. We were all looking back at him by now, confusion etched across our faces.

"You've got to be kidding me!" Tyler shrieked. "I'm freaking tiny, man!"

"Don't blow a gasket, Tee," Matt replied. "The system's designed to scale us down on Deck Three and back up again as we pass through. That didn't happen. Meg will find out why and fix it."

Tyler laughed nervously. "I think we need a little more explanation on this one. You can't just change a person's size like you change your underwear."

Matt's badge beeped. "Matt, access logs show the elevator's supercapacitor is fully drained. It discharged as you passed from Deck Four to Deck Three."

"How is that possible?" Matt replied, holding up a hand toward us to keep us silent.

"I'm not sure yet. You know my understanding of how the sigils work is relatively limited. Keep always said the self-contained unit in the lift didn't need maintenance and wouldn't use much power. I need to run additional diagnostics to figure out why that didn't hold true."

"Sigils?" Tyler muttered into my ear. "This is getting weirder and weirder."

"How could he be so wrong?" Matt responded. "The capacitor is supposed to have enough juice for hundreds of cycles. If it broke…" He shook his head. "I don't even want to go there. Can you recharge the battery?"

"It's already recharging, and keeping it powered from the reactor shouldn't be a problem. But it means a delay moving in or out of Deck Three."

"At least that's just temporary," Matt said, relief clear in his tone. "Can we add another capacitor?"

"We don't have any spares right now, but we can pick some up next time we go home. Anyway, that's a hack, not a solution. For now, I recommend returning to Deck Three. Everything should be reset by the time you're ready to head down to Deck Two."

"Copy that. Thanks, Meg." Matt tapped his comm badge to end the call. He turned to the controls, directing the elevator back up to Three.

"Two questions," I said. "One, if the elevator cab is half-size in the shaft, how is it still functional? And two, what did Meg mean by sigils?"

"The elevator uses gravitational control mechanisms to move through the shaft. Basically, unequal gravitational adjustment, pushing and pulling, from either end, with enough friction to hold it laterally in place. Sigils…" he trailed off with a sigh. "I know this doesn't come close to the day you've had, Noah. But compared to how smoothly things usually run around here, we're getting kicked in the teeth on this one."

The elevator slowed to a stop and I braced myself, unsure what awaited us. The doors whisked open, revealing Deck Three at proper scale, at least from our viewpoint. Allie bolted out, nearly bowling Matt over in her haste. I joined Tyler in scurrying after her, my thoughts still racing, trying to keep up with everything I had experienced in less than twenty-four hours. I tried to ignore the subconscious fear of my mental outcome once my mind grasped everything that had happened.

Matt faced us wearing a look two parts apology, one part embarrassment. "I'm sorry this is happening to you. I know you're all pretty freaked out."

"No kidding!" Alyssa huffed. "I could have been hurt! We shrank! That's impossible!"

"You're actually still shrunk," Matt said, wincing in anticipation of Ally's continued panic. When she remained silent, he drew a deep breath, visibly centering himself. "Something's glitching, but you heard Meg. We just need to wait for the supercapacitor to recharge before moving off Deck Three. The scaling sigil should be fine in no time."

"Glitching?" Tyler challenged. "Elevators don't glitch people into midgets, Matt. That's not a software bug."

"Technically, it might be. Head Case uses technology called Sigiltech to manipulate quantum effects, like scaling."

"So…magic," I said bluntly.

Matt shrugged. "It seems like magic, but so does AI the first time you encounter it."

"I don't think ChatGPT is going to shrink me to half size," Alyssa said.

"Look, I'm not an engineer like Meg or Leo, but I can tell you that Sigiltech channels chaos energy from the Void, which we just passed through, into specific sigil patterns. The design of those patterns create the specific effect. Sort of like computer programming."

I stared, thoughts whirling. Sigils. Quantum manipulation. Chaos energy. Wait a second…

"Are you saying this ship can change size? Is that how you hid it from us in the cornfield?" Awe overwhelmed my lingering unease.

Matt grinned and nodded. "You're no dummy, Noah. I was waiting for you to put two and two together."

"The scores on the inside of the hull. Those are sigil patterns, aren't they?"

He nodded again, still smirking a little.

"And the rift… The ship did that through Ben somehow?"

"No, Ben did that himself. He can channel chaos energy without sigils."

"Holy crap!" Tyler exclaimed. "That's insane! How is that even possible?" He looked at me. "You were right. He's freaking Gandalf."

"It's all pretty unbelievable. But in the four years since we bought Head Case, we've never had a problem with any of the sigils." Matt regarded her reassuringly. "We've got it under control."

"After I almost fell to my death," Alyssa retorted.

"We'll have it all straightened out in no time, I promise. Until then, we just need to exercise a little patience. Deck Three contains our general living spaces. Recreation, bedrooms, head, galley, and assembler. Let's go to the kitchen. We can grab refreshments and talk. Maybe finalize that rental agreement, too."

He headed down the corridor while the three of us stared at each other.

"Is anyone else majorly freaking out right now?" Alyssa whispered. "Giant spiders, blue squirrels, magic space-warping ships? And now, honey, the ship shrunk us kids. This is more than I signed up for!"

"Are you kidding me?" Tyler retorted. "This is epic! Matt just admitted they're playing with forces beyond physics. I wonder what else he hasn't told us yet?"

I silently agreed with Tyler's unspoken fascination. My wheels spun faster than Levi's fifty exaFLOPS. If Sigiltech could resize objects and open rifts through a void in spacetime, what else could it do? The possibilities staggered me.

"You can't actually be enjoying this, Noah!" Alyssa argued when I shared my thoughts. "This ship is danger-ous! First we're attacked and nearly killed. Then we go through some crazy portal and I feel like I'm going to lose my mind. Then I try to do something as simple as stepping off an elevator, and I almost fall into a pit. And we've only been here for half an hour."

"True," Tyler jumped in before I could respond. "But we also have no reason to think any of that stuff will happen again. Whoever attacked us probably thinks we're space junk by now. And like Matt said, they can fix the problem with the elevator."

"You don't know that for sure," Allie insisted stubbornly.

"No," I disagreed, with a slow shake of my head. "We don't know anything for certain yet, but I believe Matt and Ben are good guys running into some bad luck. That's enough for me to want to keep following this yellow brick road."

Ally threw her hands up helplessly. "You two are insane."

Further argument was forestalled by Matt's return, once he realized we hadn't followed him. "Are you guys coming?"

"Yeah," I said for the group, hurrying to catch up to him. Tyler stayed with me, while Alyssa hesitated for a moment before throwing her hands up and trailing along behind us. Reaching the end of the corridor brought us to what had to be the lounge Matt had referenced multiple times. A pair of beat-up sofas sat in an L formation near the center, a shaggy orange ottoman between them. One end table looked to be made from stone. The other, made from some kind of yellow composite, hovered in midair, holding my attention for more than a few seconds. At the front of the lounge, a huge cathode television on a massive articulating mount hung just above another long, wide viewport. To our right sat a piano, a guitar stand with a pair of guitars, a drum set, and behind it, a bar and foosball table. There was also a loaded bookshelf, and as I turned full circle in the room, I noticed stairs leading up to a second floor.

Suddenly, scaling to half-size made sense in the most ridiculous way I could conceive.

"So this is our main lounge area," Matt said. "The sofas recline and have built-in massagers. Alyssa, you strike me as someone who enjoys books." He indicated the shelves inset along the exterior bulkheads. "We've got some great paperbacks, and the slabs all have access to our data store, which has its own extensive media library."

He turned to point up the stairs. "Berthing is up there. We have five bedrooms in total. I'm sure you won't be here that long, so we'll keep that private space." He smiled. "Now you understand why the sigils scale us down. Otherwise, we wouldn't have anywhere to sleep or relax. This isn't a military ship, so R and R is important."

"You have an awful lot of guns for not a military ship," Alyssa pointed out.

"And we need them," Matt replied. "Space is too big to rely on anyone else for protection. Ninety-nine point nine percent of the time, things run smoothly and there are no complications. It's that point one percent that will get you killed if you aren't prepared for it."

"What kind of threats do you encounter?" I asked. "Besides unidentified ships slinging missiles at you just outside of Earth's orbit."

"We made enemies of some pretty powerful warlords when we first reached the Spiral. They haven't stopped plotting to destroy us, despite a consistent lack of success."

"I want to know more about that," Tyler said.

"Yeah, me too," Ally agreed.

Matt smiled. "You walked right past the galley. Let's grab some food and drinks and make everything legal."

CHAPTER 18

Matt's dodge around Tyler's question about his and Ben's exploits didn't get me any closer to understanding their way of thinking. Considering the capabilities they had at their disposal, I couldn't imagine why anyone would be dumb enough to keep a target lock on them.

I let it go for now as we backtracked to the first door on the left just before the lounge. A galley kitchen occupied most of the space. White counters gleamed under recessed lighting, and a simple metal table and four chairs occupied the center of the compartment. The cabinets contained plates, cups, and cutlery, but there was no sign of a fridge or any other food, or anything to cook it in for that matter. The only thing that even vaguely resembled an appliance was a simple brushed steel door that interrupted the backsplash and occupied half the area behind the counter.

"Talk about sparse," Tyler commented as we entered. Matt motioned to the chairs, and we each took a seat. "I don't see a fridge. Where's the promised grub at?"

"How can you be hungry? We pigged out on Miyaki's four hours ago."

"You pigged out. I didn't bring any for me, remember?"

"To be honest, I hadn't noticed."

"You definitely had some other things on your mind."

"I'll worry about all of that once I'm back on Earth. Until then, I'm going to shoot for denial. I want to enjoy this."

"Alyssa, what's your favorite food?" Matt asked, moving to the galley counter.

"I'm not sure I should say," she replied. "I don't want to give Tyler any more ammo to Google me with."

"I wouldn't do that," Tyler said. "I use DuckDuckGo." He shot her his signature impish grin.

"Spaghetti and meatballs," Alyssa admitted. "With a spicy marinara."

"That's a great choice. I love meatballs." Matt's smile set Ally's cheeks afire once more. He turned away from her, retrieving a plate from the cupboard and lifting the metal door. The plate easily fit into the space behind it. He put a cup in it as well before closing the door again. "What about beverage?"

"Root beer?" she said.

He nodded. "Hey Asshole, give me a plate of spaghetti and meatballs in a spicy marinara, with a root beer."

"Spaghetti and meatballs?" a voice with a heavy Brooklyn accent replied. "Mama mia, that's a tasty meal. Comin' right up, ya filthy animal!"

Tyler and I laughed. Alyssa looked stunned. "I thought the AI's name was Levi?"

"Oh, it is. Asshole isn't really an AI. His responses are dynamic but mostly canned. Ben programmed the system to think it works at a Manhattan deli. Don't ask me why."

"Order up, Sweetcakes."

Matt opened the steel door. The smell of perfectly made spaghetti and meatballs immediately wafted to my nose. I breathed in deeply. "Is this Sigiltech too?"

"No, just regular tech. A molecular assembler."

"There's nothing regular about that," Tyler said.

"Not on Earth," Matt agreed. "It uses raw materials to produce meals from a molecular recipe database."

"That's amazing," Alyssa said as Matt put the spaghetti in front of her, along with the root beer and cutlery.

"No way! It's like a super microwave," Tyler said.

"Better. It's perfectly cooked every time. And, if you want to add something to the database, you don't need to do the chemical breakdown yourself. Just give it a sample, and it can figure out how to assemble it."

"How does it work?" I asked.

Matt laughed. "Beyond providing it with raw resources, I have no idea. I just tell it what I want to eat."

I watched Ally take a bite. She smiled and nodded, signaling it wasn't only edible, but tasty.

"Noah, what's your flavor of the day?" Matt asked.

"Rice balls," Tyler answered for me.

"Asshole, can you make rice balls?" Matt asked.

"Nope," it answered simply.

"It's okay," I said. "I'm not hungry. I ate a few hours ago."

"How about a drink?"

I considered and then nodded. "Asshole, can you do a cold brew?"

"Absofreakinlutely. You want one or what?"

I paused, Matt's earlier words resonating in my mind. "When you say raw materials, what does that include?" I asked.

"Pretty much anything that would otherwise go in the trash," Matt replied.

Alyssa lowered her forkful of spaghetti. "I'm eating garbage?"

"Technically," he answered. "And also anything that would go down the toilet or the shower drain."

"You're kidding." Her fork clattered on the table, and

she pushed herself away from her food. "I think I'm going to be sick."

"It's all perfectly safe. The assembler breaks it down to base molecules, like you'd find on the periodic table, and reassembles your order from there. It's like how the wheat that's grown to be made into spaghetti is fertilized with manure. You eat that, right?"

Alyssa thought about it before pulling her chair back up to the table. "When you put it that way," she said, picking up her fork and shoving another bite into her mouth.

"Believe me, I had the same reaction when I first learned how it worked. T-bone, what's your pleasure?"

"Asshole," Tyler said. "How about a burger, medium rare, two patties. Pickles, ketchup, mustard, and potato chips. Oh, and peanut butter. Plus fries, nice and crispy. And a beer."

Matt laughed. "I have a feeling you and Ben will get along just fine. He's also a burger connoisseur."

"A beer?" Ally said. "You're only seventeen."

"No alcohol laws in space, am I right?" Tyler asked.

"You are correct," Matt answered.

"Yo, Mattie. Can you get me a plate and a mug?" Asshole asked. Matt stuck the dishes in the assembler and closed the door. Less than thirty seconds later, Tyler had the best-looking burger I'd ever seen. It was almost enough to make me hungry despite my full stomach.

"I'll be right back," Matt said. "I'm just going to grab the rental agreement." He hurried out of the galley, leaving us alone again.

"I wonder if there's any way we can bring Asshole back to Earth with us," Tyler commented before biting into his burger, groaning as he tasted it.

"I can only guess how much energy it uses to break things into molecules and put them back together," I replied.

"What do you guys think of Matt?" Alyssa asked.

"Like, is he into you? I don't think so," Tyler answered. "You're not his type."

"How do you know what his type is?"

"Look at him. He's like a young Chris Hemsworth, except American."

"Maybe he cares about more than looks. Not every man is as shallow as you."

"I think this is the last thing we should be talking about right now," I said before they could start arguing. "We aren't going to be on board long enough for you to date him, whether he likes you or not. Unless…"

"Unless what?" Tyler asked. "I don't like the look on your face."

I opened my mouth to answer, the wheels of logic picking up speed as everything I'd observed since we boarded Head Case coalesced in my subconscious. My brain had worked out the math while I'd been marveling over the technology, but the final answer had yet to make its way to my lips. Matt came back before it could, leaving all three of us hanging.

"Here's our standard rental agreement," he said, dropping a too-thick stack of legal papers in the center of the table. "I know it's pretty much a formality at this point, since you can't disembark if you wanted to, but once you sign on the dotted line this whole deal will be official."

"Is that supposed to make us feel better?" Alyssa griped.

"No, but it'll make me and Ben feel better," he replied.

I leafed curiously through the document. A lot of terminology sounded almost boilerplate, something any business might use. Arbitration. Assumption of risk. Yada yada yada. Of course, no other business on Earth talked about itineraries to Mars and Venus, or claimed they weren't responsible should we get sucked into a black hole.

"I think we need to change this part," I said, pointing to

a line right at the beginning. It stated the tour would be three hours long. We'd already burned one of them and were still drifting in the middle of nowhere, waiting for Ben to feel better.

"Yeah. You're probably right," Matt agreed. "Let me cross that part out. We'll just change it to indefinite, okay?"

"I don't like the sound of that," Alyssa said.

"It's just a formality. We'll get you home as soon as we can."

"Okay."

He crossed it out, handwriting in the change. I read the rest of the document. Other than clearing the employees of Head Space Star Tours of liability for pretty much anything and promising us we would visit Mars and Venus, there really wasn't much to the contract despite Matt's earlier claims.

I didn't care. I signed it without reservation before sliding it toward Tyler.

"Try not to get any ketchup on it," Matt warned as T-Bone plated the remaining half of his burger to scribble his name beneath mine. He passed it over to Alyssa.

"So, if I don't sign this, you'll throw me off the ship?"

"Not really," Matt replied. "But I'll probably have to lock you in a closet or something. I'd rather not have to do that."

"Come on, All-red," I said. "Don't gum up the works."

She looked at me. "I'll sign after you tell us what you were going to say before Matt came back."

Matt turned his attention my way, curious. Then all eyes were on me.

"Unless…" Ally reminded me when I hesitated.

"Well, Ben used sigils to open the rift and get us here, wherever here is. Then he collapsed and had to go to sick-bay. The elevator also uses sigils and drained the batteries after a single resize. To me, that suggests however Sigiltech works, it's not operating very efficiently right now. Plus, the hyperdrive is damaged. Which means—"

"We might be stuck out here for a while," Tyler finished. He glanced at Alyssa. "I hope your roommate remembers to feed your cat."

"Worse," I said, stomach clenching, heart pounding. "Depending on where in the universe we are, we might be stuck out here *permanently*."

CHAPTER 19

A tense silence fell over the galley. Even Matt's face paled. He'd yet to consider the ramifications of our frantic escape from certain destruction.

Alyssa dropped the pen. "I'm not signing this. What the hell does it matter, anyway?"

"It's only a theory," I said. "Maybe when Ben comes back, he'll be able to tell us I'm totally wrong and that he can get us back to Earth easy-peasy."

"I'm done waiting for Ben to make an appearance," she complained, her patience worn thin. "Can we just go to sickbay and talk to him? He doesn't need to use much energy to move his lips. And we need answers. Now."

Matt bit his lower lip before nodding. "Yeah. We might as well head down there. The transit did a number on him, but I'll see if I can wake him up. I kind of want to know what he thinks about all this, too."

"My mom's gonna kill me," Tyler said. The second half of his burger rested forgotten on his plate, his appetite gone. The same went for what remained of Alyssa's spaghetti.

Matt pushed his chair back and stood, hesitating there.

He picked up the pen and held it out to Alyssa. "I'm sorry, but unless you want to be locked in the spare bedroom, you need to sign the contract."

"You have to be kidding."

"Until you sign, we're liable for anything that might happen to you. That's not a risk we can afford to take."

"Yeah, well, if you don't get me back home in the next twenty hours, I'm going to lose my job, my apartment, and maybe Kaiju."

"Your cat's name is Kaiju?" I asked. "That's awesome."

"Thanks." She flashed a smile my way before her sour-puss swung back at Matt. "If I don't sign, you're responsible for re-homing me, right?"

"Uh…" He swallowed hard. "Like I said, none of this is even admissible in an Earth court. Who would believe you're suing a starship tour operator, anyway?"

"But I can sue you in the Spiral."

"If you can file the lawsuit and appear in front of the judge."

"Which you would help me do, because you're not a scammer, right?"

Matt sighed in frustration. "Ally, I promise when we get back to Earth if you've suffered any losses, we'll do our best to make you whole. We're not scammers, but accidents do happen."

"Apparently, so do ambushes from starships that shouldn't exist," Tyler added.

Matt pointed to him. "Exactly. We had no way to predict this would happen."

"Yes, you did," Alyssa insisted. "You admitted you have enemies in the Spiral who keep trying to kill you. Why wouldn't you expect them to follow you to Earth?"

"They would need someone who knows how to use Sigiltech to open rifts. Ben and Keep are the only two people that can do it, and Keep would never betray us."

"How can you be sure they're the only ones?"

Matt opened his mouth, but no guarantees spilled out. "Please, just sign it," he begged instead.

"No," she replied.

"Ally," Tyler snapped

"Don't," she snapped back. "There are only two adults in this room, and I'm one of them. So butt out of it."

"Ouch." Tyler clasped his hands over his heart in response to the vicious rebuke.

"If that's how you want it," Matt said. "Stand up. Leave your ticket on the table."

"Why?"

"I told you. I need to lock you up. It's for your safety."

"Red, you may want to just sign it," I said, taking a softer tack than Tee had tried. "We're a team, and I don't want us to split up."

She looked at me, and for a second I thought she might relent. "I'm sorry. I want to. But if this ends up costing me everything I've worked for, I need a backup plan. Crossing the galaxy to file a lawsuit is the best I can do right now."

"I'm sure I have money coming my way. I can help you out."

"That's sweet, Katzuo. Really. But you need that money. I'm sure the last thing your folks would want is you to skip out on college to help a total stranger pay her rent."

"You aren't a total stranger. You're a Stinking Badger."

She looked down at the signature line, then at the offered pen, then at me. Completing the cycle three more times, she sighed and finally took the pen.

"Matt," Levi said, the computer's voice breaking in over loudspeakers in the galley. "We have an unidentified contact on long range sensors."

Instead of signing, Alyssa threw the pen across the galley. This time, Matt didn't care. He had bigger fish to fry.

We all did.

"ETA?" Matt snapped, already moving for the exit. I jumped up behind him. Tyler and Ally followed.

"Twelve minutes at their current heading and velocity."

I expected Matt to turn left toward the elevator, and head to the flight deck. Instead, he hung a right, and we chased him into the lounge. He picked the television remote up from one of the sofa cushions and turned the TV on, flipping to a channel that displayed the sensor grid. Sure enough, a ship was headed straight for us.

"Levi, can you get me a visual?" he asked, turning and opening the drawer of the end table next to the sofa. He didn't find what he was looking for there, so he tried the other end table. Still nothing. He rushed over to the bar, looking behind it. "Damn it, Ben. Where'd you leave the RFD?"

Meanwhile, Levi turned the channel into a split screen of the grid and a camera feed looking out into space. The camera steadily zoomed in, painting a red outline around the ship to make it more visible against the black.

The good news was that it bore no resemblance to the ship that had attacked us near Earth.

That was also the bad news.

Matt ran up the steps to the bedrooms while the three of us stared at the screen. The ship appeared to be a few hundred feet long and nearly equally wide, composed of multiple bulbous spheres that made the entire thing look like a metallic tumor. There were no obvious viewports. thrusters, or energy trails, leaving its means of propulsion questionable. Fortunately, I also didn't see any gun batteries or turrets, but I imagined not every vessel would make their weapons as obvious as Head Case did. As I stared, I noticed how the exterior of the ship's hull appeared as if it was covered in reflective dragon scales, which shifted and moved across the surface of the craft, appearing to constantly morph their form.

"That thing is sick," Tyler said beside me.

"I'm going to be sick," Alyssa commented, her face pale. She looked over her shoulder as Matt hopped down the stairs, grumbling about Ben being a slob. "Do you recognize this one?" she asked.

He eyed the incoming ship. "No. I've never seen a ship like that before."

"Wrong answer," Tyler said. "How are we supposed to know whether or not it's friendly before it starts shooting at us?"

"We need to go up to the flight deck and try hailing them. I could have done it from down here, but I can't find the RFD pad."

"And RFD stands for...?" I urged.

"Remote Flight Deck," Tyler answered for him. "I thought that was obvious."

Matt tapped his comm badge. "Meg, Leo, is the elevator ready to go?"

"Aye, it is," Leo answered. "But it will still need a recharge after you use it."

"Good enough." He looked us over, gaze pausing on Ally while he considered whether or not to leave her in one of the bedrooms.

"Look," I said, my eyes still on the ship. The forward bulbous protrusions were shifting, collapsing in on each other and reconfiguring into a new shape, creating a long snout at the front of the vessel.

"Great," Tyler said. "Ben sent us through the void and into the Transformers' universe."

Still morphing, sleek protrusions that looked way too much like gun barrels sprouted from the front of the ship beside the snout, taking on an appearance similar to a sea urchin.

"That doesn't look very friendly to me," Alyssa said.

"That doesn't mean it isn't friendly," Matt countered. "Just cautious."

"If you say so."

"I hope so," he answered. "Come on."

"Are you sure hailing them is a good idea?" I asked, giving Matt pause. "Since that ship doesn't look at all like it was made by humans, there's a very good chance they don't speak English. Not to mention we have no idea where we are in this universe."

"Considering our shields are still pretty beat up," Matt said, "fighting isn't an option. We can't go FTL, so running isn't viable either. Our only other option is to try to talk our way out of this."

"It's kind of amazing," Tyler said. "Space is so gigantic, and yet these guys found us in less than an hour."

"Amazing and terrifying," Alyssa added.

"It also means they were already nearby or have FTL tech also," I said.

"Or Sigiltech," Tyler offered.

"Maybe we're near an occupied ILF planet," Alyssa suggested. "Maybe this is a good thing."

One of the sleek protrusions suddenly glowed in bright orange before spewing energy across the gap between us and them.

And there was absolutely nothing we could do about it.

CHAPTER 20

All four of us froze, nowhere near close enough to the flight deck to do much about the orange plasma heading straight for us, and since Levi didn't try to fly the ship, I had to assume it was beyond the AI's programming.

The energy crashed into Head Case, the shields flaring blue but holding steady against the stream. It ended within a few seconds, without so much as rattling our cage.

"That looked a hell of a lot like a warning shot to me," Tyler said.

"Aren't you supposed to miss when you fire a warning shot?" Alyssa asked.

"Or dial down the power so it doesn't do too much damage," Matt answered. "Either way, friendlies don't usually shoot first and roll out the welcome mat later."

"So what do we do?"

Matt shook his head. "I don't know. I think I should go check on Ben."

"There's no time," Tyler said. "We need a plan, now."

"I'm the pilot, not the planner. That's Ben's area of expertise."

"And Noah's," Tyler volunteered. "Come on, man. Give us an idea."

All eyes turned my way. The sudden pressure of having everyone's fate in my hands should have left me frozen in fear. It was one thing to plan a strategy for a video game, entirely different to play with other people's actual lives. But after the day I'd already had, after the bad luck that had put us in this situation, it didn't seem as though I had that much to lose. Best case? We remained potentially lost, the ship damaged, her captain incapacitated, with no obvious way home. Worst case scenario, we all die and this horrible, incredible, terrible, amazing day would come to an end.

"Can't fight, can't run, can't talk," I said. "The next best thing to do is hide."

"Kind of hoping for something that makes a little more sense there, Katzuo," Tyler said. "We're drifting through open space. There is nowhere to hide."

"I didn't mean the ship," I explained. "I meant us."

"You mean play possum?" Ty looked skeptical. "They just blasted the ship's shields. They know we have power."

"Maybe, but that doesn't mean anyone is home. What if life support failed? What if we took an escape pod and abandoned ship? We're under power in the middle of nowhere. For what reason?"

"Noah's right," Alyssa agreed. "If everything was just fine, there would be no reason for us to be drifting aimlessly out here. But what if that ship has life sign detection sensors? Or what if that beam wasn't an attack but a way of scanning us?"

"You've watched too many Star Trek episodes," Matt said. "That kind of sensor not only doesn't exist, it can't exist. It would need to be able to pass a signal fine-tuned enough to read DNA or pick up small atmospheric changes across a vacuum, not to mention through energy shielding, the hull, and all of the bulkheads, pipes, and wires." He shrugged. "At least, that's what David told me when I asked about life sign detection."

"It's supposed to be impossible to open rifts in space-time, too," Alyssa rebutted.

Matt laughed. "Yeah, I can't argue with that. It may be that they can sense us, but it seems like a chance we have to take. Good thinking, Noah."

"Is it?" Tyler asked. "No offense, Noah-san, but what if they think Head Case is derelict?"

"Maybe they'll come in for a closer look and then move on," I answered.

"And what if they don't? What if they decide to board us? Even if they believe the ship is abandoned, they may decide they want this sweet, sweet, salvage…what then?"

"There's a good chance that could be the case," I agreed. "But what other choice do we have? It's the best of the bad options."

"I agree with Noah," Matt said. "And believe me, I've had to pick from that menu before. The good news is, we aren't entirely defenseless." He tapped his comm badge. "Leo, what's your sitrep?"

"Hey, Boss," Leo replied, barely audible over the background noise. "I'm knee deep in burned out wiring on that lost thruster. What's up?"

"You didn't hear Levi's alert?"

"No. In case you can't hear it, it's kind of loud down here. Don't tell me we're being attacked again."

"Not yet, but there's an unidentified ship approaching."

"Two in one day? What'd we do to get so lucky? It's going to take me at least a day to work through this mess. Another day to replace everything, assuming we have it all in supply."

"Drop all that and head to the flight deck. We're going to play dead, but if this interloper gets aggressive again, we'll need to cut and run."

"Aye aye, boss," Leo said. "Be there in two shakes."

"Try to make it one, and give me an update on our new friend when you get there."

"Sure. What happened to the RFD?"

"I can't find it."

"Maybe Shaq has it in his nest again. He likes it because it's warm and smells like Ben."

"I looked there. Get moving."

"On my way."

Leo had just disconnected when Matt tapped the badge again. "Meg, how's the elevator supercapacitor?"

"One hundred percent, Boss," she replied. "You're free to move about the ship."

"What about the hyperdrive? Do you have an ETA?

"I haven't had a chance to look at it yet. We're in trouble again, aren't we? I heard Levi say something about an unidentified contact."

"Yeah, we may be in a little trouble. It wouldn't hurt to have the hyperdrive back."

"I'll go take a look and see what I can do."

"Thank you." He disconnected again, turning to us. "Now that the elevator's back online, I can show you what's on Deck Two."

"Aren't we a little busy dealing with the mighty morphin' space aliens?" Tyler asked.

"Not too busy to go down to Deck Two," Matt answered with a wink.

Tyler smiled. "Well, now I'm curious."

Matt hurried us back to the elevator at a near-run. We all piled in, save for Ally, who stood at the threshold, suddenly more concerned with being left half-size again than the incoming vessel.

"You can stay here by yourself if you want," Matt said, out of patience over her attitude. He hit the control pad to send the cab to Deck Two.

Ally frantically eyed Tyler and then me, obviously waiting for one of us to come to her rescue, I guessed. Tyler waved to her. I shrugged. She made a frightened, annoyed face before jumping in as the doors started closing.

"I hate you both," she said.

I put a reassuring hand on her shoulder, only removing it once we reached Deck Two. "We'll be fine," I told her, feeling the same static charge I had the first time the sigils in the elevator triggered.

"Meg," Matt said, hitting his badge again. "What's left of the energy stores after our resizing?"

"Looks like fifty-five percent," she replied. "You have enough to go back up to Three again, but then you'll need to wait for another recharge."

"I don't plan on going up to Three right away, but it's good to know we can bounce to the flight deck if needed." The cab doors opened, and we stuck behind him as he took off running down the corridor, finally pausing in front of a heavier steel blast door that looked like it had been ripped from the front of a bank vault. "This is the armory," he said. "Levi, open it up."

The locks on the door clanged when they released, the thick door slowly swinging outward on motorized hinges, revealing the prizes inside.

"What is it you do when you aren't running space tours for charity, again?" I asked, staring in at the racks of long guns, with more shelves of odd looking weapons and ammo visible behind them and along both sides of the compartment. This wasn't like a gun safe in a hunter's basement. They had more firepower here than the entire Cedar Rapids and Des Moines police departments combined.

"Hop racing," Matt answered, adding, "and a few other minor incidental things when they crop up."

"Like what? Full-scale rebellions?"

"Something like that. I can explain later."

"You're assuming there will be a later," Ally said.

"You could at least try to be positive," I replied.

"This is me trying, Katzuo," she answered. "I'm scared."

"We're all scared," Matt said. "Hopefully, we won't need any of this stuff. But it's better to be prepared."

He led us into the vault, pulling out a dark rifle that vaguely resembled an AR-15. Only this one had a counter on the side next to a dial labeled single, burst, and stream. It didn't appear to have a magazine of any kind. Instead, what looked like a battery pack hung below the body. "This is a P-150 plasma rifle," he said. "One of the most abundant and easy to use rifles in the Spiral. Standard issue for the Royal Marines. Have any of you ever fired a gun?"

"Plenty of times," Tyler boasted. "In *Fortnite.*"

"A real gun," Matt specified.

"Nope," Tyler replied. "My little brother was shot to death in a parking lot. I hate guns."

"Tee, you never told us that," Alyssa said. "I'm so sorry."

"I don't really like to talk about it, but I don't want you guys getting the wrong ideas about why I don't want to touch a rifle."

"Tyler, I get it," Matt said. "Really. But I think your brother would want you to use a gun to save your own life and the lives of your friends."

"You didn't know him."

"No, but I know that people who love others want them to fight to survive. I don't think your brother would want you to join him wherever he is if you had a choice."

The comment was directed at Tyler, but it hit me just the same. It felt good to have that perspective confirmed by someone who had obviously been in some bad situations.

"How does it work?" I asked, reaching out for the gun. Matt handed it to me and a second one to Ally. She didn't look comfortable holding the rifle either, but at least she was trying.

"Are you sure, Tyler?" Matt asked, picking up a third gun.

"Matt," Leo said, breaking in over Matt's comm before Tyler could answer. "I'm on the flight deck, at the pilot's station. Geez, that thing is weird. I've never seen a ship like it. Wherever Ben sent us, I don't think it's the Spiral or the Milky Way."

"That doesn't matter right now. What's the ship doing?"

"Closing in and decelerating. It looks like whoever they are, they plan to dock and board."

"Yeah, that's what I was afraid of. We're in the armory."

"Are you sure you don't want to try to outrun them?"

"I'm pretty sure we can't outrun them. Every option is risky, but Noah's idea feels the least suicidal."

"Copy that. They'll need to synchronize with us and find a way through our forward shields to board. You probably have another fifteen minutes or so if you're aiming to provide some nasty surprises."

"That should be plenty long enough. Let me know when they start working on disabling the shields."

"Will do, Boss."

"Last chance," Matt said, still holding the rifle out to Tyler, who looked torn between the trauma of his brother's murder and his desire to defend himself. Finally, he relented, snatching the weapon out of Matt's hands. "We have target dummies and reinforced plating in the gym for practice, but there's no time for that. Do your best. Just like any other gun, aim, hold your breath, and pull the trigger."

"Explain the three settings," I pressed.

He tapped each labeled position in turn. "Single bolt per squeeze. Three bolts per squeeze. Steady stream of super-heated plasma, kind of like a flamethrower."

"I see armor back there," Tyler said, pointing to the rack behind the rifles. "We could probably use some of that."

"Powered armor has a learning curve," Matt replied. "And there's no time to train you. If we need more than these rifles, we're already screwed."

"That's not reassuring." Tee blanched, his face losing all color.

"I'm not trying to be reassuring, I'm trying to be honest. Come on. We need to get in position before they arrive."

Once more, we trailed after Matt, racing down the passageway. Tyler glanced over at me. "Are you having the adventure of a lifetime yet?"

I remained silent. As frightened as I was, I didn't want to admit to him—or anyone else, including myself—that despite the newest threat to our lives, this was still a hell of a lot better than sitting in a hospital room, waiting for some bureaucrat to seize control of my future.

CHAPTER 21

The elevator doors slid open on the upper level of the hangar deck, and I swallowed hard as Matt waved us forward, the metal gridwork clanging under our feet as we moved toward the railing. Still kneeling below us on the hangar deck, its fists planted on the decking, the looming head and shoulders of the Hunter mech hid us from view from anyone breaching the hangar entrance.

"We'll take positions here," Matt said. "Hopefully we can catch them by surprise if they decide to lock on and board us." He tapped me on the shoulder. "I want you and Allyssa there." He pointed to the gap where the left arm met the torso. The location provided a narrow lane of fire and viewpoint to the deck below. Tyler followed our de facto leader to the other side of the upper level where he and Matt took up the same positions behind the mech's right shoulder joint.

Once we were in position, the hangar bay fell still, so silent I could hear every labored, frightened breath Ally took.

"Boss," Leo said, his sudden voice so loud over Matt's comm badge it nearly made me jump out of my skin. "The contact just hit us with another volley of…something. No damage, no shield degradation. I don't know what to make of it."

"Are they still approaching?" Matt asked.

"Aye. Still decelerating. But their course has shifted. If they stay on their current trajectory, they'll slide past us at less than a kilometer."

"They probably saw how Head Case is patched together with shipping containers and decided the salvage wasn't worth the effort," Alyssa whispered.

"I hope so," I replied.

"How long until they're past?" Matt asked.

"Three minutes."

The silence returned, thicker and tenser. Beside me, Alyssa's whole body trembled. I shook just as badly while I questioned my prior decision that I was better off out here than back in the hospital. If this entire adventure to this point had proven anything, it was how much I wanted to live to become the man my parents had always tried to teach me to be. I felt like I owed them that much. I wasn't thrilled about the idea of using deadly force against another living being, but I also had no intention of letting some alien assholes harm my new friends or rob me of my future.

One minute passed. Another. The seconds seemed to tick away like hours, every one of them raising another hair on my arms and cutting my ragged breathing just a little shorter. Anticipation had me on the verge of panic. I wanted to scream at the alien ship to either move along, grab on, or blow us to bits, so long as it did *something* already.

"Boss," Leo said, again making me twitch when he broke the uneasy silence. "The contact just stopped."

"What do you mean, stopped?" Matt asked.

"Yeah, I guess that's technically not the right term. They're matching our velocity and heading and floating beside us, about a hundred meters past the flight deck transparency."

"And doing what?"

"Nothing."

"That doesn't make any sense."

"Do they want us or not?" Tyler asked, clearly on edge. Not that I was one to talk. I was ready to jump out of my skin to get away from this predicament.

"Maybe they're scanning us," Ally suggested, sticking to her guns.

All of the lights in the hangar went out.

The sudden darkness elicited a whimper from Alyssa, begging to go home. I felt the same way, but I clenched my jaw to keep from crying out. On the other side of the Hunter, Tyler's harsh whispers suggested we were all in the same boat.

"Boss, the reactor just took itself offline," Leo said. "We're on backup power for life support."

"What do you mean, took itself offline?" Matt asked. "Levi, what's your status?"

The ship's AI didn't answer.

"I probably don't need to tell you this, but shields are down," Leo continued. The pilot station is offline too, but I can see the alien craft outside. They're vectoring to board."

"See?" Alyssa hissed. "They scanned us and saw that we're in here. They shut down everything but life support."

"They hacked us?" I asked, finding it hard to believe the ship's Primary Control System was that poorly protected from intrusion.

"Prepare to be boarded," Matt said, his voice unbelievably calm. The guy definitely knew how to keep his cool under pressure. I wondered if I would be so zen after years of interstellar firefights.

I wondered if I would live long enough to find out.

"What should we aim at?" Tyler asked. "I can't see a

damn thing in here." He didn't have time to take a breath after he finished talking before emergency backup lighting activated, offering a weak glow from various positions around the hangar. It wasn't much, but it was enough.

It had to be.

Crouching behind the railing, I nestled the stock of the plasma rifle against my shoulder and peered through the electronic sights. The targeting system lit up with a red reticle, but so far there was nothing in the hangar to shoot at. Ally's body quivered even more than before, her rifle reticle probably bouncing around like she was on a bucking bronco.

"We can do this, Red," I whispered. "I've got your back." It was a line I had used plenty of times during online matches. I'd never seen Ally in a tense situation before, but her voice had always betrayed her nerves. Of course, once the bell rang, she would turn cold as ice and start clearing the board like the Terminator. I could only hope that part of her digital persona translated.

She nodded, her lips pressed into a thin line. At the other end of our position, Tyler stared intensely at the hangar doors as if he could summon the enemy through sheer willpower. Matt knelt with his palms resting lightly on his thighs like he was meditating, his weapon leaning against the railing. I could picture him scooping it up, aiming and firing in a single smooth motion for a quick and easy kill.

"Boss," Meg said. "I'm up on Seven. Bad news. I'm locked out of the PCS."

"What?" Matt replied. "How?"

"See, hacked us," Alyssa confirmed.

"If they hacked us, they could have shut down everything," I replied. "Including life support. Including the comms." I froze, realizing our mistake. "Damn it."

"What is it?"

"They know we're here. They're coming for us."

Instead of further panic, Ally nodded, refocusing her attention on her targeting. Her hands quieted considerably.

"Meg, can you reset the PCS and reboot?" Matt asked.

"I can manually pull the plug, but it'll be twenty minutes before everything's back online."

"That has to be better than letting these guys do any more damage to it."

Silence followed while Matt waited for Meg's reply. "Meg? Are you there?"

"There go the comms," Alyssa softly intoned.

A heavy clang echoed through the bay, signaling that the aliens had locked onto our hull. I sighted along my rifle, finger resting beside the trigger guard. I was mostly the opposite to Ally. More calm before the fight, too full of nervous energy during it. I struggled to control my breathing, not wanting to hyperventilate.

There were no sparks from laser cutters punching through the sealed bay doors. No creaks or groans of strain from the locked barrier. Instead, the smaller door in the larger hangar door opened without incident or complaint, ordered to do so through the impossibly compromised PCS.

I tensed, ready to unload hot plasma death on the first ugly mug to show itself.

A handful of seconds ticked past. Then alien forms spilled through the doorway in an organized deployment, weapons clutched in misshapen hands. They looked like cyborg ogres from some nightmare realm, heavily muscled, greenish-hued bodies rippling with unnatural veins of metal that immediately made me think of lab grown meat, where scaffolding provided the mold to shape the cells inside. Their flesh seemed to press against the lines of alloy, trying to break free.

Dressed in drab brown military-style fatigues, their menacing teeth jutted out from an overgrown lower jawline. One of their two deep-set eyes was black, the other a pale white with a soft yellow glow behind it, suggesting it was cybernetic. They carried rifles, too. Larger, bulkier punishers. I was immediately certain I didn't want to see used against us, not that I had much of a choice.

The overall effect was both fascinating and deeply disturbing.

As the dozen-strong alien squad fanned out across the deck, sweeping their exotic weapons back and forth, I sighted the closest ogre's chest and moved a shaking finger to the trigger. As horrifying as these creatures were, they were still living things. Most likely ILFs from a nearby planet, possibly investigating because they had registered our sudden arrival as a likely threat. I held my fire, waiting for Matt to signal the attack by launching it.

Looking over at him, I saw he had his rifle in hand, aimed toward one of the aliens in the back, whose better-fitting brown uniform, stature and positioning suggested he was the unit's leader. Even with all of his experience, he hesitated to squeeze the trigger.

The ogre sergeant spun toward our position, his mouth opening impossibly wide. "We know you're up there, soft-skins!" he bellowed in a deep, throaty growl, his English thickly accented by his physiology but still understandable. How the hell did he know English? "Throw down your weapons and come out with your hands over your head. You do not need to die today."

"Are you friend or foe?" Matt asked.

"That depends on you."

"No friend says anything like that," Alyssa whispered.

"What are your intentions?" Matt questioned instead.

"You will be honored by an audience with the Warden. He will determine your fate."

"And who is this Warden?"

"The one who determines your fate."

"Sounds like an NPC," I said.

Alyssa bobbed her head in agreement.

"And if we refuse to surrender?"

"I think that's pretty obvious, softskin. You'll be incinerated."

I kept one eye on the ogres, the other on Matt. He crouched with his rifle pointed at the lead ogre, considering the options. My idea to hide was a total bust. We were screwed the moment the aliens had gained access to the PCS. My first real decision, and I had blown it completely.

What would Matt decide?

He didn't move a muscle, tense seconds passing while everyone in the hangar bay, regardless of species, waited on his final word.

When he delivered it, he delivered it decisively.

His single plasma bolt streaked across the hangar, a perfect headshot that should have hit the ogre sergeant clean between the eyes, killing him instantly. Instead, it hit a personal force field that flared as it caught the projectile, dissipating its energy without leaving a trace the shot had ever been fired..

In the next instant, searing energy blasts peppered our hiding spot, scorching the deck around us. We all hit the floor, scrambling deeper behind the dubious shelter of the Hunter. Return fire lanced from Matt's position, catching one of the ogres squarely in the chest and proving that only the leader had a shield. With a wet thump, the creature toppled backward, fluids leaking from the sizzling wound.

All hell broke loose. Ogres shouted curses in their native tongue, and while I didn't understand the words, the tone was crystal clear.

Finding courage I didn't know I had, I snapped off a few wild shots in the ogre's general direction while their weapons belched more chaotic beams our way. The intensity of their barrage turned the Hunter's armored shoulders red-hot, forcing us to make sure we weren't touching any part of the mech.

"We're pinned down!" Tyler yelled above the cacophony. "This was a terrible plan!"

I risked a glance over the railing. The aliens had taken up superior positions behind cargo crates and Head Case's shuttle. One of the ogres launched an incendiary grenade that arced high and landed on the deck near Matt's position. He managed to kick the explosive device off the platform before it released its volatile payload, the metal sphere exploding against the far bulkhead and spewing white-hot flames across the open floor.

"Fall back!" Matt ordered, switching his rifle's setting and spraying a burst toward the largest concentration of enemies. "Get to the elevator!"

I needed no encouragement to abandon our position. Scrambling toward the elevator with Alyssa, I grabbed her and ducked instinctively as energy bolts flashed above our heads, their trajectory suggesting the aliens were on their way up both sets of stairs. Tyler reached the elevator, dropping low, his eyes wide with fear as Matt snapped off a few more shots before rolling away from the railing. Crouching, he headed our way.

"What the hell are you waiting for?" he yelled, slapping the call button that, in all the chaos and panic, none of us had thought to hit.

The three of us stood frozen there as the first of the ogres made it to the top of the steps, his chest barely in view when it absorbed a burst from Matt's rifle. The alien tumbled back down the steps, a second one reaching the top level on the other side. Matt bent low and spun, his whirling leg clipping the ogre in the side of the head as if he were John Wick.

"Why isn't the cab already here?" he cried in frustration as he rotated back our way. The control panel signaled the cab was on Deck Two. No doubt, the enemy had used the PCS to keep it out of reach.

The three of us cowered against the back of the hangar bay as Matt swept both sides of the upper level with his rifle, ready for the next ogre to show its ugly face. When they came, they rushed up the stairs, two on each side, fully synchronized, their advance so clean Matt immediately dropped his rifle and threw his hands up.

Following his lead, we did the same.

"An honorable effort, but you'll pay for every Prall you killed today," one of the ogres grumbled in garbled English as he approached cautiously but confidently with his three squadmates. Each one had one of us squarely in their gunsight, fingers on the triggers.

The soft tone of the elevator cab's arrival took me by surprise, but I didn't dare look back. My only hint of what was happening came from the expressions on the ogres' faces as the doors slid aside with a soft hiss. Their expressions reflected shock equal to mine, their rifles quickly changing direction to aim at whoever had come. Ixy, I assumed. That's how I would have reacted to her, even now that I knew she wasn't dangerous.

To us, anyway.

The ogres were still trying to adjust their aim when something hit them as if they had each stepped in front of a moving car. It threw them backward with such force they vanished over the front railing or tumbled back down the stairs to the lower deck.

"Yes!" Tyler shouted excitedly, looking back into the cab before I did.

Ben stepped out onto the upper deck, hands glowing with saving power. He just barely made it over the threshold before the effort of channeling chaos energy overwhelmed him. His eyes rolled back in his head and he pitched forward. Matt caught him before he smashed face-first into the platform's metal gridwork.

The ogres rushed up both sets of stairs en masse and stopped, their rifles trained on us point blank.

"No," Tyler lamented, the word uttered quietly beneath his breath.

There was nothing more we could do.

CHAPTER 22

The ogres moved us to the hangar's lower deck, one of them easily carrying a delirious Ben down the steps as if he were an infant. He laid him out on the deck in front of their leader, the hulking brute looming over us with a look of furious disdain as the others tended to the wounded and dead. Only five of the twelve who had boarded remained unharmed. Not a bad showing for the Stinking Badgers, even if I hadn't managed to hit anything but plating during my pathetic defense. Most of the damage had been done by Ben in the span of a few heartbeats.

With a dip of his rifle, the leader ordered us to kneel. Tyler surprised me when he jerked his chin up and started to take a step forward.

"No…" Matt reached for his arm, his firm grasp stopping him in his tracks. "…do what he wants."

As we complied, I found myself strangely grateful I hadn't inflicted any of the evident pain on the aliens. Not that I'd been holding back or intentionally missing my shots. And not that I was glad we'd lost. If I could trade our defeat for victory by confirming a kill, I would have gladly taken it and dealt with the resulting emotional fallout. But seeing as how I'd given my all and still failed spectacularly, I could at least take solace that I didn't need to suffer that kind of remorse.

"So, we tore holes in spacetime to reach a new part of the universe and wound up captured in less than an hour," Tyler said, still sore about the defeat. "That has to be a new record if anyone keeps records on that sort of thing."

"Not helping," I replied, trying to settle him.

"I mean, how could things get any worse?" he continued.

"Don't jinx us," Alyssa hissed. "Things can always get worse."

I craned my neck over my shoulder when I heard the elevator doors open. A moment later, Meg and Leo appeared at the top of the steps with one of the ogre soldiers at their backs, directing them down to us.

"Ben!" Meg cried, rushing forward and dropping to her knees at his side. She smoothed her palm over one side of his face and looked up at the sergeant. "What did you do to him?" she hissed at the sergeant, fearless despite their massive size and strength differential.

"We didn't touch him," the sergeant replied. "He hasn't learned the rules yet, that's all. He'll be fine."

"What do you mean he hasn't learned the rules?" Matt asked. "What do you know about chaos energy?"

"I know your friend will only get himself killed if he keeps trying to use it like that. I don't need to know more than that. The Warden can explain, if he so chooses."

"Is he coming any time soon? My knees are getting sore."

The sergeant huffed, the hot shot of his breath blasting me with the smell of rotten meat. I didn't want to know what these guys ate. "You killed three Prall and injured four others. You're lucky it's only your knees that are sore. My boys would love to rip you apart with their bare hands.

So would I. But the Warden would never allow it." He exhaled another burst of fetid air. "I give you credit. You put up more of a fight than I expected. You have my respect for that."

"So glad we didn't let you down."

"How is it you speak English?" Tyler asked as if that was an important answer to have right now.

"Do I?" the sergeant replied cryptically, following up with a laugh. "The Warden says your language is primitive. Deciphering it required almost no effort. Defeating the encryption of your vessel's command and control unit was easier than that."

"Are you calling us stupid?" Alyssa asked.

"No. The Warden says that technology is a terrible proxy for intellect. Every species evolves in similar ways. Some are simply further along in that process than others. Then again, perhaps you should be more evolved than you are by now."

I narrowed my gaze, peering into the Prall leader's glowing cybernetic eye. His answer seemed off to me, as though the words had come out of his mouth, but he hadn't spoken them. Could it be? "Do you plan to speak to us through your proxies indefinitely, or are you going to make a personal appearance?" I asked, staring into the eye.

The sergeant froze, as did the two Pralls flanking him.

"What did you do?" Tyler asked, staring at the suddenly inactive aliens.

"I don't know," I replied.

"Should we run for it?" Alyssa asked.

"And go where?" Leo said. "They have full control of the ship. They could self-destruct Head Case if they wanted."

"They threatened to cut off the oxygen flow to the flight deck if we didn't come down," Meg added.

"What about Ix—"

My glare cut Tee off mid-sentence. He grimaced when he realized he'd almost given away the presence of Ixy or Shaq on the ship. Apparently, the aliens didn't know the two other ILFs were on board. Probably because they hadn't used the comms or stormed the hangar.

But they still might.

"What do you think they want?" Alyssa asked. "If they only came for the ship, they could have killed us already."

"Maybe they'll haul us off to mine asteroids," Tyler suggested, "or force us to become members of their slave army. That's what happens in the books I read."

"You guys realize that the Warden is listening to everything we say, right?" I said, pointing at the frozen Prall sergeant's eye. "The Warden's also remote controlling these soldiers at least some of the time. None of them speak our language. But the Warden does."

"How do you know?" Tyler asked.

"It's pretty obvious."

"No, it isn't. But then maybe that's why they want us alive. So they can do the same thing to us."

"I don't think so," I said. "All of the soldiers are of the same species. And they look like they might be clones, or at least grown rather than born."

The sound of clapping from deep within the alien starship's docking corridor interrupted any potential response from the others. The shadows prevented us from finding the source right away, but it wasn't as though the Warden didn't want to make himself known. It seemed like he had just been waiting for an opening to make his grand entrance.

The clapping erased any doubts I might have had that the Warden was at least humanoid, perhaps a Prall himself, if not full-on human. Large flat appendages that could be smacked together to make noise were prerequisites to the action of clapping. With that in mind, I expected a uniformed military commander, or maybe someone like Emperor Palpatine or Darth Vader. A spine-chilling bad guy dressed all in black, serious and stiff, with an icy glare and an aura of power.

Instead, I got a scrawny little fop dressed as if he had just escaped a minstrel show at a Renaissance Fair.

He continued clapping as he approached, nearly blinding in a blue velvet coat covered in sparkling gems over a simple white tunic. Curly brown hair bled out from beneath a floppy blue cap, his laced, knee-high leather boots making absolutely no sound as he moved toward us, his feet seeming to barely touch the deck.

"What…the…hell?" Alyssa intoned beside me. "Please tell me we were murdered by a serial killer at Jackson Farm. At least then, this might make some kind of sense."

The Warden stepped past his frozen Prall sergeant, positioning himself directly in front of me, still clapping. He wore a huge grin on his small, pale face, his warm brown eyes looking up at me with amusement. He remained like that longer than was even close to comfortable before finally coming to an abrupt stop.

Silence settled over the hangar. The Warden continued staring at me until his grin completely faded.

"Every group has a smart one," he said, finally breaking the silence. "You're it, aren't you?"

"I doubt that," I replied. "Ben is—"

"Too slow to realize that his admittedly impressive abilities are limited here," the Warden interrupted. "I've got my eye on you, Noah. You're going to be trouble. I can tell already."

"I…I don't understand."

"Kind of dumb for the smart one, aren't you? Well, no matter. I suppose an explanation is in order." He stepped back so he could address everyone, his grin reappearing as his eyes flashed over us in turn. "Welcome, all of you, to—"

He didn't get to finish his sentence. Like a bullet, Shaq launched from somewhere beneath the folds of Ben's clothing, his leap bringing him to the Warden's shoulder before the man could react. Sinking his teeth into the tiny man's flesh, he quickly bit the Warden before leaping off and landing on my nearby shoulder.

The Warden went as stiff as the Pralls, mouth stuck open mid-syllable, eyes quickly glassing over.

He collapsed on the deck. Dead.

CHAPTER 23

"Well, that was easy," Tyler said, already numb to the violence as he got to his feet. The rest of us proceeded to do the same. Shaq remained perched on my shoulder, still huffing with anger, his attention fixed on Ben.

I eyed the frozen Pralls, curious and frightened by their potential to reanimate. They remained locked in place as we all stood nearly as still as the aliens, unsure of what to do next.

All our attention turned to Ben when he released a low moan, his eyes fluttering open. He blinked a few times, head swiveling to take us in from his prone position on the deck. His eyes widened as they settled on the Pralls, and then his brow crinkled in confusion. He couldn't see the Warden from where he lay. "What happened?" he asked.

"Shaq killed the Warden," I replied, pointing to the body on the deck. I had yet to process how quickly and easily Shaq had downed the wannabe bard. The bite had barely broken the skin, and the Warden's death had been almost instant. "Remind me never to get on your bad side," I added softly to him. He buzzed lightly against my cheek, his mood improving now that Ben had awoken.

"Who's the Warden?" Ben asked.

"Who cares?" Matt answered. "He's dead. Let's find a way to jettison his ship before the other big green uglies come back."

"Did we make it to Mars?" Ben questioned. "I'm totally lost right now."

"We'll get you up to speed once we're out of here. But no, we didn't make it to Mars. Or Venus. Or the Spiral. I don't know where you delivered us. We can figure that out later, too. T-bone, All-red, Katzuo, Shaq, we need to cover Meg and Leo while they figure out how to unhook the bubble ship from our hangar bay."

"Yes, sir," I replied, looking back in search of my discarded rifle. "What about these…things?" I poked one of the static Pralls in the chest. It didn't react.

"That one has a personal forcefield," Matt said. "Ben, maybe you can figure it out. It might come in handy."

Ben stared at the Prall sergeant, trying to make sense of everything all at once. Impossible, when I still had no idea what the hell was going on. "I get the feeling we aren't in Kansas anymore."

"Or Iowa," Tyler added.

Matt grabbed the sergeant's rifle out of his hand while Alyssa retreated to the rear of the hangar, rushing up the steps to retrieve our rifles. Shaq hopped from my shoulder to Matt's, crouched and ready for more action.

"My, my, you are a spirited bunch, aren't you?"

The question echoed in Levi's voice from all around us, the loudspeakers in the hangar bay cranked up to what sounded like eleven. We all froze in place as if we were playing *Red Light, Green Light*, while Levi's overtly malicious laughter reverberated across the bulkheads and vibrated the deck.

"Look," I heard Tyler say, so I turned back toward the link between Head Case and the alien ship.

A somewhat familiar silhouette became visible there. Levi's laughter diminished while the Warden's image materialized.

"I really want to go home," Tyler muttered nearby. "I hate this ride, and want to get off."

The Warden stepped into full view. He looked mostly the same, save for a wardrobe change. Instead of bright colors and sparkle, this new iteration had opted for a plain black suit that immediately called North Korea to mind.

Despite his laughter, he didn't look amused this time around. "You," he said, pointing a finger toward Shaq. "I didn't appreciate that."

"Maybe you'll appreciate this," Matt said. He squeezed the trigger of the Prall rifle. It didn't fire.

That drew a measure of mirth from the Warden. He mimicked Matt, pantomiming his movements with the rifle and mocking him in a nearly perfect imitation of his voice. "Maybe you'll appreciate this. Blurp! Hahahaha!"

A plasma bolt suddenly arced down from the upper deck, a well-aimed shot that hit the Warden squarely in the chest. His eyes widened and he clutched at the smoldering hole the bolt had left, looking up to where Alyssa stood with rifle in hand. His mouth twisted in anger just before he collapsed.

Dead.

Again.

"Nice shot, Red!" I shouted. She removed one hand from the rifle to wave, but otherwise kept it trained on the hangar bay entrance.

"Anyone want to take bets that another Warden's coming?" Tyler asked.

"I just want to get the hell away from him," Matt replied. "I hate clones." He tossed the useless Prall weapon aside.

"If there are multiple Wardens, why haven't the Pralls come back to life?" I asked.

"Do you know how embarrassing that would be for me?" the ship's computer said, the Warden's voice once more booming from the loudspeakers. "For shame. You'd think by now, you'd accept that violence won't solve anything,"

"He's baaaaccckkkk," Tyler said, eyes on the hangar bay door.

Allie tried to shoot the new Warden as he came into view. The bolt hit a forcefield and dissipated.

"Of course, I learn from my mistakes," the Warden said, clothed now in a white Yoda-like robe and looking more than a little perturbed. "Unlike the lot of you." He sighed. "I have total control over your ship. Does that not register with any of you? I could disengage while the hangar doors are still open and suck you all out into space. I could turn off life support, and watch you all suffocate. I could let my Prall kill you."

Before I could react, the sergeant's hand shot out and wrapped around my throat. I was sure he could crush my larynx and spine if he wanted, but he didn't exert any pressure. The Warden just wanted to show us that he could end us in the blink of an eye. He let go just as quickly as he'd grabbed me.

"I could trigger your ship's self-destruct, as that one noted earlier." The Warden pointed at Leo. "So please, stop killing me. It's extremely annoying."

"Who *are* you?" Ben asked. "And what do you want from us?"

"I'm the Warden," he replied. "What I want from you, what I want from everyone in the universe, is entertainment." He laughed and clapped his hands.

"Wait, what?" Tyler said, as confused as the rest of us.

"Entertainment," the Warden repeated. "I just learned

your language five minutes ago and I understand the word. I expect you to amuse me. Despite the…" He motioned with his hands as if he could pull the right word to him. "… challenge you've presented so far, you're actually off to a pretty good start."

"This can't be real," I whispered to no-one in particular, my mind struggling with its current predicament. Maybe Ally was right. Maybe we *were* better off murdered by a serial killer.

"We don't even know where we are," Ben said, keeping his composure.

"But you know how you got here," the Warden replied. "You reek of chaos energy. This is a perfect example of why you shouldn't play with things you don't really under-stand." He paused, a thoughtful expression crossing his face. "Hmm, but the signature doesn't match your profile. Interesting. Very interesting."

"What does that mean?" Ben asked.

The Warden shrugged. "It doesn't matter. What does matter is that you're here. I haven't had visitors for a long time, so you can imagine I'm pretty excited." He said it with a completely flat affect and no fluctuation. "Look, despite your intense desire to murder me for a third time, I'm actually not your enemy."

"You hacked our ship's computer and attacked us," Matt said. "How does that not make you an enemy?"

"I know what it looks like, and I know it's pretty incrim-inating. But, I never intended any harm, which should be plainly obvious by the fact that you're still alive. In fact, if you rewind your minds and replay the sequence of events from the moment you first saw me coming, you'll realize the only ones who have caused any actual harm to anyone is…*you*." He emphasized the last word accusingly.

And it worked. Thinking back, I realized he was right. The Prall had threatened us, even shot at us and thrown a grenade our way. But they hadn't landed a single hit. Hadn't even singed a hair on my head. My eyes shifted to the Prall sergeant's rifle at Matt's feet. Could it be?

"Ah, there it is again," the Warden said. When I looked back at him, his eyes were on me. "I have to keep a closer eye on you than the others."

Part of me wanted to beam as though he had offered a compliment. I'd figured out the Pralls were essentially firing blanks, or at least weapons that only did harm against objects that weren't us. Then again, I was pretty sure I didn't want more attention from the strange alien.

"No offense, Mister Warden," Ben said politely. "But we don't plan to stick around. I need to get these passengers home." He motioned toward me and Tyler.

"And how do you propose to do that?" the Warden questioned. "I should hope you've realized chaos energy isn't so easily accessed here as it is in other parts of the universe. Your technomancy is gimped here, Ben. You don't have the juice to open another rift, but you're welcome to try. That should prove amusing for a short while."

Ben's expression told me he believed the Warden's words. He had been able to get us here, but he couldn't get us back.

"Does that mean we're stuck out here?" Tyler asked. "You guys said your hyperdrive can do a hundred light years an hour or something, right? How far from Earth are we?"

The crew of Head Case remained silent long enough that the Warden jumped in. "Bottom line, you won't make it. All of you are stuck here. But we don't need to frame the situation in such negative terms. Consider this an opportunity. The adventure of a lifetime."

"Where have I heard that before?" Tyler deadpanned.

I ignored him, looking back over my shoulder for Alyssa. She'd vanished from her spot near the railing. I could only imagine how she'd just reacted to the news. For my part, I was almost pleased. I didn't want to go back to Earth. I had nothing to go back to. Shifting to Tyler, I could see he was pissed, his body tense, jaw clenched.

Maybe I was wrong. Maybe there was a reason to go home.

"I don't accept that," Ben said.

"I don't expect you to accept it," the Warden replied. "What fun would that be?" He snapped his fingers, and a group of Prall emerged through the hangar bay door. In one hand, each of them carried a velvet pillow with a small, metallic pill resting in the center, a glass of what appeared to be water in the other. They stopped in a line behind him. "Here's how it works. Each of you will swallow a pill. The pill will allow me to keep tabs on you without needing to be overly intrusive. I'm even going to return full control of your ship's computer to you. Once we're done here, you'll be free to roam about the galaxy to your heart's content.. However, should you become boring, I'll have no choice but to assign tasks for you to complete. Whether you pass or fail the tasks are of no concern to me. What is important is that you try to do them to the best of your abilities. If you refuse, one of you will die. If you refuse again, two of you will die, and so on and so forth until there's no one left. The pill contains a toxin similar to the venom your little pet releases. I can trigger it remotely at any time, but I have no reason to do so as long as you comply with the few directives I issue. Do you understand?"

Our heads bobbed in acknowledgment. Tyler put up his hand.

"Yes, Tyler?" the Warden said.

"Can you give us an example of a task?"

"No. Any other questions?"

Tyler put up his hand again.

"Yes, Tyler?"

"What's in it for us? Other than not dying, I mean? Like, what do we get if we're entertaining?"

"You'll be rewarded with boons based on your performance."

"You mean like a loot box?"

"Something like that. Are there any other questions?"

Tyler put his hand up a third time.

The Warden sighed heavily. "Yes, Tyler, what is it now?" the Warden said, visibly losing his patience.

"If we do your assigned tasks and keep you entertained, will you help us get home?"

The Warden hesitated before answering. "I will consider it. What else?"

"What if we refuse to take the pill?" Matt asked.

"You can take the pill, or you can die. There is no third choice."

Tyler's hand went up again.

"What now?" the Warden snapped.

"Space is really big, and we don't know our way around this part of the universe. How will we know where to go?"

"A star map of the surrounding galaxy has been added to your ship's database. It will get you off on the right foot."

Tyler nodded. "I think that's all I have right now. Anyone else?"

When no one spoke up, the Pralls approached, one for each of us, Shaq excluded. One of them even went to the back of the hangar and up the steps to give a pill to Ally.

"Bottoms up," the Warden said.

Tyler was the first to pick up his pill, stick it in his mouth, and down it with a sip of water. We all stared at him, and I, at least, waited for him to change into an ogre. He didn't.

I picked up the offered pill and stuck it on the tip of my tongue. It tasted like a dirty penny, so I quickly grabbed the water and forced it down. Within a couple of minutes, the others had all done the same.

"That's all for now," the Warden said, silently ordering his Prall back onto his ship. "Welcome to Warexia. I do hope you enjoy your stay. I know I will." He smiled like a fox in a henhouse before spinning on his heel and following the Prall back to his ship.

We all remained silent while the small door closed behind him. Head Case vibrated slightly as the Warden's craft disengaged.

"Captain," Levi said over the loudspeakers. "The contact is moving away from us. The threat is averted."

The absurd severing of our silence barely served to jog us from our stunned stupor. It was only after Tyler spoke that we finally broke the Warden's spell.

"Well, wasn't that a bitter pill to swallow."

CHAPTER 24

"What now?" Alyssa asked, approaching us from the back of the hangar, clutching her plasma rifle like a security blanket. We'd reacted to Tyler's bitter pill comment with nervous laughter that had all but died out by the time she reached us.

"Okay, what the hell just happened? Shaq jabbed his claws into me to wake me up because the RFD was freaking out." He retrieved it from his pocket. It looked a lot like a Steam Deck, with thumb controllers on both sides and a bright screen in the center. As it activated, it projected the sensor grid into the air, showing we were all clear. The Warden's ship had vanished. "Everything seems normal out there now."

"You had the RFD this whole time?" Matt said. "I was looking everywhere for it."

"I always carry it when we go Earthbound. You should know that."

"I never needed it before, during or after a pickup. Until now."

"Well, now you know."

"We already know what happened to us," I said, a bit more boldly than normal for me. It had to be what remained of the adrenaline. "What happened to you?"

Ben looked at Matt. "Do they know about Sigiltech?"

"Yeah, I already went over the basics. But I deferred a lot to wait for your participation."

Ben nodded wearily. I could tell he was still exhausted, but he knew he had a responsibility to his passengers. "Did you sign the rental agreement?"

Alyssa huffed. "You're still worried about that damn contract? I didn't sign it."

"Yeah, I guess the agreement doesn't matter at this point," he agreed. "Sorry, I'm not fully myself right yet."

"I don't think any of us are," Tyler said.

"Yeah." Ben paused, glancing at Ally, Tyler, and me. "I owe you a major apology, and even that isn't nearly good enough for the situation we're in, but it's the best I can do. We've done the Earth to Mars run over a dozen times without a hitch. There was no reason to expect this one would be any different. I don't know who attacked us in Earth's orbit or why. I don't know where it came from. Once we're more settled, we can start digging into the sensor data we collected on it to determine the origin, but that's not a high priority right now. That ship's a long way away. I also don't know what happened with the rift. I've done the transit from Earth to the Spiral dozens of times, again without a problem before today."

"The Warden said the exit rift had a different signature," I told him.

"In simple terms, it means I didn't open the same rift that brought us out of the void. I thought I had because of the volume of chaos energy I absorbed. I would still think I had, except we should be near Neptune, not wherever here is. Someone either opened the barn door for us, or at the very least interfered with my chaos energy and redirected it to bring us out here." He paused again, likely considering the possibilities in his own mind before voicing his thoughts. "The thing about creating holes in spacetime is that you need to know your exit point beforehand. I can't just say I want to visit the Trappist system and transit there unless I have a visual of what the transit destination looks like. Either from personal experience or an image or something. And I can't just think about deep space, because that could take us anywhere."

"So whoever interfered already knows about this place," I surmised.

"More than that. They know about this specific location. Which, looking at the sensor grid and the lack of uniquely identifying markers like planets, stars, nebulas, and the like… I don't know how they managed it. Unless…" He stopped to consider again.

"Unless what?" Tyler pressed. "The suspense is killing me."

"Unless we didn't come out where they wanted us to," Ben finished. "The Warden said the signature change was interesting. He didn't act like he expected or understood it. I think the interference from the second party muddied the water rather than sending us down a different fork in the river."

"If that's the case, we're lucky we came out anywhere near anything," Meg said.

"Considering what just happened, I'm not sure that means we're lucky," Leo countered.

"If our arrival was an accident, how did the Warden find us so fast?" I asked. "We've been here less than an hour."

"He understands chaos energy," Ben said. "He might be a technomancer himself. He could have sensed the shift in the flows."

"Or maybe it wasn't an accident," Alyssa suggested. "Maybe he took advantage of the muddy water to catch us by surprise."

"We can't rule it out," Ben agreed.

"Who would interfere with your rifts?" I asked. "I know you have enemies in the Spiral galaxy. Could they be responsible?"

"We can't rule that out, either."

"The question that's stuck in my mind is if that ship near Earth was there to destroy us, or if it was there to force us to make a quick getaway," Matt said.

"They targeted the area of the ship where a solid hit would knock out the hyperdrive," Meg said. "But it's near the direct line from the thrusters to the reactor, so it's not a guarantee it was the target."

"Who's to say blowing us up wasn't Plan A, and casting us off across the universe wasn't Plan B," Tyler said. "The point is, we're here now, and I think I speak for Ally and myself at least when I say we want to go home."

"And that's my highest priority right now," Ben said.

"You heard the Warden," I said. "You can't create a rift here. And we're too far away to go the FTL route. We're stuck."

"I don't accept that," Ben said. "We got here. There has to be a way to get back. Maybe I just need to rest up and get back to full strength."

"It's not just you," Matt said. "We noticed the problem with the sigils on the elevator, too. It's drawing way too much power to scale between decks. Something's up with the chaos energy here, just like the Warden said."

Ben shook his head. "That makes no sense. Chaos energy comes from another dimension. Once you have the tap open, it should always flow the same." He closed his eyes and almost immediately began trembling. "It's like trying to drink milk tea with a boba wedged in the straw." He opened his eyes. "Something is blocking the transfer."

"How is that possible?" Matt asked.

"It shouldn't be."

"I bet the Warden knows," Alyssa said. "He talked about this galaxy like it's his own personal playground."

"Maybe it is his playground," Matt suggested.

"And we're his new toys," Tyler agreed. "This sucks."

"I promise, we'll figure all this out," Ben said. "We seem to be okay for the moment. Let's just try to take a few breaths, get our heads straight, and regroup."

"That's all we can do right now," Matt added. "What do you three think?" He looked at us.

"I'll do whatever I can to help," I replied. "I don't blame you for any of this." I turned to Ally and Tyler. "I'm sorry. This is my fault. If I hadn't dragged you out to the farm—"

"Don't, man," Tyler cut him off. "You couldn't have predicted this. I hate the situation, but like you said, there's not really anyone to blame. Sometimes, bad stuff just happens."

"Yeah," Alyssa agreed. "I'm worried about Kaiju and my rent. But continued whining won't get us anywhere. I need a quiet corner to go cry in, but once I calm down, I want to help."

"I appreciate that," Ben said. "And I appreciate your understanding. This is as bad for us as it is for you. We have people who will worry about us, too. And Matt has a race in three days."

"With a killer entry fee that I've already paid," Matt added. "I'm out of the money whether we show up or not."

I did my best to keep my emotions steady. Everyone had someone to care about them, who would miss them, except me. I was sure my auntie and granny would once they heard about Mom, but it wasn't quite the same. Beyond the occasional FaceTime and a couple of trips overseas when my age was still in single digits, they didn't know me at all. Death had stolen my parents. It hadn't sapped me of my compassion or empathy. I wanted Tee and Ally to get home. I wanted Ben and Matt to get back to their regularly scheduled lives.

As for myself, at this point I figured I would just take whatever life threw at me and run with it.

"Meg, Leo, I want you to get back to the repairs," Matt said. "Once you're done with the physical fixes, let's focus on the PCS. We need to harden it as best we can, and also make sure there's no residual zero-day hiding in the logic."

Ben scoffed. "Did you understand a word of what you just said?"

"Only the first part. Not quite as geeky as you, but it sounded good, didn't it?"

"Pretty good," Ben agreed. "Matt's right. If you don't mind."

"Of course not, Captain. We're on it," Meg said, turning toward the stairs.

"Let us know if any more bubble ships full of clones show up," Leo added, following Meg as she hurried up the stairs to the elevator.

"We'll need to give the elevator batteries time to recharge once they go back up to Three," Matt said. "Ally, there's a dark corner back there for you, if you need some privacy." He pointed to the rear corner, beneath the upper deck where the lights didn't penetrate.

Alyssa half-smiled. "I was half-joking about the corner. But I do sense a breakdown coming at some point before the day is over. It won't be pretty."

"I second that emotion," Tyler said. "I'm still in a bit of shock."

"Me, too," I agreed.

"Since it seems you'll be stuck with us for a while, we'll show you to quarters as soon as we can," Ben said.

"In the meantime," Matt said, motioning to the small ship in the hangar. "Have you ever seen a hop racer before?"

CHAPTER 25

By the time Matt finished giving us a quick tour of his hop racer and explaining how it worked, I was more than ready to give the sport a try.

The goal of hop racing, like any other race, was to reach the finish line ahead of your opponents. It required a combination of quick reflexes and precision timing. In this case, that was accomplished by making multiple quick hyperspace jumps where a millisecond of latitude on either side could make the difference between victory and defeat. A poorly executed maneuver, on the other hand, could send a racer careening irreparably off course.

Advanced racing, a newly introduced form of hop racing, added additional tasks like target shooting, vectoring maneuvers, and obstacle courses between hops. By the way he spoke about it, I could tell how much Matt had been looking forward to the race. Unfortunately, he would miss the inaugural event unless he made it back to the Spiral in three days. It was too bad his odds of making it back in time looked slimmer by the minute.

He didn't let that disappointment affect the way he handled Alyssa, Tyler, and me. Both he and Ben were kind and easy to be around, their attitudes generally positive despite everything that had happened. As the adrenaline wore off and the truth of my personal situation returned with full force, I aimed to mimic their demeanor instead of letting my emotions turn me bitter and angry.

Once the elevator batteries recharged after Meg and Leo used it, Ben and Matt returned us to Deck Three, bringing us up the stairs to the guest rooms adjacent to the lounge. There were five rooms in total, including one at the end of the corridor with a fancier outer door against a wider bulkhead. As captain's quarters, I thought that one would be Ben's room, but Matt told us he had claimed it, and Ben would have to pry it out of his cold, dead hands.

"Ally, I'd like you to bunk with Meg, if that's okay," Ben said, pointing to Meg's door to the right of the captain's quarters. "I know it isn't ideal, but—"

"It's no problem," Alyssa broke in. "I have a roommate back in Des Moines, and our apartment only has one bedroom. I'm used to sharing space."

"I appreciate your flexibility." He tapped his comm badge. "Hey, Meg."

"Hey, Captain," she cheerfully replied as if the whole episode with the Warden had already been forgotten. "I know you don't expect me to have finished with the hyperdrive yet, so what's up?"

"I'm just planning out berthing for the duration of our stay in Warexia. I want to pair you with Alyssa. Is that okay?"

"Sure," she replied without missing a beat. "It sounds like fun."

"Do you mind if I have Levi open your door for her?"

"Go right ahead. I'll be busy here for a while, but Alyssa if you can hear me, my quarters are your quarters."

"Thank you," Ally replied.

"I'm picturing you wearing Meg's clothes," Tyler said

with a grin, the elfish engineer a full head shorter than her. "Sexy." She gave him an annoyed look. "Or maybe not."

"Levi, open the door to Meg's room," Ben said.

The lock clicked and the hinged door swung open, revealing a very tidy and bright room. White and pink wallpaper surrounded a pink duvet on a pink acrylic queen-sized bed, a pink steamer chest at the end of it. Pink curtains hung over a large display along the side of the compartment, currently displaying the limited view outside the ship. A pair of pink doors were on either side of the bed. The open one led into a personal pink bathroom, or *head* considering we were on board a starship. The other likely went to a closet.

"It's very, uh…"

"Pink," Tyler finished for her.

"It's very pink," Ally agreed.

"I hope you like Barbie," I said.

"Have I ever come across to you as someone who might like Barbie?"

"No, but we don't know the real you, remember?" Tyler said.

Alyssa pressed her lips together, caught red-handed. "Touche, damn it. No, I don't like Barbie. The pink will take some getting used to."

"I'm sure Meg would be willing to change it if you ask," Ben said. "She's understanding like that."

"From the look in your eye and the tone of your voice, you're speaking from experience," Tyler said.

"We were together for a few months," Ben admitted, "before we decided we're better as friends."

"Only one bed though," Alyssa said, moving to the threshold. "That's different."

"Meg doesn't take up much space."

"You've never shared your bed with anyone before?" Tyler asked.

Alyssa whipped her head toward him, flashing her dagger eyes, cheeks darkening. "What are you trying to suggest?"

Tyler's face flushed as he took a flinching step back. "Uh. I…uh…nothing." He waved his hands in front of him as if he were warding off the devil himself. "I swear, it was an innocent question."

"Uh-huh," she replied. "That's something zero people on this ship need to know the answer to."

"Matt, why don't you teach Ally how to use the assembler while I show Tyler and Noah to their room?" Ben suggested.

"Sure," he answered, winking at Ally.

"Yeah, I'm not…really hungry," she said hesitantly, her face reddening further.

"Besides, we already met Asshole," I said, figuring I'd rescue her. "Matt already showed us how to order food."

"You met Chef Asshole," Ben said. "That's like a mini-assembler. You haven't seen anything yet."

"Follow me," Matt said. "We'll get you set up with some fresh clothes and whatever else you think you'll need."

"Okay," she hesitantly replied, giving Tyler one more dirty look before trailing Matt back down the passageway toward the lounge.

"I think saying the wrong thing might be my superpower," Tyler said once they had gone.

"Been there, done that," Ben answered. "This way."

He did a one-eighty in the corridor to open the unlocked door across from Meg's room.

"Wait," I said before he could open it. "Please don't tell me there's only one bed in there."

"Okay, I won't tell you." Ben opened the door.

Looking at its drab gray walls, I was instantly reminded of the hospital. And then I saw the bed. Not a queen like Meg's bed. It was a single-sized bunk. Considering I kept getting whiffs of Tee's stinky gym clothes, not to mention he probably snored and farted a lot, I definitely didn't want to share anything beyond the room, let alone a single bed, with him."

"I know it needs some work, but—"

"There's no way in hell we can both sleep in that." My now steady finger pointed directly at the tiny bare mattress.

"I know it's not much to look at right now. But you'll have a chance to make it your own with the assembler, and—"

"It's not even big enough for me to sleep in, let alone both of us," Tyler complained.

"Unfortunately, the assembler isn't big enough to make an entire twin mattress, let alone a bigger one, so for now, you'll have to make do with a mat on the floor."

"Of course, I get the floor," Tyler griped as he moved through the doorway.

"It's better than sharing," I pointed out. Ben remained behind us, in the doorway.

"We can get a second bed in here later," he said, closing his eyes. He swayed a little, reaching for the doorframe to keep his balance.

"Ben?" I moved closer to him, just in case one of us had to catch him before he hit the deck. "Are you okay?"

"Yeah," he replied. "I'm just exhausted."

"Why don't you sit?" I said, motioning to the bed. "I'd love to hear more about Sigiltech."

"Maybe another time. You can make a mat, some blankets and pillows, and just about anything else you want to decorate your room, even some new threads to wear, with the assembler. Just head down to the first level. I'm going to collapse in my bed for a few hours. Again, I'm very sorry for everything that's happened."

"Don't worry about it," Tyler said before I could. "We'll

figure it out. As my granny always said, at least we have our health."

Ben's weak smile suggested only partial agreement with the statement. "Yeah, maybe. I'll see you two in the morning. Try to get some rest."

"Goodnight," I said as Ben left our room, closing the door behind him.

"He's thinking it, too," Tyler said.

"Thinking what?"

"The bitter pill. We have no idea what it is, or what it will do to us. Just that the Warden said he could kill us with it whenever he wants. But how do we know he won't trigger it as soon as he gets bored?"

"We don't."

"I think Ben's worried about it, and so am I."

"I'm not. The Warden didn't keep us alive just to poison us on a whim. Maybe Ben's worried about something else? He didn't exactly have the best day today."

"Neither did we. Especially you."

"No, and I'm going to lose it again as soon as things get calm. So let's decide what color sheets we want before that happens."

Tyler laughed. "I definitely didn't wake up this morning thinking I'd be having a sleepover with you."

"That makes two of us. I should be home right now. In my own bed. With my parents asleep in the room next to mine." I sighed, lowering my head into my hands and fighting back a wave of emotion.

"I've always wanted black sheets," Tyler said, pulling me away from my darker thoughts.

I lifted my gaze. "Black? That's horrible. How about tan or gray?"

"Congratulations, you've cornered the market on boring. Come on, Noah-san. Live a little."

"Fine, we'll do black. I don't really care that much." I

moved to the edge of the mattress and sat, sudden exhaustion threatening to overwhelm me, too.

"That's the spirit," Tyler joked, sitting next to me. "So, on day one we rented a starship, were ambushed by a UFO, crossed through a hole in spacetime, were attacked by cyborg ogres, and wound up toys for an alien madman. Does that sound about right?"

"Pretty much. "

"Dorothy's definitely got nothing on us," he chuckled, elbowing me playfully in the ribs. "I wonder what tomorrow will bring?"

"Are you sure you want to find out?"

He smiled. "Hell, yeah. It still beats sitting around, feeling miserable, right? I'm going to find Ally and Matt and get a look at the main assembler. You coming?"

"It beats sitting around, feeling sorry for myself," I replied.

"See, now you're speaking my language."

CHAPTER 26

By the time we found Matt and Alyssa inside the assembler compartment—directly across from the galley—Ally was already holding a folded yellow flight suit with red stripes down the legs. She had several scrunchies for her hair circling her left wrist and calf-high white boots with chunky soles. Magboots, Matt called them, explaining that they were a necessary piece of apparel on a starship for those moments when gravity went by the wayside. Slide-stepping to move across the deck beat the hell out of being tossed head-first into the overhead. She also had a small stack of neatly folded undergarments near the door.

"So, just to clarify," Tyler said. "You throw whatever kind of extra stuff you have lying around into a receptacle, and Asshole breaks it down to its component molecules to make new, useful stuff?"

"Exactamundo," Matt replied.

"So why is it called an assembler, instead of a re-assembler?"

"Which one rolls off the tongue more easily?"

"Good point. So what if you only threw, say, gummy

bears into it, and then asked it for a shirt? Would you get a gummy shirt?"

Matt stared at him like he had two heads. "You know, we never thought to try that. Asshole complains when he needs materials to make an item. He'll say something along the lines of, 'Yo, jabroni, I need some hydrogen and iron if you want me to fill that order.' So my guess is, no."

"That's too bad. It might be fun to wear a gummy shirt. Especially if you get hungry and Asshole's out of raw materials to make more food."

"Very funny."

"I try."

"Try harder." I watched as the wall in front of us moved aside, revealing a larger compartment. A second folded flight suit, this one orange with white stripes, rested on the floor.

"This is so awesome," Alyssa said, entering the compartment to retrieve it. "If you get tired of an outfit, you literally throw it away and make a new one."

"You look like you're all set for hop racing," Tyler said.

"I just wanted something I couldn't find at Macy's," she replied. "I think I saw Taylor Swift wear something like this."

"If anyone can recycle one thing to make another thing, does that mean there aren't any stores in the Spiral?" I asked. "Or do they only sell recipes and raw materials? Or what?"

"There are still stores," Matt replied. "Most people in the Spiral can't afford a medium assembler like this one, never mind an industrial version. For the most part, businesses use them to make the products they sell to customers. They have specialized recipes that they guard with Coke-level secrecy, meaning only they can provide the specific, authentic item. Mini-assemblers like the one in the galley are more common, but for personal use, they might only hold enough material for a few meals at a time, so people need to be more aware of what they're tossing in."

"It's incredible."

"Two outfits and some intimates are enough for me right now," Ally said. "I'm sure you're both eager to try the assembler out. Especially you, Noah. You could use some clothes that fit."

I looked at Tyler's hand-me-downs. I needed new threads. "You don't want to stick around to see what I make?" I asked.

"Tempting, but it's way past my bedtime. I'm hoping once I lie down, I'll wake up and realize this was all a bad dream."

"Do you hate us that much?" Tyler asked.

"Only you," she replied with a smile. "Seriously, do you actually *want* to be stuck in this scenario?"

"Point taken. Right now, the bad outweighs the good. But who knows, maybe that'll turn around."

"Or maybe I'll just wake up in my own bed. Wish me luck."

"Good luck," I said, waving to her as she vanished out the door.

"And there she goes," Tyler said. "So, Matt. What do you think of our All-red?"

"What do you mean?" Matt asked.

"She has a bit of a crush on you," I said, "if that wasn't obvious."

Matt nodded. "I don't want to sound arrogant, but I'm kind of used to that. She seems nice." He shrugged, looking away from us. "Asshole, scan a new user, filed under Katzuo." He winked at me, though I didn't know if it was because of his use of my handle or the way he changed the subject, or both.

"What?" Asshole replied. "You got another mouth to feed? Geez. I'm already underpaid as it is." He let out a deep sigh. "Fine. Which one of these two unidentified meat sacks is Cat Suo?" The synthetic voice separated the word like it was a first and last name.

"I am," I replied.

"Okay. Hold onto your assets, Cat Suo. Here we go."

A trio of green lasers appeared at the top of the rear bulkhead, creating a triangle that slowly descended over me. I closed my eyes when it hit my face, and then waited while it finished the scan.

"All done. You're a scrawny little chicken, aren't you? I barely need any materials to cook up an entire wardrobe. What'll it be, Mac?"

Tyler cracked up. I ignored him and frowned at Matt, who shrugged again. "Hey, don't look at me. Ben programmed the voice."

"I'm not really that picky. Just give me something similar to what Ben and Matt wear."

"Fugly duds comin' right up," Asshole announced.

"I suddenly feel like I made a big mistake."

"You're fine, as long as you don't mind blue jeans, hoodies, and rock band t-shirts."

"Yeah, it's all good. That's the least of my worries right now. As long as it fits better than this." I tugged at the loose material of my current attire. "And smells better."

"So, about Ally," Tyler tried.

"Give it a rest, T-bone," Matt answered.

"Let me ask you a serious question," I said. "When we talked to Ben before, he seemed worried about something. Tyler figured it was the pill the Warden made us swallow, but I got the impression there was something more to it."

A ripple of tension swept across Matt's face before vanishing. "That's not for me to say. I think the pill is worrisome enough on its own."

"Any guesses what the pill does?"

"Beyond the toxin the Warden's using as an incentive?"

Matt answered. "A tracking device of some kind, at the very least. Maybe something that wires to the optic nerve and broadcasts what we see back to his ship."

"That's terrifying," Tyler said.

I snorted. "Says the guy who live-streamed himself break-dancing. You can't make a bigger fool out of yourself than that."

"That video got over a thousand views," Tyler replied. "And you're wrong. I can totally make a bigger fool out of myself." He turned to Matt. "You said all that like it's no big deal."

"It's not my first rodeo," Matt answered.

"Ding dong, order up!" Asshole shouted before we could ask him to expand on the statement.

The front of the wall slid open, revealing my fresh clothes dumped in a disorganized pile.

"Hey, what gives?" I asked. "You folded Ally's clothes. Why not mine?"

"She has manners," Asshole replied. "Please and thank you. You just make demands. That's what I think of your demands."

I scowled as I scooped up the two sets of clothes. They were well-made, and I could tell the fit would be good without putting them on. A couple of pairs of boxer briefs and magboots waited underneath the clothing, and I picked those up, too.

"Asshole, scan a new user," Matt said. "File under T-bone."

"Like the steak?" Asshole replied. "Oh baby, you're makin' my mouth water. Hold onto your assets, T-bone. Here we go."

The assembler repeated the same scanning process. Tyler chose clothes that matched his current outfit, leaving us waiting for them to complete. He didn't repeat my mistake, making sure to ask nicely so Asshole would fold them for him. When that was done, he ordered a mat, blanket and set of bed sheets, along with two pillows for us and linens, which I'd forgotten for myself, all in black.

"Geez, are you two planning on whacking someone?" Asshole asked.

"No, why?" Tyler replied.

"Black hides bloodstains. Comin' right up."

"I never thought of that," I said, glancing at Tyler.

"Don't get any ideas," he replied.

The assembler spit out his order, everything nicely folded. Tyler collected them, and we followed Matt back up to berthing.

"You two should get some rest," he said. "And try not to worry too much. We'll figure out how to get you home."

"It's not me I'm worried about," Tyler replied. "But I appreciate the positive attitude."

"Thank you, Matt," I answered. "I'm sure you'll do your best for us."

He nodded and headed to the captain's quarters. I closed the door to our room and helped Tyler make up his pallet on the floor before putting my sheets on my bed. We turned the light out and lay down, too tired to even strip down to our underwear.

"You should do something about your bandages in the morning," Tyler said. "You don't want those cuts to get infected."

With everything going on, I had nearly forgotten about my physical wounds. My strained muscles were hurting more than my cuts. A good sign. "Yeah, I'll mention it to Ben. They have a sick bay, so they must have fresh bandages. Right now, I just want to close my eyes and pretend that everything is wonderful so I can fall asleep."

I don't know if Tyler answered me. Exhaustion took over the moment my head settled on the pillow. I didn't even have enough energy to think about my parents before I drifted off...

A shrill alarm jolted me awake, I don't know how much later, leaving me disoriented while I struggled to wake up. Tyler stood beside the bed, roughly shaking my shoulder.

"Noah, get up!" he shouted. "We're under attack!"

CHAPTER 27

Alarms blaring all over the ship, my heart instantly racing, I scrambled out of bed. "How the hell can we be in trouble again already? It's been five minutes."

"Try four hours," Tyler shouted back. "I don't know what's going on, but Levi said there are new contacts incoming. We need to get to the flight deck."

"Contacts?" I asked. "As in more than one?"

"That's what Levi said."

I couldn't believe we were in trouble again so soon. It was as if I had become a black hole of mayhem, pulling it every shred of nearby strife. I also couldn't believe I had been sleeping for four hours. When my head hit the pillow, I felt certain my parents would haunt my dreams. Instead, it had seemed as though there had been no time to dream.

"Let's go," I snapped, eager to do whatever I could to help and grateful Tyler had reacted the same way.

We rushed out into the corridor, nearly colliding with Ally as she exited her room. Tyler adjusted his momentum to avoid her, winding up with his arm around her waist, spinning her around as though they were on a dance floor. They settled with their faces only inches from one another.

"Hey," Tyler said as comically as he could manage, one eyebrow arching high as he winked.

Ally groaned and shoved him away. "What's happening?"

"We don't know," I replied. "We're going to the flight deck."

"You should be going to sick bay," she said, pointing at the bandage on my forehead. "You're bleeding through it." She glared at Tyler. "Didn't you notice?"

"I just woke up," he complained.

I didn't know how the wound could have opened up while I slept. I tried not to panic over it. We had enough to panic about already. "I'll deal with it later. Come on."

We raced down to the lounge and then toward the elevator. Flashing emergency bulbs bathed everything in a Christmas glow. As we waited anxiously for the elevator, the alarm cut off abruptly. An ominous silence took its place.

I remembered my comm badge as the elevator doors slid open and we hurried inside. "Wait," I said to Tyler before he could direct the cab to Deck Four. "We don't know when it was last used."

"Damn, I almost forgot," he replied.

"Meg, are you there?" I said.

"Noah, is that you?" she answered. "Is this important? I'm a little busy—"

"We're in the elevator on our way to Four. Do we have enough charge?" I asked at lightning speed.

"Yes, you're clear," she replied.

"Do you know what's going on?" I asked as Tyler hit the button.

"No. Only that someone else somehow found us in the middle of nowhere and I need to finish repairing the hyper-drive ASAP."

Her answer knotted my stomach with dread. This had

disaster written all over it. We stepped onto the flight deck to find Ben, Matt, and Shaq already present, grim expressions on their faces.

"What's happening?" I asked.

"We've got company," Matt replied, pointing out the wide transparency.

I moved closer to the window, my mouth falling open. Three oblong, scaly ships surrounded Head Case at a distance, glowing veins of orange visible beneath their pearl-hued hulls. More of the Warden's forces? They bristled with what appeared to be quills—shards of crystal that jutted from their spiked carapaces.

"Have you tried contacting them?" Tyler asked.

Ben nodded. "No response. Probably because they can't understand a thing we're saying."

"Then what do we do?" Alyssa asked.

"Right now, we're waiting to see what they do," Matt replied. "We aren't in the business of shooting first. Hopefully, they picked up our arrival or our heat signature and just swung by to check us out."

"That's what we hoped about the Warden," Tyler reminded him.

"That's why I've got the guns and thrusters ready."

"And why I'm sitting in the co-pilot seat while Meg and Leo are busting their tails to get the hyperdrive working," Ben added.

"What can we do?" I asked.

"You look like you should be in sick bay," Ben replied.

"In the middle of this? Not a chance."

"This is our responsibility. You don't need to do anything."

"Like we're supposed to just stand here and watch while you fight for our lives?" Alyssa said. "We did that before. It sucked."

Ben smiled. "Noah, take over for me," he said, releasing

his restraints and rising from the co-pilot seat. "Ally, take the systems console. Use the control pad to navigate to the status screen. I need you to keep an eye on our shield status."

"On it," Alyssa said, rushing to the station.

"Obviously, green is good. Orange is meh. Red is bad," Ben summarized.

"Simple enough."

"Tyler, I don't have anything for you to do right now. But I promise that once we're out of this mess, I'll get you up to speed on all of Head Case's systems so you can help us with the next one. I thought we would have more time."

Tyler didn't look happy about being sidelined again, but he nodded and slid into one of the stadium seats to mope. I hurried to take Ben's place at the co-pilot station.

"That doesn't look like a benign maneuver to me," Tyler noted, drawing my attention to my sensor grid.

Outside, the alien ships shifted formation, moving to surround us in a triangle in an effort to prevent our escape. The tips of their spines gained the same orange glow that radiated beneath their translucent hulls. They looked ready to deliver blistering volleys of plasma or magma. Or something.

"Unidentified contact," Ben said into what looked like a CB transmitter that could have been ripped out of a big rig. "Please respond. We mean you no harm. We are not a threat. If you fire on us, you will be fired upon."

"I'm glad Leo got the shields back up to snuff," Matt commented.

"What are you waiting for?" Tyler cried. "Hit them before they hit us, or we'll be trapped."

"We don't shoot first," Ben reiterated.

"Then don't shoot, just move! You don't have your magic to protect us, if that's what you're thinking."

I glanced back at Ben. Apparently, Tyler had hit the nail on the head. "Matt," Ben said softly. "Go."

"Aye aye," Matt muttered. "Brace yourselves!"

He jammed the throttle forward. Head Case leaped toward the nearest enemy ship in a blur of acceleration, vectoring thrusters pushing us toward the center of one of the triangle's sides. Almost immediately, plasma pulses sizzled through the space we'd just occupied in a heavy barrage that would have turned Head Case, and us, to slag. We slipped out of their kill box, leaving the aliens scrambling to give chase.

"Return fire!" Ben barked.

At his command, Matt unleashed a barrage from the lower pair of cannons. Blue energy hammered the nearest alien hull, met by crackling orange energy attempting to absorb or deflect the charged ions. Partially failing, shards of their shimmering armor plating exploded outward.

"Nice shot!" Ben cheered. I was equally pleased to see our weapons do some actual damage.

Our brief surge of optimism evaporated as the other two ships unleashed strafing runs across our starboard cheek. The deck shuddered under dozens of hits while klaxons blared a damage report neither Matt nor Ben needed to hear; the situation was painfully clear.

We were in real trouble.

"Starboard shields at thirty percent," Ally said. "Assuming I'm reading this right."

"You probably are," Ben answered.

"Damn, they punch hard," Matt added.

Outgunned three-to-one, Matt threw Head Case into a punishing dive, coaxing every bit of speed from her thrusters. Despite the dampeners, the G-forces still dragged at my body, bringing fresh pain to my cuts, bruises, and sore muscles. Behind us, the aliens gave chase, continuing their blistering assault.

"Can't this bucket go any faster?!" Tyler shouted.

"Not at the moment!" Matt shot back through gritted teeth. He yanked us hard to port, narrowly dodging another salvo meant to slice us in half.

"We can't keep this up forever," I said. "Sooner or later they'll land another solid hit."

Matt ignored me, angling us onto a new vector using the debris from our one and only successful strike against the enemy as chaff gave us cover. We slipped behind the spinning shrapnel, the wreckage absorbing a few rays of orange plasma meant for us.

"Hold onto your lunches," Matt hissed. "I've got an idea."

He cut some of the thrust, allowing our pursuers to close the distance, still maneuvering wildly to keep as many shots from hitting us as possible.

"Rear starboard shields, fifty percent," Ally announced.

"Come on," I heard him mutter beside me. "Just a few seconds more."

"Forty percent," Ally updated. "Port shields, seventy percent."

"This is going to be tight," he announced. He yanked the main throttle all the way closed while using the stick to activate vectoring thrusters, a second thumb-throttle allowing him to push them to maximum output. Our forward velocity decreased in a hurry, causing the trio of enemy ships to overshoot us. As they struggled to come about, Matt opened the throttle and swung Head Case in a wild rotation, until our weapons aligned on the nearest target.

"Fire!" Ben shouted

Matt unleashed a full frontal assault with all of Head Case's firepower. Unable to handle the powerful barrage, the alien shields winked out. Almost immediately, armor boiled away under the massive attack. Debris poured out of the ship's rear, followed by a quick fireball before the whole craft split in two, its orange glow dying out.

"Hell yeah!" Tyler pumped a fist. "That was amazing!"

I stared at Matt in awe, developing my own kind of crush on the real god of Thunder.

Of course, it wasn't time to declare victory. The remaining ships swept back in, angry and intent on punishing us for our success. Matt's maneuver had let us take out one of the ships but left us more vulnerable on the tail end of it. Crossfire slammed Head Case from both sides.

"Rear shields are out again!" Alyssa cried.

"Better keep them on our forward shields," Matt said. "We'll make our stand here. Noah, take the stick."

"What? Now?" I started shaking, unprepared for the order and freezing up.

Noticing my utter failure to perform, Matt threw the ship into a desperate corkscrew evasion, trying to spoil the aliens' aim. No longer worried about flanking attacks, they tightened their fire despite Matt's efforts. Space transformed around us into a deadly stew of crisscrossing orange rays. It was all Matt could do to keep us ahead of the destruction, juking madly through space.

"Forward shields are nearly gone!" Alyssa's hands shook like bowls of Jell-O.

I was sure that this was it. The end of a wild ride I could barely believe I'd embarked on. We were about to pay the ultimate price, annihilated by alien legions from some obscure corner of the galaxy. All because we accepted charity tickets for an impossible voyage gone horribly awry. If only I could undo the awful mistake that had doomed us to…

My panicky lament broke off as Matt threw Head Case into a bone-crushing high-G turn. Thrown sideways against my restraints, agonizing pain shrieked through my already sore ribs. Somehow, it was strangely cathartic; knowing this would be our final maneuver somehow calmed in our final few seconds of existence.

But somehow, it wasn't the end.

Matt led the aliens into a trap of his own design, one that left them firing on Head Case from nearly opposite angles. While the forward shields held up to the punishment, Alyssa had already confirmed that the rear shields were gone. Yet, the energy rays from the alien ships never contacted the rear shields. Instead, they vanished into nothingness. I knew it was Ben's doing before I even looked at him. His body was lit like a candle, his forehead soaked in sweat. I knew at that moment what it looked like for a man to be ready to die to protect his family. I knew Dad would have done the same. He just never had the chance.

"Ben, now!" Matt shouted.

Ben dropped the defense at the same time Matt fired the overhead vectoring thrusters to rotate Head Case downward, pushing us away from the two approaching ships at just the right moment. The two enemy ships fired at where Head Case had been, orange rays passing each other and smashing through each other's shields, carving out armor. Trailing debris, the two ships swung away from one another to avoid colliding, but for one of the ships at least, it was already too late. A sudden fireball burst from the side of its hull and the entire ship went dark.

The remaining alien craft peeled away, its outer shell badly damaged, its propulsion system, hidden somewhere on the ship, seemingly offline. It didn't gain velocity, relying on only vectoring maneuvers to take a relatively straight path away from us.

"Whooooooooooo!" Tyler screamed from the nosebleeds. "Yeah! Take that you sons of bitches! Ya-hooooooo!"

Ally cheered as well, while Matt relaxed back against his headrest and expelling a relieved breath. Ben had a weak smile on his face, though he looked ready to again pass out.

I wanted to enjoy the victory, too. Instead, I slumped in my seat. Matt had asked me to take the stick, and I'd blown it. Maybe it would have changed the outcome and spared Ben the need to use chaos energy to bail us out. Maybe not. The point was, they'd given me a job and I'd failed to execute.

"Matt," I said. "I froze. I'm sorry."

"No," he replied. "I shouldn't have put you on the spot like that. I was only thinking about my next move, not the person in the co-pilot seat. You're a hell of a VR pilot, but you aren't ready for this yet."

It felt like a backhanded compliment, but I decided I hadn't earned the right to take offense. "I don't think I want to be ready for this."

"I said the same thing once. Sometimes, we don't get a choice. Anyway, we won this round. And like Ben said, if we can get a breather around here, we'll get you ready for whatever comes next. As ready as any of us can be, anyway."

"Thanks, Matt," I said, appreciating his understanding. He responded by putting his fist out. I bumped it, matching his grin.

"Meg…damage report." Ben's listless voice reflected his fatigue.

"Well, they pretty much just undid everything Leo and I spent the last five hours working on, and then some. But we're alive, so there's that."

"Hyperdrive?"

"Somehow, it escaped damage. Which a good thing because if it had been hit, Leo and I would be literal toast right now. We should have it back online in the next fifteen minutes or so."

"I'm glad you're both unhurt. I hate to ask you to start repairs once you finish with the drive, but..."

"It's okay. I hate sleeping anyway."

"Once we're in hyperspace, we'll have time to repair, rest, and recover."

"Aye, Captain."

Ben looked wearily forward. "Nice job," he said, eyes switching from Matt to me, as if I had actually done anything.

I didn't want to take credit for my failure. "I didn't—"

"Nice job," he repeated. "You'll get more action next time."

"I hope not," I answered. "I don't want a next time."

Ben smiled. "That makes all of us. Matt, I need to go pass out again."

"Understood."

"Noah, Tyler, Ally, you three were probably sleeping. I don't know if you can after this engagement. Maybe once the adrenaline wears off. If not, I recommend pizza and a movie to help calm the nerves."

"Do you have the Last Starfighter?" Tyler asked.

Ben laughed. "We sure do. It's—" He froze, his eyes on the forward transparency.

Or at least, I thought they were going to the view outside. Turning back to see where Ben was looking, my eyes widened when I saw the holographic projection of the Warden's face floating in front of the pilot stations.

"Ugh, not him again," Ally groaned.

"Congratulations," the Warden said, seemingly sincere. "That was a pretty impressive and decisive win, if I do say so myself. And very entertaining, indeed."

"Of course," Ben said. "You did this."

"Technically...yes. But not directly. You see, the Achai are visiting Warexia too. And, well... let's just say they were starting to bore me. So, I gave them a task."

"To destroy us?" Tyler asked.

"Not specifically you," the Warden countered. "To attack and defeat a ship of their choosing."

"So why did they attack us?" Alyssa asked. "We're in the middle of nowhere."

"I may have passed them coordinates to your location, since you were the ship closest to them. But I didn't expressly tell them to attack the ship that looks like a giant robot head. They made that choice of their own free will." Since he was only a head, I couldn't see him shrug, but the shifting of his expression suggested he had. "Obviously, it was a bad choice. Be right back."

The hologram vanished. Through the forward viewport, we watched as the surviving alien ship suddenly went dark.

"And that, my friends," the Warden said, his head reappearing, "is the price of failure."

"Wait a second," Matt said. "Before, you said it was good enough that we tried to carry out the task, not that we had to succeed."

The Warden wrinkled his face. "Hmm. That's right, I did say that. Well, I didn't say the same to them. Probably because I thought they looked much tougher than they turned out to be. I'll honor my word with you. As long as you try."

I could tell by Matt's face that the promise held no consolation for him. The same went for me.

"In any case, I wanted to offer my congratulations on your first success. I expected you to die within the first few seconds, so I'm very excited to see what will happen next. Oh, and as a reward, one of you has been randomly selected to receive a boon. I'll be seeing you."

He vanished again.

"Check, please!" Tyler cracked.

CHAPTER 28

Our narrow victory and the reappearance of the Warden left us all shaken. A million thoughts blasted through my mind like a storm of asteroids, each crashing into the other, making it hard to sort out any specific idea. No doubt, the others felt the same. I drew a deep, shaky breath, wincing as my bruised muscles protested.

"Well, that was fun," Tyler quipped, breaking the uneasy quiet a second time. I was used to his attitude from our matches. He always tried to lighten the mood, no matter the situation. He couldn't stand silence or tension. For him, it was always better to air complaints and concerns than let negativity fester. Or when all else fails, crack a joke. "Anyone else ready for round three?"

"Not really," Alyssa muttered. She slumped back in her chair, rubbing at the dark circles beneath her eyes. Despite her evident fatigue, I doubted rest would find any of us easily after such a close call.

"At least we survived," I offered. "It could have been much worse."

Tyler snorted. "Sure, we survived. This time. But for how much longer? You heard the Warden; he fully expected us to die against those 'Achai' or whatever he called them. This is nothing but a game to him. A way to alleviate his boredom. His freaking boredom!" He slammed his fist on the tray table of the stadium seat, releasing his tension, fear, and frustration. "Who knows what he'll throw at us next?"

"He did say he'd reward us for succeeding," Alyssa pointed out.

"He said he'd give one of us a boon," I said. "We have no idea what that means. How can he single us out from a distance?"

"The pill," Tyler said. "It must be able to do more than we thought."

"Which is even more terrifying than before," Ally said. "What if it turns us into mutants? What if one of us grows wings or something?"

"I think wings would be kind of cool," Tyler answered, reaching behind his back to see if anything was growing there.

"We need more information," Ben said. "We don't know anything about the Warden. His purpose, motivation, capabilities. He obviously has pretty advanced technology. Is that common here, or is he the only one who possesses it? Does he control this entire galaxy, or is he just one Boss out of many? How many people has he pitted against one another, and is it really just for entertainment, or does he have a greater purpose? What is that purpose? He said chaos energy doesn't flow properly here. Why not?"

"That's a pretty hefty brainstorm for a guy who can barely stand up," Matt said.

"You know me. Once the challenge presents itself, it's hard not to run with it."

"Could the disruption in the chaos energy have something to do with the Warden?" I added.

"Another great question," Ben agreed. "I like the way you think, Noah."

"While you two rub your brain cells together, the rest of us need a plan," Tyler cut in. "The Warden already proved we're sitting ducks out here."

"I agree," Ben said. "We'll have time to process all of our questions later. We need to get moving so we're less of a target. Once we have the hyper—"

"Captain," Meg's voice crackled over the comms. "The hyperdrive is back online."

"Music to our ears, Meg," Matt said. "Your timing is amazing."

"I know," she replied lightly. "Leo and I are shifting back to the shields. Holler if you need anything."

"Thank you both," Ben said.

"Now we just need a destination," Matt said.

"Levi, project the star map the Warden provided," Ben added.

"Projecting," Levi replied.

An expansive web of star systems dominated the projection that appeared where the Warden's face had been minutes earlier. Each like a primitive organism, the systems were outlined in rough circles, with an apparent primary star in the center—though some of the systems were binary or even trinary in nature—with the planets cast around *the solar luminescence.*. A small red robot-head occupied the far left of the map inside one of the amoeba-like borders, indicating our position in the known galaxy, which itself stretched for what appeared to be millions of light years. I couldn't begin to wrap my head around the full extent of Warexia's scope. If we were back on Earth, the Solar System would be a single amoeba out of thousands.

"I think we need to zoom in a little," Ben said. "Levi, magnify the area around us. Keep the nearest three systems in the projection."

"Aye, Captain," the AI replied. "Processing." All the other systems disappeared before the area around Head

Case quickly expanded inside the hologram. The nearest three systems were composed of nearly sixty planets in total, all of which were represented as plain blue orbs of similar size. Eight of the planets had numbers floating above them, that ranged from a little over thirty-thousand to nearly eight hundred million.

"What do you think those numbers mean?" Alyssa asked.

"I'm going with population," Ben answered.

"The only clue the Warden's giving us about the galaxy, it seems," Matt added. "Assuming they're even accurate." He tried to air-tap on one of the planets, but they didn't appear to be accessible.

"So what do we do, just pick one?" Tyler asked.

"We don't know anything about them," I said. "Or about the galaxy in general. We have no idea if this place is generally peaceful or if it's a chaotic hive of scum and villainy. If we choose the wrong planet, we could stumble into yet another bad encounter."

"All part of the show," Matt said. "The more we know, the less fun it is for the Warden, I'm sure."

"I think we should avoid the more populated systems for now," I said. "Smaller worlds are likely to have smaller militaries or at least less opportunity for someone to pick another fight."

"It'll also be easier to avoid attention," Matt agreed.

"Theoretically," Tyler said. "With the luck we've had so far, we're going to wind up picking the Warexia equivalent of Sparta."

"Wherever we go, we'll approach with caution," Ben said. "Come out of hyperspace some distance away and do a full sensor sweep. It won't tell us anything about the general attitude, but right now every puzzle piece we can put in place helps."

"Maybe we should expand the map a little more," I

suggested. "Give ourselves more options."

"I'm sure one of these planets has to be okay," Alyssa countered. "The sooner we can land somewhere, the happier I'll be."

"I'm with Red," Tyler said. "We should pick one of these. The sooner we reach civilization, any civilization, the faster we can learn about this place, and the quicker we can get back where we belong."

I shied away from his suggestion. "I don't know…"

"Come on, Katzuo," Tyler cajoled. "Some of us want to be here for as short a time as possible."

"I know, I just think that running for the nearest inhabited planet is exactly what the Warden expects us to do. He could be handing out a task to kill us to another group in these clusters right now."

"I'm with Noah," Ben said. "We can't know for sure, but there's no technology I'm aware of, Sigiltech or otherwise, that allows a ship to be tracked in hyperspace. We need time to repair our damage and get our feet under us. And the further we go, the more time we have. Plus, there may be a chance we can move outside of the Warden's influence. A place where he may not have other groups under his thumb."

"So what…we're supposed to spend weeks in hyperspace while Kaiju is all alone?" Alyssa said.

"I thought you have a roommate," I replied.

"I do, and she'd never let anything happen to him. But I want my kitty."

"I feel badly for you, Ally," I said. "I really do. But I also think there's a greater risk you'll never see Kaiju again if we stick too close to shore. Remember, someone redirected us here. To this spot. On purpose. As far as I'm concerned, we can't get far enough away from it."

"I'm with Noah, too," Matt said.

Tyler threw up his hands in frustration. "Fine, fine. I can't argue your logic, even if I hate it."

"Ally?" Ben said, looking for a quorum.

She sighed. "Okay, but if we end up in a bad spot again, I'll be sure to point out that I was ultimately against this decision."

Matt chuckled. "I'll be sure to note that under *I told you so* in the Captain's log. Levi, zoom out to two weeks' distance via hyperdrive."

Since the map wasn't two-dimensional, nearly twenty new systems were added around us, with almost a hundred inhabited planets.

"Geez, this place is huuuuuuggggeeee," Tyler commented.

"That's only two weeks out. The whole thing stretches over a year," Matt said.

"I'm going to die here, aren't I?" Alyssa said.

"No," Ben replied firmly. "I won't let that happen."

He believed it strongly enough that I was willing to believe it, too.

"Should we close our eyes and point?" Tyler asked.

"Let's just take a few minutes," Ben said. "Levi, cycle through each system."

The projection jumped to the next system. We looked over the populations. It was all we had to go on. "Next," Ben said, skipping us to the next one. We repeated the process a few more times.

"How are we planning to choose like this?" Alyssa asked.

"Gut instinct," Ben replied. "If you feel strongly about one of them, you'll know it when you see it."

We hopped through four more systems before Tyler became the one to single a planet out. "That one," he said. "Goldhaven."

I checked the population. Sixteen thousand three

hundred and eighty-seven. Definitely on the smaller end, but not the smallest we'd seen.

"Why that one?" Matt asked.

"Like Ben said, it's just calling to me."

"Seems as good a spot as any," Alyssa said.

"Noah, any objection?" Ben asked.

"No. I trust Tee's instincts."

"Thanks, man."

"Then Goldhaven it is. Matt, make it so."

"Aye aye, Captain," he replied with a grin. He entered the remote coordinates while we returned to our seats. "Next stop, Goldhaven."

I watched through the forward surround as space began twisting around us, bending into a fisheye view as a soft hum emanated from somewhere within Head Case. Within no time, the distorted space seemed to compress in on itself, the stars collapsing together as if they'd been placed in a blender, until only darkness remained.

CHAPTER 29

"Compression complete," Matt said. "We're on our way."

"Really?" Tyler replied. "I didn't feel a thing."

"What did you expect to feel?"

"I don't know. Butterflies in my stomach. A tingle down my spine. Something."

"Sorry to disappoint."

I sank back with a weary sigh. "Maybe now we can relax a little."

"Some of us," Ben replied. "But you seem to have forgotten something." He pointed to my forehead.

"Right." The bloody bandage clinging to my forehead. The hectic action had distracted me from the wound.

Matt whistled low through his teeth. "Damn. I can't believe you're walking around like that. Let's get you patched up." He motioned toward the exit.

I didn't move. Matt was a nice guy, an amazing pilot, and obviously skilled with a rifle. A fighter, to be sure. But to me, that meant he couldn't be good at everything. Noticing my hesitation, his expression softened with understanding.

"If you prefer, Ben can show you to sickbay instead. He probably needs some time there himself."

Equal measures of relief and embarrassment warred within me. I shouldn't need pampering over basic first aid. What the hell was wrong with me? "I-I'm okay," I stammered unconvincingly. "Just tired, you know?"

"He's right," Ben said gently. "I do need to run a new health scan after pulling more chaos energy. If we can get a baseline, it'll help me understand my limits. Noah, you're with me."

"What should we do?" Alyssa asked.

"You can either return to Deck Three for free time, or we can check with Meg and Leo, and see if you can help them with repairs."

"I can't relax right now," Tyler said. "I might as well make myself useful."

"Yeah, me too," Ally agreed.

"Don't worry," Matt said. "I'll find some way to put them to work."

Ben nodded, motioning toward the exit. I shuffled after Ben, feeling like the world's biggest wimp. I had to believe exhaustion was the culprit. I'd been so eager to help after Tyler woke me up. There was no other reason I should feel so weak now.

We took the elevator down to the medical level in silence. My thoughts continued their collisions in a tug-of-war between our current predicament and darker ruminations about all I had lost. Ben likewise seemed preoccupied, his thoughts likely turned to the Warden and our distant destination.

The elevator doors whisked open on Two, allowing the deck lighting to chase away my darker sentiments. I followed Ben around the elevator shaft and down a short passageway to an unmarked door.

"Just through here," he directed.

I ducked through, bracing for olfactory assault. Instead, a light smell of flowers or lavender, or something similar, immediately made me think of a spa instead of a hospital. Three doors waited against the rear bulkhead, all of them open, leading to small available treatment compartments. The only thing in them appeared to be diagnostic chairs, sporting non-threatening instruments and an attached terminal to run scans and review the results.

My gaze snapped to the room's current occupant. Ixy rested behind the counter, pedipalps clicking in greeting as we entered. Her dark eyes glittering above curved fangs conveyed warmth rather than menace, but only because I already knew she was friendly.

"Hey Ixy," I offered. "What are you doing here?"

"Hellosss." She completed her greeting with an approximation of a bobbing bow. "Comesss to ssseee Bensss. Fixing yousss?"

"That's right," Ben confirmed, entering behind me. "If our stubborn patient cooperates." He glanced my way. "Ixy came down while I was still here. I told her to stay while I went to confront the Warden. I figured she'd be a nasty surprise if the boarders tried to breach further into Head Case. I guess she decided she was comfortable."

"Yesss," Ixy agreed.

"I'm glad you're here. You can assist."

"Yesss."

I wanted to question how an oversized arachnid would assist with my wounds, but I didn't want to hurt Ixy's feelings by questioning her abilities. Instead, I followed Ben into the first compartment without comment. Ixy trailed behind us, only able to fit her front half into the small space.

"Have a seat," he said, pointing to the diagnostic chair.

I did as he ordered, resting back in the surprisingly comfortable seat.

"Turn your head toward me." He opened a nearby

cabinet to pull out what I assumed was an antibiotic and some clean rags. "Any idea why your cuts opened?"

"None at all," I replied, tilting my head obligingly as Ixy reached toward my head. It took some effort not to pull back from the giant spider limb stretching toward me, but somehow I managed to remain still. She hooked the end of her appendage beneath the soiled dressing, peeling it back as gently as I'd ever experienced bandage removal.

Ben took her place, dabbing away crusted blood with an alcohol wipe. The abrasive sting barely registered.

"It looks like it's getting infected," Ben murmured. "You probably shouldn't have left the hospital when you did."

"I thought you wanted me to leave the hospital so you could scoop me up and carry me to Never-Never Land," I replied.

"We did try to plant the idea in Tyler's mind. Subliminal messaging doesn't always work."

"How did you do that?"

"We intercepted the broadcast and inserted some extra packets. The messaging referenced Tyler directly, so it didn't bother anyone else. Actually pretty simple for Levi to accomplish."

"How did you know Tyler would be so compliant?"

"We looked up his family history, and we knew you went to school together and played on the same eSports team. The Stinking Badgers, right?" I nodded. "I love it. Tyler's a good guy. A little lonely. All his friends are screen names."

"It's not easy for us geeks," I admitted.

"Believe me, I know. I got to ride on Matt's coattails some of the time, but I've been in your shoes, too."

"How did you and Matt end up friends?"

"My dad died when I was young. My mom raised me, two brothers, and a sister. Matt's mom left him with his father when he was young. We lived in the same apartment building. His dad didn't really care what Matt did, as long as he wasn't giving him any trouble. He pretty much ignored him. Matt was at our apartment more than he was at his, so my mom and Matt both like to say she raised four boys."

"Sounds like he had a tough go of it."

"At times. We made it work. Anyway, we monitor police bands, among other things. Levi picked up on your accident, did some digging on you, and our algorithm pulled your name for the ride of your life. Only, it wasn't supposed to be this kind of ride." He paused to tap on the terminal's touchscreen. "Rest your head back. I'm going to have the auto doc run a scan on you. If it is an infection, it'll tell me how best to treat it."

"Seriously?" I asked. "That's so cool." I let my body go slack, my head resting against the chair. Ben used the touchscreen to recline me a bit more.

"Close your eyes," Ben said as the machine came to life, a light shining down over my head. I did as he asked, able to sense the light as it passed over my face. "Tell me more about your parents. What were their names?"

"My dad was Noah, too," I said, emotion bubbling up at the mere thought of them. "My mom's name was Natsuki. It means summer moon."

"Beautiful."

"Yeah, she was." Talking about them in the past tense, thinking about them, started the waterworks all over again. Maybe it was exhaustion. Maybe it was adrenaline with-drawal, or maybe this was the first time I had let down my guard since it happened. At that moment, all of the pain and loss came flooding out, and I found myself bawling like a baby. I didn't care that Ben and Ixy witnessed it.

Ben handed me some tissues, and then Ixy comfortingly stroked the hair on the top of my head. I don't know how long I cried, but I was glad I wasn't alone this time. I couldn't hold onto the emotion forever. When the tide flowed back out, it left my eyes feeling puffy and probably red. I blew my nose, looking up at Ixy, whose eyes had somehow gained a rippling expression of sorrow and compassion despite their inability to change. I glanced over at Ben, whose own tears had streaked his cheeks.

"I didn't get to tell you very much about them," I said, sniffling.

"Yes, you did," he replied, reaching out to squeeze my shoulder.

"So Doc, what's the diagnosis?" I joked lamely, seeking distraction. "Will I live?"

"No question about that," Ben assured. "Though you may end up with a thin scar. Chicks dig scars, or so I'm told."

I barked out a surprised laugh. "Not sure that matters since the only candidates around here are Ally, Ixy and Meg. Ally and Meg are too old, and Ixy, well…I think that goes without saying."

Ixy clacked with laughter while Ben paused thought-fully. "True enough. But once we get you back to Earth, I'm confident you'll need to fend off admirers with a stick." He turned his attention to the screen. "Ixy, I need the Hilasol. I think there's some in Room Two."

"Yesss," she replied, backing out of the compartment to retrieve whatever Hilasol was.

"Normally, I could heal you myself," Ben said. "But we're outside of normal right now."

"With Sigiltech?" I asked.

He nodded.

"What else can you do with it?"

"Not much, here."

"I get the sense there's more to it than that," I said, seeing the same distracted fade in his eyes when he said it.

"You're pretty perceptive; you know that?"

"Mom always said I had her heart and Dad's mind. I wasn't always sure that was a good thing."

"I think it is. Can you keep a secret?"

"I'd rather not, to be honest."

He hadn't expected that reply, but he seemed to appreciate it. He considered how much to tell me before sighing. "I suppose you're going to find out sooner or later. The thing is, I have a malignant brain tumor."

The reveal caught me fully by surprise. "What?"

"My ability to channel chaos energy is the only thing that keeps me alive," he continued. "Without it, the tumor would grow and spread to the rest of my body."

"They never cured cancer in the Spiral?"

"It's complicated. But no."

"And not being able to channel chaos energy as easily means—"

"I'm not entirely sure what it means right now," Ben said. "I restore myself almost subconsciously at this point. A constant flow of energy to hold back the tumor. Maybe I can pull enough so it won't be a problem. Or maybe it'll become increasingly difficult over time. I don't have those answers either. But I'm worried about it."

"So is Matt."

"Yeah."

"I'm so sorry, Ben."

"Thank you."

Ixy conveniently returned with the Hilasol at that moment. I had no doubt she had overheard the conversation and decided to give us a moment of privacy. She passed him a small bottle. He opened it and dumped out a single, orange pill.

"Not another pill," I said.

"This one is guaranteed to help you. It'll fight the infection from the inside out, and prevent any of your other scrapes from suffering the same fate. One pill should be enough."

Ixy used her other limbs to pass forward a glass of water, handing it to me. "Thank you."

"Welcomesss."

I swallowed this pill more eagerly than the last one while Ben opened another cabinet, handing me a bottle of pink liquid. "Take this to the shower. Remove the bandages and wash yourself with it. Anything bad on the surface will die. Put on boxers and come back here. Ixy will patch you up again."

"Doctor's orders?" I asked.

"Yep." Ben lowered his head, weariness bleeding through his otherwise friendly visage. Dark smudges underscored his bloodshot eyes. Using chaos energy to help fight off the Achai had clearly depleted reserves even a solid night's sleep wouldn't restore. Yet he'd shoved his personal discomfort aside, putting me first. Even after I was the one who had frozen and forced him to use his special abilities in the first place. Things hadn't gone the way he and Matt had planned, but they'd given all of themselves trying to make it right so far, and I had no doubt they would continue to do the same going forward.

"I really appreciate everything you've done for us," I mumbled awkwardly. "You and Matt. And I appreciate you asking me about my parents. It helped some, I think."

Ben blinked, clearly surprised by my spontaneous confession. "I'm glad it helped. I'm sorry everything went sideways. I give you my word I'll do everything in my power to return you and your friends safely home."

"No, you won't," I replied.

The comment surprised him. "Of course I will."

"I mean, you won't do everything in your power. We'll do everything in our power. We're all in this together now. Whether you like it or not."

He smiled. "Fair enough. I know you feel like you let everyone down. But you did your best, and you learned something, I'm sure. Next time will be different."

I nodded emphatically, determined to prove him right. "It definitely will. You should get some rest. You need it as much as I do. Maybe more."

"Excellent advice," Ben replied with an exhausted yawn. He put out his hand, helping me off the diagnostic chair. "I hope I'm not out of line when I say that I think your parents would be proud of you."

"No, you're not out of line," I replied, tears threatening once more. "They would be."

Ixy scuttled ahead while Ben and I returned to the elevator. He jabbed the call button with heavy eyes, sagging against the bulkhead. By the time metal doors opened, he would have fallen into the cab if I hadn't caught him. Totally depleted, Ben didn't resist help onto the elevator or down the passageway and up the stairs toward his quarters. Ixy remained behind, waiting for me to come back after I showered with the pink goop. I found her lack of concern for Ben comforting. Once he got some rest, I imagined he would be fine.

"Levi, open Ben's door," I said, approaching his quarters.

"Only Ben and Shaq have access," she replied.

"Do you have cameras? Can you see me holding him up?"

Apparently, the system did, though I couldn't spot their location. The door unlocked and swung open. I steadied Ben over the last threshold, easing him gently onto the wrinkled bedding. He didn't resist. Shaq poked his head out from beneath the blankets.

"He's just exhausted," I said.

"Mmmhmmm," Shaq replied, nuzzling Ben's face. He

looked at me, his buzzing voice emulating "thank you" as best it could.

"You're welcome," I whispered, ducking out of the room and pulling the door shut behind me. I leaned against the bulkhead and closed my eyes, conjuring an image of my parents. For the first time, rather than all-out sadness, I was grateful for everything they had done for me.

No matter what happened from this moment onward, I resolved to always make them proud.

CHAPTER 30

While the ghosts of my parents would never fully stop haunting me, the hour I spent with Ben, both in sick bay and afterward, had a therapeutic effect I doubted sitting in an office and chatting with a therapist could ever replicate. With some of my demons subdued, if not settled, I more easily fell into a routine while we made the trek across the Warexia Galaxy toward the distant world of Goldhaven.

As the current renters of the starship Head Case, Ben and Matt gave us options on how we wanted to spend our unexpectedly extended stay. If I'd wanted, I could have slept all day and watched movies all night, with intermittent breaks to eat pretty much anything I had a craving for. I could have sat back and let the real crew of the starship handle all the work while I lazed around with little motivation. After all, I had done the same at home plenty of times, taking advantage of my position as a high-schooler to skip out on as much responsibility as I could.

But things had changed.

Everything had changed.

I had no desire to take advantage of our situation. No inclination to let anyone else do for me what I could do for myself. I quickly came to self-discover that the old Noah had died with my folks, replaced by the newer, more mature version who would spend the rest of his life fending for himself. I didn't expect it to always be a smooth ride, but there was no way I would let sorrow, mourning, and loss get the better of me. No way would I let it turn me into a man I didn't want to be, one who wouldn't make Mom and Dad proud.

With that attitude permanently in mind, I dove full-bore into being as helpful as I could. I educated myself on everything Head Case, offering my services wherever they were needed and in whatever capacity I could provide them. At first, Tyler and Alyssa were less inclined to do the same. While they too didn't expect the crew to do everything for them, they had a harder time overcoming their frustrations about what they had left behind on Earth. Their lives that were on hold back there. It wasn't that I didn't understand their perspectives, but at the same time, I knew they were spending too much time looking in the rearview mirror. Of course, we were all nervous about what would happen once we came out of our hyperspace safe zone, but I knew the best thing we could do about what happened next was to be as prepared for it as could be.

I convinced Tyler to tag along with me by the second day, and Ally finally relented by the fourth. I could sense Ben's approval when I arrived on the flight deck early that morning with both of them in tow, my new recruits groggy but open to the training I had already been receiving on the intricacies of starship operation and maintenance.

That day, and in the days that followed, we spent long hours on the flight deck, each of us learning to pilot Head Case. A patient and confident teacher, Matt instructed us on all of the main functions available through the pilot station that went above and beyond flight control. We learned how to plot hyperspace courses, add filters to the individual surrounds, monitor shield status, and of course everything about weapons and fire control.

By the end of the sixth day, I had memorized the entire pilot station settings menu and its related gestures and could carry out tasks nearly as smoothly as Matt. He still owned all three of us as we worked our way through a series of increasingly complex simulations run by Levi, but my scores had improved enough that I was consistently coming within a few hundred points of his leading score. Not bad for a newbie, and Matt said he had total confidence that I would overtake him in time.

While my bat-to-ball skills had been non-existent, my fast-twitch reflexes and positioning instincts in three-dimensional space were surprisingly refined. Even Ally conceded grudging appreciation for the smoothness of my vectors and my success at the computer's simulated space slalom course.

She was hardly a slouch herself.

Our education expanded beyond flight operations once Meg finished the most critical of Head Case's many needed repairs. She and Leo provided crash courses on damage control methodology and common quick-fix techniques. We learned to splice fried conduits, replace gel packs, recalibrate sensors, and fabricate replacement parts with the assembler.

While Tyler struggled somewhat with the flight controls —his scores were consistently behind the rest of us—he took an immediate lead in quickly picking up the more technical aspects of starship repair. It didn't surprise me. He'd always handled the hands-on assignments in class with natural ease, something that had made up for my stunning lack of focus in that category. It's what had made us a great team on school projects. He would do the manual work, while I would write the reports and handle any equations. Together, we had generally put out grade-A work. It pleased both of us that the same held true when it came to starships, and our previously loose friendship continued to solidify into a tighter bond.

What I didn't expect was how more mundane shipboard chores managed to fill the gaps between study sessions. On the seventh day, Matt started posting a duty roster assigning different cleaning and routine maintenance tasks on a rotating schedule. I didn't mind swabbing the decks or scrubbing the head, especially after sampling more of Asshole's culinary masterpieces. If getting more familiar with mops and dust rags than I'd ever planned was the price for spicy chicken sandwiches and spot-on Reese's milkshakes whenever I wanted, I considered it a bargain. My only gripe was that while Asshole had a pretty extensive array of recipes in his arsenal, the assembler didn't know how to make onigiri or takoyaki.

Overall, life aboard Head Case quickly fell into a comforting routine. We woke bright and early for a group workout under Matt's demanding supervision. Breakfast followed and then morning lessons capped by lunch, with more training in the afternoon. Evenings brought dinner and socializing as a crew. Even Ixy, who generally only popped up for random jump scares as she carried out her own set of tasks, would come down from Deck Five to spend time with us. She especially enjoyed it when Ben and Matt would play their instruments in the lounge. It turned out they'd had a band back on Earth, and on top of being a great pilot and uber-handsome, Matt had a solid singing voice. While Ally had overcome her initial stuttering crush on him, she still had a tendency to swoon when he covered Post Malone.

My favorite diversion was reading late into the night, sprawled across the bed I now took turns sharing with Tyler. We still intended to add another bunk when the opportunity presented itself, but our daily itinerary left us both too exhausted to go through the trouble. We kept the black sheets but added a brighter steel gray paint to the walls, along with dark furniture that appealed to our shared gamer aesthetics. I switched off the glowing overhead panel when Tyler started keeping me awake with his snoring, immersing myself in anything and everything I could learn about the Manticore Spiral through the documents and hypernet caches within the ship's data stores. Of course, I'd sucked as much info as I could out of Ben and Matt, who had given us all a full retelling of how they had ended up in the Spiral in the first place. It made it easier to ignore darker ruminations about all I'd lost, which tended to hit me hardest during those late nights.

All things considered, life was pretty good. Routine camaraderie balanced lingering trauma. I missed my folks, of course. But I was learning to live without them. My new, unintended surrogate family helped ease that pain.

With three days to go on our long haul to Goldhaven, I found myself waiting in the lounge with Tyler and Alyssa, my tapping foot trying to release the tension created by an equal blend of fear and excitement. Ally played with her hair beside me to do the same, while Tyler rested on the adjacent recliner with his eyes closed, somehow immune to this particular brand of the unknown.

My foot stilled when I heard Meg's familiar light footsteps coming down the hall. Looking over my shoulder, she grinned and waved to me as she hopped down the three steps into the sunken lounge. Steps that were almost giant-sized for her and her brother.

"Good afternoon, Space Cadets!" she cheerfully greeted us as she put a hand on my shoulder and her other one on Ally's. Her voice pulled Tyler out of his nap, his eyes sliding open and his head lifting.

"Hey, Meg," I replied, smiling back at her. Ally smiled back at her, and Tee waved at her.

"Ooh, I can feel how nervous you two are," she said, giving us each a comforting squeeze before stepping back. "Does that mean you're ready for your first spacewalk?" Despite sporting coveralls smeared in hydraulic fluid, her enthusiasm shone brighter than a dwarf star.

"Yeah, sure," Ally answered, her reply failing to come close to Meg's level of excitement. "That would be…great."

I knew she had been dreading this moment from the first time Meg mentioned it. She wanted to go out into space, but she was also terrified of being jettisoned from the hull to be lost in the empty vacuum. It didn't help that since we were within a hyperspace compression field, leaving that field would mean instant implosion even deep-sea pressure couldn't come close to matching. On the upside, at least that kind of death would be quick and painless.

"You'll be fine," Meg reassured. "We've never lost a crew member to a spacewalk."

"Yet," Tyler added.

"Stuff it, T-bone," Alyssa snapped.

"I, for one, can't wait," I said, hopping to my feet.

"I'm ready," Tyler agreed, lowering the footrest and sliding out of the recliner. Ally took a deep breath and stood, too.

"Then let's boogie," Meg said with an inviting hand wave. We trailed behind her slight form, taking the elevator from Level Three to Five, which excited me almost as much as our imminent extra-curricular adventure. After nearly two weeks, this was the first time we'd been granted access to Level Five, and only now because Meg was with us.

The elevator doors opened, light from the cab revealing the nearest part of the deck and leaving the forward area in light shadow. Still, I could see well enough to distinguish Ixy's web. The multiple layers of webbing, thick and gray, covered the entire forward curve of the ship. Thankfully, it was bereft of any giant insects or other captured treats. I think Ixy rested in the center, but it was hard to be sure.

Between us and the web, a huge mound of sand covered most of the metal decking, interspersed with a variety of random objects that looked as though they had been picked from a dumpster. It was definitely an odd sight within the otherwise tidy ship. We circled behind the elevator shaft and entered an engineering compartment, following it back through a second hatch and into a staging area.

"This is so cool," Tyler commented, rushing over to a row of space suits hanging from a rack attached to the bulkhead.

Sleeker and less bulky than anything NASA could offer, the suits provided flexible protection using lightweight meta-materials that didn't exist on Earth. Meg pointed out the flat oxygen rebreather hidden cleverly within the high collar before explaining the emergency thruster pack and a battery that fit snugly across our shoulders and back. I donned my suit quickly, fumbling only slightly with the hidden closure seam. Magnetic gloves and boots completed the ensemble.

"Looking sharp, Red," Tyler quipped to Ally once we were all suited up.

"Again, stuff it, T-bone," she shot back, her voice still quivering with nervous energy.

"Both of you stuff it before I turn off your comms," Meg warned. Despite the stern tone, her expression remained upbeat. She showed us how to secure our helmets, a sharp hiss signaling their seal.

HUD projections flickered to life across the inner surface of my visor, offering necessary data like oxygen levels and battery life. It would take practice to filter necessary data from flashy distractions. For now, everything enchanted me. Just on the other side of an airlock door, space beckoned.

Meg ushered us from the staging area into the airlock. My heart began pounding once the inner door closed and she tapped the controls to depressurize the airlock. Glancing over at Ally, her terror-stricken face and wide eyes remained obvious through the glare of her faceplate.

"Remember," Meg said. "The magboots work the same outside the ship as they do inside. Toes first to release the lock, then slide-step and plant the heel to re-engage." We'd practiced with the soles all week in preparation. I had found myself walking that way more and more even without the electromagnetic coils engaged. Meg reached for her large toolbox, tethering it to her suit before placing her hand on the control that would open the outer airlock door and finally reveal space in all its amazing nothingness. "Same with the gloves," she reminded us, her voice crystal clear through everyone's helmet speakers. "Lift your fingers first to disengage, palm pressure to engage. Are you ready?" We all flashed thumbs-up in response. "I'll go first. Just follow my lead, go slow, and most importantly, enjoy the view!"

The inner lock cycled open and then Meg opened the outer hatch, giving us our first unimpeded view of space.. Not even stars were visible inside the HCF. Meg propelled herself through the opening with easy grace. Staring out into the total darkness I held my breath without realizing it.

"So cool," Tyler repeated, his voice my reminder to breathe. My spirit soared higher than our velocity as Meg showed us how to use our gloves to crawl out of the airlock. Awkward as newborns, yet no less awestruck, Tyler and I followed her out, planting our magboots on the curved patchwork hull, the entirety of it bathed in LED service lights. The angle to turn sideways was the hardest part to navigate, and Meg made sure to do it slowly for our benefit.

Tyler followed close behind her as she made her way

aft, but everything was so silent, eerie yet unbelievably peaceful—amazing beyond what I had ever expected—I stood there and stared, soaking it all in.

"Step aside, Katzuo. I want to come out, too."

Ally's voice snapped me out of it, and I scrambled, almost too fast, to get out of her way. As my right foot released, my left foot lost grip on the hull. For a brief moment, I separated completely from Head Case, floating fully in the expanse. Automated systems took over, the vectoring nozzles on my pack quickly spitting out a brief burst of compressed air to shove me back to the metal before I even thought to be afraid.

"Noah, are you okay?" Meg asked. She had stopped and spun around, the networked suits alerting her of my total disengagement.

"Yeah," I replied. "Nothing to worry about. Just got a little ahead of myself." I waited for Ally before trying to move again, suddenly eager to have someone else nearby in case I messed up again. A second look in her direction revealed a total shift in her demeanor. She was all smiles now that she was outside, her eyes glittering with amazement, her grin stretching from ear-to-ear.

"This might just make being lost in space worth it," she said softly.

"Enough lollygagging, space cadets," Meg finally said. "We've got shield node fuses to replace."

Under her guidance, we made our way along Head Case's spine toward an absence of service lights, indicating the damage we intended to repair. When we arrived, Meg tugged her toolbox to her and nimbly retrieved the palm-sized replacement from her utility pouch and pointed toward an external access panel.

"Who wants to pull the circuit and replace the bad fuse?"

I slide-stepped forward before Alyssa or Tyler could

reply. Accessing the panel took three frustrating attempts before Meg patiently reminded me to release the safety latch first. Hot embarrassment flushed my cheeks when the panel slid aside easily on the second try. I wrestled out the damaged sensor and handed it to Meg, who pushed it into the box to feed to Asshole later. Inserting the replacement was easier than expected. The service lights activated as soon as the fuse locked into place.

"Nicely done!" Meg praised. "I knew you could do it."

"Thanks. I couldn't have done it without you."

"That's one fuse down. Sixteen more to go."

"Sixteen?" Ally said, surprised by how many of the shield relays had been damaged. "How are we even still alive?"

"It's magic," Tyler replied, wiggling his fingers in front of his faceplate.

"You'll all get plenty of chances to practice replacing the fuses. This is the most common source of external damage we deal with. And not only from being shot at. Sometimes, space junk can sneak in, or a fuse can just burn out." She grinned behind her faceplate. "The next outage is that way. Last one there is on toilet-cleaning duty!"

She used her pack's vectoring nozzles to propel herself into a skipping jog down Head Case's starboard side, leaving us space babies crawling along in her wake.

Maybe getting thrown halfway across the universe by some unknown force wasn't such a bad thing, after all.

CHAPTER 31

Returning to the reality of our situation after a week and a half of blissful ignorance hit us hard. We needed to learn how to shoot, and hit whatever we were shooting at.

"Today you're going to learn basic firearms skills," Matt said as he stood before us in the training room. A line of plasma rifles and ballistic long guns resembling AR-15s rested on a nearby table. After ten days in hyperspace, I had finally healed enough for him to move beyond less strenuous lessons in starship control, maintenance, and repair to teach us the self-defense skills we needed to survive in this hostile environment. Not that I wanted to learn to kill for real—I knew for sure Tyler didn't—but the incident with the Pralls had proven, at least to me, that it was a skill I needed to protect the people I had come to think of as friends.

"I know you've handled the plasma rifles before," Matt continued, "and Ally even scored a solid hit on the first

Warden, but it's important that you have a full breadth of training across different firearm types and the targeting skills to make efficient use of any and all of the guns in our armory. I know you aren't all that keen to fire at another living thing, or to be fired upon, but all things considered, it's unfortunately a very real possibility that both may come to pass." He motioned to the weapons. "I don't need to go over the details of using the plasma rifles with you again." He picked up the other rifles. "The MM-50s are more tradi-tional projectile firearms. They fire .22 caliber rounds, similar to an M-16, but generally with a smart payload that drills into the target before detonation. I've loaded these rifles with gel rounds so they can mark your hits without further damaging the bulkheads. We'll do pistol, laser, and blaster training at additional sessions, until you've carried, maintained, and fired every weapon in our armory. Sound good?"

I nodded eagerly. After barely contributing last time trouble found us, I wanted to properly pull my weight. Tyler was less committed, but he still bobbed his head, ready to learn. Ally didn't have much of an outward reac-tion at all.

"We'll start with the plasma rifles since they're simpler and you've held them before." He motioned to the table. "Pick one and let's see how accurate you are."

We each stepped forward to claim one of the weapons before stepping back to wait for further instructions. Tyler obviously felt uncomfortable holding his, but once Matt adjusted his awkward grip, he began to handle it with more efficiency. Alyssa easily lifted hers in both hands, immedi-ately comfortable with it.

Matt retrieved his personal access device from his pocket, using the pad to activate an overhead projector. At the front of the room, three target outlines appeared in front of the thick metal bulkhead that showed plenty of scorching from past shooting sessions. The targets had roughly human proportions with bright red bullseyes at center mass. "Go ahead and line up. From here to the target is about thirty feet. I wish we could go longer, but obviously Head Case isn't big enough."".

"How come you don't have simulation modes for the plasma rifles at least, like you do for the pilot station?" Tyler asked once we'd lined up in a row in front of the projected targets. "They seem pretty high-tech."

"Because firing live ammunition gives you a better feel for how the weapons respond," Matt replied. "It's especially important with the MMs. Go ahead and power on your rifles." Again, we did as he said, activating the guns. "Make sure to take your time aiming. Right now, this isn't a race. You'll pick up speed as you gain experience. When you're ready to shoot, exhale as you squeeze the trigger. PRs have no recoil, so you'll find them easier to shoot than the MMs or the RGs."

"RG?" I asked.

"Railguns," he replied. "We'll get to those later. Right now, nothing fancy. Aim for center mass, nice and easy."

I shouldered my plasma rifle, sighting down the barrel to the projected reticle at the end, realizing as I did that the weapon had painted a dot on the target's center mess. I did my best to align the dot inside the reticle. I exhaled slowly and squeezed the trigger. A bolt of plasma erupted from the weapon. It streaked past the target, missing it by over a foot. I swallowed hard and glanced to my right, embarrassed by my pathetic aim.

Beside me, Tyler aimed more carefully, squinting with one eye closed. He pulled his trigger after a few seconds. A bolt of plasma grazed the target's left side, nearly spearing the outer edge. Not a solid hit, but way closer than my wild shot.

"Nice!" Matt praised.

Alyssa turned out to be the steadiest and by far the most accurate shot. Firing after barely a pause, her bolt struck almost dead center with a satisfying sizzle. The target flashed and faded, apparently indicating a kill.

"Hell, yeah!" Tyler shouted. "Nice going, Red."

Alyssa grinned, clearly pleased by her precision.

Even Matt looked impressed. "Well done, Alyssa. I've got a feeling you have a knack for this." He looked my way and then at Tyler. "Your first shot was pretty good, Tee. Once you get the fundamentals down, you'll both get better with practice."

My initial embarrassment shifted to third-party pride over Ally's nearly perfect shot. Whatever else happened, at least we were learning necessary skills. With enough time and training, we wouldn't need to feel so powerless should we find ourselves in another situation like the one with the Pralls.

"Again," Matt instructed, summoning a fresh target for each of us.

Within an hour, confidence had replaced my initial awkwardness and uncertainty. While I was still the worst shot of the three of us, I had at least managed to start hitting the target with regularity, scoring plenty of shoulder and leg wounds to go with my occasional center mass hits. I had gone from questioning whether or not I could improve with practice to certainty that I could and would. Of course, Ally remained the leader in this particular challenge, even after we finally graduated to the MMs.

Magazine after magazine vaporized the humanoid projections, putting her high atop the leaderboard. As she had explained, doing her best not to sound like she was bragging, a decade of handling PlayStation controllers had honed her fine motor reflexes and hand-eye coordination, leaving her well-suited for wielding automatic death-dealers. That explanation might have held up, except both Tyler and I had both done the same, and we were nowhere near as fast or efficient with our shots as Ally was.

Alyssa dropped her final target with a triple tap to center mass. I didn't know the system was keeping an actual score until it appeared where the targets had been. Hers flashed what I imagined was an impressive 12,571. Tyler managed a respectable 10,803, while I surprised myself with what I considered a serviceable 8537. As far as I was concerned, that put me well in the below-average to average range. And for today, I was happy with that.

"Enough pew-pew for now," Matt said. "Let's move on to hand-to-hand."

"Now you're in trouble, Red," Tyler said, setting his pistol aside. "You aren't going to make Noah-san and me look bad again, like you did with the target practice."

"You might be surprised," Matt replied. "Hand-to-hand combat is more about form and technique. Brute power helps, but it isn't the be all, end all."

I bit my lower lip to avoid smug commentary, recalling my years of aikido and karate under Sensei Watanabe's instruction. I'd been throwing other kids around the mat since I was eight and had no doubt I could do the same to Tee and Ally. For now, at least, that was my stance.

"What if they have us seriously outgunned?" Alyssa wondered aloud. "Like, say, alien warriors with four arms?"

"If they have more arms than we do, we either run like hell or sick Shaq and Ixy on them."

Alyssa laughed. "Of course. Why didn't I think of that? Why do we need to learn this stuff when we have them for backup?"

"What if they aren't around and you have no choice but to defend yourself?" I asked.

"That's what guns are for."

"What if you don't have a gun?"

"Why wouldn't I have a gun?"

"What if guns are prohibited on Goldhaven and you need to defend yourself?"

Ally looked at Matt. "Are guns prohibited on Goldhaven?"

"I have no idea," he replied past his amused grin. "You don't want to learn hand-to-hand?"

"I do. It's just that I don't think I'll be very good at it. Brute strength may not be everything, but I have zero." She flexed her rail-thin arm without producing even the hint of a bicep.

"Maybe you don't have a lot of physical strength today," Matt said. "But that doesn't mean you can't in time."

"I really hope we aren't stuck here long enough for me to transform into She-hulk."

"Me neither. But it might be worth starting strength training, anyway. I can help you get started. In private, if that makes you more comfortable."

Her face flushed so brightly, I thought Ally might collapse. She offered a sheepish smile. "Uh…um…sure."

"Great. I studied martial arts back on Earth, and I've picked up some additional training from a Royal Marine since then. I'll run you through the same regimen she ran me and Ben through. Sound good?"

"Matt, full disclosure here," I broke in. "I have black belts in both karate and aikido."

"What?" Tyler said. "Since when?"

"Since I was thirteen. I picked up a third-degree black belt in karate last year."

"You never told us about that," Ally added.

"It was never relevant before. Even Bruce Lee might have sucked at *Fortnite*."

"In that case, it's up to you if you want to participate," Matt said.

"No, I'll go through the motions. I just wanted you to know upfront so you pay more attention to Tee and Ally."

Matt nodded his appreciation. What followed was Self-defense 101, simple locks, strikes, and throws. We cycled through basic techniques, starting with arm bars and wrist releases against a single opponent. Even one-armed, Matt deftly foiled Alyssa and Tyler's attempts to control him. My extra experience showed quickly, escaping his grip or putting him in peril with minimal effort. Not that I thought I could beat Matt in a real fight, but at least I was sure I could hold my own for a short while. There was still something to be said for raw power, and he had a lot, while I had little.

After thirty minutes of drills, we finally switched to sparring. Already braced for embarrassment, Tyler insisted on being my partner. Alyssa battled invisible opponents under Matt's watchful eye. She threw her wild, ineffective punches with more enthusiasm than ability.

"Keep tension here and here," Matt reminded her, adjusting her wrist and shoulders. "You don't want to hyper-extend the joint or pull a muscle."

Tyler faced me wearing his trademark impish grin, wiggling his fingers in invitation. "Shall we dance?"

I dipped into a ready stance. "Whenever you're ready."

He rushed me immediately, faking left before throwing a sloppy right cross. I pivoted from the obvious strike, seizing his overextended wrist and yanking down while sweeping his leg. He slammed flat on his back with a startled grunt, wincing when my knuckles pressed warningly against his windpipe.

"Um...ow?"

I rolled away, letting him rise. He bounced back to his feet, and we went again, with the same result. He let me send him to the mat a few more times before tapping out. By then, Matt had gotten Ally throwing quick jabs with a semblance of technique. Seeing we had stopped, he glanced over at me. "Noah, you look bored."

"No, I'm fine," I replied.

"I'm not much of an opponent," Tyler said. "You were right. All this beautiful beefcake is ineffective against the flying tomato over here."

"Flying tomato?" I said, grinning.

He laughed and shrugged. "First thing I thought of, man."

"Ally, Tee, why don't you two take a breather?"

"Gladly," Alyssa replied. She was the sweatiest among us, though she seemed to be having a blast.

"Have you ever seen the Matrix?" Matt asked me.

"Who hasn't?" I replied, doing my best Neo impersonation. "I know kung-fu."

"Show me," Matt added. He dropped into a fighting stance, turning his hand and waving me toward him, just like in the movie.

I dropped into my own stance with a huge grin on my face. I didn't care if I won or lost.

I don't think I had ever been happier in my life.

CHAPTER 32

I wouldn't have known Head Case had dropped out of hyperspace if it weren't for the changing view outside, which shifted from all black to nearly all white. At first, curving like we were looking out at infinite space from inside a fishbowl, the stars began separating before finally settling into pinpricks of light against the endless black. My body lagging behind my brain, the physical effects of the disorientation didn't hit me until we were at sub-light speed for nearly ten seconds. I closed my eyes, tightening my grip on the armrests of the co-pilot's seat while the sudden bout of nausea and dizziness passed. Behind me in the command chair, I could hear Ben tapping on his control surface, likely checking the initial sensor readings as the data started pouring in.

My eyes went directly to Goldhaven, centered on my surround and also visible near the edge of our long-range sensor grid. At first little more than a tiny white globe reflecting the light of its nearby star, a well-practiced hand gesture zoomed in one of the auxiliary cameras, changing only my personal view of the planet.

"Nice job, Tee," I summarized, beyond unimpressed

with the place. "Of all the planets in this galaxy, you picked Tatooine."

Goldhaven wasn't exactly Tatooine, but it was close enough in appearance. Predominantly a pale brown mass, there was little sign of water from orbit, though the shadows of the topography suggested that oceans might have once occupied a swath of what looked like sand near the equator. Mingled with gorges where rivers had once flowed, darker smudges of brown and gray, with occasional splotches of green mixed in, indicated once verdant forests that had mostly dried out and died. No matter what Gold-haven had been in the past, it now appeared to be an inhos-pitable desert—bleak and barren.

Hearing my comment, Ben replaced the natural view through the forward transparencies with the zoomed-in feed, revealing the planet to the rest of the crew.

"I told you we should have gone somewhere closer," Alyssa said. "We just wasted two weeks."

"Jump to conclusions, much?" Tyler replied. "I admit, it looks inhospitable, but that doesn't mean we can't get what we came here for."

"The atmosphere seems thin but breathable," Ben said. "Comparable to Earth. We aren't close enough for surface temperature readings, but I'll go out on a limb and guess that it's probably pretty hot."

"What do you think happened here?" Ally asked.

"The system's star is a red giant," Leo said. "It's old, and at the end stage of its life cycle before going supernova. I bet the planet is billions of years old. The climate was prob-ably fine before the star's rise in temperature, but now it's no longer in the Goldilocks zone."

"Seems like that might've happened pretty recently," Tyler said. "There's still evidence of large cities down there."

"Celestial bodies don't do anything quickly. This

process has probably been happening for centuries. If people still live down there, I bet they have underground aquifers or moisture condensers to keep them going. But it can't be all that comfortable unless they live underground. I'd guesstimate they have maybe another thousand years before they'll have no choice but to abandon the planet."

"Sensors aren't reading any other planets or moons nearby," Ben said. "No ships in orbit either, including satellites or debris."

"So you're saying that whoever lives here, they don't have space flight?" Tyler guessed.

"They might not have flight or technology of any kind anymore, but judging from the sizes and configurations of those cities, the civilization here was probably well-developed at one time. And now, who knows what they have left if it's all underground."

"Probably why no one's answering my hails," Alyssa said from the comms station.

"Maybe no one's home at all," I said. "We have no idea if the Warden's data is accurate. It could be totally outdated, or a complete fabrication. This could be a totally dead planet."

"Gee, I can't believe the Warden would lie to us," Tyler announced, his words dripping in sarcasm.

"It does look pretty quiet down there," Ben admitted. "But..." He drew a circle on the feed, around a faint smudge of light spilling westward from the darkened curve of Goldhaven's nightside. "Those look like lights to me."

The thin swath of illumination fringed what I assumed had once been a lake or inland sea. The dim illumination failed to penetrate far past a ridge of towering cliffs fronting dry oceanfront property. Yet that wasn't what grabbed my attention. Instead, I found myself squinting toward the darkness beyond the distant shoreline. If I unfocused my eyes just right, the blackness there seemed to ripple...to almost flow.

What was out there?

"I'm not seeing any other light, but that doesn't mean there aren't other settlements on the far side of the planet," Ben said. "We'll know more when we get closer."

"Are we sure we want to get closer?" Matt asked. "I'm with Noah. This place feels like a bust."

"Luke Skywalker came from Tatooine," Tyler said, defending his pick. "He wasn't a bust. You never know."

"I'm with Tee on this one," Ben said. "There are lights, which means there's intelligent life. Considering we know zero about Warexia or the Warden, even folk tales would be helpful right now. Otherwise, our next pick could be just as bad. Or worse."

"Not if we pick a larger population," Meg said.

"That's not a given," Leo countered. "We could drop into the middle of a war zone or something. Tyler's right. This planet doesn't look like much, but that may not be a bad thing."

"Thank you, Leo," Tee said.

"It can't hurt anything to swing in for a closer look," Matt said, opening the throttle on the main thrusters. I felt the light shift as we gained velocity. The last two weeks had allowed Meg and Leo to repair most of the damage to the ship, including the thruster Head Case had lost to the unidentified ship that attacked us in Earth's orbit. The whole ride felt smoother for it, though it was a subtle change.

Having intentionally come out of hyperspace at a distance from Goldhaven where we couldn't be taken by surprise, we remained quiet and introspective as we burned toward the planet. Soon enough, we were at the natural distance of the original zoom-in.

"Let's see what we've got," Ben said as the PCS shifted

from less accurate long-range sensors to the primary arrays. His fingers tapping on the control board was the only other sound on the flight deck as we waited for the main display to show a satellite view of Goldhaven's northern subcontinent.

It zeroed in on an isolated concentration of crumbling structures tucked into a sheltered cove along the dried-up coastline. Now that we were closer, I could see that nothing but encroaching badlands surrounded three sides of the settlement. Some water still remained of the ocean, though it had receded from the old shoreline by hundreds of feet. Other than the faint glow, little else suggested this lonely outpost hosted any living things.

"Tricky approach for a landing," Matt said. "It's such a treacherous location, I wonder why they settled here."

"I doubt it was so treacherous a few hundred years ago," Ben replied.

"True. How do you want to play this? For all we know, whoever lives here has never seen a spaceship before."

"And they might not be friendly to unidentified visitors," Alyssa added.

Ben turned toward Alyssa and Tyler. "I don't suppose either of you happened to pack a WE COME IN PEACE banner?"

"No, sorry," Tyler replied. "Never got around to packing. Period."

"We did leave in kind of a hurry," Alyssa added, tongue-in-cheek.

"You mean you don't keep banners like that in storage?" I asked, joining in. "You know, for the little green men on Mars."

Ben grinned. "I really should have had Asshole print a couple of those up."

"I doubt whoever is down there can read English," Leo said, apparently missing the nature and point of our banter.

"I'm still not convinced there's anything down there," Meg added. "Those lights could be the remnants of civilization, not proof a civilization still exists."

"Since we aren't getting an answer on the comms and our sensors aren't picking up wireless activity, there's only one way to find out," Ben said. "Matt, take us down, but stay ready to bail if things go south."

"Aye aye, Captain," he replied, guiding Head Case into a gentle descent, angling toward the settlement. We plowed through the thin atmosphere, violet skies giving way to an endless, ugly brown landscape.

"Readings show the surface temperature is close to a hundred and ten degrees Fahrenheit," Ben announced. "Humidity is ten percent."

"Sweater weather," Tyler joked.

"There's a reason no one lives in Death Valley," I added. "I don't suppose you guys have climate controlled underwear?"

"Actually, we do," Matt said. "But let's worry about that later."

I watched the arid wasteland gaining definition as we continued our descent. Goldhaven was nothing like what I had envisioned as our first destination outside the Milky Way. In my daydreams, I'd imagined something picturesque, with all kinds of alien creatures and exotic humanoids in a range of colors, perhaps selling overpriced souvenirs in glistening cities. Of course, that expectation was stupidly naive, but right now even the real Tatooine looked more appealing than this grim proxy.

Our shadow swept in a hurry across the barren landscape, the ragged peaks ahead growing steadily larger in the forward viewport. Matt banked gently, dropping us low over the crumbling stone spires, the deep gorges and sheer cliff faces, clearing one last rise before dropping down over the flat coastline. He cut the throttle considerably, letting friction slow our approach.

Finer details of the settlement emerged as we neared it. Instead of civilized streets and powered structures, we discovered only the remains of what might have once been the city from my daydreams. A pack of animals resembling hairless coyotes lifted their heads from small piles of refuse to look in our direction. There were no immediate signs of life beyond the naked doggos.

"No way sixteen thousand people live here," Tyler groaned as Head Case swept over the settlement at a few thousand feet. "No way anybody lives here," he corrected.

"The Warden's population stats are completely wrong," Alyssa agreed.

"Are we sure this is where civilization should be?" I asked.

"Matt, bring us back around, and find somewhere to land," Ben said.

"Are you sure that's a good idea?" Alyssa asked.

"Not at all," Ben replied. "But we have to work with what we've got."

Matt slowed Head Case even more, making a slow, wide arc over the dwindling ocean to come about on approach to the settlement. "I can put us down there, near the edge of the plateau."

"I feel sorry for the sucker who paid oceanfront prices for such scenic property," Tyler joked about the landing zone. Rubble speckled the area, confirming a structure had stood there at some point in Goldhaven's history. "Oh, crap!" He threw his hand out, pointer finger aiming toward an unseen target.

All eyes followed the line of his finger toward a pair of figures emerging from the blowing dust. Even at a distance their alien nature was obvious. With a height rivaling the Warden's Prall, combined with an awkwardly slight build, it seemed as though we'd stumbled on a society of Slender-men. Rubbery black skin glistened under the harsh sunlight, draping their elongated skulls and apparently naked forms. Their large dark eyes fixed unblinkingly in our direction.

"At least we know now this place isn't abandoned," Ben said.

"No, but they're moving right to where I planned to touch down," Matt answered.

"Maybe they're friendly," Meg suggested without enthu-siasm. "Coming out to greet us."

"Yeah, right," Matt replied, putting the external guns on standby. "We didn't get a chance yet to print out any of those banners."

The comment drew tense laughter from a couple of us. Otherwise, his remark fell flat.

"I'm going down to the armory," Ben announced. "Matt, you're with me. Noah, take the stick."

"You want me to land?" I replied, surprised.

"You don't think you can do it?"

I shook my head. "No, I can do it."

"Good, because I want Matt to meet the natives with me." He tapped his comm badge. "Ixy, meet us in the hangar."

"Yesss, Captainsss," she replied.

"What about us?" Ally asked, motioning to herself and Tyler.

"Wait here," Ben answered.

"Sidelined again?" Tyler questioned. "Come on, man. We've been training for two weeks so we can be useful."

Ben considered before nodding. "If that's what you want, let's go. Noah, you have the stick and the flight deck."

"Aye, Captain."

Tyler grinned as he jumped out of his seat. Alyssa was a

little more restrained, but she rose and hurried to join them as they exited the flight deck. Within seconds, I was alone with Meg and Leo.

"What does that mean, I have the flight deck?" I asked them.

"It means you're in charge," Leo replied. "You get to boss us around."

"That doesn't seem right. You're actual crew. We're just renting the ship."

"Exactly. Which means you have command when the owners aren't around."

"And sometimes when they are," Meg added. "If you read the contract in its entirety."

I swallowed hard. "Uh…I never did."

Meg offered an adorable, spritely chuckle. "You probably should."

"Noted. I'll do a closer read-through once we're out of trouble. If we're ever out of trouble."

"Ben will bend over backwards to make everything right. That's who he is."

Returning my attention to the camera feed in my surround, I noticed that our presence continued to attract attention I wasn't sure we wanted. More elongated forms converged from hovels and rubble piles, massing like an angry mob. They clutched wicked looking spears, though at the moment, their three-fingered hands held them non threateningly. It didn't matter that the spears were ancient technology, I got the distinct impression the mob could shift into a lethal threat within a single breath.

"That's quite the welcome wagon," Leo remarked.

Part of me was grateful Ben had left me behind. As excited as I was to make contact with another alien race, it seemed this one was no less aggressive than the Prall, and I wasn't in the mood to have a hole punched through my chest. Hopefully, these aliens were at least in control of themselves and their decisions.

"Have you guys done anything like this before?" I asked, adjusting the throttle to slow Head Case further, while increasing power to the anti-gravity plates tucked below the hangar bay decking. I could hear their faint throbbing as the ship came to a near-hover a few hundred feet over the aliens' heads.

"You mean make contact with a technologically inferior alien race?" Meg said. "No. This is our first time, too." That didn't make me feel any better. "Don't worry. Ben knows what he's doing," she tacked on after reading my tense expression.

"Noah, do you copy?" Ben said, his voice loud and clear over the comms.

"I copy. What do you need, Captain?"

"Nothing right now. I'm just testing the comms. I'll keep my channel open so you can hear what's happening. If things get ugly, get the ship out of here. Don't get caught, too."

I didn't want to acknowledge Ben's order to abandon them, because then I would feel compelled to follow through. "I'll do what I have to," I replied instead.

"Copy. We're on our way to the hangar. Bring us in for a landing."

"Aye aye, Captain," I replied in the same tone Matt used to affirm commands. "Initiating landing sequence."

"You don't need to say that," Matt said. "Just tell us when we're skids down."

"Right. We're on final approach. Skids down in twenty seconds."

"And try not to crush any locals beneath the ship," Matt added. "That doesn't tend to get relations off on the right foot."

"Ten-four." I adjusted the flight controls, bringing Head

Case ever closer to the arid ground. The aliens had stopped emerging from their shanty town, but there were enough out there that I couldn't easily count them all. Four hundred? Five? Not quite the sixteen thousand the Warden's map had promised, but enough to overwhelm us if things got out of hand.

Then again, how bad could it get when there was no way we each spoke the others' language?

The aliens stopped their advance less than twenty feet from the landing zone, leaving me enough room to safely bring the ship down. Despite their primitive appearance and living conditions, their composed demeanor suggested they had seen spacecraft before.

I focused on the final fifty feet, repeating the motions I had practiced in simulation dozens of times over the last fourteen days. Hand steady on the stick, I reached over and flipped the switch to extend the landing skids, the vibration through the hull confirming the release. A few seconds later, Head Case settled gently on its tripod legs.

"Nice landing," Matt praised through the comms. "I knew you had it in you."

"It's not like I just blew up the Death Star or anything." I replied.

"Still impressive for your first time. Except you forgot to tell us we're skids down."

"You didn't give me a chance," I complained.

"How do the natives look?" Ben asked, waiting to make their appearance.

I eyed the aliens. Three of them had stepped forward, implying they were the leadership. Now that we were so close, I could tell that the rubbery black I took for skin from a distance wasn't skin at all, but a protective covering of some kind, like a wetsuit for the sun. A sunsuit? The skin-hugging material clung to their faces, revealing only their large eyes, while giving no hint as to their male or female gender or even if there was that kind of distinction between them.

"They don't look like they're itching for a fight," I told Ben, noting the aliens with the spears remained back with the rest of the group. "If I had to guess, they seem like they want to talk."

"From your lips to their ears," Ben replied. "Let's hope that's true. Stay ready to launch just in case. With or without us."

I didn't respond this time. In the back of my mind, there was no *without us*. Ally and Tee were here because of me. I would rather die than leave them, not to mention Ben and Matt, behind.

Head Case vibrated a second time as Ben opened the main hangar door. My eyes alternated between the ramp extending to the ground and the alien reps. They didn't change position or posture, including when Ben and company began their descent down the ramp.

Even though my heart beat like a kettle drum, my hands rested solid as a rock on the stick and gravity controls. I remained ready to bounce off the surface at a moment's notice. Ben and the others approached the three alien reps. They came to a stop less than ten feet away from them. I half-expected Ben and Matt to unfurl a WE COME IN PEACE banner despite their claims they didn't have one.

Instead, the two sides stared at one another in silence, each waiting for the other to speak first. It didn't take long for Ben to break the stalemate. "Greetings," he said, his voice clear, his annunciation crisp. As if that would facilitate communication. "My name is Benjamin Murdock. I'm a traveler from a far away star. My friends and I came here by accident. This galaxy is called Warexia, and this planet is named Goldhaven. That's all we know of this place. I really hope you can help us."

None of the aliens reacted. It was no surprise they

didn't understand English. I was curious to see how Ben would manage the language barrier.

He tapped his chest with his hand. "Ben," he said. "Ben." He pointed to Head Case. "Starship." Using hand gestures, he started trying to signal how we had wound up in Warexia by mimicking a crash.

"Enough," the lead alien said. I nearly fell out of my seat when I realized I could understand what sounded, by his voice, like a male. How the hell was that even possible? "You are servants of the Warden," he said.

"The Warden," Ben said, growing excited. "Yes. He attacked our ship. He—"

"If you are servants of the Warden," the alien interrupted, "then you are enemies of the Oron, and you must die."

CHAPTER 33

The spear-carrying Orons advanced, the others stepping aside to make way for them. The leader backed up a step, and with lightning quick reflexes, he reached behind his back, producing a nasty looking knife. The obsidian blade glinted in the sun as he brandished it at Ben.

My hands shifted to the pilot station controls, activating the cannons and aiming them at the gathered aliens. Unless the sunsuits contained hidden shields, one barrage from the guns would end the conflict lickety-split. Even so, I had no intention of squeezing the trigger. Ben had made it clear we never, ever fired the first shot. Self defense was one thing. Murder, something entirely different. Something I was certain I didn't want any part of.

"Wait!" Ben cried, throwing up his hands. "We come in peace! Please!"

I had no doubt he could hear the turrets swiveling into position behind him, and I saw that Matt already had his rifle shouldered, while Tyler and Ally were in the process. Shaq, maintaining the element of surprise, had yet to emerge from his hiding place in Ben's sleeve. Ixy had remained in the hangar, but had already made it halfway down the ramp when she froze in response to Ben's plea.

The cry succeeded in halting the Oron as well. They remained in place, some with their javelin-like spears lowered to charge our away team, others with their weapons raised to throw. Their leader clutched his dagger, his body tensed like a spring waiting to uncoil.

"We aren't servants of the Warden," Ben continued. "We're victims. He attacked us. He attacked our ship. He sent his Pralls on board. We fought them, but we lost. He made us swallow some pills. I don't know what they're for. We came to Goldhaven to try to get as far away from him as we could. We're newcomers to Warexia. We know nothing about it, or about the Warden, except that he seems to be evil. Please, we need your help."

The lead Oron continued glaring at Ben. I figured their reluctance to attack had to be a good sign.

"Everyone, drop your weapons," Ben said to Matt and the others.

"Ben, I—" Matt started to argue.

"Do it."

Matt tossed his rifle down. Tyler and Ally did the same. Ben again locked eyes with the Oron leader, still pleading with him to stand down.

For a moment, I felt certain the Oron would relent. His tension eased slightly. His posture loosened. Movement near the back drew my attention, and I noticed one of the armed Orons at the back of the gathering had finished cocking his arm back, ready to let his weapon take flight.

My finger rested on the trigger. The slightest twitch, and I could have ended the alien's life before he released the weapon. It was one option. The easiest, and safer choice. But it meant killing not just the fighter, but the others around him as well. Instead, I shouted to Ben through the comms. "Captain, watch out!"

The last word was barely out of my mouth as the spear launched in a low, powerful arc toward Ben, its velocity leaving him only a couple of seconds to react. His eyes narrowed when he caught sight of the spear, but he didn't move. I could almost feel him reaching for chaos energy, dragging it through the clogged hose and pushing it out through his body. He didn't glow this time. Maybe he hadn't siphoned enough to become ethereal, but he had enough to yank the spear from the sky, sinking it into the ground between himself and the Oron leader.

Matt was already reaching for his discarded rifle, so Tyler and Ally did the same. They again came to a sudden stop as the Oron unexpectedly fell to their knees, bending forward and planting their faces against the rock in sudden supplication. Their leader didn't go quite that far. He settled for an upright position on his knees, his expression toward Ben one of awe.

"You weave Chaos," he said. "That is…impossible."

"Difficult," Ben answered, wiping a line of sweat from his brow. "But not impossible. Believe me, we're no friends of the Warden. Please, help us. And please, stand up."

The Oron leader regarded Ben for a few more seconds before returning to his feet. He turned to face the other Oron. "On your feet. This is not the Ora Kai. Stand up." They did as he said, returning to their feet. The fighters pointed their spears to the sky, no longer threatening violence.

"Ora Kai?" Ben asked.

The leader pivoted back to Ben. "An ancient prophecy of our people. The coming of one who heralds the new dawn. *They will burn the galaxy with Chaos, and Order will follow.* It is a foolish superstition."

"How do you know he's not the Ora Kai?" Tyler asked, drawing a sharp glare from Ben.

"The Ora Kai is of Warexia. You have said yourself that you are not."

"I'm glad that settles it," Ben said. "How is it you speak our language?"

The leader shook his head. "I do not."

"I can understand you. And you can obviously understand me."

"As a servant of the Warden, you have been granted the gift of tongues. Any language the Warden speaks, you are able to speak and understand."

"I'm pretty sure I'm speaking English right now," Tyler again commented, drawing the same reaction from Ben. "Sorry. Bad habit."

"It is such in your mind, but not on your lips," the Oron answered.

"You said that as servants of the Warden, we need to die," Ben said. "Why?"

"You are Ben," the leader replied, tapping his chest. "I am Ocha, First of the Oron."

"These are my friends, Matt, Tyler, and Alyssa," Ben said, pointing to each in turn. Tyler mimicked Ocha's chest slap, which bothered Ben but seemed to impress the Oron.

"While you are not Ora Kai, I believe your ability to weave Chaos is a sign, perhaps of his imminent coming. You will visit our community. I will answer your questions. Then you will leave, and you will never return."

"Thank you," Ben replied. "We're grateful for your hospitality."

"As you should be. Come."

"Before we go, I have one more person on my ship I'd like to attend," Ben said.

"We will begin walking," Ocha replied. "Your person will catch up." He made a loud gurgling sound, and the other Oron turned away from Head Case, shuffling back toward their hovels.

"Noah, let's go," Ben said. "Tell Leo he has the stick and the flight deck."

"Are you sure?" I asked, barely able to contain my excitement. I was proud to be in charge of Head Case, but I really wanted to be out there with my friends.

"I'm responsible for you being dragged across the universe. You should at least get to experience everything firsthand, once the danger has passed. Leo can handle the ship, and I have the RFD as a fallback."

"On my way," I replied, reaching for the seat's restraint release.

"Don't forget to stand down the guns," Ben added.

"Right." I tapped the controls to disengage the cannons before jumping out of the seat. "Leo, you have the stick. And the flight deck," I called out as I ran to the exit.

A quick trip in the elevator brought me out to the hangar. I nearly fell down the steps to the lower deck in my rush to go outside. I expected the air to be hot, based on the ambient temperature when we touched down, but the atmosphere slipping into the ship didn't have the punch I imagined. Other than that one trip to Japan, I'd never been outside of Iowa. The dry heat brought Arizona to mind.

The Oron were far ahead by the time I hit the ramp, their black drysuits rendering them as retreating ghastly silhouettes in the dusty haze. Thankfully, Matt had lingered halfway between them and Head Case, waiting for me to catch up. I waved to him, hitting the bottom of the ramp and stepping out onto the parched ground. The heat became more noticeable, but the waning light had killed the sun's intensity, and without humidity, the air would cool in a hurry. I paused once my feet hit the dirt, kneeling to touch the ground as my heart thudded with excitement, a million thoughts racing through my head. I was touching alien soil. Another planet. I'd experienced interstellar travel in a robot head spaceship and made contact with an alien race.

Amazing.

"Katzuo, let's go!" Matt shouted, stealing away my brief moment of awe. I straightened and ran toward him. He didn't wait for me, instead keeping distance between both me and the Oron until he had reached the edge of their settlement. I was sweating by the time I caught up to him, only to see he looked unbothered.

"EV underwear?" I asked.

He laughed, tugging the collar of his light green fatigues to reveal a thin, rubbery material beneath, not altogether different from the Oron coverings. "Spiral tech. It'll keep your internal temperature steady as long as the environment isn't too extreme. One-ten is hot, but it's not hell. The material's also bullet, plasma, and energy resistant."

"Like body armor?"

"It is body armor. A second layer that goes under the heavier suits in the armory."

"Why didn't we grab those against the Prall?"

"It would have been useless against the sledgehammers they carried. Come on. Ocha already took Ben and the others inside."

CHAPTER 34

I followed Matt into the settlement, if it even deserved to be called that. The Oron dwellings appeared to be nothing more than holes in the surrounding rubble. The debris came from what I imagined were once grand skyscrapers had been gathered and arranged to disguise the entries while maintaining their natural look of desolation. As when we had landed, there was no sign of the Oron now that they'd returned to hiding. Even the hairless coyotes had vanished.

"They really don't want anyone to know they're here," I said.

"It seems that way," Matt replied. "But then, why the lights?" He pointed to the higher piles of rubble and semi-intact frames of the pulverized architecture. Large spheres of contained illumination perched at regular intervals, beaming out into the darkening sky. "It's totally giving them away."

With everything else going on, I had missed that key detail. It directed my mind to another overlooked fact. "This city didn't fall into drought. It was destroyed."

"Yeah," Matt replied. "I know what the Oron appear to be. But I don't trust it."

I nodded in agreement. "I think that's a wise course. What about Ben?"

"He sees the good in everything and everyone until proven otherwise. In some circumstances, it's a superpower. In others, it's kryptonite."

"I prefer trust but verify."

He tapped the side of his rifle. "Then that puts you right in the middle because I don't trust anything."

"You must balance Ben out really well, then."

Matt laughed. "I would, if he ever listened to me."

"Ben told me he has a brain tumor."

It felt like a strange time to mention his affliction, especially when it hadn't come up during our hyperspace journey. I hadn't promised Ben to keep the secret, but I chose discretion over blabbing about it to Tyler and Ally. Still, Matt and I were having a moment as we traversed the deserted Oron camp. I didn't want to waste it.

"He uses chaos energy to keep it under control," Matt replied. "With how hard it is to access here…" He trailed off. "I've thought about it before. I'm sure he's concerned too. But so far, I don't see any sign the tumor is growing again. I'm sure he's testing himself in sick bay every day. He would tell me if there was a problem."

"If there's anything I can do to help, just let me know."

"Thanks, Noah. I appreciate that. I'm sure Ben does, too. I'm sorry we got you into this mess."

"Are you kidding? Outside of being shot at, this is all so amazing. You know, I wonder what Child Protective Services or the hospital thought when they came looking for me and I was gone. I can only imagine the looks on their faces. Do you think they're trying to find me?"

"With six months to your birthday and plenty of other cases to deal with? No offense, but probably not."

"Good."

We passed through the other side of the settlement

without spotting any of the Oron. If not for Matt, I would have been totally lost, with no idea where Ben and the others had gone. He had either seen where they went or had some way to track them, because he led with confidence until we stood just outside the remains of a large structure near the cliff edge. Despite missing walls and a sagging roof, it was high-end by local standards. Ocha sat cross-legged on the floor—Ben, Tee, and Ally arranged around him—with space for Matt and me to join the group. A second Oron stood behind Ocha, clutching an upright spear. I didn't get the impression the Oron leader lived here. Rather, this seemed to be their official meeting place.

"You will sit," Ocha said to Matt and I. His tone suggested his annoyance at our delay.

I popped a squat next to Tyler, with Matt between me and Ben. Ally was on Ben's left side. Shaq had also emerged from his hiding place and was currently curled around Ben's neck like a scarf. "My apologies," I said to Ocha, more to try out the weird translation than anything. My mind thought in English. My ears heard English. How could we be speaking another language?

"I need no apology. Instead, let us make haste. Because I too once needed help and help was granted to me, so I have agreed to help you. But I do not want you here, both for your sake and for the sake of the Oron."

"I understand," Ben said. "And again, we thank you for your willingness to render aid. The Warden—"

"The Warden," Ocha repeated before Ben could finish the question. "Once, the Oron were strong. An entire world, we called our own. Many starships, we possessed. But from the dawn of our age until its darkest night, the Warden was, and is, and always will be."

"You're saying the Warden is immortal?" Ben asked.

"And more. Before the Oron was the Warden. Before

Warexia was the Warden. There is no Warexia without the Warden."

"You're saying the Warden is a god," Tyler said.

"And more," Ocha again said. "Yet the Warden asks for no sacrifices. The Warden requires no followers. The Warden makes no rules. Yet the Warden's eyes are everywhere. The Warden's hands are on everything. The Warden shapes us. The Warden guides us. The Warden torments us. The Warden destroys us." Ocha trailed off, eyes downcast. "None desire to become servants of the Warden. It is a fate worse than destruction."

"Because things weren't bad enough already, right?" Alyssa said. "We're not even supposed to be here."

"What happened to you?" Ben asked, ignoring Ally's complaint. Right now, we needed data. There would be time to process it all later. "What happened to the Oron?"

"All begins and ends with the Warden," Ocha replied. "The Oron, nearly extinct from the Warden. A civil war. Oron against Oron. Violence. Famine. Death. The Warden commands it. The servants obey. Until the servants do not obey. Until the servants weep. Hidden, until they are forgotten by the Warden. Few are we. Escape. Beg for help. A new home. Goldhaven, already destroyed by the Warden. Goldhaven, where little remains. Goldhaven, forgotten by the Warden."

I swallowed hard in response to his tale, fear pricking my skin like knives as I remembered to exhale. "How long have you been here?" I asked breathlessly.

"No more are the servants. The free Oron only remain. The Warden forgets, but the Warden does not forgive. Difficult is our life in the baking star and the dwindling water. Forever, we cannot remain here. But also, we cannot leave. Only the Ora Kai may set us free. He who makes Order from Chaos. We shall not live to see it."

Ocha lowered his head, his posture heavy with sadness.

"So there's no way to get the Warden off our asses?" Tyler said. "Just freaking great. What about a way to get back to Earth? Do you know anything about that?"

"Of Earth, I know not," Ocha said. "Escape you may, if you are fortunate. If you find a place to hide."

"I don't want to hide," Alyssa said. "I want to go home."

"Do you know which planet belongs to the Warden?" Ben asked. "Which one is his homeworld?"

"All worlds belong to the Warden," Ocha answered.

"But is there one that he returns to, when he isn't flying around in his ship forcing people to do drugs?" Tyler questioned.

"The Warden has no ships."

"Sure he does. Didn't you hear Ben earlier? We were attacked by one of them."

"Of ships, there are none. There is only the Warden."

"I think he's saying the Warden is the ship," Alyssa said.

"That would explain the clones," Matt added. "And his control over the Prall."

"A ship that makes its own crew?" I said. "Or do they only exist to recruit new servants?"

"How do you know the Warden is the ship," Ben asked Ocha, "instead of commanding the ship?"

Ocha didn't answer. He didn't seem to understand the question. "Maybe it's all the same to him," I said.

"It pretty much is all the same," Alyssa agreed. "Who cares if the ship is a god or the god lives on the ship? He's still a malevolent asshole."

"We don't know that he's malevolent," Tyler said.

"What?" Ally screeched. "Are you not paying attention? The Warden destroyed the planet we're standing on. He also made the Oron kill one another. What if he can make us kill people? Or each other!"

"How does anyone force an entire civilization to eat

itself?" Tyler said. "No way. I don't buy it. And we have no proof the Warden was responsible for Goldhaven either."

"So you're calling Ocha a liar?"

"No. Warexia is a big universe. He can't possibly know everything about it, and no offense, but the Oron don't seem like the most advanced society. I'm saying what he believes is true might not be."

"We can't rule it out," Matt agreed.

"Ocha, what do you know about chaos energy?" Ben asked, forging ahead with his questions instead of engaging in arguments that could just as easily happen back on Head Case.

"Legend only. Before the Warden, much Chaos. After the Warden, none."

"Not none," Ben corrected. "But very little. Do you believe the Warden stole it?"

"Perhaps Chaos belongs to the Warden. Perhaps the Warden is Chaos."

I could tell by Ben's face he wasn't sure what to make of the statement. Me either. Based on Ocha's replies, I believed the Warden had done something to the chaos energy. If that was true, then as of right now there was only one way home.

Through the Warden.

We needed another way.

"You will go," Ocha decided suddenly. "You are no longer welcome."

"I have more questions," Ben said.

"You will go."

The Oron behind Ocha stepped forward and banged the end of his spear into the dirt to emphasize Ocha's request.

"Please, two more questions," Ben begged.

Ocha's concealed face shifted slightly beneath his drysuit as he considered the request. I suddenly realized why he hadn't removed the cowl of the suit now that we were out of the elements.

"Two questions. No more," Ocha agreed.

"One, can you recommend a planet where we can learn more about the Warden and Warexia without attracting his attention? A place with a data store or archive, a library, or similar?"

It seemed to me like a much too advanced question for the simple alien. And when Ocha didn't answer right away, I was certain he didn't understand. Until he started to speak.

"Once, the Oron begged for aid. The Oron received aid from the Gemmen. The world of the Gemmen is Nocturne. Seek out the Gemmen, yet understand. Everywhere you go, the Warden will be. Nocturne is no different. You will be quick. And you will be cautious."

Ben nodded. "Thank you. That's more than I hoped for. I don't have another question."

"I do," Matt said. "You're trying so hard to hide out here. What's with the lights? We saw them from space. That's why we came to the surface."

"When the Warden knows, when the Warden comes, the Warden will see not lights. The Warden will see only the Oron. The lights are for the lost. A memory of home. A pleading for forgiveness. A beacon to Ora Kai, so that one day, the Oron will be truly free."

The answer left us in momentarily stunned silence. Ben moved first, pushing himself to his feet. We quickly joined him. "Thank you again, Ocha," he said. "We'll never forget your hospitality in spite of the risk to yourself and your community."

"Hear this," Ocha replied. "Should the servant ignore the Warden, pain will follow. Should the servant please the Warden, great reward awaits. Until it awaits no longer. Now, you will go."

Ben glanced at Matt, nodding his agreement with Ocha's edict before leading us from the meeting place. We walked at a brisk pace, an understood agreement among us to remain silent until we returned to Head Case.

My body shivered in response to all that Ocha had said, my mind still not fully able to come to terms with the kind of trouble we had fallen into. Remembering what Ben had said about the rift only chilled me even more. None of this was an accident. Someone had delivered us to Warexia.

To the Warden.

But who ? And why?

We might as well have tied a big red bow around Head Case that said: HERE WE ARE. COME AND GET US!

Halfway back to the ship, something in Ben's pocket buzzed. His brow crinkled, and he reached for the source of the noise, pulling out what I imagined had to be the RFD. The screen was already active.

The Warden's face filled the frame.

CHAPTER 35

"Ah, there you are," the Warden said, his eyes alight with malevolent mirth. His Cheshire Cat grin sent a shiver down my spine. "I've been looking all over for you. Kudos on making it surprisingly more challenging than I expected. You aren't letting me down so far."

"So glad to hear it," Ben replied flatly.

"Let me see here," the Warden said, glancing down as if checking notes. "Goldhaven. Interesting. Out of all the planets on the map that I provided, why Goldhaven?"

"I think the question is, why not Goldhaven?" Tyler remarked.

The Warden laughed. "Indeed. Why not Goldhaven." His smile vanished instantly. "But really, how did you come to choose it? I'm sure, in part because it allowed you to spend two weeks in FTL, which you rightly assumed would buy you time to repair your ship and avoid my admiring gaze for a short while. But there are plenty of other more populated planets that fit the bill."

"I liked the name," Tyler said. "Simple as that."

The Warden cracked up at that. "I love it. Simple. Straightforward. How are the Oron faring these days?"

I could see Ben attempt to hide his surprise. Ocha had claimed the Warden didn't know they were on the planet. Had he always known, or had us discovering them here revealed them? "I don't know what you're talking about," he lied, turning the RFD in a manner that suggested he was showing the Warden the landscape. "There's nothing here."

"So you landed your ship on a deserted planet? Why?"

"We weren't confident it was deserted."

"You're a terrible liar," the Warden said. I had to agree with him. Ben had the worst poker face in the universe. "Don't get yourself all worked up. I'm sure you spoke to Ocha, and I'm sure he told you that I don't know the Oron are there. But I do know. I've always known. There's a lesson for you and your crew here." He paused dramatically, his voice dropping a few octaves and becoming monstrously threatening. "I know everything." He cracked up again.

Ben gave up trying to cover the truth. "If you knew they were here the whole time, why haven't you destroyed them? Ocha is convinced you will."

"Have you looked around? Goldhaven is in the throes of its own demise, a victim of the end of its star's life. The atmosphere is on the verge of collapse. Its ocean's drying up. What could I possibly do to them that could be worse than a slow, agonizing extinction? To send a ship to blast them all to ash and dust would be a boon, not a curse."

"How can you be so cruel?" Alyssa asked.

"My dear, I have no idea what you mean."

"Seriously? You forced the Oron into a civil war. You destroyed most of their civilization. You did the same to Goldhaven."

"Did you see the number of planets on the star map?"

"Yes, so."

"So, I'm responsible for every inch of Warexia. Thousands of planets. Hundreds of intelligent life forms. Who are you to tell me that I'm cruel? How do you know that the destruction of these two populations didn't save a hundred more?"

"I...I don't," Alyssa admitted. "Did it?"

The Warden shrugged. "Who knows?" He again cracked himself up, proving he had no intention of giving us any hint of where the truth might lie. Somewhere in between his and Ocha's perspectives, if Dad's wisdom was anything to go by. "I'm sure Ocha painted me as a monster. You can't tend a garden without pruning."

"You sent the Achai to attack us purely for entertainment value," I reminded him. "That doesn't spell benevolent god to me."

"Ah, you again," the Warden said. "Noah, whatever will I do with you?" He sighed. "I never claimed to be benevolent or malevolent. If I had to choose a word, I would say indifferent. But I don't have to choose a word. I am what I am. My motivations are mine alone and no concern of yours. I provided you with the necessary path to survive in Warexia. The only question is whether you'll follow it. Which is my purpose for contacting you now. While you've entertained me with your efforts to escape my attention, if only for a short while, I want to see more from you. You've had two weeks to prepare your ship, and you're clearly comfortable making contact with other races. It's time for your first task."

"How can you be bored with us already?" Tyler complained.

"Let's call it a preemptive strike. I don't want you prancing off into FTL for another two weeks and leaving me behind."

By Matt's expression, I had a sense that's exactly what he'd hoped we would have a chance to do.

"You never said we had to stay out of hyperspace," Ben said.

STARSHIP FOR RENT 277

"That's because it's all so much more fun when you think for yourselves. But every action has a reaction. Cause and effect. You reap what you sow. And so, your first task. I want you to deliver a message. The planet and contact are accessible through your ship's log."

"You have an entire universe at your disposal, and you need us to play messenger?" Tyler asked. "What gives?"

"I don't *need* you to play messenger. I *could* deliver it myself. I choose not to. As I said, everything you need is in your ship's log."

"Is there a time limit on this delivery?" I asked.

"An excellent question, but I suppose I should have expected as much. Yes, Noah. There is a time limit. And if you fail to deliver the message within the allotted time, there will be consequences."

"I have an unrelated question," Ben said.

"Then I'll give you an unrelated answer," the Warden replied. "Go on."

"Ocha believes your arrival coincided with the drought of chaos energy in this galaxy. Is that true?"

"If you ever find yourself on Vislsiv, beware the spotted cughra. You have your task. Bye-bye for now."

The RFD's screen went blank.

"What the heck kind of answer was that?" Tyler moaned.

"An unrelated one," I replied, amused by the Warden's response despite myself. "He warned us."

"I hate that guy," Alyssa said.

"So, what do we do now?" I asked.

"Get back to Head Case," Ben answered. "Leave Gold-haven before the Warden can tell the Oron he knows they're hiding here and to kill us if they want to stay alive."

"Can the Warden be that predictable?" Tyler asked, glancing back at them over his shoulder.

"Who knows." Motion from the far end of the settlement drew my attention. A single Oron had emerged from his hole in the rubble. He stood motionless, watching us closely, as if Ben's premonition were already coming true.

"Let's move," Matt said, breaking into a jog toward the ship. Thankfully, we weren't that far away.

"Leo," Ben said. "I want us off the ground as soon as we're all on board."

"Aye, Captain," Leo replied.

A few more Oron spilled into the open. All of them held spears.

"Maybe they're just making sure we leave," Ally guessed.

"I don't think so. Leo, let's go," Ben said, the Oron right behind us as we ran up the ramp leading into Head Case's hangar bay. Remaining just outside the door while the rest of us boarded, Matt opened fire as I crossed the threshold. A quick glance behind me revealed his plasma bolts kicking up the parched earth just in front of the approaching aliens.

"Hold on!" Leo warned us.

Anti-gravity systems vibrated the deck. Matt squeezed off a few more rounds as the ramp started coming up. A spear hit it just before it closed, revealing both the weapon's sharpness and the strength of the thrower when it sank all the way through the metal.

Head Case lurched skyward, hopping back and away like a jackrabbit from a coyote. I activated my magboots just in time to stay on my feet. A couple more spears thunked into the hull before we made enough distance to escape their range. Or perhaps Leo had activated the shields. The main thrusters ignited, rattling the ship even more. Even with dampening and my magboots locked to the deck, the sudden acceleration dumped me on my butt.. Matt grabbed my arm, pulling me up as we climbed up and away from Goldhaven.

"Thanks," I said.

"Anytime."

"Let's head up to the flight deck and see where we're supposed to go next," Ben suggested once the inertia flattened, our escape assured.

"So that's it?" Tyler said. "The Warden says jump, and we jump? No questions asked?"

"I'm not too keen on defying a god," Alyssa replied.

"He's not a god."

"Then what is he?"

"I don't know. I just know he's not a god."

"You heard Ocha," I said. "Ignore the Warden, suffer the consequences. Do as he says, reap the rewards."

"You reap what you sow," Ally agreed, paraphrasing the Warden.

"Until the Warden gets bored with you," Tyler said. "Ocha said that, too. Discarded like an old toy. I bet it's like a video game. Each task gets a little harder until it becomes damn near impossible. Never mind what we do at the end."

"Any video game is beatable," I said.

"Yeah, with save games and retries. I don't think we have that luxury here."

"So you want to defy the Warden to do what? Close your eyes and point at our next destination?"

"No. We should go to Nocturne. Visit the Gemmen. Ocha said they could help."

"Yeah, he also said they helped the Oron escape the Warden, which they obviously haven't. Their usefulness seems limited."

Tyler opened his mouth to continue arguing, but Ben shut him down. "Enough. Both of you. Let's just go see what we're looking at. We don't have enough information about anything yet to make any decisions."

Tyler glowered but remained silent as we followed Ben

into and off the elevator. "Leo, I have the flight deck," he said as we took our seats.

"Aye, Captain. You have the flight deck."

"This gets crazier by the minute, doesn't it?" Meg said.

"Understatement of the year," Tyler mumbled.

"We've dealt with worse," Ben answered.

"Have we?" Matt questioned. "I'm not so sure about that, bro."

"Levi, the Warden said he left some data for us."

"I don't know who the Warden is," Levi replied. "There is no new data within our storage units."

"Of course not," Tyler grumbled.

"We already picked apart the PCS," Meg said. "Both the hardware and the OS. We didn't come across any malicious code, corrupted memory, or unexplained code execution."

"And the hardware showed no signs of tampering," Leo added.

"If Levi is compromised, we don't know how," Meg continued. "And if we can't see it, then Levi can't, either."

"The Warden's seized control of the ship's systems twice already, and you have no idea how?" I asked.

"No," Meg replied. "Believe me, we're not happy about it. We're still trying to figure it out."

"However he's doing it, he said he left us the data we need," Alyssa said. "But Levi just said she doesn't have it."

"Let's assume the Warden told us the truth," Ben said. "The data is there, but in such a way that it isn't obvious to the PCS' algorithms."

"He would have needed to provide a who, what, and where," I said, working the problem from the top down. "Person, place, and message."

"Bingo!" Ben agreed. "The only piece we need right now is place. Levi, bring up the star map."

The map projected at the front of the flight deck, centered on our position.

"Considering the Warden didn't want us disappearing into hyperspace for another two weeks, I think it's relatively safe to assume our destination is within an area of that size or smaller," Ben continued.

"That's still a big area," Meg said.

"Yeah, I'm sure we can narrow it down. Levi, reduce the view to two weeks of hyperspace travel."

The map zoomed in, still leaving us with hundreds of potential destinations including our point of origin, which Levi also highlighted at the edge of the projection.

"Is figuring out where we're supposed to go a puzzle, then?" Tyler asked.

"It wouldn't surprise me," I answered. "Everything seems like a game to the Warden."

"Levi, how many populated systems are within range?" Ben asked.

"Seventy-one," the AI replied, highlighting each of them in blue. Of course, they were scattered all over the map.

We all stared at them. Nobody spoke.

"What now?" Ally asked, first to voice the question on everyone's mind.

"If this is a puzzle, we need to work out the next piece," I said. "Any ideas?"

We passed around a lot of questioning glances without any solid answers. Meanwhile, Head Case punched through Goldhaven's atmosphere. "Captain, should I keep us in orbit, or just fly out into deep space?" Leo asked.

"Don't you mean sail out into deep space?" Tyler asked.

"Are you really going back to that now?" I countered.

Tee shrugged. "Seemed like as good a time as any."

"Going back to what?" Ben questioned, having missed the initial conversation two weeks earlier.

"Let's settle this once and for all," I said. "The ship that fired on us in Earth's orbit before we went through the rift,did it shoot missiles or torpedoes?"

"Torpedoes," Ben replied.

"Missiles," Matt said.

Shaq buzzed what sounded like "torpedoes."

"Hah!" Tyler said. "See?"

"You're just agreeing with Ben," I said to Shaq.

"So?" Shaq replied, to my chagrin.

"Fine. Ixy said missiles. Meg? Leo?"

"We don't want to get involved in this," Meg said.

"We've seen people have this argument before," Leo agreed. "It's destroyed friendships."

"Better to just let it go," Meg finished. "Maybe call them projectiles?"

"But that's so vague," I complained.

"Why does it have to be a binary choice?" Leo asked. "Why can't it be interchangeable?"

"I don't believe we're even having this discussion right now," Ally said. "Of all the dumb things to—"

"Wait," I cried excitedly. "Leo, I think you're onto something."

"I am?"

"Levi, are any of the planetary populations composed solely of ones and zeroes?"

All of the highlights vanished except one. We all stared at it in shock.

"Bingo bango boingo," Ben exclaimed. "Give the kid a prize!"

"How the hell did you do that?" Tyler asked.

"I don't know," I answered, ignoring the wave of heat washing through my cheeks from all the attention. "It just kind of popped into my head."

"I bet you're great at those escape room games," Ally said.

I shrugged. "I'm okay at them."

"Levi, convert the binary to English," Ben said.

"It might not be a name that can be converted to English," Meg warned.

"The binary code translates to Levain," Levi said.

"Le Vain," Tyler repeated in a bad French accent. "Sounds like a bakery."

"Ooh la la," Ally added.

"Interesting name for a contact," Matt agreed. "Like Madonna, or Ye."

"What planet is Levain on?" I asked.

"The name of the planet is Cacitrum. Population 01101100011001010111011001100001011010100101101110." The AI read the binary as individual ones and zeroes, instead of converting it to a count.

"Levi, locate and highlight Nocturne in red," Ben said.

The AI highlighted the Gemmen planet, putting it in the opposite direction from Cacitrum.

"Levi, what's the hyperspace distance from Cacitrum to Nocturne?"

"Eight days, fourteen hours, thirty-one minutes."

"And the distance from our current position to Cacitrum?"

"Five days, twelve hours, forty-nine minutes."

"Too far by a little over three hours," Ally said, surprising me with her quick estimate.

"Why am I not surprised?" Matt said. "Do you think maybe the Warden doesn't want us to pay the Gemmen a visit?"

"He knew the Oron were on Goldhaven," Ben said. "He must know the Gemmen helped them get there. If they were a threat, you'd think he would have dealt with them already."

"I bet it's all part of the game," I said. "We obviously can't visit both locations inside of two weeks."

"Barely," Alyssa said. "Is there any way we can increase our hyperspace velocity?"

"No," Meg answered. "It's not really a matter of velocity, it's compression levels. The equation is logarithmic, which means it would take immensely more power to go even a fraction faster. Three hours might as well be three weeks."

"Unless we can find an impossibly dense power supply in the next two hours and fifty-nine minutes," Leo added.

"I doubt the Oron have anything like that," Matt said.

"So we have to make a choice," Ben said. His eyes shifted from the star map, dancing from me to Tyler to Alyssa. "Or rather, you three need to make a choice."

"What?" the three of us said at once, joined by Matt and Shaq in the question.

"You're renting Head Case. It's your call."

"Nocturne," Tyler said.

"Cacitrum," I simultaneously countered.

"Cacitrum," Ally said.

"Sorry, Tee," I followed up. "You lose."

He thrust his finger at Alyssa. "She doesn't get a vote. She never signed the agreement."

"I'm stuck out here, too," Ally complained. "And I paid for your ticket. I think that earns me a vote."

"Agreed," I said. "At least half a vote, in which case you still lose, Tee."

"You're only agreeing because she voted for Cacitrum," he complained.

"So?" I replied. I heard Shaq's amused buzzing in response to my answer.

"So that's bull," he replied.

"What's bull is picking a fight with an entity that fits certain characteristics of a god," I snapped back. "An entity that pwned us once already. All the Warden asked us to do is deliver a message, not destroy a civilization. This should be an easy call."

"I don't trust the Warden."

"And I do?"

"I also don't like being told what to do. I'm not a freaking delivery boy."

"You are today." I turned to Ben. "Cacitrum."

He gave Tyler a couple of seconds to continue bitching. When he glowered silently instead, Ben nodded.

"Matt, make it so."

CHAPTER 36

The next three days were relatively uneventful. Our training continued, as did our work with the various weapons available in the armory. We even had our first session with the powered armor. Tyler mastered the bulkier suit quickly, while Ally and I struggled to get a feel for the enhanced strength it provided at the cost of overall agility. I mostly preferred the lighter feel of the environmental underlay Matt had shown me on Goldhaven, which offered some protection from plasma, bullets, and blades. My only problem with the base layer was its skin-tight fit. Asshole had nailed it when he called me a scrawny chicken, especially compared to Matt and Tee. The underlay accentuated their muscular builds. It only served to advertise everything I lacked. Even so, Matt stressed the benefits of getting comfortable around one another in the tight-fitting armor, so that we could get over our discomfort in a controlled environment. Not that he had anything to be embarrassed about. While Ally initially felt self-conscious about her body too, it had only taken some positive encouragement from Sensei Matt about the benefits of her athletic build to see her through the crisis. He couldn't do the same for me. I had to solve the equation for myself, and putting the situation in perspective came to the conclusion that I had two choices. Live with it, or do something about it. The training area included free weights and Tyler was happy to start torturing me with them, especially after our disagreement on our next destination.

Finishing my first weight training session, I hit the showers, changed into a pair of sweats and a plain white t-shirt, and headed for my room. Tyler had invited me to watch an action movie with him, but I wasn't in the mood to spend an hour finding something in the datastore we could agree on and two more watching it. Mindless entertainment had its place, but with so much to learn, I felt like I could make better use of my time. Without him around, I lay sprawled on my bed, slab in hand, browsing the technical manual for Matt's hop racer. He'd promised to let me fly it one day, but only if I at least knew the basic maintenance procedures. I knew distraction was part of his motive for the promise, hoping to keep my mind from drifting into dark places. I appreciated the effort, but no matter how hard I stared at the schematics, my thoughts kept drifting back to our bizarre encounters with the Warden, mixed with memory snippets of Mom and Dad.

A knock at the door made me jump. I didn't need to ask who it was. Tyler would just come in. Ben and Matt would use the comms. Ixy would wait for me to exit and sneak up behind me. Meg, Leo, and Shaq tended to keep more to themselves, the twins because they were always busy fixing or fiddling with something, and the Jagger because he was always either with Ben or in Ben's room.

"Levi, open the door," I said, glancing up to find Alyssa hovering in the passageway wearing a sheepish expression. "Hey, Noah. Mind if I come in?"

I sat up, setting the slab aside. "No problem. What's up?"

She entered hesitantly, remaining at the threshold, her

eyes drifting to take in our decor. We'd recently had Asshole make a few posters of video game characters and added RGB lights in strategic places to cast the space in colorful glows. "I just needed someone to talk to. You're the lucky target."

Her tone worried me. We'd all been stretched to our emotional limits over the last couple of weeks, and while I had noticed the strain in her face and behind her eyes—and had checked in on her a few times—she'd always claimed to be okay. Now fatigue shadowed her eyes, and her shoulders sagged beneath some unseen weight.

"I've always got time for a teammate," I said gently before adding, "and a friend. Did you want to talk here or maybe go for a walk?"

"A walk would be great if you don't mind. I know every inch of this ship by now, but at least moving makes me feel like I'm getting somewhere."

I turned off the slab and followed Alyssa from the room. We headed through the lounge unnoticed by Tyler, his gaze fixed on a scene from The Fifth Element. We meandered aimlessly through Head Case's passageways with no particular destination in mind, sticking to the lower decks so as not to discharge the elevator's batteries.

"Sorry if I'm being mopey," she said after a few minutes of silence. "I'm trying to keep it together, I swear. It's just harder some days than others, you know?"

"Believe me, I get it. Some days are definitely harder than others." I thought of my own struggle to maintain composure in the aftermath of my parent's death. Most days I succeeded, but sometimes emotions ambushed me when least expected. "But I'd rather be here than in a foster home or something."

"I wish I had your optimism," she admitted quietly. "You've rolled with all this craziness way better than me or Tyler." She stopped abruptly, turning troubled eyes my way.

"Don't get me wrong, I'm glad one of us is holding it together. It can't have been easy losing your parents right before getting swept halfway across the universe."

"It's been...an adjustment," I hedged, discomfort crawling beneath my skin. Talking about my loss still felt like it would never get any easier. Especially when she and Tyler viewed me as the emotionally strong one. "Honestly, I try not to think about it too much, or I'll fall apart."

"I'm sorry to bring it up. I guess I just...I don't know how you do it. I'm looking for some advice, I suppose."

"How do I do what?"

"Not fall apart. I'm trying, but it's getting harder with every day that goes by. I can't stop thinking about my responsibilities. Kaiju, my bills, my parents. I'm sure they know I'm missing by now." Tears rolled down her cheeks, though her face strained to remain composed. "I know there's a part of you that enjoys all of this, but I'm scared to death we're going to die out here. The Warden is going to kill us."

She lost it completely, falling into my chest and sobbing. We were alone in this part of the ship, out of earshot of anyone else. I had the sense she'd come looking for a shoulder to cry on, someone to comfort her, when she stopped by my room. She just held out until she knew we would be alone.

I took her in my arms. It felt awkward at first, like it had when I walked into the training room in the armor under-lay. But when I stopped making it about the awkwardness and more about her pain, the strangeness of holding her faded away. We'd become friends over the last few weeks. Real friends, not just online gaming teammates, and she needed me.

We stayed like that for a good ten minutes, her tears wetting me through the t-shirt, her nose running onto it, too. I held her close, stroked her hair, and offered soft words of encouragement. I couldn't change the situation. And I understood her upset. I still had responsibilities back home, too. I had no idea if my parents had had a funeral, and if they did, if anyone had come. If the police were looking for me or thought maybe I was dead. If anyone cared to find me. If anyone cared that I had disappeared.

I had to stop myself from traveling that road, or I'd wind up like Ally. Frayed loose ends could unravel me if I let them. I focused on her instead, and eventually the tidal wave of worry, guilt, and frustration subsided to a more gentle lapping at the shores.

"We aren't going to die out here," I said once she'd calmed a bit. I held her by the shoulders and looked into her eyes. "We'll find a way back to Earth. I won't give up until we do. Neither will Ben, Matt, or the others. In the meantime, we continue looking out for one another. That's all we can do. What we have to do."

She nodded, offering a meek smile. "When we first met, I thought of you like a little brother. But the way you handle everything, the maturity you've shown. You're more like a big brother to me now. And I appreciate that."

"I had good teachers," I replied, thinking of my folks.

"I'm sure they were amazing," she agreed. "I'm sorry I never got to meet them. I'm sorry we never really talked offline. I didn't know what I was missing, even with Tee. He's a goof, but he's generally a kind-hearted goof, and it's not like you lived so far away. In any case, I think they would be proud of you."

"I hope so," I replied. "That's what I'm aiming for."

"Well, you're off to a great start."

"Do you want to go back to the lounge, finish off the movie with T-Bone?" I asked.

"Not really," she said, threading her arm through mine. "I'm kind of enjoying our moment, and like I said, Tee can be a bit too eager to lighten the mood sometimes. Do you have any other ideas?"

"I was looking at the technical manual for the hop racer when you knocked. Maybe we can go down to the hangar and see if I can locate the components on the real thing. It's not a party, but—"

"It sounds perfect," she interrupted. "I don't want to be alone, but I don't want a lot of noise either."

We resumed walking in silence, each of us finding our own comfort in the company of the other. Eventually, we reached the hangar deck where Matt's racer sat on the port side, next to where the Hunter's fist was planted. I'd pored eagerly over every byte of data on the sport I could access through the datastore and had picked Matt's brain as much as possible. No amount of study had conveyed the thrill I knew awaited me once he made good on his promise to let me fly her. Imagining the gut-wrenching sensation of popping in and out of hyperspace, through obstacle courses and other challenges served as the best distraction I had.

Kneeling beside the craft, I pointed out various components, explaining their purpose to a semi-attentive Alyssa. She didn't share my enthusiasm for the sport, but she seemed to enjoy how much I enjoyed talking about it. At least up to a point. I was in the middle of explaining the intricacies of the hop timing mechanisms and the importance of an AI trained to the specific pilot when I noticed she had stopped listening and had turned her head away from me.

"Red, are you okay?"

Her eyes snapped back to me. "Huh? Yeah. Sorry, Noah." She pointed to the only shadowy corner in the hangar. "I was just looking at that deck plate."

I followed the direction of her finger. At first, I didn't understand what had caused her such distraction, but the longer I stared, the more I realized that something was off with the deck plate. "Let's check it out."

We went straight to the plate. The light barely penetrated the area, so it wasn't until I leaned over the plating that I realized it was dented in. That didn't seem right considering the location, but I reasoned it could be easily explained away. Maybe it had somehow taken damage during one of Head Case's prior adventures. It could have simply resulted from Meg or Leo dropping a heavy wrench on the deck, but looking closer, a glint of *something* caught my eye.

"Do you see that?" I asked. Normally, only wires, pipes, and other infrastructure hid beneath the grillwork. "There's something down there."

"What do you think it is?" Ally replied. "A dropped screw?"

"I wish I had a flashlight. It looks too big to have fallen through the grating."

"Should we move the plate and get a closer look?"

I figured whatever the object's purpose, it was probably supposed to be there, but some of the life had returned to Ally's sad eyes, and I didn't want to dismiss the therapeutic effect of a good mystery. I tried shoving my fingertips into the narrow crevice between the plates to pry up the damaged one. I didn't stand a chance. "I think we need to call for backup."

She hesitated before nodding. "Go for it."

I tapped my comm badge. "Hey Tee, you done watching your movie?"

"What's up, Noah-san?" Tyler replied. "Don't tell me you need me to tuck you in."

Alyssa snorted. "As if. Get down here to the hangar. We found something and could use your he-man muscles." She smirked over at me. "That is, if you can get off your dead end for five minutes."

Tyler's eye roll was practically audible through the link. "When did you two sneak away without a chaperone? I'm on my way, Your Majesty."

By the time Tyler loped down the stairs from the elevator a couple of minutes later, I'd located a toolkit and retrieved a pair of pry bars. I waved him over impatiently.

"It's about time! Help us move this deck plate."

"I had literally two minutes left in the movie. You wanted me to miss the ending, didn't you?"

"How many times have you seen it?"

"Not the point." Tyler dropped down beside me, eying the object beneath the deck. "What is that?"

"No clue, but the deck plate won't budge without both of us. Take that side," I said, handing him one of the pry bars. We wedged bars under opposite edges of the damaged plate, throwing our combined strength into lifting up the unyielding metal. I gritted my teeth at the strain, glad when the plate finally lifted enough for Alyssa to wiggle her fingers underneath it.

"Almost there! Push harder! Ally, lift!"

Finally, the panel lifted free. I sprawled backward, pry bar slipping from numb fingers. Tyler whooped triumphantly. "Hah! Take that, you dastardly deck plate!"

We gathered on three sides of the open square, looking down at the object nestled among multi-colored wiring. Metal, pill-shaped and a little smaller than a football, the sight sent an immediate dread coursing through me, raising goosebumps and shivering my spine.

"Does anyone else think that looks like the pills the Warden made us swallow?" I asked.

"Sort of," Tyler agreed. "But how would it have gotten down there?"

"Maybe the Prall put it there," Alyssa suggested.

"When did they have the chance? It took us five minutes to lift the panel out of the way and it made a racket. I know those ogres are strong, but I think we would have heard something."

"Maybe the Warden is responsible," I said. "Maybe not. Whatever it is, whoever it belongs to, I could be wrong, but I don't think Ben knows it's here."

"Should we bring it to him?" Ally asked.

"I don't think we should touch it," Tyler answered. "What if it's a bomb set to explode when it's moved or something."

I tapped my badge, fighting to steady my nerves and my voice. Our benign distraction had become something potentially more serious. "Captain, do you have a minute? We found something in the hangar I think you'll want to see."

CHAPTER 37

Ben rushed through the elevator door at the rear of the hangar and trotted down the stairs to the hangar deck, skirting the Hunter's massive form as he hurried toward us. Shaq rode his shoulder, bluish fur standing on end. Apparently, even the Jagger sensed the gravity of our discovery.

"What did you find?" Ben asked breathlessly as he dropped to his knees at the edge of the opening in the deck plating. His eyes widened as he took in the metallic ovoid nestled in the wiring below. "What the hell is that?"

"Obviously, we have no idea," Tyler said. "We just found it under the deck plate. We were kind of hoping you knew it was there."

Ben shook his head. "No. I didn't know it was there. Have you tried moving it?"

"Are you crazy?" Ally retorted. "What if it's a bomb or something?"

"Valid point." Ben's brow crinkled. "It's definitely concerning to find tech like that embedded in the ship without knowing how it works, why it's there, how long it's been there, or who left it." He reached for his comm badge. "Matt, Meg, Leo, are you busy?"

"Not at the moment," Matt responded immediately. Meg replied similarly a few seconds later. "Leo's in the head reading his horoscope," she responded. "What's up?"

Tyler chuckled. Ben didn't break a smile. "The three of you meet me in the hangar ASAP. We've got a mystery on our hands."

A few minutes later, Matt slid down the ladder rail and strolled casually across the deck toward us, the last to arrive. As usual, nothing seemed to faze his perpetually calm attitude. Even the sight of our ominous discovery earned only a raised eyebrow and a low whistle.

"Any theories on the football of doom?" he asked.

"All the markings on it are in another alphabet, and I guess the Warden's translator only works on spoken language. Our best guess is that it's some kind of transmitter." Ben rubbed his jaw contemplatively. "Noah thinks maybe the Warden planted it onboard, which would explain how he's able to track us wherever we go. Only none of us can come up with a plausible idea how it could have gotten it down there without anyone noticing." His eyes shifted to the twins. "Meg? Leo?"

"Don't look at us," Meg replied. "If we dropped something that big into the hangar wiring, we'd remember."

"Is it safe to move?" Matt asked.

"Your guess is as good as ours," Ben answered.

"It isn't connected to anything," Leo said. "I think as long as we lift it gently and without changing its orientation, we should be safe."

"Should be?" Tyler said. "That doesn't inspire confidence."

"I mean, we've been pushing some pretty high-G maneuvers lately, even after the Warden's visit," Matt said. "If nothing's holding that thing down, I bet it's already been tossed like my lunch when Ben flies the ship."

"What?" Ben grumbled. "Do you remember the first time we played *Star Squadron*?"

"Yeah, but I was a different person back then. Point is, all signs point to yes with regards to the football being safe to carry."

"I concur," Leo said.

"Okay," Ben decided. "Matt, you're the jock. It's your ball."

"Meg and Leo are the science geeks," Matt deferred. "They should handle it."

"I'll get a cart," Leo said. "That'll keep it mostly stable while we transfer it to sick bay for analysis." He came out of his crouch and ran back up the stairs to the elevator.

"These lines look familiar," Matt said, leaning in to trace some of the alien writing with the tip of his finger. "I feel like I've seen them somewhere before."

"They resemble sigils," Ben agreed. "That may be why they look familiar to you. But they aren't sigils."

"Maybe," Matt conceded.

Leo returned with the hover cart in no time, guiding it to a stop directly adjacent to the open deck plate. He had arranged some towels in the center, creating a secure nest for the alien egg. "Ready when you are, Boss."

"You should all stand back," Matt said, crouching over the object. "Just in case."

"If that thing blows, we're all dead anyway," Ben replied. "There's only a few inches of steel beneath those wires. That's all that's sitting between us and compressed space."

"Are you trying to scare me more than I already am?" Alyssa asked.

"Sorry," Ben replied. "Matt, do it."

Matt nodded, dropping to a knee and leaning beneath the level of the decking. He gently wrapped both hands around the bottom of the object, interlocking his fingers to ensure his cradle remained tight. Scooping the ovoid like it might be as brittle as an actual bird's egg, he quickly stood and transferred it to the cart, lowering it quickly onto the towels. The flex of his muscles, followed by the sinkage of the towels, indicated the heavy weight of the device.

"The object's secure," Leo announced, allowing all of us to breathe a sigh of relief. Not that any of us felt truly relieved. Not with a discovery of something hidden right under our noses, and who knew for how long it had been there.

An ominous silence settled over the group as we rode the elevator up to Deck Two, our strange cargo secure on the hover cart in the center of the cab. If not for the occasional thrum synchronizing with fluctuations in the onboard reactor, I wouldn't have been surprised if another malfunction in the elevator sigils had somehow caused time to stop. I wasn't the only one. Both Tyler and Alyssa looked equally inpatient during the short ride, eager to either be rid of, away from, or at the very least identify the football's purpose.

"What do we have in sick bay to help us identify this thing?" Ben asked, looking to the twins for answers.

"We can modify the autodoc to run a deeper penetration scan," Leo said.

"That'll at least tell us what's inside," Meg added.

"Like explosives?" Tyler asked.

"Including explosives."

"How long will the modifications take?" Ben questioned.

"A few minutes," Leo said. "We just need to change a few of the system settings through the interface. Our autodocs are older models, the kind that were initially produced as quality control for robot manufacturing, software updated to handle organic machines."

"That's a chilling thought," Ally said.

"That's what we are though, right?" Meg said. "At least, once you take out the soul. Organic machines. We all function the same." She glanced at Ben. "Well, most of us."

I didn't know if she was referring to his ability to channel chaos energy or his brain tumor. Or maybe both. He was both supernatural and malfunctioning at the same time.

Reaching sick bay, Leo guided the cart into the first room, the same one Ben had scanned me in. Matt transferred the football onto the examination chair, careful to keep its position stable, while Meg tapped on the interface, cycling through menus long memorized. We waited with bated breath until she clicked her tongue in satisfaction, again glancing toward Ben. "We should be all set, Captain."

"Run the scan," he replied.

She initiated the autodoc. Multiple appendages shifted from overhead, red and green lasers sweeping over the seat and down to the object. The tools slowed once they made contact, taking their time examining the outer shell while invisible wavelengths pushed deeper into the metal. Multiple windows cluttered with metrics I couldn't decipher overlaid one another on the autodoc's display. Meg's sharp intake of breath hinted at her ability to understand the datastream.

"Figured it out already?" Ally leaned closer, head cocked.

"These readings suggest a self-contained cryostasis system," Meg explained.

"Cryo...you mean whatever's in there is alive?" I eyed the container uneasily. "Alien lifeforms haven't worked out very well for us so far."

"Assuming these readings are accurate."

"Cryostasis requires incredibly precise calibration," Leo protested. "Even minor disruption risks permanent systems failure and biological termination. All the jostling this egg must have been through during our run-in with the Achai probably killed whatever's inside."

"Normally I would agree," Meg admitted. "But look at this." She pointed to data that might as well have been a smiley face for as much as it meant to me. "The inner containment chamber is filled with gel that likely stabilized the system. What's really interesting is that the stasis is only pulling a few watts of power. I've never seen a hibernation system draw such little juice."

The autodoc finished the scan, now showing another screen on the display. This one I could at least begin to understand. A three-dimensional rendering of the object, all of its guts visible in the scan.

"There are two batteries," Meg said, pointing to spheres at either end of the football. "One is depleted. The other charged to eighty percent. Leo, do the math."

"What math?" he asked.

"The battery size divided by power draw, Leodiot. That'll give us an estimate on how long the object has been running on internal power."

"Oh. Sure." He stared at the screen. "About fourteen years."

"Wait, what?" Ben said.

"Sorry, no. That's wrong. I forgot the drain on the second battery. Sixteen to eighteen years."

"That's almost as long as Head Case has existed," Ben said. "There's no way it's been hiding down here that entire time."

"Why not? When have we ever looked under the deck plating in the back corner?" Matt asked. "There's hardly any light back there."

"That's the hibernation chamber," Meg said, pointing to an apparently open cavity in the center.

"It's tiny," I said. "What the heck could fit in there?"

"Looks empty to me, man," Tyler said.

"We need to dial in the resolution," Meg explained, returning to the settings screen. She changed some variables and re-initiated the scan. I could hardly breathe, pulse pounding in excited anticipation of glimpsing the capsule's mysterious occupant. Beside me, Alyssa tapped her foot impatiently. A form finally took shape within the cavity, small enough to easily fit inside my palm.

Everyone gathered closer, staring at the entity.

"Gross!" Ally grimaced at the image. "Is that some kind of mutant squid?"

I shared her assessment. The diminutive alien appeared to have a bi-lobed body with numerous tendrils that it had wrapped around itself. Despite its initially grotesque appearance, I found its delicate nature appealing.

"There's our little stowaway," Tyler quipped. "Someone smuggled an intergalactic jellyfish on board."

"No," Ben said. "It can't be…" He trailed off, his nervous response suggesting he recognized the creature. "Meg, can you get a composition analysis out of the autodoc?"

"Let's not get ahead of ourselves, Ben," Matt warned. "Remember what you said about the external markings? Just because it looks like something familiar, that doesn't mean it is."

"Yeah," he agreed. "I'm with you. But what if it is what it looks like? Meg?"

"Working on it," she replied, entering the system's command line and entering instructions that weren't in the user interface. "I should be able to extract what we need, but it might take a while."

"I don't have anywhere else to be right now," Ben replied. "The rest of you are free to continue whatever it was you were doing before we found the container."

"I'm not going anywhere," I said, enjoying the mystery.

"Me either," Alyssa agreed.

"My movie just finished. I might as well hang out with you guys," Tyler said. "I can go to the galley and grab us some pizza, if you want?"

"We need to keep sick bay clean," Matt said. "But thanks for the offer, Tee."

"What do you think that is inside, Captain?" Alyssa asked.

"Let's worry about that if I'm right," he replied.

"Is it a good thing or a bad thing if you're right?" I questioned.

"Honestly, I'm not sure."

"While we're waiting, maybe we can match the external markings to a known alphabet," Leo suggested. "Considering the age of the capsule, it must have come from the Spiral. Meg, can you shoot a trace of the engravings over to Levi for processing?"

She sighed, leaving the terminal to enter a different set of screens and carry out his request. "Done."

"Levi, match the capsule engraving to known alphanumerics used across the Spiral," Leo said.

"Processing. Standby," the AI replied.

We were left waiting impatiently once more, tension and excitement building. I expected Tyler to drop another quip or crack a joke, but he remained strangely quiet, as intrigued by the find as the rest of us. Levi won the race to provide the first answers.

"I have compared the engraving to every alphabet, iconography, and related character usage stored in our database," the computer announced. "The symbols appear to be unique, but most closely match ancient Hiberian."

"I've never heard of the Hiberians," Leo said. "Are you sure?"

"There is a ninety-six percent probability my deduction

is correct. The marking roughly translates to Asmarin Klatamin Gruck."

"That's not English," Tyler said.

"Obviously," Alyssa huffed.

"Levi, that can't be an accurate translation," Ben said. "It's gibberish."

"I am ninety-six percent certain it is Hiberian."

"Where in the Spiral is Hiberia?" Matt asked.

"I can project the location on the flight deck or in the conference room. There are no projection systems in sick bay."

"I'll go up to the flight deck to check it out," Matt said. "Levi, project the Spiral star map there, with Hiberia highlighted."

"Projecting."

Matt hurried out of sick bay. The door had just closed behind him when Meg finished her work.

"Okay, I'm running an analysis against our dataset of known organisms," she said. The screen showed the organic composition of the hibernating organism on one side, a flow of known DNA patterns flipping past on the other in rapid succession. It surprised me how many different life forms Head Case had such intricate data for.

"I feel like I'm in a Vegas casino," Tyler said in response to the visual.

"You're too young to have been to a casino," Ally replied.

"I've seen Ocean's Eleven," he answered. "Luck be a lady. Give us something good, not some kind of super human-devouring tentacle monster."

The images finally stopped cycling, pausing on one. At the same moment, Matt burst back into the room.

"Ben, Hiberia is the original name of the planet Demitrus," he said, his voice tight.

"It's a match," Meg said, her voice equally tense. "There's an Aleal inside."

Ben's face paled. His eyes narrowed. I couldn't tell if he was excited or angry or both.

"Alter," he whispered.

CHAPTER 38

"We need to get Alter out of that thing," Ben said eagerly.

"Whoa! Hold on there, bro," Matt countered. "Let's not be too quick to open that can of worms. If that thing's an Aleal, we're better off dumping it out of an airlock and forgetting we ever found it."

"But it may be Alter," Ben insisted. "An earlier version, before—"

"As far as we know, there is no before version," Matt said. "And even if there was a before, we can't trust that before is really before."

Their conversation sounded like gibberish to me, and judging by Tyler and Ally's faces, it sounded the same to them. Meg and Leo were kind of caught in the middle, giving me a sense that they had no idea how to react to the discovery. Only that they had knowledge of the species, and it definitely wasn't all sunshine and roses.

"What's an Aleal?" I asked, interrupting another back-and-forth between Matt and Ben.

"An alien race," Matt answered. "That thing you see inside the capsule isn't an individual organism, even though it looks like one. It's a colony of self-sustaining single-celled organisms with a shared intellect and memory."

"That's so cool," Tyler said.

"Not as cool as you might think," Matt continued. "The Aleal aren't intelligent life forms."

"Yes, they are," Ben countered.

"Come on," Matt complained. "You know as well as I do, the Aleal aren't spacefaring, and they don't have an intellect of their own. Not in the traditional sense. They gain intelligence, personality, and memory by absorbing it from others."

"That still sounds pretty cool," Tyler insisted.

"They have to devour the creature in the process. I've seen the end result, it's disgusting."

"It's not their fault," Ben said. "That's how they're designed."

"It's not influenza's fault it's designed the way it is either," Matt argued. "That doesn't mean anyone wants it around."

"I'm really confused," Alyssa said.

"Me, too," I agreed.

"It's too long a story to get into now. The point is, Aleal are dangerous and unpredictable. They can mimic anyone they absorb, and there's no way to know their true motivations."

"I take it Alter was an Aleal?" I guessed. "And she broke your heart, Captain?"

"Aleal don't have genders," Meg said. "They are whatever they're mimicking. But what you see in the scan is what we understand to be a protective state outside of their natural environment."

"We all nearly died because of an Aleal," Matt said. "I'm not too eager to risk that happening again. That one's in hibernation. It won't know the difference if we jettison it from the ship."

"The capsule came from Demitrus," Ben said. "Alter may have severed part of herself to preserve a copy, and then left it on Head Case for someone to find."

"One, that would have been long before it ever knew you existed," Matt argued. "Two, you don't know how or why it was left here. Three, even if it is a copy of Alter, Alter was very different back then. You're letting your sentimentality get the best of you, Ben. And this is the absolute worst time for that. You said it's my ball, right? We all know we need to punt it out an airlock."

Ben glared at Matt but didn't continue arguing. He didn't seem to be able to bring himself to verbally agree with Matt's suggestion.

"How can that thing be dangerous?" I asked, looking at the scan. "It's so little."

"It seems harmless enough until it's attached to your face, sucking your brains out through your nose," Leo said.

"Ewww, seriously?" Ally said.

"It's worse than that," Matt confirmed. "At least for a human-sized colony." He looked at Ben again. "I'm taking it back to the hangar bay and getting rid of it."

Defeated, Ben nodded.

"It's just too risky," Matt added, laying his hand on Ben's shoulder. "I'm sorry."

Ben nodded again. It was obvious Matt hated hurting his friend this way, but what choice did he have? We couldn't afford a brain-eating alien running amok on the ship.

"Uh, guys?" Tyler said, getting our attention. He pointed at the capsule, which had started emitting mist from its opening seals. "I think it's hatching."

The capsule halves split open, the ice surrounding the chamber evaporating more quickly and bathing the immediate area in fog. Several tendrils writhed languidly upward through the hazy air, their delicate tips curling as if tasting the atmosphere. Beside me, Matt reached for one of the nearby cabinets, searching for something to use as a weapon. Or at least a vessel to contain the creature.

Ben had stiffened, staring at the emerging Aleal. If push came to shove, would he exhaust himself to use chaos energy against the diminutive threat? In the back of my mind, I hoped this tiny alien wasn't what Matt claimed. It seemed so helpless, so harmless, though Shaq had already proven size didn't matter when it came to how deadly a creature could be.

The Aleal's body appeared over the top of the capsule, pulled up by its tendrils, which continued writhing in the air above it. The melting ice haze had dissipated, leaving the little squiddy in full view. It turned slowly as if taking us in without any outward sign of eyes, ears, or mouth. What did it use to sense and understand the world?

Matt retrieved a scalpel from the cabinet, turning it on the Aleal.

"Matt, wait!" Ben cried.

Too late. Matt lunged at the alien, which slipped aside before wrapping its tentacles around his throat and beginning to pull itself toward his face. Matt managed to get his hand up before the Aleal reached his nose, blocking its access to his nasal cavity. It reacted by dragging a barbed tentacle across his face, drawing blood.

Ally cried out in terror. Ben stared in tense shock. Brow furrowed, it seemed as though he wanted to access chaos energy but couldn't get his mind in the right state to succeed. Meanwhile, the Aleal released itself from Matt as he tried to stab it with the scalpel, propelling itself from him to Tyler, tendrils quickly carrying it up his arm toward his face.

"Help!" Tyler cried, trying to shake it off before attempting to knock it off with his free hand. It stretched out a tentacle, and Tyler cried out in pain as the Aleal caught his wrist, its barbs digging painfully into his skin.

"Stop it!" I shouted without thinking. "We're not your enemies. We aren't going to hurt you."

I didn't expect much to come of my pathetic orders. Incredibly the alien hesitated, its body tilting toward me before it seemed to relax. Its tendril fell away from Tyler's wrist. The tendrils on his arm followed. Still reacting rather than thinking, I put my hand out toward the Aleal. It gathered itself and jumped the gap, landing smoothly in my palm. It hunkered down there, wrapping its tendrils back around itself.

"Matt, are you okay?" Meg asked.

He had a long laceration spilling blood down his cheek. It dripped off his chin to his shirt, but it was nothing a few stitches wouldn't fix. He glared at the Aleal in my hand. "I'll be fine. Noah, we have to—"

"No," I replied, cupping my other hand over the creature. "I just promised it we wouldn't hurt it."

"Noah," Ben said. "Matt's right. It's too risky. It already attacked us."

"It probably heard you saying you wanted to toss it out of the airlock," I replied. "Maybe that's why it opened the capsule."

"How do you know *it* opened the capsule?" Meg asked.

"I don't. It's just a guess. How do you know it didn't? Anyway, it seems to me that Matt made the first move. What happened to not firing unless fired upon?"

"You don't understand," Matt said.

"You're right, I don't."

"We didn't realize your rules were only applicable when it suited you," Alyssa said, jumping to my defense. "The way I see it, we're renting the ship from you. So this is our call. Or does that also only apply when you're otherwise indifferent?"

Matt's jaw clenched in frustration. Ben laughed softly. "She's got you there," he said.

"This is a mistake," Matt said. "Noah, please listen to reason, before you get us all killed."

I lifted my hand away, revealing the terrified alien colony beneath. "I can't believe you're frightened of this. My vote's to let it stay."

"Mine too," Ally said. "Tee?"

His wrist and throat both sported bleeding cuts, though they looked relatively superficial. "It seems pretty dangerous to me," he said. "That might be something we can use against the Warden, if or when the time comes. It seems to like Noah-san. I think we should keep it."

Matt exhaled a harsh breath, shaking his head. "Fine. Because you obviously know better than the people who have been through this before. This is the part where I would normally storm down to sickbay and have the autodoc stitch me up. Since we're already in sickbay, maybe the rest of you can leave, and take that thing with you." His angry eyes turned my way. "Just remember, Noah. An Aleal isn't a pet."

"I get it," I replied.

"No, you really don't. But I hope you do before it's too late."

He turned his back on me. We slowly filed out of sick bay, leaving him to fix his face.

"Don't worry about Matt," Ben said. "I'll circle back and talk to him. He'll be fine. He doesn't hold grudges."

"Do you think I'm doing the right thing?" I asked.

"You have a good, compassionate heart, Noah. Keep following that, and at least you'll know you were always true to yourself, right or wrong."

The answer made it clear that despite his misgivings about air-locking the Aleal, he still believed it to be the most prudent course of action. He also clearly understood why I couldn't agree to the same.

I didn't mind. I believed in myself, and I knew what my parents would think of my decision.

That would have to be good enough.

CHAPTER 39

The Aleal rode my palm back to my quarters without complaint. Alyssa and Tyler crowded close on either side, their shared glances betraying emotions oscillating between curiosity and apprehension. My courage began failing with every step. Maybe I'd gone too far. Matt clearly worried that this tiny organism was a huge risk. His experience with the species dwarfed mine. But even if justified, ruthlessly flushing the Aleal into compressed space where it would be obliterated seemed cruel.

I cupped my free hand over the Aleal as the door to my quarters slid open. Ally came in with us, and Tyler locked it immediately behind us to ensure the little alien couldn't escape. I crossed to our shared desk in the corner, where Tyler had left a food container. "You can rest in here for now," I said, gently tipping the alien toward its new nest. It seemed reluctant to leave my hand, still clinging to me like a frightened child.

"Looks like you're its safe place," Alyssa said.

"You can't ride around in my hand forever," I said gently to the Aleal. "I need it back. You're safe here."

It stretched a tendril out to the container, feeling the

edge and checking it for signs of danger before gripping on and launching itself into the enclosed space, where it cowered on the bottom. Wondering if it would prefer somewhere to hide more fully, I grabbed a few tissues from a box on the desk and stuffed them in the corners, laying a couple on top of the alien. It reacted positively, tendrils grabbing the paper and pulling it around itself until it was nearly invisible.

"That's right," I said. "There you go." Once secured, I turned my worried eyes on my companions.

"Are you having second thoughts?" Alyssa asked, reading my concern.

"Yeah, kind of," I admitted, keeping my voice low so it wouldn't startle the Aleal. "Not because I don't want it here. But...what if Matt's right? What if I'm putting everyone in danger by letting my heart overrule my head?"

"Does your heart actually believe this little jellybean means us harm?" Tyler scoffed.

"Asks the guy with the ring of dried blood around his wrist," I answered.

"Which should only serve to emphasize my point. I'm not holding it against the little booger. It's obviously scared."

"It's not about what I believe. It attacked Matt pretty viciously for something so small."

"Only because Matt threatened it first," Ally defended. "From the Aleal's perspective, a giant creature lunged at it with a weapon."

"Again, it was scared," Tyler insisted. His defense of the creature didn't surprise me. Ben thought I had a kind heart, but Tyler had the softest heart of us all, though he'd never outwardly admit it.

"Matt knows these things way better than any of us," I argued, seeking to justify my decision. "If there's any risk, shouldn't we play it safe?"

We fell into an uneasy silence. We had no idea what we were dealing with here, only that it seemed innocent and harmless. Matt was unequivocally convinced otherwise. I peered into the makeshift nest. The tissue wad shuddered as the Aleal shivered out of sight.

"Nice job, man. Now it's even more terrified," Tyler said. "I think maybe it senses our feelings toward it."

"We haven't exactly made it feel welcome." Ally gently pushed my shoulder. "It likes you the best. Say something reassuring."

I leaned close without crowding its sanctuary. "I promise Tyler, Alyssa and I won't let anyone hurt you. I know Matt seems scary, but his bark is worse than his bite. Well, usually." I forced an awkward laugh. "You're among friends here as long as you promise not to...you know...eat our brains or anything."

Its trembling eased marginally in response to my lame apology. A single tendril unfurled, curling almost in question. Taking that as a positive sign, I smiled encouragement and slowly extended a hand. The appendage brushed my fingertips, wrapping loosely around my thumb. A sensation similar to pins and needles tingled up my arm.

"Is it shocking you?" Alyssa asked nervously.

I grinned wider. "More like it tickles. I think everything's okay now."

I glanced around the room, considering options to make the Aleal more comfortable. My eyes landed on an extra blanket I had cast off the bed because it left me too hot. Grabbing it from the floor between the bed and Tyler's mat, I shoved it into the corner next to the desk, bunching it so that it had plenty of folds and wrinkles for the Aleal to hide in. "Let's give this a try instead," I said to it. "You'll have a bit more space here, and more freedom to move around. And it'll keep you warm."

The alien pushed the tissues aside and climbed out onto

my offered hand. Before I could lower it toward the blanket, it sprang away from me, landing and quickly vanishing into the blanket's wrinkles.

Alyssa's face softened, residual doubt fading behind a smile. "Aww, it seems much happier now! We should give it a name."

I studied our diminutive guest. "I think it's too soon to give it a name. We need to see more of its personality."

"Maybe it already has a name," Tyler replied. "It seems to understand English. I wonder if it can talk?"

"I think it would have spoken already if it could," I countered.

"I didn't see a mouth anywhere," Alyssa agreed.

"Or ears, or a nose, or eyes," Tyler added. "But it still manages to locate itself. And lack of a mouth doesn't mean it can't make sound. Crickets, anyone?"

"I still think it would have by now if it could," I repeated.

Tyler shrugged. "Maybe. I'm just going to call it Squidworth until you come up with something better."

"I was thinking of Alfonse," Alyssa said. "Alfonse the Aleal."

"That's terrible," Tyler said.

"Seconded," I agreed. "Not that Squidworth is any better."

"Admiral Ackbar?" Tyler offered.

"He's more like a fish," Ally said.

"Squidoo, Squiddie, Squid game," Tyler rapid-fired.

"That's like saying you should be named Mandoo, or Humany or something," I countered. "Matt was right about that much. It's not a pet. But hopefully a friend."

"Fine, we can drop the name thing for now," Tyler said. "I'm too hungry to come up with anything good, anyway. Anyone else up for some grub?"

Alyssa's stomach growled loudly before she could respond, sparking soft laughter.

"I could eat," I admitted.

Several of the Aleal's appendages perked up at the mention of food. It abandoned the sanctuary of its blanket, climbing to the surface of the desk.

"Well, you're definitely hungry," I said. Uncertainty quickly replaced my flash of good humor. "But what do you even eat?"

Its body tilted toward me, tendrils wavering expectantly.

"I don't think Asshole has a receipt for brains in its data-banks," Tyler said. We exchanged uneasy glances. I wasn't thrilled by the notion of what it might take to satisfy our guest's appetite. For all we knew, nothing but living brain tissue might suit.

The thought sparked an idea. "Hang tight, I'll be right back," I told the others.

"You're going to leave us alone with it?" Alyssa asked.

"It's obviously hungry. I doubt it's waiting for me to leave before eating your brains." I looked at the Aleal. "Right, bud?"

It vanished back into the blanket, suggesting it would stay out of sight until I returned.

"If it did want to eat someone's brain, I think yours is the best choice," Tyler said.

"Shut up," Ally replied with an amused glare.

"I'll be right back," I repeated before practically sprinting from the room. A couple of minutes later I exited the elevator on Deck Five, gaping at the sprawling master-piece of webbing completely enshrouding the forward bulkhead. There was no sign of Ixy within the strands.

"Ixy?" My query echoed unanswered through the gloom. "Are you here? I need your help." I sensed Ixy's dark bulk descending behind me with predatory silence, accompanied by an inquisitive trill. I flinched despite expecting her amused attempt to scare me witless. "Damn it, Ixy! Even when I'm expecting it, you still get me to jump."

She chittered in amusement. "Greetingsss Noahsss." One deadly limb reached past my shoulder, delicately caressing crystalline strands. "Likesss web?"

I nodded my appreciation. "It's incredible. You're very talented."

She plucked the line, sending shivers across the entirety of the construction. Somberness drifted into her tone. "Websss remindsss me of homesss."

"Do you miss your planet?" I asked.

"Yesss. And noessss. Likessss Bensss. Likesss Noahsss. But sometimessss lonelinesss."

"You can come down and hang out with us whenever you'd like. You don't need to hide up here all the time."

"Not hidingsss. Feedingsss."

I only noticed the half-dozen cocoon-wrapped packages on the deck amidst her web after she mentioned it. I tried to disguise my sense of disgust, but her clattering laughter suggested I'd failed miserably.

"That's actually kind of the reason I came looking for you," I said. "I don't know how much you keep up with current events, but Ally and I found a capsule under the deck plating in the hangar. It turned out there was an Aleal inside."

"Alealsss?' She replied, surprised. "Altersss?"

"No, I don't think so. It's a tiny one, like a blob with tendrils. Matt said Aleal only eat brains, but I figured since you probably knew Alter and you're more of a carnivore that you might have a better idea of what we should feed it. I'm sorry if that comes across like you're some kind of monster or animal or something."

She clattered amusement in response to my awkward apology. "It'sss okay. I havesss what you needsss."

"You do?"

"Yesss. Alterssss and I atesss the samesss."

"That's great!" I exclaimed excitedly. "I'm so glad I came to you first."

"Yesss."

She skittered into her web, deftly maneuvering through the strands and scooping one of the cocoons off the deck. She returned with it clutched in her pedipalps, holding it out to me. "Thisss should do the trickssss."

"What is it?" I asked.

"Ratsss. Bensss letsss them on boardsss for me to eatsss. Aleal can eatsss."

I didn't ask her if that meant the rat was still alive under the webbing. In this case, ignorance was bliss. I held out my hands to accept the macabre gift. Ixy passed it over, the outer webbing slightly tacky. "Thanks, Ixy. You're a life-saver. Let's just hope the little space slug didn't decide to eat Alyssa's brains while I was gone."

Ixy clattered in laughter again. "Good lucksss."

My quarters had never seemed so far away. What kind of madness had I invited by sheltering the Aleal, that I was carrying a gift-wrapped rat down for it to devour? And why hadn't anyone mentioned the rats before now? There had to be rules against vermin on starships, didn't there? But then, rats had been present on sailing ships from day one. Why not starships? Ixy kept the rats down on Head Case just like cats did on sailing ships.

I had joked with Ixy about the Aleal attacking Alyssa while I was gone, but Matt's conviction over the alien's threat sent a wave of doubt and dread through me as I exited the elevator. What if my friends lay bleeding out, their lives and brains forfeit to the Aleal's appetite? Grisly fates assailed my wild imagination during the seconds I spent navigating the lounge and dashing up the steps. It seemed ridiculous. A side-effect of hunger and exhaustion.

Still, I threw open the door prepared for anything.

Anything except both Tyler and Alyssa strewn across my bed, gentle snores serving as proof of life. The Aleal was nowhere to be seen. My breath caught nervously until a tiny tendril poked from beneath my pillow. It had moved closer to the pair when they conked out while waiting for me, overcoming its fear to seek comfort in companionship. How could Matt be so worried about something that wanted to be near people like that? I decided with finality that despite any past history with an Aleal, he had to be wrong about this one.

"I've got a treat for you," I said, holding up the cocoon for the Aleal to see. Its tendrils perked up, as if it already knew what lay beneath the arachnid mummification.

My voice woke Ally, who bolted upright when she saw the little guy near her head. Her screech frightened it back under the pillow while also waking Tyler.

"Huh? What's going on?" He growled, head whipping back and forth in search of the threat. "Do I still have my brain?" He clutched at his head.

"You never had a brain," I replied. "It's okay. I've got something for the Aleal to eat."

"What is that, and where did you get it?"

"It's a rat. Ixy gave it to me. Apparently, Ben lets them run around parts of Head Case so she can catch and eat them. Now our new friend can eat, too."

"Gross," Alyssa said.

"Yet fortuitous," Tyler added. "Did she jump scare you?"

"Does she ever not jump scare me? I think she practices her attack moves on us." We all shared a laugh at the Xixitl's favorite pastime.

"It's okay, bud," I said to the Aleal. "They were just startled awake. I'm going to put the takeout under your blanket." I lifted the bottom of it and stuck the cocoon beneath. No sooner had I hidden the package than the Aleal crawled across the bed and jumped to its hideaway, going after the morsel underneath. Thankfully, whatever it did to feed didn't make any sound.

"I don't know if I'm more tired or more hungry," Alyssa said.

"More hungry," Tyler decided. "Let's go eat."

"I'm going to sleep now," I said. "You two go on without me."

"I think I'll hit the sack, too," Alyssa said. "I can barely keep my eyes open."

"How is it, sharing a bed with Meg?" Tyler asked, wiggling his eyebrows suggestively.

"Get your mind out of the gutter, T-bone," she snapped angrily in reply.

"You could have put a mat on the floor like I did," Tyler said in defense.

"Yeah, because that looks so comfortable," she hissed, rolling her eyes. "Meg's been so busy fixing Head Case, she's hardly ever there. When she is, I don't even know it until I wake up and she's in the bed next to me. And, she told me I can redecorate however I want. But the pink is growing on me. Anyway, we get along pretty well, so it's all good."

Tyler slid off the bed. "Well, you two enjoy your slumber. I'm going to have Asshole make me a huge plate of nachos and start rewatching phase one of the MCU. Toodles." He wiggled his eyebrows at Ally again before slipping out of the room.

"What a day," Ally said once he had gone. "Have a good night, Noah. Thanks again for being there for me, earlier."

"Any time," I replied.

She stood, her eyes drifting to the Aleal's new nest. "Goodnight, Alfonse."

"Please don't call it that," I said.

She laughed, offering a wave before following Tyler out of the room.

Fear and adrenaline subsiding, my eyelids abruptly felt leaden. It *had* been a long day. Hopefully, everything would make more sense in the morning. My adventurous optimism returned. Nothing had killed us yet, not even a ravenous, carnivorous alien. That had to count for something.

I stretched out on my bed, beyond caring I was fully dressed. My eyes slipped closed. Almost immediately, I felt a slight shift on the bed. Opening one eye, I watched the Aleal approach from my feet. It seemed slightly larger than it had before, its previously translucent innards were tinged with red. I did my best not to think about the processes leading to the discoloration, instead monitoring its advance toward my head. I wasn't afraid, so much so that I closed my eyes again as it reached my neck.

The Aleal nuzzled my jaw, tendrils twining loosely around my neck like a living scarf. Any lingering question about its intentions evaporated. Comforted by the closeness of an unlikely new companion, I drifted off to sleep.

CHAPTER 40

None of us knew what to expect when we reached Cacitrum. We had no idea what this planet would even look like.

I gazed at the forward transparency in anticipation, my heart pounding in tense excitement, my stomach—stuffed with butterflies—churning nervously as Head Case emerged from its hyperspace compression field.

"Shields up, weapons hot," Matt said, frosty as usual while entering the unknown. We had to be ready for anything, including an immediate fight.

The curve of space regained its infinite flatness as the hyperdrive disengaged and the stars expanded away from us. Instead of a field of black, the space ahead of us bustled with activity.

"Whoa, look at that traffic!" Tyler exclaimed. "This definitely ain't Cedar Rapids."

"Or Goldhaven," Alyssa murmured appreciatively. "So many ships coming and going. It's like JFK at rush hour."

Hundreds upon hundreds of vessels swarmed around an Earth-like world, ranging from small personal craft barely larger than Matt's hop racer to titanic dreadnoughts that dwarfed even the largest craft in Earth's collective navies.

"When did you ever visit New York?" Tyler asked.

"I went to New York City with three friends after high school graduation," she explained. "We did Broadway, the Statue of Liberty, all the good stuff."

"I didn't know nerdy gamer girl had any real-life friends."

Her mood soured slightly. "Yeah. We kind of drifted apart after that trip. They went off to college, and I... didn't."

I toggled magnification on my surround display, zooming in for a better look at the planet. Brilliant white clouds swirled across emerald continents and sapphire oceans, speckled with the tell-tale silver gleam of several dozen metropolises scattered across the globe. Even from high orbit, I easily spotted slender towers and elegant arches hinting at masterful and intact alien architecture.

"It looks amazing," I said, marveling at the view.

"The planet's a beauty alright," Matt agreed. "It's hard to believe the Warden controls a world like this after seeing Goldhaven."

"However many worlds he controls, at least one of them has to be legit." A hint of hope tinged Ben's words. "If this Levain person is down there waiting for us, maybe we'll finally get some straight answers."

"Even if he isn't down there," I said. "They must have something like the Internet, or at least libraries or something."

"Captain, we're receiving a hail," Alyssa said from the comms station.

"It's probably whatever passes for Orbital Control or Planetary Defense," Ben replied. "To put it in Spiral terms, anyway. Open the channel."

"Channel open."

An unfamiliar voice filled the flight deck. "Unidentified freighter, this is Cacitrum Orbital Defense. You have entered Cacitrum space on an unauthorized approach vector. Reduce speed to one-quarter and transmit identity credentials immediately."

I glanced at Matt. He had allowed me to handle the drop from hyperspace and our approach to the planet. "Should I put us into evasive maneuvers?" I asked. Having witnessed Matt handle our disastrous first encounters, I was pretty sure I could mimic a few of his tricks if needed.

"Not yet," he replied, swiveling his head toward Ben. "We don't have identity credentials. What do you want to do?"

"Are you sure?" Ben answered. "Levi, do we have identity credentials for Warexia?"

"Affirmative. Shall I recite them to you?"

Matt's mouth dropped open. Ben smiled sheepishly and shrugged. "I didn't think the Warden would send us here with no way to land. Noah, cut our velocity as requested." I did as Ben asked. He put a finger to his lips to keep us quiet before re-opening the comms. "Cacitrum Orbital Defense, this is independent starship Head Case requesting permission for landing. I'm transmitting our credentials now." He turned the comms off again. "Levi, send the credentials on the active comms channel."

"Confirmed. Credentials sent."

We held our collective breath. In the updating sensor projection, a dozen larger ships had started angling our way, no doubt part of the Orbital Defense fleet.

Thankfully, the reply came quickly.

"Credentials accepted. However, your ship configuration is not recognized in the COD database. You will proceed to Traffic Control Zone Three for further screening and provisional clearance. Do not deviate from the assigned trajectory. Compliance is mandatory."

"Acknowledged. Following guidance as directed."

"What does configuration not recognized mean?" Alyssa asked.

"It means they've probably never seen a starship that looks like a robot head before," Tyler answered.

A squadron of sleek, smaller craft with obvious offensive capabilities swung into flanking formation around Head Case as COD transmitted additional navigation data to us. Per instructions, I adjusted our course toward a waystation hovering at the edge of the planet's upper atmosphere.

"Armed escort, not a good sign," Tyler muttered beside me. "Worse, they're toting torpedoes on their bellies. Are we sure these folks aren't just a different brand of Warden groupies?"

"We have to assume everyone in this galaxy is a Warden groupie until proven otherwise," Ben answered.

"And those are missiles they're carrying," I added. "It doesn't get more clear-cut than that."

The traffic control station grew rapidly from a silver speck to an asteroid-sized construct. Beneath a sleek central tower, six levels of curved docking arms spilled a rainbow of running lights into the black. Dozens of ships of all sizes and shapes were already docked there, a constant flow arriving and departing, threatening to unnerve me. This was the first time I'd had to fly Head Case through such dense activity.

An authoritative female voice filled Head Case's interior. "Unregistered vessel Head Case, you're cleared for docking on level six, berth nine. Once you arrive, power down and stand by for inspection."

"Cacitrum Orbital Defense, Head Case acknowledging and complying." Ben answered smoothly.

The assigned docking station flashed red and green to identify itself and help guide our approach. Our weapons-heavy entourage split formation, clearing a path for us to maneuver gently into the waiting berth. Rather than panic, I did my best imitation of Matt, forcing myself to stay calm and guiding the ship toward the solid object with confidence I didn't really have. Firing vectoring thrusters, Head Case continued shedding velocity as I closed on the target.

"Their docking arms aren't designed for a ship like ours," Matt said. "You'll need to do a hard turn and burn to slip us in head first."

"Maybe you should take over," I replied.

"No, you've got this," Matt insisted.

I exhaled sharply to exorcize my nerves. Perhaps sensing my tension, the Aleal shifted in my pocket, a pair of tendrils snaking into the open and shivering questioningly. "I'm fine," I said. "Just a little nervous."

The station loomed over us. I didn't wait for Matt to signal the turn, trusting both the telemetry on my surround and my instincts to choose the moment. Swinging Head Case in a tight one-eighty, I killed the main thrusters and fired the retros at max power, eyes wide as we quickly closed on the docking arm, certain we were coming in too hot. I was just about ready to close my eyes and brace for impact when the station's docking clamps stretched out, grabbing hold of Head Case and bringing us to a stop. An umbilical immediately extended toward the hangar bay. Through the rear feed, I watched the interceptors pull back but remain close.

"Looks like the welcome wagon is waiting," Tyler quipped.

Ben stood as Matt completed the shutdown sequence. "Let's head to the hangar and put on our best smiley faces. We don't want anyone to get the wrong impression."

"It just occurred to me that because of the Warden's translator service, we have no idea who or what we're speaking to," I said. "Or in what language."

"Yeah, they could be sentient trees or something, for all we know," Tyler agreed.

"If a maple greets us at the hangar bay door, I think I'll wet myself," Matt said.

"I already did on our approach," Alyssa remarked. "I thought we were going to crash."

"I wasn't worried," Tyler said.

"That was a nice piece of flying, Noah," Ben said.

"Thanks," I replied, heat flushing my cheeks. I had to admit, I'd even impressed myself. And it sure was fun.

We trailed Ben from the flight deck down to the hangar. Tyler, Alyssa and I, despite the peaceful days spent in hyperspace, had taken to mimicking Matt. We wore armored underlays beneath our clothing and carried sidearms within quick reach. I'd grown so accustomed to the feel of the blaster at my hip and the fit of the protective fabric against my skin that I felt naked without them.

We'd just finished descending the hangar stairs when a loud rapping echoed across the compartment. Our guests had arrived.

"Levi, open the smaller hangar door," Ben said.

The control panel chirped before the door whisked open. Ben stepped forward to greet whoever passed through.

"If the Warden steps through that door, I'm going to wet myself," Tyler said, winking toward Ally.

Thankfully, the Warden didn't make another grand entrance. Instead, a quintet of humanoid robots filed across the threshold, gleaming alloy chassis topped with featureless mannequin heads. Clutching sleek rifles tight to their steel chests, they shifted into a perfect line in front of us..

"Uh, welcome aboard Head Case," Ben greeted politely. "I—"

"We will survey the interior of your vessel," one of the

robots announced. "Please, stand aside. This will not take long."

"They don't think much of privacy here, do they?" Tyler quipped as we stepped aside, allowing the robots to spread across the hangar. They quickly scanned the deck and climbed the steps. All but one vanished into the elevator.

"What are you looking for?" Ben asked the sentinel left behind.

"Illicit or stolen goods. Contraband. Outlawed technology," the robot answered.

"We have weapons on board," Ben announced. "An entire armory full of them."

"Your disclosure is appreciated. Protective ordnance is permitted by both the Cacitrum Governing Council and the Warden."

I shivered at the machine's mention of the foppish pseudo-god.

"What can you tell us about the Warden?" Ben asked.

"All must follow the edicts of the Warden. No more needs to be said."

"Who is he, though?" Alyssa asked.

"No more needs to be said," the robot repeated.

"You can't tell us anything else about him?" Tyler inquired.

"No more needs to be said."

"It kind of does," he pressed.

"I am detecting unnecessary hostility," the robot said, shifting its weapon toward Tyler.

"Whoa! Sorry," Tyler cried, putting up his hands, palms out. "I'm not hostile at all, see?" He spread his lips into a huge grin. "I'm very friendly in fact."

The robot returned its rifle to its original position. "This will not take long."

It was right. Within a couple of minutes, the rest of the

machines emerged from the elevator and descended the steps to join it. The chief pivoted smoothly to address Ben.

"Preliminary inspection complete. This vessel matches no known configurations in our database, but internal systems are unremarkable. I detect no obvious contraband nor indications of potential hostility against Cacitrum interests. You are conditionally granted surface access for a period of thirty days. You may apply with the local Port Authority in any of our beautiful cities to extend your stay."

It extended a slender metallic card emblazoned with an official government seal and strings of alien symbols. Smiling, Ben accepted it.

"That is your temporary entry pass," it explained. "Do not lose or damage this pass prior to completing planetary registration. Display your entry pass to starport officials upon arrival. I will relay orders to orbital defense releasing you from detention. Safe travels, Captain."

"Thank you."

It nodded crisply and exited toward the umbilical corridor, its companions falling silently in line behind it. The station's airlock door hissed closed in their wake.

"Well, that was easy," Matt said. "Anyone else think those robots looked familiar?"

"Too easy if you ask me," Tyler replied.

Ben waved the entry pass, frowning. "Let's get this bucket registered so we can find Levain and get this side quest wrapped up. Getting back to Earth is the priority, not running errands for the Warden."

We had to wait at the top of the steps for a couple of minutes while the elevator batteries recharged to power the sigils. After a short silence, Tyler once again broke the ice.

"So, do you think this whole planet is populated and run by machines?" he asked. "I have a vision of little robot babies in floating bassinets, like ugly steel Baby Yodas."

"Why would machines need cities?" I asked. "They could exist entirely as unique programs within massive data centers. The only machines that would need to take physical form would be the ones responsible for providing power to run the data centers."

"What if they're sentient machines? They might like the nightlife."

"They could build simulations of any experience they wanted to have. If their intellect is a construct, then all of reality can become a construct."

"You mean like the Matrix."

"Sort of. The Matrix was a prison for the human mind. The free machines all lived in the post-apocalypse outside. Kind of a crappy existence, when you think about how it was depicted."

"That's why Cypher had it right," Tyler agreed. "I even wrote a paper about it for my social studies class."

"This conversation is even a little too geeky, even for me," Alyssa said.

"Ben's tried to have similar conversations with me," Matt said. "I just nod my head and smile until he wears himself out."

"I'm not that bad," Ben argued.

"You used to be. Not as much anymore."

The elevator cab arrived, and we hurried back up to the flight deck, retaking our positions at the different stations.

"Station Control," Ben said. "Requesting permission to disembark."

"Permission granted, Head Case," the same voice as the Orbital Defense controller replied. "You are clear for departure to the surface. Please select a spaceport so appropriate approach coordinates can be provided."

"Apologies, Control. I'm not that familiar with Cacitrum. I don't really know where to go."

"What is your business on the planet?" Control replied.

"If you seek trade, you will land at Caspsus. If you seek recreation, Iona. If you seek employment as a cargo transport or mercenary, Portus."

"Employment as a mercenary?" Tyler said. "That sounds fun."

"What if we're looking for a specific individual?" Ben asked. "We don't know much about them. Only a name. We were hired to deliver a message to him."

"Provide the name."

"Levain," Ben said.

"Are you certain this is the individual you have been hired to contact?"

Ben's expression reflected sudden confusion and concern. "Yes, why?"

"You are cleared for departure," Control replied, ignoring the question. "Do not deviate from the assigned approach coordinates, or you will be considered in violation of your clearance and considered hostile. Thank you for visiting Cacitrum. Have a nice day."

CHAPTER 41

The comms disconnected and the docking clamps released. A small burst of air shoved us away from the docking arm, sending us drifting out toward the incoming traffic before Matt had a chance to ignite the main thrusters.

"Damn it,' he cursed, scrambling to prep Head Case for flying. "Noah, grab the stick."

I didn't hesitate, ready to take control the moment the engines fired up. Some quick cajoling kept us from slipping outside the approach vector station control provided. Good thing, too. The orbital defense starfighters had adjusted course to intercept.

"Like sharks circling a seal," Tyler said, noticing their movements.

"Atmospheric entry in fifteen minutes," Matt announced, checking our flight path.

I kept my attention glued to my surround feed, careful to remain in the designated lane while our escorts flanked us. Cacitrum's continents—the broad mountain chains, verdant forests, and green plains giving way to silver cities heavy with activity—gained definition as we descended. Outgoing starships, launched from the same spaceport where we'd been cleared to land, climbed past on our left.

"Does anyone else think it's weird that control knew who we were looking for from a single name?" Tyler asked.

"Maybe Levain really is famous," Alyssa suggested. "That would explain why the request surprised him."

"And why control didn't answer your question, Ben," I added. "He's probably like, *who the hell doesn't know Levain?*"

"If that's the case, Levain won't be easy to reach," Ben said. "Famous folks have entourages, bodyguards, maybe even a security detail. The whole nine yards."

"We still have plenty of time to deliver the message before the Warden gets restless."

"That worries me, too. He probably expects it to take days for us to get an audience. And I'm sure it won't be easy or there would be no entertainment value watching us try."

"Have I mentioned that I hate this yet today?" Ally said.

"You just filled your quota," Tyler replied.

Matt's estimate for atmospheric entry was right on the mark, and within fifteen minutes, we were pushing through the upper layers, the ship's shields easily deflecting the heat. Completing our ingress, I shifted my view to take in the landscape below, eager for a closer glimpse of the city we were approaching.

Perched at the end of a continental peninsula, the gleaming metropolis stood out like a beacon of prosperity. I'd never seen such incredible architecture. Impressive in size, shape, and material, every towering skyscraper had a different appeal. Every green space was perfectly designed to merge with the lower-lying structures. It was definitely a purposely designed city, not one that had merely sprung haphazardly up at a convenient spot.

My gaping jerked up short as the spaceport came into

view. I had expected a continuation of the opulent design. Instead, my eyes landed on a utilitarian enclosure taking up miles of precious waterfront property. The concrete tarmac intermingled with a huge, blocky terminal structure and its support structures created the most severe-looking checkerboard I had ever seen. Landing bays, lined with cracked asphalt that was thick with weeds, occupied every other space on the board while ancient-looking control towers looked down on the facility, their stone walls crumbling like the buildings of ancient Rome.

"What a dump," Tyler muttered, voicing my own thoughts. "Are you sure we've got the right place?"

"These are the coordinates station control gave us." Matt shrugged.

"The spaceport doesn't look like much," Ben said. "But the city proper beats anything I've ever seen before."

"Apparently, this is Portus," Alyssa said.

"The mercenary city?" Tyler asked. "Sweet."

"I guess that explains the gunships at the far end of the tarmac," I said, pointing to a trio of sleek gray vessels bristling with firepower, nestled within three of the landing bays.

"And the line of cargo transports sitting in the loading zones," Matt agreed.

"Incoming starship Head Case," the familiar voice said over the comms. "You're cleared to land in bay thirty-seven."

Like before, lights activated to indicate the proper bay and our positioning on our final approach. Unlike before, I handled the landing without fear. Head Case settled gently onto the tarmac, surrounded by the concrete walls of the spaceport. A pair of blast doors within one of the walls parted. A single humanoid robot marched toward the ship.

"Here we go again," Tyler said.

"Relax. It's probably just coming out to greet us and

answer any questions we might have," Ben said. "Noah, do you want to wait here or come with us?"

"Are you kidding?" I replied.

Ben tapped his comm badge. "Leo, I need you on the flight deck to manage the ship."

"On my way, Captain."

"Poor Leo never gets to be part of the away team?" Alyssa asked.

"He's fine with it," Matt replied. "His idea of adventure is tearing apart a new hyperdrive."

"That does sound pretty fun," I said. "But not as fun as checking out a new alien world."

"One more question," Alyssa said. "We're supposed to deliver a message to Levain. But either the Warden didn't give us one, or we have to find it."

"There's no hidden message in the datastore," Ben said. "Leo and Meg spent most of the trip looking for it."

"Isn't it possible they missed it?"

"Well sure, it's possible. But then it's not a message that wants to be found. Anyway, we're out of time searching for it. The way I see it, if the Warden wants us to deliver a message, he'll make sure we have it when the time comes."

"That's really what we're going with?" Tyler asked.

"The Warden said as long as we tried," I said. "We tried."

"I wonder why he made that promise to us when he didn't make it to the Achai," Alyssa said.

"I guess he just likes us better," Tyler said. "I don't blame him."

"We need to go," Ben said, rising from his station.

For the second time in half an hour, we headed down to the hangar. Ben had Levi open the entire hangar bay door, splitting Head Case's grin into a huge open mouth, the ramp descending to the tarmac like a tongue. I thought maybe I should leave my blaster behind until I noticed Matt still had his, and I figured he knew better than me. I also thought about leaving the Aleal behind, but I knew Shaq was hiding somewhere in Ben's coat, and besides, I was sure the little guy wouldn't be any trouble.

"Greetings. Welcome to Cacitrum," the robot waiting for us said as we descended onto the planet's surface.

Overhead, unlike on Earth, the nearly cloudless sky took on a turquoise cast. Hanging front and center, the planet's star seemed larger than ours, or perhaps it was closer to Cacitrum than our sun was to Earth, but it shone more white than yellow. Unlike the stifling heat and humidity of Goldhaven, a springlike breeze kept the environment nice and comfy.

"Please present your access credentials for processing," the robot continued. Ben handed the robot the card he had received earlier. It touched the card with its palm. "You have thirty days remaining on your current credentials. Please see a local port authority if you require an extension. Enjoy your visit." The robot turned to leave.

"Wait," Ben said. It stopped and turned around, waiting expectantly. "We've never been on Cacitrum before. We don't know where we're going. We could use some directions."

"Of course. Once you enter the terminal here, you will either walk or take a transport to the main processing facility. If you intend to apply for employment or contracting work, buy, sell, or trade goods, or otherwise earn an income from your visit to Cacitrum, you must be fully processed. If you are here purely for leisure, you may advance through the processing facility and board a high-speed transport into Portus."

"And is there a directory or something I can use to locate a specific person? I'm looking for Levain."

"Are you certain?" The robot asked.

"Yes," Ben repeated. "Why?"

Before the machine could answer, the twin blast doors into the terminal parted again. A handful of different style robots marched in, carrying weapons. These were black instead of the greeter bot's silver, with smaller heads and no activity lights.

"You are dismissed," one of the new bots said to the greeter. It didn't argue, turning and walking away as if everything about this was perfectly normal.

"Captain?" I questioned nervously.

Ben turned his head to glance up and back at Head Case's closest camera, signaling to Leo. While the turrets behind us didn't move, I could visualize him activating the systems in preparation.

"You are here to see Levain?" The lead bot asked.

"That's right," Ben replied.

"We are authorized to transport you to him. You will leave your weapons behind."

"I'm not sure that's an agreeable demand," Matt said.

"You will leave your weapons behind," the bot repeated.

"It can't be this easy," Tyler said. "Something's up."

"It's the Warden," Ally added. "There's a trick to this. There has to be."

"We are authorized to transport you to him. You will leave your weapons behind."

"Yeah, we heard you the first time, man," Tyler said. "And don't think about turning your weapon on me. I might be a visitor, but I feel pretty confident you aren't allowed to just gun me down in cold blood."

"You are correct," the bot replied. "Murder is prohibited in this venue."

The modifier sent a chill down my spine. Tyler's face paled.

"We are authorized to transport you to Levain. You will leave your weapons behind."

"Who is Levain?" Ben asked.

"You will meet him soon. You will leave your weapons behind."

"Repetitive, aren't they?" Alyssa said.

"Seriously, even Grok has more varied responses," I replied. "Ben, what should we do?"

"You and I will go with the bots," Ben answered. "The rest of us will wait here, just in case."

"You want to bring Noah instead of me?" Matt asked, confused.

"No. But the Warden has given Noah more direct attention than anyone else. If this is a game or a trick, I think it's better to have him with me to help figure things out."

"You should at least let me come with you, then," Tyler said. "You might need a little muscle, and let's be honest. Noah doesn't have any."

Ben considered before nodding. "Okay, Matt, you stay here with Ally. Stay ready for Plan B."

"What's Plan B?" Tyler asked.

"Hopefully we won't need one," Matt said. "Be safe. All of you."

"We are authorized to transport you to Levain. You will leave your weapons behind."

"Geez, we know already," Tyler groaned, undoing the straps to his sidearm. He passed the holstered weapon to Matt. I did the same.

"You will follow us," the lead bot said. It turned on its heel and marched away, the other robots right behind it.

"Noah!" Ally said before we could follow. As I turned, she threw her arms around me, hugging me tight. "Be careful."

"I will," I replied.

"Where's my hug?" Tyler complained after she backed away.

"I'm sure the Aleal would be happy to hug you," Alyssa replied.

"Uh, no thanks."

"Come on," Ben urged. "We don't want to lose them, and they aren't waiting up." The robots had already vanished inside the terminal.

"This is a bad idea," I said as we hurried to catch them. "And I don't trust any part of it."

"Me neither," Ben replied. "But we have to play the Warden's game, at least for now. We don't have a choice."

"For now," I agreed.

CHAPTER 42

The robots marched swiftly across the landing zone, disappearing through the open doorway. Ben, Tyler and I scrambled to catch up before we could lose them. Crossing the threshold into the structure, the next thing I noticed after catching sight of the robots was a large banner hanging from the high ceiling. In full color and printed so that it appeared fully three-dimensional, I was only mildly surprised to find the Warden's larger-than-life grin beaming back at me, his pearly whites gleaming and his eyes glittering like stars. The message beneath his mug, on the other hand, did come as a shock.

AT YOUR SERVICE

"Who is he kidding?" Tyler scoffed, noticing the banner at the same time. "Seriously? This has to be another one of his stupid jokes."

"At least we have proof that he holds real status in this galaxy," Ben said. "Or at the very least, on Cacitrum."

We passed beneath the banner, picking up speed to fall in close behind the robots. The corridor seemed to stretch on forever, running the full length from the terminal to the farthest spot in the spaceport. It remained curiously vacant, the intersecting corridors showing little to no activity as well. "You'd think they would have hover trams," Tyler said as we hoofed our way along the corridor. We had to be a mile out from the terminal, probably a little more. "Or a golf cart. Or a robotic rickshaw or horse or something."

"I'd guess they only want serious visitors, especially anyone wanting to see Levain," Ben replied.

"Maybe that's why the corridor's so empty. None of the other visitors were serious enough. They left their ships, stepped inside, looked down the length of the passageway and tapped out."

"There was so much activity in and out of the place during the descent, the surrounding emptiness has to be intentional," I said.

"What would be the point of that?"

"I have no idea. I'm sure the Warden does, though."

"Or Levain," Ben said. "Seeing how everyone knows the name, he might be powerful enough to clear a path for us."

"Good point," Tyler agreed.

As we continued down the long, empty corridor, following our robotic guides, the silence and emptiness were starting to feel ominous, putting me on edge. There had to be something untoward waiting for us, some twist or turn we wouldn't be expecting. Things had gone smoothly up to this point, almost too smoothly. Each junction we crossed left me on high-alert, anticipating that the next would reveal the true surprise. Another ambush? I could imagine the Warden's face on the banner, the grin morphing into uproarious laughter as we were unceremoniously gunned down without warning.

Despite my worries, the trek remained uneventful as the end of the passageway came into view, where a pair of huge, weathered blast doors marked the entrance to the main terminal.

"Finally," Tyler remarked. "Do you think they have any food kiosks inside?"

"Didn't you eat just before we dropped out of hyperspace?" I replied.

"Yeah, but I want to sample some local cuisine. Real alien food. I don't care what it is. I'll try it."

"Even if it's a stinky green fungus?"

"Tryin' it."

"Fried spider?"

"Tryin' it."

"What?" Ben asked. "How could you, knowing Ixy?"

"Sorry, Captain. Tryin' it."

"Live parasitic alien worm?" I offered.

"Totally tryin' it."

"You're full of crap."

"If there are food kiosks through those doors, you'll find out."

"Except for one thing," Ben said. "We don't have any local currency."

Tyler slumped. "Maybe Levain can give us a loan or something. Or maybe they'll take American dollars. You did."

The robots reached the blast doors, which rumbled and creaked softly as they parted, allowing the machines to walk through without slowing. We hurried to close the distance we had kept behind them, scooting through the doors close on their heels.

"Now this is more like it!" Tyler commented, his shock and awe gaze joining mine.

For as dank and foreboding as the walk-in had been, the explosion of color, light, and activity that followed drove a stake through the heart of my earlier ambush fears. In a single step, we'd gone from a dark alley at two in the morning to the middle of Central Park at midday. Overhead, thousands of panels cast a calming light on an unexpected throng. The light constantly shifted colors in a dizzying kaleidoscope in sync with strange music that reminded me of whale song.

The humanoid bots remained present in large numbers and appeared to be in charge of every job within the spaceport, including managing the storefronts lining the back half of the terminal's ground floor and upper mezzanine. They handled baggage, ticketing, and information. Armed white and red models similar to the black bots leading us to Levain also patrolled the space. The alien lettering emblazoned across their chests impossibly translated to *security* in my mind, though I shouldn't have been able to read it at all.

The guards maneuvered smoothly around hundreds of arriving passengers hurrying to get wherever they needed to go and departing travelers waiting for transportation... The diversity of humanoid species all but overwhelmed me. Unfamiliar with all of them, the best I could do was categorize them in more familiar terms.

The mingled scents of multi-species body odor, ozone, and grease burned the inside of my nose as diminutive gnomes swerved around towering rock-skinned behemoths. Slim, graceful elves waited in a queue marked for processing while a gruff goblin family tried to push past. A marble-skinned woman in rainbow-colored robes strode regally through the masses, a werewolf entourage clearing a path for her. Further away on my left, a cluster of trolls in fatigues waited in line to apply for hire.

Automated, hovering, holographic billboards drifted through the crowds, flashing advertisements for local attractions alongside the Warden's ever-present grinning visage. Messages like TO PROTECT AND SERVE scrolled beneath his face in multiple alien languages.

"Whoa," Tyler breathed at my shoulder, head swiveling to absorb the chaotic spectacle. "So much for empty corridors. I feel like I just stepped onto the set of Shrek: A Space Odyssey."

I couldn't keep myself from laughing at that one. Even Ben failed to hide a small grin. "And we were wondering if there were any organic life forms here."

"As far as I can tell, it's only the visitors," Ben said. "But maybe that'll change when we get out into the city."

The robots guided us through the masses, who quickly moved aside to let our armed escort through. When a small elven child failed to move quickly enough, one of the bots grabbed him roughly by the arm and shoved him away, sending him sprawling.

"Hey!" Ben shouted, voicing his displeasure. "What the hell?"

When the bot ignored him, he raised his hand in a way I had come to recognize meant he intended to channel chaos energy.

"Ben, wait," I said. "Not that I don't think these bots are assholes, but we might need that later."

He glanced at me, fury in his eyes. It faded quickly as reason had a chance to take hold. "Yeah. You're right."

Distracted by the bot's action, we nearly collided with the back of our escort, which had come to an abrupt stop. Looking past them, I saw the marble-skinned woman and her group blocking their path. Or depending on perspective, we were blocking hers.

"Move aside," the woman snapped. "Or my grithyak will shred you to scrap."

"You will move aside," the lead bot replied.

"I do not take orders from machines," she hissed. "You have five seconds to step out of my way."

The werewolves, grithyak, didn't just extend their claws. They reached to their belts first, grabbing metal extensions and sliding them onto their already sharp fingernails.

"You will move aside," the lead bot repeated. It and the other bots shifted their rifles toward the woman and her escort. The grithyak tensed, ready to spring at them.

One of the security bots put itself between the two sides. "Halt. Violence in the terminal is unauthorized. You will be detained and prosecuted."

"You can't prosecute a machine," the woman growled. "And you can't prosecute me. Do you know who I am?"

"Yes. You are Princess Goloran. You have diplomatic immunity. Do you know who these bots belong to?"

"No," Princess Goloran sneered. "Nor do I care."

"We are registered to Levain," the lead bot said.

Princess Goloran's mouth closed tight. She stared at the bots briefly before finally stepping aside without another word. The bots continued through the terminal as if nothing had happened. I did my best not to look at the princess as we passed, but I couldn't help myself. I glanced over, only to find her already staring at me.

"Is there a problem?" she huffed, even though she had been looking at me first.

"What? N…no," I replied, looking away as my cheeks heated. "Sorry."

Tyler laughed, draping an arm on my shoulder. "Nice one, Katzuo. Smooth."

I grimaced at him, lowering my head in embarrassment. That didn't stop me from looking back at her one last time before we reached the other end of the terminal. I expected her to be lost in the crowd. Instead, she had yet to make a move, her gaze still cast in our direction. My direction. I didn't get the sense she was into me. It was more like a cat eying her next meal.

The look and the way she had instantly deferred to mention of Levain left me thoroughly terrified. What the hell had we gotten ourselves into?

CHAPTER 43

The robots led us to an elevator at the far end of the terminal, which descended into a garage. The walls and ceiling were rough concrete, and the air smelled strongly of oil and metal, but there wasn't a single car to be seen. Nor was there any other mode of transportation present that bore any resemblance to anything I might have expected.

Instead, our guides led us to Cacitrum's version of an ornately carved, horse-drawn carriage, with a posh interior of red velvet behind tinted glass. The vehicle rode on a set of wide tires that, by their looks, were airless and shock-absorbing, and the "horse" was clearly a robot. With six legs and four red eyes, it was made of glossy steel that mimicked something larger and thicker than a live horse. Though it had both a mane and tail, each individual strand was an illuminated fiber in a mix of colors. It flicked its tail as its head swiveled our way, its voltaic eyes brightening at our approach.

My quick look around revealed more of the strange steampunk steeds, tied to a row of hitching posts along the outer wall of the building. Some were hooked up to carriages like the one sitting in front of us. Most were saddled to accommodate one or two riders,

"This is crazy weird," Tyler commented.

"And kind of cool," I added.

"That, too," he agreed.

"You will get in the carriage," the lead robot announced, its door swinging open as he gestured toward it.

After we took turns looking at each other, silently questioning whether we should or shouldn't, Tyler shrugged and climbed in first, plopping down on the plush seat. I slipped in after him, still marveling at the overall unlikelihood of the entire spectacle.

"Do you think they have robot cowboys, too?" Tyler asked me as Ben climbed in, settling on the seat beside me, opposite Tee. "You know, wrangling robot steers, drinking grease sarsaparilla at the saloon, getting into gunfights at the corral."

"I'm open to anything at this point," I replied.

"You will remain seated for the duration of transit to your destination," our escort added.

The other bots fell into step behind the carriage, marching along in rank and file as the horse cantered forward, pulling us through an abbreviated tunnel that dipped down in front of us. Mechanical torches came on as we moved forward and then went off again behind us. What had to be a main thoroughfare leading out of the installation ran above us. We could hear the clomping of hooves, louder than the quiet whir of wheels.

The tunnel swung around to the left, dumping us out onto the thoroughfare. Our carriage merged with other multi-legged traffic nowhere near as nice as ours. The robot guards began to run to keep up as our horse broke into a trot. Faces of all shapes, sizes, and colors, some as robotic as the guards, turned to look at us from inside simple carriages, the hard seats of basic wagons, and the cramped quarters of horse-drawn rickshaws.

"So, if Goloran is a Princess, and the Warden is in charge, does that mean she's the Warden's daughter?" Tyler mused out loud.

"I don't think the Warden fancies himself a king," Ben replied. "Warexia is so large, there are probably dozens, if not hundreds, of different governments and class systems in use, none of them directly related to him."

"But she could be his daughter," Tyler said.

"It's possible," Ben agreed. "Why?"

"I just think it's weird if he has a daughter. I wonder what she thinks about him making so many copies of himself. I wonder if she has copies, too."

"I'm more curious about all the aliens," I said. "I didn't expect there to be so many different humanoid species in one place."

"It's not that strange for most ILFs to share similar traits," Ben said. "Walking upright and opposable thumbs, for example. Based on our experience in the Spiral, evolution tends to steer toward the same end result, skewed primarily by the environmental variables surrounding that evolution. Of course, that doesn't mean there aren't exceptions like Shaq and Ixy, but it's true for the majority there and apparently here as well. And if it looks even somewhat human, we've probably already envisioned something similar in our minds and given it a name, like an elf, or an orc, or an ogre."

"Or a werewolf," I said, referencing the grithyak.

"Bingo."

"Well, then, what are the odds we'll run into a dragon at some point?" Tyler asked. "Or a beholder like in *Dungeons and Dragons*?"

"They're not humanoid, so probably pretty low. But we can't rule it out."

"Awesome. I've always wanted to behold a beholder."

"Pretty sure you don't," Ben said.

"You mean they have beholders in the Spiral?"

"No, I mean I'm pretty sure you don't want to be petrified or disintegrated."

All discussion ended as our carriage took us into Portus City, the thoroughfare evolving to a wide central avenue that split the center of the city. I'd never seen a place with so many buildings look so pristine. The tall skyscrapers lining the avenue didn't have a speck of dirt or grime on them, nor did the high glass arches that hooked from one side of the avenue to the other. The patches of greenery along the roadway were beautifully manicured, the flowers in full bloom and the light gray pavement so free of litter it suggested you could eat off it.

I didn't need to guess how the city stayed so clean. Out here, as in the spaceport, robots handled everything, from gardening to washing windows and scrubbing walls. At one point we crossed a wide boulevard of upscale boutiques and posh market stalls teeming with thousands of nonhuman ILFs. I leaned over Ben to gawk out of his window, mouth agape at the activity before realizing that even the storefronts and restaurants were manned by machines catering to visitors.

"We should stop and try one of the food joints," Tyler remarked as we passed through. The bots behind the carriage ran ahead, wailing like sirens to clear slower-moving tourists out of the way.

"I don't think these bots are going to stop so we can sample the local cuisine," Ben replied.

"Why not? I thought we still had like a week to meet with Levain. We have plenty of time, and look over there." He pointed to a table at an outdoor restaurant, where a group of pixie-like humanoids with tiny noses and sharp ears shared a massive plate of something with a gooey white sauce over it. "That looks soooo good."

"Levain is expecting us. Maybe after."

Tyler sat back in his seat. "I'm holding you to that, Captain. You owe us some foreign food after getting us stuck here."

"I'll make sure you get to try something exotic," Ben promised.

We turned onto progressively less crowded avenues, eventually entering a district where no living thing could be readily seen. No vendors called to passing prospects. No maintenance or custodial staff made rounds over empty sidewalks. Even the worker bots had thinned considerably. Only the rhythmic footfalls of our escort interrupted the pervasive silence, their formation tightening as the horse-bot veered onto a narrow, tertiary cross-street.

Apprehension started churning in my gut. "I feel like we're being led somewhere we don't want to go," I said.

"It's definitely getting creepy out there," Tyler replied.

Ben didn't reply, but I could tell by his worried look that he had already come to the same conclusion. His hands fisted in his lap, and his brow crinkled slightly as he worked to slowly draw in chaos energy.

Two of the bots split from our convoy, stopping mid-street without warning. The rest of the escort reacted in kind, shouldering their rifles. Our carriage rolled to a halt behind them.

Tyler turned in his seat and rapped on the carriage above him. "What's wrong?" he shouted at the driver. "Why did we stop?"

"Rerouting to our final destination," the lead bot announced, avoiding Tee's question. The robo-horse resumed its aggressive trot, our escort moving in closer to the carriage than before.

"Something's up," I said. "Something our escort didn't

expect." Judging by everyone else's tense expressions, they had already reached a similar conclusion.

We made it three more blocks before the carriage made an abrupt left turn, pausing again as we entered a dirty alley, the cracked and pitted asphalt covered in strewn debris. Two rows of double-hung awning windows were set into the high gray walls on each side of the narrow passageway.

All the way to its ominous dead end.

The lead bot climbed down from the driver's box and swiveled his head toward us. "You will remain inside the transport." The glass muffled his voice, but we could hear him well enough. "You will not attempt to exit until cleared," he advised us.

"What's going on out there?" Ben asked. "If there's trouble—"

"You will remain inside the transport," the robot repeated. "We will handle this intrusion."

"That remains to be seen," Ben muttered as the bots fanned out in both directions. His wary eyes connected with mine. "I have a suspicion this is about to get ugly."

I'd already figured that out for myself. My heart started pounding as I looked across at Tyler, a silent message passing between us. Who could be brazen enough to threaten a convoy on its way to see Levain at the Warden's request?

We hunkered down in our seats, straining to make out details through the lower row of windows. Maddening minutes trickled by. I flinched when the comm badge chirped against my breastbone, followed by Matt's query. "Ben? How's everything going? Did you meet Levain yet?" Suddenly, before Ben could respond, the situation went sideways.

Bots painted in jagged red and yellow stripes exploded into view from both ends of the alley. More slid down off the rooftops on both sides of us, landing around the carriage as if leaps like that were no problem at all. Some fired plasma rifles at our escorts; others wielded some kind of energy swords. Our escorts fought back, turning the alley into an instant war zone.

It all happened so fast. Fifteen seconds, twenty tops, and all five of the escort bots and our driver were nothing more than scrap metal and sparking electrodes spread across the asphalt. Amidst the acrid smoke of their demise, plasma bolts scorched the carriage, shattering windows and burning holes in the upholstery. Tyler howled as a bolt hit just inches from his head.

"We can't stay here!" Ben shouted, kicking open the door. "Stay low!" He flung himself face-first into the alley.

Tyler and I looked at one another, both stricken with fear. "You first," Tyler said, growling when another plasma bolt sizzled into his shoulder. It pierced his clothes but not his underlay. "Well, what are you waiting for?" he shouted. "Christmas!"

I shrugged and followed Ben, Matt's training succeeded in keeping me from full-on panic. Tyler landed right behind me. Ben immediately grabbed my arm and dragged me beneath the carriage. I pulled Tyler after me, the smoke hanging in the alley working to obscure our dive from the carriage. "Now what?" Tyler asked, looking at Ben and then at me as rifle fire continued pouring in overhead. "This isn't part of the Warden's stupid request, is it?"

"Who knows," Ben answered, tapping the ground beside him. Or rather, as luck would have it, an old sewer access cover embedded in the asphalt. "I think those robots weren't as dumb as they looked. They stopped the carriage over this access on purpose." A soft glow lit his fingertips, and the heavy sewer cover lifted silently, rising to hang suspended against the bottom of the carriage. "Hurry."

I slid forward, peering into the darkness. Quickly

swinging my feet around, I turned over and shuffled down onto the rusted service ladder, descending it a dozen feet before my boots landed on dry metal. Only the fusty smell of old sewage remained.

Tyler came down right behind me, Ben bringing up the rear. He guided the manhole cover back down into place, his head barely clearing the top of the tunnel. His fingertips continued to glow until he twisted his comm badge, producing a backlit light. We did the same to ours, the combined illumination allowing us to see the way ahead. We started walking, moving at a brisk pace to get as far from the area as we could before our attackers realized we had vanished.

Of course, Tyler was first to break our grim silence. "You got a plan, Ben?" His inquiry echoed hollowly through the metal tunnel. "Or should I start mentally composing my last will and testament?"

"Do you have anything to bequeath?" I asked.

"I have a timeshare in a starship," he replied.

"It's non-transferable," Ben said. "Didn't you read the contract?"

"Not the whole thing."

"It's in there."

I laughed quietly. "Anything else?"

"Do the clothes Asshole made belong to me?" Tyler queried.

"No," Ben said. "Also in the contract. They go back into Asshole's inventory when you leave."

"Damn, you were thorough."

"What can I say? I'm from Earth, too."

"Right," Tyler laughed.

"We have to assume that the bots alerted Levain after they parked the carriage over the manhole," I said."He'll likely send another team to retrieve us."

"How do you know he has another team?" Tyler asked.

"Princess Goloran deferred to us at the mere mention of his name. Someone that powerful has to have more than just one armed escort unit. Even if he doesn't, he can probably hire mercs to cover the deficit. I think as long as we keep to this tunnel, someone will meet us."

Grinding metal echoed from behind us, signaling the attackers had discovered our ruse.

"The gig is up," Tyler said.

"We should run now," Ben replied.

It was the best idea I'd heard so far.

CHAPTER 44

Our footfalls rang through the dank passageway as we raced to stay ahead of the murderbots. My heart pounded, my pulse racing. Each side tunnel we approached left me certain another ambush awaited us around the next bend, but the glow from our comm badges revealed infinitely more of the same—a deserted tunnel.

"Where the…hell is…the cavalry…you predicted… Noah-san?" Tyler panted beside me.

"Any minute now…I hope," I replied, equally out of breath.

We pushed our aching bodies faster, rounding a gentle curve. My eyes strained against the dark, terrified that we'd slam full speed into a dead end before Levain could locate and rescue us from the ambushers. Mercifully, the way ahead remained open, but for how much longer? The murderbots were still trailing us, their metal feet clanging on the metal tube, continually growing closer. They already had an edge in foot speed, and we couldn't run indefinitely. With no weapons, standing and fighting wasn't an option either, not to mention Shaq couldn't work his poisonous magic against machines, and the Aleal, still tucked in my pocket, couldn't eat the brain of something that didn't have one.

It was only a matter of time before push came to shove.

We came out of another loping turn, each step leaving me more eager to locate a ladder to return us to the surface, or at the very least provide us somewhere to hide. As the minutes passed, neither of those things presented themselves. The enemy bots were still gaining on us, their footsteps so close that I kept looking over my shoulder, waiting for them to appear right on our heels. For my first eight or nine glances, they weren't anywhere to be seen. And then suddenly, the first murderbot rounded the bend behind us. Hideous red eyes gleamed within its expressionless faceplate. It raised its rifle, and I winced, anticipating blistering rays piercing my back.

Just as it fired, Ben's burst of chaos energy knocked the robot back into those behind it. The wayward plasma bolt slammed into the tunnel just ahead of us, offering a brief glimpse of a ladder a short distance away.

So close, but still so far.

"Pick up the pace!" Tyler shouted, our view of the ladder fading as quickly as the light that lit it up. Looking back again, six sets of yellow eyes untangled themselves from the pile Ben had left them in, rising to resume the chase.

I shifted my attention from the machines to Ben, wondering if he had enough energy left for one more push. His sweaty brow and tired eyes answered the question for me. It was all he could do to keep up with Tyler and me. Our only shot was to reach the ladder and climb back to the surface before the bots caught us.

Which meant we didn't have a chance.

My body tensed in anticipation of the end. I nearly gave up and skidded to a stop. The underlay would absorb one or two hits in the executionary barrage, and then it would be over. I glanced at Tyler, feeling more sorry for my friend than myself. He was here because of me. Because he had a soft heart. Because he cared. He didn't deserve to die like this, so far from home without a chance to even say goodbye to his mother.

My footsteps slowed, and just as I stumbled, a shadowy form that hadn't been there seconds earlier stepped out of the shadows ahead, an RPG-like weapon balanced on his shoulder. "Get down!" he shouted in an enhanced voice.

I didn't need to be told twice. A flash of azure light nearly blinded me as we dove to the tunnel floor. I threw my hands over my head and squeezed my eyes shut as a rocket streaked past. In less time than it took to draw my next breath, the tunnel quaked under the concussive force of the hit. Still ready to die, I expected the thunderous detonation to bring the entire tube down around us.

Silence followed for a handful of seconds... I cracked an eye open, peering over at Tyler through the dust and smoke created by the blast. Sprawled beside me, his eyes connected with mine. "What the hell happened?" he coughed out, gingerly sitting up. I followed his shocked gaze to where the tunnel had mostly collapsed behind us, burying our would-be killers, or least cutting off their access to us. "Damn. Score one for Levain," he said.

"Noah? Tyler? Are you okay?" Ben's voice drew my attention to where he crouched on the floor a few feet away.

"I'm fine," Tyler replied. "Thanks to the Mandalorian there."

"I'm good, too," I answered, before remembering the Aleal in my front pocket, the one I had landed on. I jumped to my feet, poking a finger in to check on the little booger. A reassuring tendril poked into the tip, sending a tingle up my spine.

The clearing of a throat drew all of our attention to the newcomer. He stood with feet braced in a ready position, clutching the unfamiliar rifle in black-gloved hands, the rocket launcher discarded. A man, I guessed, based on his broad shoulders and height, though his helmet obscured all facial features beneath a black faceplate.

After a tense pause, the mysterious figure straightened from his combat stance. Slinging the rifle over his shoulder, he strode toward us, stopping less than a foot away. Regarding us briefly, he gestured back the way he had come.

"Let's go," Ben said. "I think he's Levain's cavalry."

We trailed our rescuer toward the end of the tunnel.

"Um, thanks for the assist back there," I said. "Are you with Levain?" The question seemed rhetorical, but I didn't see any harm in asking it.

His helmet shifted marginally toward me before our guide faced forward again without response. It was as much of an affirmation as I would get. Reaching the ladder, we climbed from the depths back into muted daylight, emerging in a nondescript alley choked with refuse. It was even dirtier and dingier than the one we had escaped by the skin of our teeth.

"Where are we?" Tyler asked.

Once more, our new escort ignored the query. He crossed the trash-littered pavement and climbed aboard what looked a lot like an Old West buckboard. He sat down in the middle of the front bench, giving the three of us little choice but to squeeze onto the bench behind him. Tyler's butt was still a foot above the seat when our escort slapped the robot horse with the reins. Steam rose from its polished nostrils as it surged forward, momentum slamming Tee's rear down on the seat.

"Hey! Jerk!" he shouted, rubbing his butt as he threw our rescuer' a disgruntled look. Ben hid his grin behind his hand as he and I exchanged amused looks. Mando merely ignored him.

After passing several small buildings, the buckboard angled toward a hulking warehouse hunkered behind a twelve-foot stone wall topped with razor wire. Robot guards patrolled the outside of the wall's perimeter. Heavy steel doors parted to allow us entry, and we crossed a large courtyard, passing a few similar wagons before moving toward the warehouse and a second set of blast doors. They too opened in front of us, bringing us into a sparse antechamber. Glaring white lighting chased away the outer decay, while pale walls and gleaming tile floors transformed the space into what could pass as the reception area of a wealthy business. A quartet of burlier, crimson-painted robots stood outside an elevator, its doors open on the brightly lit interior. They came alert at our entry, snapping to attention.

Our escort dismounted the wagon, leaving us to jump down and hurry after him as he walked past the formation and into the elevator without acknowledgment. The guards remained at stiff attention while we boarded the elevator. I stared at our rescuer the entire way up. Who was he? Why hadn't he removed his helmet? Might *he* be Levain?

The elevator stopped three floors up. The doors whispered open, revealing a carpeted reception lounge appointed in plush black velvet furnishings. Neatly arranged statues and gilt-framed artwork lent the space an upscale ambiance. Potted greenery and baskets of exotic flowers added visual interest and a pleasing aroma. My muscles relaxed some, the peaceful atmosphere calming the tension of our violent escape and nick-of-time rescue.

Full-length windows dominated the exterior wall, the gauzy ivory curtains over them creating a hazy, less-than-ideal view. We obviously weren't in the best neighborhood, and the surrounding construction reinforced the down-trodden nature of the immediate area. It seemed like a strange place to meet someone with the kind of influence Levain seemed to hold over the city, if not the planet.

"Do you think Levain's office is here?" Tyler asked.

"I hope so," Ben replied.

Our guide stepped past the lounge seating toward a back hallway. We followed him down several corridors to a closed circular portal guarded by another pair of crimson bots. When the barrier slid aside, my pulse jumped with excitement. After so much build-up and danger, we'd finally reached the mystery figure waiting at the end of our quest.

We passed through the doors, into a large but simple office. Heavily laden bookshelves ringed nearly the entire room, save for the parts of the wall broken up by doors and windows. Fancy rugs lay strewn across a gleaming hardwood floor. A large lump of fur rested on one of them, its midsection rising and falling. A thick wood desk occupied the back of the room, its surface clear. An oversized high-backed chair faced the window directly behind it. A thick white-clad elbow rested on the right arm.

Our guide raised his hand, pointing at the floor near the door. We stopped on the spot as he continued toward the desk.

"I don't suppose we've gotten the message the Warden wanted us to deliver," Tyler whispered close to my ear.

"Not that I'm aware of," I replied, looking at Ben. He shook his head. We were twenty feet from the man I presumed to be Levain, and we were still flying blind. Another of the Warden's games?

Our helmeted ninja friend knocked twice on the desk to get Levain's attention. My heart rate kicked up another notch in anticipation.

The chair swiveled around to face us.

CHAPTER 45

A behemoth of a man in both size and shape, the man in the chair instantly became the most intimidating entity I'd ever encountered. He regarded us the way an elephant might regard an ant, his deep-set eyes shadowed by a thick brow beneath a bald, oversized forehead and crown. A wide nose led to a thick, leathery pout that didn't look as if his lips were capable of ever cracking a smile. His square jawline and strong chin gave way to two softer ones beneath, which themselves vanished into a deep purple scarf he wore around his neck, tucked under a white vest beneath his white coat. His glare alone left me eager to retreat with or without completing our task.

His chair groaned, seeming to exhale as he lifted his massive bulk out of it with a surprising ease. We waited for him to speak, but he seemed in no hurry to do so. He leaned forward, planting his jackhammer fists on the bare desk. I waited for it to buckle under his massive bulk, but it held up better than me.

"Are you Levain?" Ben asked, his eyes narrowing with speculation.

"Are you human?" Tyler asked. I couldn't help

wondering the same thing myself. He looked the part, save for his oversized cranium.

"Nobody comes looking for Levain by name unless they have some sort of death wish," the man finally said, ignoring Tee's question. The bass zen of his voice surprised me. "Do you have a death wish?"

"The Warden sent us," Ben answered. "He—"

Levain cut Ben off with a deep, throaty laugh that rumbled across the office, ready to shake the books from the shelves along the side walls. "The Warden sent you, did he?" He paused thoughtfully. "The Warden sent *you*?" He pointed at Ben, waving his finger back and forth to encompass all three of us before glancing at our rescuer. "Maybe you should have left them down in the tunnel with Zariv's bots." The other man shrugged. "That bastard owes me for trying to rob me of what's rightfully mine." His head swiveled back to us, landing on Ben. "So the Warden is sending children to do men's work now," he continued. "You poor bastards. You probably have no idea what you've gotten yourselves into."

"Maybe you can tell us." Tyler said. "The Warden was... light on details."

"We aren't even supposed to be in this galaxy," Ben added. "Our ship—"

"Yeah, yeah, I get it," Levain interrupted. "If you're here on behalf of the Warden, and you've never heard of me, then you must be newbies, visitors from another part of the universe. Where did you come from, and how did you get here?"

"How many visitors come to Warexia?" I asked. "We had a run-in with the Achai—"

"Kid, almost everyone in Warexia started as a visitor to Warexia. That's kind of how this place works. A thousand ways in, and no way out."

"Wait, you can't mean that," Tyler said. "There has to be a way out."

"Those are the Warden's words, not mine." He proved me wrong when a huge grin formed between his thick lips, which looked ready to crack open and bleed from the strain. "I know a way out."

"You do?" We all said it at the same time, and probably way too eagerly. Could our best hope of getting out of this place and back home be standing right in front of us? There was no way it could be that easy. Could it?

"I do," he affirmed. "But before you ask, no, I won't share."

"You don't need to tell us how," Ben said. "Just help us do it. Please. My friends here were only supposed to be gone from Earth for a few hours. They've been away from home for weeks now."

"Boo-hoo," Levain said. "Why should I care about that?" He paused, tilting his head slightly to the side. "Wait, did you say, Earth?"

"Yeah, why?"

"I'm a big fan of Earth. Especially the food."

"You've been there?"

"Not personally. But I've ordered takeout, so to speak." He repeated the same throaty laugh.

"There's no way we can convince you to help us?"

"For free? Not a chance."

"So how do we earn your help?"

Levain sighed. "This is painful. Look, you don't know enough about anything to even know why you're here, or what any of it means. The Warden is a toy collector. To him, you're a new toy. To me, you're an ignorant nuisance. Those two things don't blend well, understood?"

"Not really," Tyler said.

"You said a thousand ways to get here," Ben said. "We came through a rift in spacetime."

"Through the Void?"

"Yeah."

"You have a rift engine?"

"No. Is that a thing?"

"Could be. I don't know. How'd you get into the Void if you don't have a rift engine?"

"Chaos energy." Ben answered truthfully.

Levain straightened to a full stand, his condescending regard softening a little. "*You* know how to harness chaos energy."

"That's right."

He reached up to rub his chin with a gigantic paw. "Well, that is interesting. But…" He shrugged. "…it probably doesn't change anything. I take it you weren't aiming for Warexia. Something knocked you off course, and here you are. And you can't get out because chaos energy is choked off here."

"Yeah, we were redirected. We thought unintentionally, but maybe not. Could the Warden be responsible?"

"Like I said, a thousand ways in. All the dead end streets in the Void lead here. The Warden's responsible for that."

"Who is he?" I asked. "The Oron said he's a god."

"Kid, I wish I knew," Levain answered. "All I can tell you is that he thinks he owns this place because he's been here for so long. Could be he's a god. I guess that depends on your definition of such. Or it could be he's the first to find himself trapped here. Or could be he's something else entirely. Something harder to define."

"His banners are all over the spaceport," Tyler said.

"Yeah, most of the people of Cacitrum love him. They don't worship him, though. He's more like their fun uncle. He claims to protect them from harm, and they eat it up like candy."

"Are there any people on Cacitrum?" I asked. "Because we haven't seen any besides you two."

"Not in the cities. Not anymore. These days, the regular folk send their bots to do anything they want done while they lounge around out in the countryside, doing who-knows-what. It's people like me—people who still do the dirty work—who keep this planet running."

"But the Warden does protect them," I said.

"*I* protect them!" Levain snapped, slamming his fist down on the desk. This time, the wood couldn't take the strain. The legs on the left side buckled, the whole thing collapsing to one side. The display of strength left me stunned and frankly a bit terrified. Levain only sighed, glancing at Mando. "I'll need another new desk." The other man nodded. Levain looked back at us. "The Warden takes credit he doesn't deserve and hasn't earned. The people of Cacitrum honor him and fear me, while I'm the one working my ass off so they don't need to get off their asses. It's a thankless job, but somebody has to do it."

"And I'm sure it's all out of the kindness of your heart," Ben said.

"Wise-ass. Of course not. Who do you think builds half the bots on this planet? My point is, the Warden has almost nothing to do with Cacitrum beyond all those stupid banners and statues. Until now, anyway." He waved a noncommittal hand. "So, go ahead. You have a message for me? Let's hear it."

I looked at Ben, who looked back at me, uncertainty gripping his face. If the Warden had provided an actual message, we'd yet to discover it.

"Well?" Levain said. "I'm listening."

"Nothing?" I mouthed to Ben. He shook his head.

"I'll handle this," Tyler said, taking a couple of steps toward Levain. "We… well… we uh…. I think we're having some kind of technical difficulties. Can you give us a minute?" He motioned Ben and me into a huddle.

"That's handling this?" I whispered while Levain folded his arms across his corpulent chest and continued glaring impatiently at us.

"What else am I supposed to say?" Tyler countered. "The Warden left us high and dry."

"We need to tell him something," I said.

"We need the freaking Warden. Isn't he supposed to know where we are and what we're doing right now?"

"He's probably enjoying making us sweat. Ben, any ideas?"

"Maybe the message is that there isn't any message. Maybe we were just supposed to meet Levain."

"Why, so he can eat us?" Tyler hissed.

I risked a glance at our host. He looked amused now, but I could already sense the limits of that amusement. He wouldn't suffer fools like us for very long.

"Let's just try to bow out gracefully," Ben continued. "We tried to deliver the message. We made it all the way here. It has to be good enough."

"I agree," I said. "I just want to get the hell out of here."

We broke our huddle.

"Oh, are you ready now?" Levain asked. "Because you're about ten seconds from a pounding."

Ben stepped forward. "The truth is, the Warden told us we needed to deliver a message to you," he said. "But he never gave us an actual message. We're sorry to have bothered you. We thought we were doing the right thing. If you'll just allow us to go, we won't—"

A shrill tone sounded from Ben's pocket, interrupting him. He retrieved his RFD. A simple message had been scribbled across the screen in childish handwriting.

Tell Levain that I want his associate to remove his helmet. - W

"Wait, I have it," Ben said. "He wants your bodyguard

here or whoever he is to remove his helmet." He turned the message toward Levain.

"Are you serious?" Levain replied, releasing another rumble of a laugh. "Talk about wasting everybody's time. At least I don't have to kill you. It goes against my sensibilities to hurt children. Especially stupid ones." He turned to his associate. "Jaffie, you heard the Warden. Lift the bucket off your head." He sighed, still confused by the Warden's request as his man reached up to release his helmet. "I swear, I thought this would be about something important. Now you get why I think the Warden's such a joke."

"You know, he can probably hear you right now," Tyler said.

"I've said worse. If he wants me, he knows where to find me."

I'd already locked my attention on Jaffie. I wasn't curious who might be under the helmet. I wouldn't know him from Adam, anyway. I was more curious why the Warden had sent us here just for this. A beginner's task to see if we would follow his instructions? A means for the Warden to get under Levain's skin? The Warden worked in mysterious ways, I guess. At least we would succeed in our first quest relatively unscathed, and avoid the same fate as the Achai.

"Come on, Jaffie," Levain said, growing impatient with how slowly the man lifted his helmet. "We don't have all day. Just get it off."

The man did as his boss ordered, pulling the helmet straight up in one final jerk. I looked at him. He looked at me. In that instant, we were both transported back to the intersection in downtown Cedar Rapids, millions of light-years away. I heard the rumble of the SUV's engine, felt the tension of knowing the truck couldn't stop and we wouldn't clear out of its path in time. My breath caught in my throat recalling how the front of his behemoth vehicle made contact with the passenger side of our family sedan, crumpling it and pushing us nearly fifty feet across the intersection and into a light pole. My heart broke anew remembering that my parents were dead, and this son of a bitch, instead of checking on them, had fled the scene.

I almost laughed as I glared at him, my hands curling into fists. "You," I snarled, my pain and fear and fury rising in my throat as the most acrid bile.

No doubt, the Warden was very entertained…

———

Thank you for reading Starship For Rent! For more information on the next book in the series, please visit mrforbes.com/starshipforrent2

OTHER BOOKS BY M.R FORBES

Want more M.R. Forbes? Of course you do!
View my complete catalog here
mrforbes.com/books
Or on Amazon:
mrforbes.com/amazon

Starship For Sale (Starship For Sale)
mrforbes.com/starshipforsale

When Ben Murdock receives a text message offering a fully operational starship for sale, he's certain it has to be a joke.

Already trapped in the worst day of his life and desperate for a way out, he decides to play along. Except there is no joke. The starship is real. And Ben's life is going to change in ways he never dreamed possible.

All he has to do is sign the contract.

Joined by his streetwise best friend and a bizarre tenant with an unseverable lease, he'll soon discover that the universe is more volatile, treacherous, and awesome than he ever imagined.

And the only thing harder than owning a starship is staying alive.

Forgotten (The Forgotten)
mrforbes.com/theforgotten
Complete series box set:
mrforbes.com/theforgottentrilogy

Some things are better off FORGOTTEN.

Sheriff Hayden Duke was born on the Pilgrim, and he expects to die on the Pilgrim, like his father, and his father before him.

That's the way things are on a generation starship centuries from home. He's never questioned it. Never thought about it. And why bother? Access points to the ship's controls are sealed, the systems that guide her automated and out of reach. It isn't perfect, but he has all he needs to be content.

Until a malfunction forces his wife to the edge of the habitable zone to inspect the damage.

Until she contacts him, breathless and terrified, to tell him she found a body, and it doesn't belong to anyone on board.

Until he arrives at the scene and discovers both his wife and the body are gone.

The only clue? A bloody handprint beneath a hatch that hasn't opened in hundreds of years.

Until now.

Deliverance (Forgotten Colony)
mrforbes.com/deliverance
Complete series box set:

The war is over. Earth is lost. Running is the only option.

It may already be too late.

Caleb is a former Marine Raider and commander of the Vultures, a search and rescue team that's spent the last two years pulling high-value targets out of alien-ravaged cities and shipping them off-world.

When his new orders call for him to join forty-thousand survivors aboard the last starship out, he thinks his days of fighting are over. The Deliverance represents a fresh start and a chance to leave the war behind for good.

Except the war won't be as easy to escape as he thought.

And the colony will need a man like Caleb more than he ever imagined...

Man of War (Rebellion)
mrforbes.com / manofwar
Complete series box set:
mrforbes.com / rebellion-web

In the year 2280, an alien fleet attacked the Earth.

Their weapons were unstoppable, their defenses unbreakable.

Our technology was inferior, our militaries overwhelmed.

Only one starship escaped before civilization fell.

Earth was lost.

It was never forgotten.

Fifty-two years have passed.

A message from home has been received.

The time to fight for what is ours has come.

Welcome to the rebellion.

Hell's Rejects (Chaos of the Covenant)
mrforbes.com / hellsrejects

The most powerful starships ever constructed are gone. Thousands are dead. A fleet is in ruins. The attackers are unknown. The orders are clear: *Recover the ships. Bury the bastards who stole them.*

Lieutenant Abigail Cage never expected to find herself in Hell. As a Highly Specialized Operational Combatant, she was one of the most respected Marines in the military. Now she's doing hard labor on the most miserable planet in the universe.

Not for long.

The Earth Republic is looking for the most dangerous individuals it can control. The best of the worst, and Abbey happens to be one of them. The deal is simple: *Bring back the starships, earn your freedom. Try to run, you die.* It's a suicide mission, but she has nothing to lose.

The only problem? There's a new threat in the galaxy. One with a power unlike anything anyone has ever seen. One that's been waiting for this moment for a very, very, long time. And they want Abbey, too.

Be careful what you wish for.

They say Hell hath no fury like a woman scorned. They have no idea.

ABOUT THE AUTHOR

M.R. Forbes is the mind behind a growing number of Amazon best-selling science fiction series. He currently resides with his family and friends on the west cost of the United States, including a cat who thinks she's a dog and a dog who thinks she's a cat.

He maintains a true appreciation for his readers and is always happy to hear from them.

To learn more about me or just say hello:

Visit my website:
mrforbes.com

Send me an e-mail:
michael@mrforbes.com

Check out my Facebook page:
facebook.com/mrforbes.author

Join my Facebook fan group:
facebook.com/groups/mrforbes

Follow me on Instagram:
instagram.com/mrforbes_author

Find me on Goodreads:
goodreads.com/mrforbes

Follow me on Bookbub:
bookbub.com/authors/m-r-forbes

Made in the USA
Middletown, DE
30 March 2025

73506825R00218